THE MURDEROUS MYSTERY OF THE SARMATIAN DEMON

Felicia—An old friend of Charity Day's. When she asks for a favor, will her fatal secrets send Nevsky to his grave?

Count Dromsky-Michaux—Distinguished owner of the Hermitage Antique Shop. Betrayal has cost him his business. Will an ancient curse cost him even more?

Vasily Brunov—Successful lawyer and rising politician. His charm inspired Nevsky's interest, but does his legal specialty have a violent side?

Tod Buckcry—Broad and brawny owner of "sPots" pottery store. He asks Charity to come up to see his ceramics, but what did he actually have in mind?

Ruth Spires—Count Dromsky-Michaux's secretary. Her green eyes see more than they should about other people's business. Will her desire for a closer look prove lethal?

When Yuri Nevsky takes on a dangerous case, he knows that operating on blind trust may be deadly—especially when the motives for murder are greed, jealousy, and an object worth a million dollars.

BY THE AUTHOR OF *NEVSKY'S RETURN*, NAMED ONE OF THE "MOST NOTABLE CRIME NOVELS OF 1982" BY *THE NEW YORK TIMES BOOK REVIEW*

P9-EJT-878

Other Avon Books by
Dimitri Gat

NEVSKY'S RETURN

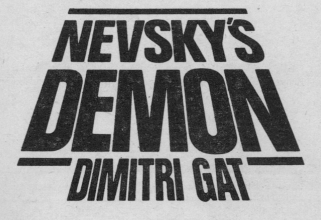

NEVSKY'S DEMON

DIMITRI GAT

AVON
PUBLISHERS OF BARD, CAMELOT, DISCUS AND FLARE BOOKS

NEVSKY'S DEMON is an original publication of Avon
Books. This work has never before appeared in book form.

AVON BOOKS
A division of
The Hearst Corporation
959 Eighth Avenue
New York, New York 10019

First Avon Printing, May, 1983

WFH 10   9   8   7   6   5   4   3   2   1

To The Memory Of My Father,
VSEVOLOD DIMITRIERICH

Chapter One

It was one-thirty in the morning when the door chimes rang. I should have been asleep but wasn't. My night thoughts lately had featured a somewhat disturbed almond-eyed beauty named Tatiana and an odd priest, Father Alexander. They had helped mark the bloody path I walked on my way to finding a kid named Nicholas Markov. I stayed in bed. Chances were it was one of the Morlande Street teen-agers ringing every doorbell on a dare. Ringing in his head, too, probably from a big share of an Iron City six-pack or a few drags on a joint. Good kids in my little borough, really, likely to run giggling home full of their own daring—to a glass of milk and a plate of mother's sandwiches.

The chimes sounded again. I sat up and groped for my robe at the foot of the bed. The nights were still cool. Early June in Pittsburgh wasn't all that warm. I wanted to get downstairs before more chiming woke my housemate, Charity Day. At least one of us might as well enjoy a night's sleep. I didn't bother with lights. I had lived in the house at 138 Morlande Street for many of my forty years. I was navigating the main staircase when the chimes rang again. So much for kids.

I glanced down the wide hall leading past the living room and the music room. Charity was coming toward me, robe and hair smudged pale blue and silver in the reflected light of the first half-moon of summer.

"Light sleeper?" I whispered.

"Night thoughts. My late family. I keep imagining their car hitting the semi."

"I was on Nicholas Markov and Company again."

I had fastened an inconspicuous mirror under the roof of the wide overhanging porch angling around a third of 138. Sometimes it was a big advantage to know who came calling without opening the door.

A woman had pressed herself into the V of walls by the front door. Her back was to the street. I couldn't see her face. I heard a shaky voice. "Charity, *please* be home. *Please* answer."

Beyond the porch and broad, sloping lawn I saw an unfamiliar station wagon by the shadow-shrouded curb. Charity snapped on the porch light. The sudden brilliance was like a flare. The woman turned her face to the V of stone-faced walls.

"Who are you?" Charity called.

"Felicia. Felicia Farrow Semanova."

"Felicia!" Charity turned the heavy dead bolt and opened the big front door.

Felicia slid in quickly. She threw her arms around Charity's neck and hugged her. "Thank God you answered!" She smelled faintly of gasoline. And badly needed a bath. "The porch light. Please turn it off."

Charity flipped the switch. Felicia hurried to the window. "Somebody tried to follow me here, I think."

"They did?" I said. "Why?"

In the gloom I sensed Felicia's eyes on me. "You're..."

"He's my housemate. My landlord," Charity said.

"What about Tom?"

"He and the kids were killed in a car accident more than two years ago."

"Oh, God..."

"You thought you were followed?" I said.

"I cut off the parkway at the Northway ramp—then went right up the on-ramp. I think that shook him."

"Felicia..."

Her face turned back toward the living-room picture-window glass. "Wait just a couple minutes, OK?"

"Can I turn on a light *inside?*" Charity said.

"In a minute, OK?"

Charity and I stood by, feeling foolish, until she heaved a deep sigh of relief and left the window.

"Can we talk?" Charity said.

Felicia took Charity's hands between hers, a gesture both pleading and childlike, as though they were pinafored tots at school recess. "I *need* to talk. Were we once close friends, Charity? I mean very close friends?"

Charity smiled. "Of course we were, 'Licia. We were bosom buddies and had some gay old times."

"I want you to remember those times and accept my apology for breaking in on you like this."

"You don't have to—"

"But I do." Felicia held Charity's hand more tightly. "I apologize because it's necessary, and for another reason."

"Which is?"

"I want you to take me in here tonight—in the name of our happy times, our being true friends what seems so long ago. And not to charge either of us with causing the drift." Even in the weak light I saw the anxiety in Felicia's face.

"I won't charge anything to anybody. For heaven's sake, *relax*." Charity looked at me. "Can she stay overnight?"

"For sure."

"There's one other favor..." Her voice weakened. "...because we were friends."

"What?" Charity said.

"I want to bring something into the house first. Is that OK?"

I looked down at her shadowed face. I couldn't see her expression, but my nose told me all about her anxious sweating. "What is it?"

"I—I can't tell you."

"Is it dangerous?"

"It's not a bomb or anything, if that's what you mean." I hesitated.

"Please make up your mind, Mr...."

"Nevsky. Yuri Nevsky. Call me Yuri."

"Yuri, then." A heartbeat's pause. *"Well?"*

Charity touched my shoulder. "Yuri..."

"Sure," I said.

She hurried out and down the long curving walk,

past the horse chestnut trees. Charity and I went out on the porch, staying in the shadows.

She lowered the station wagon's rear gate. She scrambled up and in on her knees and wrestled out a wrapped object. I started down the walk in my bare feet to help her. She carefully lowered the front end to the street. I saw the object was about five feet long. Beneath the black wrapping were irregular shapes and angles. Even in good light I doubted I'd guess what was under there.

She carefully lowered the other end onto the street. Then she levered it up over her right hip, one end still down. She struggled across the sidewalk and up the three concrete steps leading to my walk.

"Felicia, wait! I'll help you," I said. "Don't kill yourself."

"No you won't." She dragged her burden along the grass beside the walk. There was a single step before the five wooden ones leading to the front porch. She took a short breather before the last five.

"You oughta let me—"

"For*get* it, Yuri!" she said.

"OK. OK."

She dragged her shrouded load up the stairs and across the wooden porch floor. As she raised the tail end over the doorsill, she staggered. Charity reached out to steady the black shape. Felicia's free hand slapped her wrist away. "Don't touch it!" she growled.

"All *right*." I imagined Charity's pale face coloring with irritation.

She dragged her burden through the entrance hall and the smaller of the two living rooms and laid it down by the oak newel post of the main staircase.

"Can I turn on a light *now*, Ms. Mystery?"

"Not in the front of the house."

"Kitchen's in the back."

"Will we wake up somebody?"

"Those to wake are already awake," I said.

"Just you two in this big old ark?"

"Two-by-two..."

"When I saw this big house, Charity, I thought for sure Tom and your kids were..." Felicia's voice was hushed. "I—I'm sorry. You and Tom sounded so . . . happy. Oh, it's all so *rotten*."

"What?"

"Everything."

Charity led us to the kitchen. The fluorescent fixtures dazzled down on appliances, cupboard doors, butcher block counters, one ideally bald and bearded man and two ladies on the shady side of thirty-five.

Right then Felicia Farrow Semanova was looking shadier than Charity Day. Her brown curly hair was matted and tangled. Her luminous brown eyes were bloodshot and leaked tears. She was trembling. My irritation of a few moments ago faded. She was on the verge of total exhaustion. She sank down on a kitchen chair. Her jeans were stained. Her blouse wasn't exactly ready for a fashion show either. A button was missing and a crescent of what looked like axle grease decorated the center of her back.

Charity and I exchanged glances. I went into the pantry I had remodeled into a sizable bar and brought back a brandy. She was still sniffling. "Don't cry for me," Charity said. "I've done too much of that myself already."

"It's not just for *you* . . ."

"You and Alexey? Oh, *no*."

She nodded and sipped the amber liquid, the snifter held between her shaking palms. "Thinking about coming over here, seeing you, once my best friend and matron of honor, made me remember when we were both first married," she said. "And you came over on your delayed honeymoon to see us in Moscow. And how we escorted you around the Kremlin and Alexey kept saying about Moscow, *'This* is the Tartar Rome!' so often I didn't have to translate it anymore. We had the one-room apartment with the bathroom down the hall—on the floor below—and you couldn't figure out why Alexey was so proud of it. And it seemed every *day* was sunny." Her face lit up for a moment. Then the shadows and lines dug back in again. "It was all so special for me— marrying a Russian, going to live in Moscow. Getting away from my family. Starting a new life. It took a long time for it to go sour. I wouldn't *let* it go sour. Even if it was hard for Alexey to find decent work. Even if I

5

had to buy favors and bribe to get things I once took for granted, and stand in line for the rest. I could have taken all that. *Except*—being the 'Russian wife.'"

"Meaning what?" Charity said.

"Working like a dog at home with no help from him. Closing one eye"—she winked lecherously—"to his philandering, to his going down to the vodka shops during the day and out—somewhere—at night." She turned her reddened eyes to Charity's face. "Couldn't you *tell* back then he wasn't for me?"

Charity looked at her hands. "Well...when TT and I came over for dinner and he ate in his undershirt. Then...his wanting to wrestle Tom to see who'd buy the bottle of vodka...I had a feeling there were class differences there."

Felicia had a light, airy laugh. Too brief, though. "No kids made it easier to drift apart," she said. "I found a job teaching English at the local school. Alexey worked for a while in an alloys and light-metal foundry and fabrication plant, then he got a sub-sub post in import-export. He traveled a lot in the Eastern Bloc and once in a while outside. I moved back to Pittsburgh about two-and-a-half years ago. He stayed in Russia. We kept up letters from time to time. And even managed to call once in a while. But pretty soon what had been a marriage became just a spotty business relationship. Until..." A recent painful memory wrung more tears out of her. She shook her head, trying to toss off the memory like a retriever shakes off droplets. She picked up Charity's hand and squeezed it. I saw Felicia's fingers and palms were newly chapped and webbed with tiny cracks over the skin. She leaned against Charity, sighed deeply and bawled hard. "Charity, Charity"—she sobbed—"nobody ever told me how hard life was."

Her exhaustion was right on the surface. She shuddered. On the edge of collapse she pulled herself back, slugged down the rest of the brandy. "I've been in Pittsburgh all these months," she said. "I'm sorry I didn't call you. I know we were best friends—"

"We were." Charity hugged her. "Maybe we can be again."

"I was, I guess, ashamed of my...situation. But when I needed somebody I could really trust, you were the first person I thought of. I started thinking how great it would be to see you again. And your family. All those years since I last saw you."

"Seven or eight at least."

Felicia nodded. "You look good, Charity, you really do. I looked you up. You're an attorney with a big firm downtown."

"My work's helped me keep myself from flying all apart. Living here with Yuri's helped, too."

Felicia looked at us. "Are you two...?" She made a vague gesture, palm up.

"Lovers?" Charity looked at me and we both grinned like idiots.

"I don't know what we are," I said. "But it's not lovers. Colleagues, housemates, friends..." I didn't mention that a few months back, reeling and floundering in self-search, I had proposed marriage to Charity. She had the wisdom to refuse me. Depending on which side of the bed I got up on, that memory filled me either with relief or sadness.

Charity, ever the practical one, got right to it: "Why were you looking for somebody you could trust? And what's wrapped up in the black vinyl?"

"You don't mind asking a direct question, do you, Charity?"

"I get to the point fast. I don't like messing around."

"And you're a stickler, too," Felicia said. "I remember that. A stickler. You believe in doing things right. You believe in right and wrong. You have high standards—"

"Which sometimes are a disadvantage in the legal profession."

"It's not just *you* I trust. It's your values. Your ...character, I guess." Felicia looked warily at me. "Charity, what I want to ask you is confidential."

"Yuri can be trusted—completely."

Felicia looked suspicious. "This deal is not just going to be old friend-old friend. It's going to be client-attorney. I'm going to pay you. I think he ought to be included out."

"If it has to do with leaving that bundle here past tonight, I better be included in," I said. "It's my house."

"W-what makes you think I want that?" Felicia said.

"You went to all the trouble to drag it up here. I just can't see you dragging it back out tomorrow. Doesn't make sense."

Felicia said nothing. Her darting eyes said she felt trapped. Charity put her hand on her friend's wrist. "Don't *worry*. I'd trust Yuri with my life. *You* can trust him with what you have wrapped up there."

Felicia took a deep breath. "Charity, I want you to keep my bundle. I want you to hide it. Until I come back for it."

"What's in there?" I said.

Felicia put her purse on the edge of the kitchen table. She rummaged in it while Tuptim, Charity's Siamese, tried to curl around her ankle, hoping for nighttime company. She pulled out a roll of money held by a rubber band. "This is five thousand dollars. It's for you, Charity."

"That's a lot of money. What's it supposed to buy?"

"Immunity from your questions, counselor, for one thing."

"All of them?"

"Just about. And your silence. It buys your silence—and *his*. Your absolute silence."

"We hide whatever it is and keep our mouths shut," I said.

"You got it."

"For how long?" Charity said.

"One month."

"That's all you want?"

"That's all I want for *me*. That's asking more than enough in the name of an old friendship. But I also want something from you." She folded Charity's palm around the roll of bills. "Don't look inside the wrapping." She lifted her chapped palm and held Charity's face. She leaned close, her bloodshot eyes unblinking. "If it does get unwrapped, one way or the other, *don't touch it*. Promise me you won't. Both of you."

My mind's cauldron bubbled with questions. The ice in her eyes chilled every one.

"It's...bad luck. Unlucky things happen to people who touch it," she said.

Charity began: "I don't believe—"

"Do I have to *say* it?" Abruptly Felicia was nearly

8

shouting. "Do I have to say I was told it was *cursed?* Do I have to spell out that two people who meant a lot to me are *dead* maybe because they touched it? Are you that much of a stickler, Charity? Are you?" She was leaking tears again. Her knees were trembling.

"OK. OK." Charity put her arm over her friend's shoulder. Felicia was shaking all over. "I *would* like to know what it is," she said softly, not expecting an answer.

"It's my retirement," Felicia said. "And I'll come back for it...uh, what day is it?"

"Wednesday, June second. About two in the morning."

"Be back in one month, give or take a few days. Just before the Fourth. If I don't come back and don't call or write, then the bundle should go to my brother."

"You used to talk about him. And I met him once one summer on the Connecticut shore," Charity said. "But I forgot his name."

"Winston Farrow III. Win. We've never got along. Can't stand each other. But he should get it. He lives in Cambridge. He's on the staff at Harvard. Don't know what he does. Stuffs shirts or something." She got up and walked out to the foot of the staircase. "Where do you want me to put it? I'll hide it for you."

Charity and I exchanged glances. I nodded. "The White Chamber's probably the best place."

"What's *that?*"

The answer was: a former coal cellar I had converted to what amounted to a room-sized safe and sanctuary. When I had got into what I called the information business, which meant finding out things for money, it was sometimes necessary to hide people and objects for a while. A Greek master metalworker and mason from Sharpsburg did the job. I picked him because he had made his pile of greenbacks and was going home to the old country to sit under an olive tree and tell lies for the rest of his life. He collected his fee on the way to Greater Pittsburgh International.

In old houses like 138 the basement foundation and room walls are made of picked stones. The coal-cellar door had been replaced with a fake one with matching stones. Its seams were almost impossible to see. I'm handy with the electrical side of life. I installed an electronic lock. That mechanism was also hidden behind the stone facing. The lock "key" was an extra circuit wired into the components of my bedroom clock radio. It would take an electronics technician with a wiring diagram to find out how to open the Chamber.

I excused myself to go to the john. On the way back down I swung through my bedroom, wriggled a finger through a small hole in the radio back and touched the right resistor. Felicia insisted on dragging her "retirement" down to the basement. The White Chamber was gaping to swallow it. She caught a glimpse of some of the space-age life-support equipment inside.

"What the hell is *this?*" she said.

"You said 'hide,' we thought you *meant* hide," Charity said.

She laid her bundle down and came back out. I closed the door behind her. The door seemingly disappeared. Wide-eyed, she ran her hands over the uneven white-washed stones. "It's *gone,*" she said. She turned weary eyes on me. "Hey, Nevsky, what do you *do* for a living anyhow?"

"I'm in the information business," I said.

"Does it pay?"

I glanced across the basement at my newly out-of-order and unrepaired Gas King Supreme furnace. "Not enough," I said.

Storing her burden drained the last of Felicia's strength. Charity helped her upstairs. She clutched the stair railing with shaking hands. "Couple more little things in the name of friendship and my five K, old, dear friend," she mumbled. "Please, a bath and a bed."

Charity took her up the other stairs to her quarters, mumbling of bubble baths, big sponges, a soft guest-room bed and pajamas that probably fit. I heard the water running. I poured myself a finger of Sam Thompson Pennsylvania Rye Whiskey and wet my fatigue-musty mouth. I was just working up a good ponder when I heard Charity's distant voice calling me upstairs. She led me into her guest room.

Felicia was in bed—already sound asleep, despite the blazing ceiling fixture. She was snoring.

"The *same snore* I heard when we were at Radcliffe

almost twenty years ago," Charity whispered. "Like a small furry animal growling in a paper bag."

We turned off the light and, after Charity gathered up her friend's clothes, went downstairs. "I could use a little background about now," I said.

Charity provided it over a glass of White Mountain Chablis. She began talking with a distant, dreamy smile on her face. She was *so* pale and blonde that she looked like an aging cherub. "Oh, what a straight line life is when you're twenty!" she said. She described herself as filled then with some vague, do-good legal ambitions. Felicia had fallen in love with Russian art and literature—she, with a father who moved between the State Department and Wall Street. She spent her junior year in Russia, poking around the wonders of Samarkand and Moscow—and came home calling it "Moskva" and speaking much better Russian.

She sometimes invited Charity east to the Farrow summer home on the Connecticut shore—the last time the summer before senior year. They swam, gossiped on screened porches, and had tea at four sharp. Felicia was a skillful sailor. She had spent every summer of her life on boats. When she turned eighteen she earned some kind of seaman's papers. She bubbled with the wonders of western Russia and of course the art. Woven into the fabric of the story of her junior year abroad, told in bits short and long in a dozen different nooks and haunts of her summer landscape, was the thread of a man. Called sometimes "a friend," a "fellow I met," "this mad Russian," and finally "Alexey." He was clearly important to her. In those days she was a gentle, understating girl, an ocean of patience—more so when compared to the racing brook of Charity's impatience and let's-get-on-with-it-ness. So it took the better part of her summer visit for Charity to understand. Felicia, who rarely dated and was as far from man-struck as she was from the Mindanao Deep, thought she had found *the* one.

The wedding was two years later, in New York. Charity, matron of honor, drove miles through a snowstorm to the church. Things were even more confused than at the average wedding. Alexey and the best man, pried free by State Department influence, arrived late

11

on an Aeroflot flight—and spoke no English. The number of Russian-speakers, beside Felicia, was what one might expect from a Wall Street crowd—none.

Alexey, testing out the shakiest of English, said "I do" twice—both at the wrong times. But that didn't keep Charity from crying or make Felicia any less married.

When we had finished our drinks, Charity gathered up Felicia's clothes, heading for the basement laundry room. I went with her. Charity wouldn't cook, hated to clean. Laundry she didn't mind. She even did mine. She had a clothes-washing ritual. She first looked in the pockets. She staked claim to all my small change. Her soap-dish cache was on the shelf above the Maytag. She threatened me with broken thumbs if I ever reached in there. The pockets of Felicia's jeans held no money. All she found was a book of matches from the Imperial Diner, Erie, PA. The next ritual called for a look under the laundry-table light for missing buttons, tears and stains. The blue black stain on her blouse was grease, so she soaked it with Era. I held the blouse up to my nose. The whole outfit *did* smell of gasoline. Both blouse and jeans had scattered brownish stains on their fronts. She soaked them, too. Felicia's sneakers were damp, so I dumped them in the dryer to wait for the rest of the load.

I was just turning the dial to start the washer when I heard a thump upstairs—on the kitchen floor right above us.

Charity gasped. Hairs stirred on the back of my neck. I had that I-wish-I-had-a-weapon feeling. There were assorted weapons tucked into inconspicuous crannies all through 138. Mostly they gathered dust. But every once in a while... None was now within reach. "Hello! Who's there?" I shouted. "That you, Felicia?"

Silence. I held my breath, straining to hear ...anything. The house was quiet. Charity and I exchanged nervous glances. I knew what was bothering us: the thought of a cursed *something* under our roof. Nonsense, sure, but scary nonsense.

"The man always leads the way upstairs in situations like this," Charity whispered.

"You're sex stereotyping again."

I went up, feet at the far sides of the stairs, a TV trick to silence squeaky risers. Charity was right behind me. Now I was reluctant to call out. And *really* didn't want to hear another noise.

Coming up the stairs I saw the fall of light from the kitchen fixtures. No shadows broke the white glow. No movement. No one—or no *thing*—waited for us. I heard Charity's rapid shallow breathing just behind me.

I laid flat on the stairs with my head right below the top step. An old Boy Scout ploy—peeking out at an unlikely spot.

I inched my face up to where jamb bottom met kitchen floor. I peeked out—and groaned. With embarrassment. The kitchen *wasn't* deserted. Tuptim was there. She had knocked Felicia's purse off the table edge, spilling out its contents.

Charity rushed by me and scooped up her pet. Nose to nose, she said, "Another trick like *that,* you crazy Oriental, and it's dried food and water for a month!"

I picked up the purse. Its leather was stiff and smelled damp. I looked at what went back in—Pennsylvania license and Ford Fairlane station wagon registration in a Leatherette folding case. The registration number, 20B-1933, reminded me of Prohibition. I copied the address into my Harvard Coop notebook. I dropped back into the purse a pocket dictionary, a comb, a 50-cent astrology booklet (sign of Taurus), a small bottle of Bufferin, an emery board, Binaca and a payroll check stub. Felicia worked for Hermitage Decorator Antiques on Walnut Street in Shadyside. She took home $135.28 a week. She also carried a credit-card case and a billfold. I couldn't resist looking. She had given Charity five thousand dollars, but had only $9.72 for herself.

Felicia was shouting upstairs!

"Oh, God!" Charity ran for her stairs. I was right behind her. "What the *hell* is going on?" she said.

Halfway down the hall to the guest room I heard what Felicia was shouting. "Stand up, Sergei! Stand *up,* for the love of God!"

Charity eased open the guest room door. Felicia was flailing in her sleep, sailing the dark seas of nightmare. "Stand up, Sergei!" she cried again. She heaved a sigh so deep it seemed to come from the cellar of her soul—and fell sound asleep.

Charity wiped oozing palms on her robe quilting. "Aren't *we* jumpy tonight?"

"Guests who come by night dragging trouble wrapped in black ... all I'm up for at this hour is a glass of warm milk and a hot water bottle."

"You *love* it, Yuri. All you men are pushovers for a woman in trouble."

"You think she's in trouble?"

"Right now I'm too tired to think anything. I'm going to bed."

I knew my body. I wasn't ready for sleep. My heart was thumping along almost as fast as my brain. I went downstairs and eased into the sprung couch in the smaller living room and turned on a lamp. My thoughts wandered east and west, up and down. In time I began to drift off. The bells tolled 3:00 A.M. in the church belfry at the foot of the hill.

The door chimes brought me upright like a puppet jerked to life. I looked in the porch-mounted mirror.

A cop was at my door.

On the street sat a borough police cruiser, circling blue light dazzling my brain and stirring my suspicions with each blinding revolution. Felicia had given Charity five thousand dollars to keep a cursed who-knew-what for a month. Sounded like trouble. And it looked right at that moment like trouble for *me*.

I opened the door. My borough had only one chief and four officers. This officer was a familiar face. Officer Slapko. Seen regularly controlling traffic Sunday morning after church services or standing by the school cafeteria when it served as a poll.

"Mr. Nevsky?"

"Yes."

"You have a guest with you tonight?" The close glare of the porch light lit the facial moonscape of scars from Slapko's long-gone adolescent acne attacks. Below his squared brown moustache heavy lips shuddered when he spoke.

I drew a deep breath, getting hold of my nerves. Charity had been right. We were jittery. "What about her?"

"Well, it's not her..." The heavy lips split into an apologetic grin. "It's her station wagon. It's parked on the street. And it's after one in the morning. I'm sure you know the borough curfew—no on-street parking overnight."

I grunted like a dolt. "Oh, that's right."

"You have your guest move her car. Up onto your back driveway will be fine."

"I'll do it. She's asleep."

He touched the bill of his cap. "Sorry to bother you. I saw the light, figured your guest didn't need a twenty-dollar ticket."

He drove off. In his wake he left me feeling foolish. Talk about overreacting! I pulled a jacket over my robe, picked Felicia's keys out of her purse, and went out to the station wagon.

I found myself wondering what Felicia was up to, honest or otherwise. There was a flashlight in the glove compartment. I used it to go over the car's interior. All I found were four road maps, an ice scraper and two boxes carrying the Hermitage Decorator Antiques logo. It included a stylized drawing of that famous Soviet museum. The boxes held antique vases. Each was addressed in black Magic Marker to people living on the east boroughs side of Pittsburgh. So she made deliveries, whatever else she did, for Hermitage Decorator Antiques.

I moved the car onto the drive and went to bed. To my surprise I fell asleep almost at once. To my greater surprise I didn't drift toward tortured, bloody dreams of Tatiana and Nicholas Markov. The first night that had happened since I found the lad.

Charity was right: some new excitement was just what I needed.

Chapter Two

Our wake-up coffee cups in hand, Charity and I stood
over Felicia's bed. She hadn't stirred at the sound of
Charity's alarm in the next room. Nor did she stir now.
She was sunk in the deep sleep of the exhausted. I
studied her face bathed in the light of the shaded south
window. Lines branched out at the corners of her eyes
and mouth. Her skin, which Charity had described as
once unusually creamy and blemish-free, had been
thickened by the rough abrasions of the years. Like her
hands, her face had recently been chapped and reddened. She whimpered into the pillow. We tiptoed out
toward our regular morning routines.

As a bulwark against the creeping slovenliness of
those who lived essentially alone, every weekday morning we tried to meet at 7:45 in the kitchen, fully dressed
for our day's activities. I did all the cooking at 138.
Charity claimed she was "cooked out" from her years
as a wife and mother. I was a great one for eating
generally. If the only way I could get a good meal was
to cook it myself, well, right on! That morning, amid
sections of the *Post Gazette* and WDUQ radio's morning
light classics, we shared one of our favorites: fresh
mushrooms cooked in butter with a bit of Worcestshire
sauce and served on buttered English muffins. Half a
grapefruit each and two cups of fresh ground and brewed

coffee finished readying us for slaying the day's dragons.

"Felicia?" I said.

"Let her sleep. She's exhausted. I'll leave her a note with my law firm number, in case she wakes up."

We spent fifteen minutes talking through Felicia Farrow Semanova's arrival. We had learned early in our alliance in search of information that there was no such thing as a shared experience. We are all sealed into individual flesh-and-bone envelopes. Just because she and I had shared moments with Felicia didn't mean either our feelings or interpretations were the same. We found we could fill out and broaden almost any such experience by working with it.

Too, night visitors with mysterious bundles could later on lead to some kind of civilian or law-enforcement awkwardness. We needed a sensible, simple version of events that either of us could verify in case Felicia's bundle proved to be somebody else's property and they came looking for it and laying waste, hurting one of us, or worse—the survivor had to pick up the pieces and handle things. Sometimes the information business got a bit rough. Quite possibly one day it would become too rough entirely, and that would be the end of us. Having these little chats was one of our shared charms for delaying that inevitable bad time.

"What do you guess we have in the White Chamber?" I said.

"Some kind of single solid object. Heavy enough to make a hundred-and-twenty-pound woman struggle, but not too heavy for her to move it. Shape says it's not in any container."

"Want to go look at it?" I said.

"No. She's trusting us." A frown and a faint shadow of fear touched Charity's face. "Funny, but I don't want to have anything to do with it. Maybe it's that curse business. Not that I believe..." She let that drop.

"Think she stole it?"

Charity shook her head. "Not if she's the Felicia who once was my best female friend. She was a pretty classy lady, Yuri. And a worker. Her father had pots of money, but she always made *sure* she worked for everything she got. I'd say she probably has a right to what she's

18

stashed in the White Chamber. Let's keep it for her. That five thousand she gave me is gross overpayment anyway. By the way, I intend to split it with you. After all, this is your house."

"Love to say no to that, but"—I tried my most sheepish, little-puppy-dog-pet-me smile—"the information business has been slow, and then there's the furnace..."

In my little Datsun I headed for the heating company showrooms and gloomed over the death at a grand old age of Gas King Supreme. R.I.P. old friend. Its distant thumps and churnings were counterpoint to some of my earliest memories of childhood and adolescence at 138.

In early spring this year I had got out of bed and found the house cold. The furnace hadn't kicked on during the night chill. A quick look at Gas King Supreme told me nothing. The gas company man said to call the furnace company. The furnace business wasn't what it used to be—a couple of sheet-metal workers playing pitch in the back of a garage, one of their wives answering the phone and sending out the bills. When I phoned the furnace company number I found in my late mother's address book, a woman's voice with a finishing school and at least a master's degree behind it said, "Tri-State Energy Consultants—will you hold?" "Hold" played classical music. I recognized the piece: "Winter" from Vivaldi's *The Four Seasons*. They liked to rub it in.

I held a long while. When the woman came back on the line I told her my furnace wasn't working. Could they send someone out this afternoon? She did a good job of smothering her laughter. Something called the computer-controlled work-flow schedule said the earliest possible "heating consultation" would be in about six weeks.

"What am I supposed to do till then?" I said.

"Hope for a warm spell?"

I was lucky. It did turn warmish. Charity and I muddled through using the big living-room fireplace and lots of sweaters. Yesterday the heating consultant arrived in a van holding enough electronics to be part of the satellite tracking system. He was bearded and wore thick glasses and a stylish jump suit. I met him by the garage. Hands on hips, he greedily surveyed the rambling lines of 138 and its pre-Civil War architecture. "You've had an energy audit, of course?" he said.

"Let's go look at the furnace," I said.

The space-age furnace man performed exploratory surgery on Gas King Supreme with flashlight, screwdriver and voltmeter. He muttered and said, "Tsk, tsk. Hot water radiator heat is so…primitive."

"It only worked for 125 years."

He began to rattle off my furnace's pathology. I cut him short. "How about the quick summary diagnosis?"

A flicker of annoyance clouded his bearded face. I had taken away some of his chance to be professional. In his sullenness he reverted to your basic, old-timey furnace guy. He said, "You can put a fork in this one, Mac. It's done…."

The morning rush was over. My Datsun sailed along under a promising morning sun. I decided to take the scenic route, so I picked up Fifth Avenue near the Nabisco plant. I rolled down the window. They were baking that morning. The early summer air sang with sweetened yeast, and the juices ran in my mouth. What if they were making Oreos! Fifth Avenue was one of the old City of Pittsburgh arteries. On the high ground to the left, along the next two miles, long-dead captains of the steel industry had built huge mansions set on grand acreage. Forbes and Frick, Carnegie's cronies, others whose names the public had forgotten. Now those opulent buildings had passed to the public, driven there by the lash of soaring tax rates, in the form of community art centers, ill-attended museums and Hebrew schools. Newer industrialists, finding themselves out of fashion, moved to Sewickley Heights, Fox Chapel or rolling horse farms in Ligonier where behind high hedges and iron fences they could worry about unions and Japanese imports.

The energy-company showrooms were on a wide street in Oakland. One look at their new architect-original structure and the presence of a receptionist who matched me with "a sales consultant" put me in a poor mood to survey the technological wonders created in response to the energy shortage. Ed Green was squat and smirky. On his florid salesman's face I read the book of twenty-five years in the business of selling. Insurance, real estate, increasingly smaller cars, men's clothes and now energy systems had etched the meaningless professional smile into permanent lines around his eyes and mouth. His moustache was turning gray. His green eyes looked at my face and weighed my wallet.

My mood got worse as we strolled among the banks of model solar panels and combo wood-coal-and-gas furnaces. Wind-powered generators with thin propeller blades lay about like the rubble strewn from airplane crashes. The price tags on all were enough to make the most solvent quake. The cost of technology, inflation and not a little gouging by Tri-State Energy Consultants was going to make any new furnace a major investment. And right then I didn't have the capital.

The furnace Ed Green recommended was less than half the size of the late Gas King Supreme. When he told me the cost I grew irritated. When he said deliveries were four months behind, my irritation deepened. It was the extra installation charge that shoved my emotional gauge needle over into the red of anger. I told him what I thought about Tri-State Energy Consultants.

"Don't you watch TV, Mr. Nevsky?" he said. "OPEC is—"

And there I was grabbing him by his wide Anderson Little coat lapels. Scratch a Russian, find a Tartar, somebody said. "I don't want to hear about OPEC or the Arabs!" I growled into his whitening face. "Tell me about gouging mothers like you and Exxon! *That's* where it's at."

"Mr. Nevsky—"

"You've all done nothing but make more and more money off what little crisis there is. You're all ripping off everybody. And Congress is too scared or too well cut in to stop any of you—"

I felt a heavy hand on my shoulder. I turned around and let Ed Green down. Right away I saw what at least one NFL linebacker was doing off-season. He was a floor man cum bouncer for Tri-State Energy Consultants.

I left quietly

I felt embarrassed and guilty at my outburst, though

I had every right to be angry. Repression. The price we paid for helping Western civilization lurch along.

At the root of my anger was something deeper. It wasn't Felicia Farrow Semanova's bundle either. It was the ambiguity of my life situation and my shifting personality. I was sinking into one of my introspective moods. I had two places where such thinking went best. One was plunking at the baby grand in the music room at 138. The other was undergoing what I called Dinosaur Therapy. Because I was only six blocks from Carnegie Museum, today it would be dinosaurs.

The dinosaur hall was on the first floor, a high cavernous room lit by spotlights that left patches of shadow. One of the heavy polished-wood benches sat in shadow—my couch for saurian therapy. There I sat, leaned back a bit, and beheld the full assembled skeletons of the *Brontosaurus* and the *Tyrannosaurus Rex,* superstars of the Jurassic period. That those petrified bones once supported creatures who long ruled the earth, and now were gone, had a way of making everything seem less urgent. That they towered above me, intimidating even without flesh and motion, and had been swept into history by a mysterious and unexplained change in the earth's climate, gave me a good feeling for the true capriciousness of life. One final impression from those towering cages of ribs and bony armor, and tiny weak me alive to sit at those claw feet: life was an impenetrable mystery. As I sat among dinosaurs, my spirits climbed steadily. Before long I was smiling. Freud was OK. But it was monster reptiles that did the trick for Yuri Nevsky.

What did I ponder during my saurian therapy? Some token rummagings in the memory attic of my failed marriage. A bad match it had been, held together for ten years by Ann's and my total stoicism and our commitments to our daughters Jane and Clara. Complete understanding of our relationship would forever escape me. The greater the meaning we attached to the events of our lives, the further understanding retreated into the essential mystery. I knew a few things. The strands of motive and meaning ran down toward the cores of our most personal selves. There intimacy, emotion and sexual expression twisted and twined into the knots

22

coding our personalities. All through our marriage we had held back from expressing ourselves, either verbally or physically. I was inhibited by her outbursts, anger and need to command. She was insecure and intimidated by my long silences. Our emotions were shackled. We danced through the years in a dainty, false Minuet for Pussyfooters. We did the steps, the music of matrimony played, the set of 4691 Azalea Drive and the costumes were perfect. But the dance failed. We were strangers to one another. Ten years and still strangers.

My search for Nicholas Markov up and down Russian Slope had turned out to be a search for my past as well. For so many years I had put my Russianness aside. I played at being free of ancestors and ethnic blood. Then I had been forced to accept my roots in that vast land of birches and suffering. What to make of those bloodlines was part of the puzzle. I didn't know if it mattered that by the time the Mayflower sailed, my ancestors had already been living on estates for a hundred years and were identifiable a hundred years before that. The dog-eared genealogy prepared by my great-uncle in Paris and willed to me by my father listed relatives in personal service to czars through more than three centuries. Many other distant but related lives closed within the dates of the Napoleonic Wars. They had been army officers. To make connections between those long-dead half a world away and Yuri Nevsky was no easy matter. One thing was certain. I knew where I came from. Past that, I didn't know much.

When I finished telling the dinosaurs about Russia I started in on what it meant to be a middle-aged information specialist living with, but not sharing the bed of, an attractive widow. I looked up at the towering skulls, at their cement-filled eyesockets, and imagined I saw boredom there. That meant I had had enough therapy for the day. On the way out of the museum I dropped my clip-on button into the marked receptacle. Cost me a buck and a quarter—therapy anyone could afford. Only *Peanuts*'s Lucy was cheaper.

I got out of the Datsun in the garage and tensed up right away. Some time ago I had installed a gadget there. It was a grid with a little lightbulb in the center of each square. It carried no labels or other identification, but there was a bulb for every door and window of 138. I made sure that screen, glass or wood always covered those dozens of openings. That way I knew if any one had been forced. The bulb arrangement, which only Charity and I understood, told me a cellar window had been tampered with.

And Felicia was asleep alone inside.

I slid out the right short brick from an inside garage wall. The snub-nosed Smith and Wesson .38 lay in its nest of dehumidifier packets. I snatched it out and ran for the closest entrance, up the stairs to the elevated rear porch and door. I had the door key in one hand and the .38 in the other.

I slipped inside as quietly as I could. I stood listening for a few moments. I heard nothing. I walked down the hall that led to Charity's half of the house, then to the guest room. My heart was pounding. I slipped off the pistol safety.

The sound I heard relaxed me some. Felicia was still snoring away. I put my hand on the knob and eased open the door. She lay in undisturbed sleep.

But the closet door was wide open.

So were the closet doors in Charity's bedroom and study. Someone had gone through the house—or was still doing so.

It was a big house. I got plenty of thrills and chills going through every room, stopping from time to time to listen. What I found made me sense that my uninvited visitor was looking for Felicia's bundle. Larger spaces had been searched, smaller ones like drawers and low cabinets had been ignored.

I worked my way down to the first floor. Same procedure. Larger cabinets and closets gaping, holes in likely looking walls. Soon only the basement remained. Quite possibly my visitor was still there, crouched, armed and waiting.

I turned on the lights and went down the stairs one at a time. The pistol handle was cold in my sweaty palm. The laundry room was deserted. That left the main cellar area, with its cold cellar and tool room. Those two doors were open. Their lights were on.

Some random chips had been struck from the whitewashed stones of the main cellar walls. After that the pick had been thrown down. It lay on the concrete floor less than four feet from the door to the White Chamber.

My visitor's instincts had been good. But not quite good enough. He or she had given up and left....

When Charity got home at 4:30 I filled her in on what had happened. I started dinner. After a while she came down and told me Felicia was getting up at last. We both went upstairs with her clothing. She went into the bathroom and came out dressed and smiling.

"Dinner in ten, Sister of Sleep," Charity said.

"Dinner! What time is it? What *day* is it?"

I told her it was late Wednesday, June second. "I've got to leave right after dinner," she said.

We went downstairs to the pantry bar. When Charity had made the drinks, she said, "Felicia, you've got to admit there's something just a *hair* odd about all this."

"So?" Her tone was waspish.

"Oh, don't worry. I'm not going to ask any questions about the past." She smiled thinly. "I've been paid too much for that."

"Charity..."

"But I can ask questions about the future. Say July Fourth comes and you don't. Don't you want me and Yuri to find out where you are or what happened to you?"

"Not really."

"You could be just—I don't know—delayed or something."

"Charity, if I don't show, your job is to give the bundle to my brother Win. That's *it*. Do it and you've earned your five thousand."

"He'll want to know what it is."

"Just tell him it's from me."

Charity put down her glass and turned to our guest with hands on hips. "And do I tell him it's *cursed?*" she said.

Felicia scowled. "God, Charity, can't you let *anything* just lie? Just leave well enough alone?"

"I just—"

"You're right. You *are* a stickler, aren't you? You must be a wonderful attorney. OK, I'll give brother a

25

call in the next couple of days. Clue him in about it. Just in case."

"Clue me in, too. How about it?"

"No! That's part of our deal. Leave well enough *alone,* for Christ's sake!"

I said, "Charity's having trouble with the arrangement because somebody broke in and searched the house this afternoon."

Felicia's blue eyes shot wide open. "Did they find the—bundle?"

"Almost, but not quite. They left through the basement hatchway, I think."

"Who *was* it?" She intertwined her fingers, began to twist and turn them. Agitation. She was nearly wringing her hands.

"Well, it wasn't police, for sure." I studied her expression.

"I...can't imagine who it was." She slid off into a private reverie.

"No idea, then, at all?" I said.

She shook her head. Sadness slid like a shade over her face. "I'm sure you both can see I'm trying to protect myself and my retirement," she said. "But I'm protecting something else, too, Charity. It's how you see me, and how things were before. I want those memories to survive—as was." She leaned over and took Charity's hand. She looked into her face and smiled sweetly. "Remember your delayed honeymoon with us in Moscow? Remember how *I* was. Remember how Alexey was. Remember...everything just as it was."

Over dinner Charity shared with us some of those long-ago memories. Tom and she had flown to Paris on a charter, by then well along in working through the early intricacies of marriage. The Parisian tourist horror stories proved false for them. They joined the armies who had fallen in love with the Lady of the Seine. They sipped citron pressé in sidewalk cafes on the "Boul Mich," as they learned to call it. *Les bateaux mouches* chugged their tourist selves up and down that romantic river. One night they had dinner at a tiny restaurant on a dead-end street near the Pont Vert: pike quenelles and parsleyed lamb set out on a checkered tablecloth and washed down with good house wine. They sat at one of four outdoor tables. A fat-cheeked old man with a flowing white mustache and no teeth played a concertina. A gamin redhead sold roses from a round lacquered tray and called them "nature's words for love."

From Paris they traveled by train through Germany and Poland to Moscow. Deep in Germany a summer storm rattled the roof with rain and a fusillade of hail. They swigged from a bottle of Cointreau and oohed at the elements. She remembered the pleasure of her reunion with Felicia. Later the two couples went north to Leningrad. On the shore of Lake Ladoga Alexey's uncle had a motor sailer moored by the town of Sviritsa. They sailed—or rather motored—along within sight of land. Alexey couldn't really sail, and the tub had trouble coming about under his helmsmanship. Felicia, the experienced sailor with papers to prove it, sat smiling and raised her finger to her lips to silence judgmental Charity.

Some magic on the part of Felicia's State Department father freed them from Intourist. Alexey led them around Moscow. His knowledge of the narrow twisting streets and the nontourist spots impressed Charity and Tom. He had grown up in that sprawling city and wanted to impress the Americans he claimed to hold in contempt. He was a good host. Felicia was there when the Days needed a guide or advice on walking tours and shopping.

At visit's end both Alexey and Felicia stood on the railway platform, patient despite the unseasonable heat, the usual departure delays, and the hordes of elbowing and shoving Muscovites on their way west. The couple waved and blew kisses. *"Dosvedanya!"* they shouted above the station clamor. *"Dosvedanya!"* How happy they were, Tom and Charity agreed. How lucky to have found each other! "Almost as lucky as us," Tom said.

With this last, Charity began to dab at her eyes with a napkin. She smiled miserably through her welling tears. "I guess I over*did* it." She got up and rushed for the kitchen. Felicia excused herself and went to comfort her.

In a while Charity returned dry-eyed but slightly paler than usual. Right after the ice cream Felicia insisted on leaving. The moment she got behind the wheel of her station wagon she seemed wary, guarded some-how. "See you in a month!" she called.

We waved her all the way down Morlande Street as she had waved Charity and Tom off on that long-gone scorching Russian day when they were girls and called themselves women. When life was linear—straight lines with regularly placed goals to be achieved like mile-stones on the way to their own glorious purple sunsets. Nothing could go wrong for them. They were rational, educated people, dwellers in America's privileged upper middle class. They had advantages, taste, were never reckless. They practiced good health habits, brushed their teeth, exercised regularly, set their lives' sails to carry them along safe familiar courses.

Now life's essential mystery had closed in on them like a fog. There we all groped like partygoers at blind-man's buff. Our pasts and presents resisted separation. Time's reality itself could be questioned. Suffering sharpened its sword and hewed at us, shaping us against our will.

At the head of the street Felicia's station wagon turned onto the main drag and out of sight. I wished her all the luck in the world. She needed it.

So did Charity and I.

Chapter Three

Gardening time is the first two weeks in June. I spent
most of them on my "farm" in Murrysville about twelve
miles east of 138. My parents bought the thirty-six acres
and one-floor cottage after World War II. It was my
father's dacha, where he took us for weekends and summer vacations. In that arrangement—owning land and
using it in the Russian style—he must have filled up
some emptiness that only those who have lost everything in revolution can understand.

As a child I hadn't understood. I resented the iso-
lation of the hilltop, the absence of my city friends. I
was indifferent to the many chores, like weeding straw-
berries and corn and whitewashing the cottage's foundation. I did like cutting the asparagus, smoking the
bees and picking grapes.

I saw now I was never curious enough about the other
Russians who also owned nearby small cottages and
formed a summer colony. Sunny summer Sunday after-
noons all the Russians gathered. The air was blue with
the barking consonants of the language, with here and
there a pocket of thickly accented English.

When my father grew older, he rented the cottage
to Lou, who had a wife and two boys. Her reaction to
the place must have been similar to mine. She ran off
with the milkman. I always imagined him leering at
her in housecoat and curlers, saying, "Baby, I'm gonna

show you the *dairy*. And the *bottle washer* . . ." Lou stayed on with his kids. When he moved in in 1956 my father charged him eighty dollars a month. After my father died, my mother charged him eighty dollars a month. A year ago Lou retired and moved to Florida, no doubt on what he had saved in rent over the years. Ours must have been an inherited family weakness. During my brief reign as landlord I, too, had charged Lou eighty dollars a month.

Even though I had hated the farm and gardening when a child, as an adult I found growing vegetables and fruit oddly compelling. And there were worse ways to spend a gathering dusk than on the small porch with my feet up on the railing and a rye in my hand, surveying the meadows and pastures on the rolling western Pennsylvania hills across the valley.

A friend used to say, "If you want to find out what life's really like, grow a garden." There was some truth in that. Gardens had a way of lowering unrealistically high expectations. Getting through a growing season with modest success was no easy feat. Too, there was a direct parallel between those perfect photographs of perfect produce in the seed catalogs and lifelike illusions offered by TV, bad novels, and unexamined social customs. A garden, like living, shattered pretty, false mirrors with the hammer of reality.

Though one might plan carefully and work hard inside neatly fenced territory, fate could still deal out trouble: a hail storm, a bounding deer with a taste for young green shoots, the dreaded groundhog . . . Nonetheless one had to go ahead; to risk nothing was to gain nothing. Better a tomato with "shoulders" than none at all.

So I bent to setting out my tomato plants, my green peppers, my eggplants. I sowed the seeds of cucumber, zucchini, basil, corn and anise. I sweated. The droplets gathered on my largish nose and fell from its tip onto the turned earth. Sun and fresh air filled my days, books and early sleep my nights. No mistaking it: a pastoral life.

One morning of the second week at my dacha the phone rang. Charity. She was crying. "Yuri, Yuri, you have to come *home*. Something dreadful's happened."

I tried to get it out of her, but she was too upset to say any more than that it was an article in the *Post-Gazette* that morning. I locked the cottage and waved good-bye to my tomatoes. My Datsun jolted down the rocky drive as my sense of foreboding rose.

Charity was waiting in the living room with the paper folded to the second section, page five, bottom-left column. Her eyes were red, and her face trembled as though it were about to fly into fragments. She gave me the paper. I saw the report at once.

WOMAN KILLED IN ACCIDENT

McKees Rocks—A Squirrel Hill woman was killed late Wednesday afternoon after the car she was driving veered into the side of an oncoming gasoline truck on West Carson Street.

Felicia Farrow Semanova of 1700 Mount Royal Drive was pronounced dead on arrival at Allegheny General Hospital. Witnesses said Mrs. Semanova's station wagon, traveling west, swerved into the side of a tank truck driven by Anthony DiConsolo, at 5:42 P.M. The Semanova car then spun and struck an iron utility pole. Police reported the impact crushed the driver's side door, killing Mrs. Semanova instantly.

The fatality was the third of the year along West Carson Street in the half mile west of the Penn Lincoln Parkway entrance ramp.

Mr. DiConsolo, an employee of Marfar Trucking Industries, was not cited by investigating officers.

My hand holding the paper dropped to my side. "I'm...sorry," I said. "Very sorry."

Charity's control failed and she burst into tears. She came to me and I put my arms around her. "We were once such close friends. We were." She shuddered against me and I held her.

My vivid imagination saw the oil truck lumbering down the road like a great tubular elephant. I saw the light station wagon sideswipe it like a darting deer. I

31

heard the scream of rubber on asphalt, the clamor of abused metals, and the final clang of utility-pole iron slamming like a cell door on the life of Felicia Farrow Semanova. An accident. Senseless. Her number turned up on the carny wheel of the cosmos.

"A stupid accident," I said.

Charity loosened her grip and stepped back. "Probably."

"'Probably'? She was driving alone and lost control of her car. Probably speeding."

Charity grunted and went to her purse for a Kleenex. She scowled at me. "You know as well as I do there's something going on. Someone was after what she gave us to keep."

"But she said not to do anything but give whatever it is to her brother Winston. That's what she paid you to do."

"She *over*paid me, and you know it."

"Just the same..."

"Make us some coffee, will you?"

Over two cups each I got Charity to admit that she was obligated to reach Winston and tell him about the bundle. She wasn't content with that. She wanted to go further. She marshaled all her persuasive courtroom style, and of course she always had that cool beauty...

"No," I said.

"Why no? What's wrong with nosing around a little?"

I told her it took time. I needed to be free in case something that paid came up in the information line. At the heart of it all, I explained, was the furnace, the late Gas King Supreme. Money had become a priority. There was no money in working for a dead woman.

"How about a friend of a dead woman?" she said.

"Charity..."

She stood toe-to-toe with me. "I'm serious, Yuri. Deadly serious." Her red eyes locked on mine. "We owe it to Felicia to ask a few questions. To find out if it was an accident."

"The King is dead..."

"If you talk about that furnace *once more*, I am gonna *bop* you! Felicia was way more important to me than any damn furnace. I need your help if I'm going to snoop a little." She jabbed her stiffened index finger against

32

my chest. Powered by her intensity, it felt like a cold chisel. "If you don't help me, I'll never help *you* again!"

I wanted to smile, but her icy eyes put that idea out of my head. "Give me some time to think about it," I said. "Anyhow, the first thing is to get in touch with Winston."

A while back we had asked the phone company to install an amplifier unit on the kitchen phone. A flipped switch and the little box broadcast the voice at the other end. The box also picked up the sounds of the room and sent them back over the line. The gadget was useful in making sure one or the other of us heard correctly. Sometimes being sure can be very important. Charity used the switch.

She called information in Cambridge, Massachusetts, and asked for a number for Winston Farrow. No such listing. Felicia had said he worked for Harvard. She called Harvard information. They gave her the development office. A dry-voiced woman reported that Mr. Farrow had been with them for only eight months. They had no forwarding address or number. A Mr. Drayton might have that information. He would be out of the office until day after tomorrow. Would she call then. She said she would.

She called information for Pine Promontory, Connecticut, where she had been a summer guest so long ago. It was too early in the season for Mrs. Farrow to be in residence. But Charity didn't know where she spent the winters. She dialed. Someone answered. It was the caretaker. She explained who she was. She didn't tell him Felicia was dead. She asked if he had Winston Farrow's number.

"Win? Mister Win? Don't know it off hand. Might be around here somewhere."

"Mrs. Farrow then? I can phone her."

"Ain't no lines run to where she's at, ma'am. She's with the good Lord. Died of grand old age 'bout six months ago."

"I'm sorry."

"Seen her every summer, last thirty year. A fine, fine lady. Don't know who I'll see this year."

"Oh?"

"Place tied up in law, ma'am. Mrs. Farrow, she had

some debts. Place here gonna be sold. I'm now working for some court, you believe? Mister Win, he got run off by the sheriff couple, three weeks ago. He was trying to take some things meant a lot to him. No dice. I got it, one way or the other, that Mr. Winston and Miss Felicia won't see a red cent outta the place they grew up in. Ain't it a pity?"

"It is, Mr. . . . ."

"Ben Green, ma'am."

"Ben, I'd still like to get in touch with Winston. Could you look around for his address over the next two days? Maybe it's written down somewhere. I'll call back day after tomorrow about this time."

Ben Green hesitated. "Don't know, ma'am . . ."

"I'm an old friend of the family. And I have something to give Win that might be worth money. *Please* look."

He agreed. Charity hung up. "I feel like I accomplished *some*thing anyway," she said.

She went upstairs and got dressed for a day at the law firm. She was late as it was. On her way out she said, "You could open the bundle, if you have the nerve. And decide just where we're going to start."

I paced over all that, on a roughly circular path through all the rooms on the first floor of 138. First thing was . . . I hadn't agreed to help her. After forty-five minutes I decided to leave the bundle alone for a while. I wasn't buying "curse," of course. I think I was hoping that if I didn't dig deeper into what Felicia had been up to, it might somehow take care of itself. I was having a lot of trouble getting really committed. I knew peeling off the black vinyl would be an irreversible act. Like Pandora, I wouldn't be able to put back the knowledge of what was in there. I sensed it would somehow draw me further into its mystery than I wanted to go. Lying under my reluctance was the very real problem that there was no money in it for me. Reserves were getting low. I mumbled angrily to myself. How mercenary I was becoming! That made me feel small . . . but didn't wholly change my mind.

The morning mail brought a letter from Jane and Clara, my daughters. School was winding down. They wanted to come for a visit this summer. I held the letter in a trembling hand. My eyes smarted as tears gathered. Jane's preadolescent handwriting churned up my guilt like a paddle. Whatever the marriage situation had been between Ann and me, it was I who had set about to destroy it. That I was searching for intimacy and close sharing and didn't know it did not seem much of an excuse at that moment when I held my distant daughter's letter in my hand.

I went to the piano and began to play my exercises. Great for getting me thinking, though I played badly. I tortured myself with memories of the affairs that had undermined my marriage. First came a few giddy, unfocused younger women, inevitably nearsighted, who sent me quasi-feminist notes on the backs of famous-art-work postcards. The coup de grace wasn't delivered by the legendary empty-headed sexpot, but by a woman who had once called herself Ann's friend. Hopelessly conservative, she had enjoyed my passion and personality for six or eight months, then turned somber and responsible. All tears of parting were genuine.

I played away my seizure of guilt and gloom. I was well out of the marriage. My daughters wanted to see me, I them. There was the Boyce Park wave pool, night games at Three Rivers Stadium, plenty in and around Pittsburgh to keep us all busy for a week or two. Charity in her own way was a big kid. She would like romping with the three of us. Things would be OK. . . .

The door chimes rang. I checked the porch mirror. A tall salesman-type faced the front door. Snap-brim straw hat, poplin coat, dress shoes, briefcase in his left hand. On the way to the door I ran through my I-gave-at-the-office and I-can't-afford-blank-right-now speeches. I kept the aluminum screen door locked during the warm months. That would keep him from getting his foot in, I thought as I opened the heavy front door.

My caller was John F. Kennedy, 35th President of the United States.

Mask! Before I could slam the door Kennedy raised a canister and sprayed me through the screen. Mace came down on my senses like a hammer. My eyesight was gone. My breath was slammed out of my lungs. I reeled away from the screen, groping to stay conscious.

Distantly I heard a blade shredding the aluminum screening. I went down to my hands and knees.

I couldn't see and could scarcely breathe. The only reason I was conscious at all was that the screen had broken up the shaped disabling jet. I heard the rattle of the screen door opening. JFK was coming in. One more squirt and I was gone.

I lunged weakly at where his legs ought to be. I hit them but didn't knock him over. My sole effective thought was to hold on to him somewhere. He wouldn't dare Mace me up close. He didn't. He hit my head with something very hard. Stars exploded. A surge of adrenaline gave me the strength for one more lunge. I wrenched him off balance. His curse was silibant and muffled.

My sinuses and breath passageways were searing. My eyelids were spasmed with blinking. No air, no strength. He hit my head again. And again. I tumbled down, down to a cool but consuming white dwarf sun.

I woke up sputtering on the living-room carpet. JFK had just dumped a pan of water on my face. I was miserable. My head felt like it had been used as a batting practice ball by the 1979 Pirates. I was in real danger of puking from an irritated vagus nerve. My eyelids were swollen nearly shut. I started in coughing right away. One last thing: I was *pissed.*

My ankles and wrists were wired. JFK was sitting on the edge of the couch. His hat and rubber mask were still on. He had added one item to his getup—a nasty-looking little automatic. It was pointed right between my eyes.

"Felicia Semanova came here early Wednesday morning. She brought something with her. Where is it?" He held something in his mouth. It was either to protect him from the Mace or to muffle his voice. Probably both.

I guessed he or his had followed Felicia to 138. I would have to lie carefully. I groaned and shuddered with discomfort—not all just for effect. "It's gone. I never did see what it was. My housemate wouldn't keep it for her."

"I didn't see her leave with it."

"She came back later and picked it up."

"I've been watching the house," JFK said. "I didn't see—"

"Day and night for two weeks? No sleep? Come *on.*"

"I think it's still here."

"Long gone." I tried to penetrate the masked speech.

"You weren't here. Your blonde friend didn't move it."

"You looked yourself. Everywhere. With a pick and a flashlight. Right? It's not here."

JFK cocked his pistol. He wore gloves. "Then tell me where it is. Or I'll kill you."

I hadn't thought it was possible to feel more miserable than I did. But I was wrong. If I said it was somewhere else, he might take me along to that place—and kill me when it wasn't there. If I told him it was in the White Chamber in the basement, he'd kill me because I'd given him what he wanted. "What is it?" I said. My mouth burned from the Mace. It was hard to talk.

"Something valuable, Nevsky."

"I think it was hers. I think you're ripping her off."

He rapped my skull with the pistol butt.

"Did you kill her, too?"

He rang my bell again. The stars danced. If this was stalling, I was going to run out of skull before he ran out of time.

I rolled my head over and puked. Dry heaves, thank God, or I might have strangled.

"You want to insult me more?" His voice was an unidentifiable hissing mumble. The pistol moved into my limited field of vision. "I'm getting impatient."

I heard distant footsteps on the upstairs porch. Live with someone long enough and you know their step, the way they approach a door to unlock it.

Charity was home very early.

I had to gamble or we were both going to be in big trouble. The rubber mask had dimmed JFK's hearing some. But he would hear the door open....

The instant it did, I shouted, "Charity, trouble, run!"

The pistol jabbed my temple. "Another word and you're dead!" Behind the mask JFK's mouth opened to shout to her.

Before he could, Charity screamed, "I'll get the police!" The door slammed again and she was gone. Clever lady, I thought. Now she was gambling—with my life, bless her heart. Out of earshot, no threat to me could cow her. She *had* done some fast thinking. I was alive, even if I was in trouble. My trouble would be waiting for her with every advantage. I knew she wasn't running for the police. She had dug out the little derringer she carried at the bottom of her purse and was readying an ambush by one of the doors. Trouble was, there were five exits from the first floor.

JFK gave me a nasty poke in the temple with his pistol barrel. "You're dumb lucky, Nevsky," he hissed. He put away his pistol and snatched up his briefcase. He hurried out of the living room. He picked the big front door as an exit. I wriggled to my knees, hoping to catch a glimpse through the picture window of my housemate getting the drop on him. But he left the porch running and I heard nothing special in his wake.

My head spun and I decided to lie down again. To my surprise, miserable as I was, I fell asleep....

"Dozing on the job!" Charity said as she plied the wire cutters. "Can't trust *you* to man the home front."

"He got away?"

"I guessed porch door rear. He picked front. By the time I got around the side of the house, he was a speck in the distance." The bits of wire fell away. When I tried to sit up she shoved me down. She had a bowl of hot water, towels and a washcloth. While she cleaned me and surveyed the damage, I told her what had happened. I finished and added, "I *owe* you. Why'd you come home?"

"I couldn't concentrate. I kept thinking about Felicia. I decided to take the day off. I told them I'm going to take a few of all the vacation days I have coming. I'm going to use them to try to get to the bottom of whatever Felicia was involved in." She grabbed my bearded chin with long white fingers. "You *with* me, Yuri Nevsky?"

"I said I owe you."

"You *will* help then?"

"And I owe somebody else, too." I waved toward my lumpy skull.

"You're holding a grudge?"

"Russians are experts at it."

She helped me upstairs. She dosed me up with headache pills and carefully washed my swollen eyes. I was still coughing frequently. My air passages were going to stay irritated for a while. I fell asleep the moment she closed the door.

I woke up when she came in with tea and Pepperidge Farm Lido Cookies on a tray. "Light food for people with head injuries." She looked into my eyes with the house flashlight. "You made me nervous sleeping so much," she said. "You look OK, though. You want a doctor?"

"Not if I can help it."

She made me lean toward the bedside lamp to better check my lumps and eyes. "My eyes sting," I said.

"They're not *as* swollen."

She read the highlights of the evening's *Pittsburgh Press*. Listening to her with my stinging eyes closed, I heard her voice with new clarity. I found it very soothing, with a mellow vibrancy supporting her lighter tones. I should ask her to read the Bible to me sometime, or Shakespeare. We could take turns. Maybe this was the start of a new tradition at 138.

About then I started to feel drowsy. "You need your beddy-by time, sweetie," she said. "Tomorrow we start on Felicia Farrow Semanova."

"*Where* do we start?" I said.

"Hermitage Decorator Antiques," she said. "Where else?"

I slept for a long while, then woke in blackness. I wondered what had wakened me. Then I heard them and knew—that distant rumble in the night and the long blast of a diesel air horn. A night freight was running through Marland Borough up the north-south line. I had grown up in Homewood, where the big trains groaned at night all through my childhood. My father used to ride them to Chicago on business. He left from the terminal of the Pennsylvania and Lake Erie— "Peeandlee" to the locals—on the North Side. Now that stone and marble monster had been remodeled. It was inhabited no longer by hissing engines and conductors with pocket watches, but with chichi restaurants and trendy boutiques.

My father rode the commuter train to work in downtown Pittsburgh. I went down the street to meet him at 5:40 in the afternoon, favorite stuffed animal in arms. Those trains had long since quit running. I had noticed in my travels around the city that they had torn up much track. Where before six and eight sets of rails curved in shiny strands to the horizon, now only two or three remained. The ballast, rails and ties were gone. The beds remained. Gandy dancers rode along them to their jobs in two-and-a-half-ton pickup trucks.

Despite everything some trains still ran. Last month Charity and I had stood down at the foot of the hill while a long freight lumbered by, boxcar stencils offering a crash course in the names and logos of the remaining lines. We had counted cars, as we had once done as children, long years back. "One hundred and *ten!*" we chorused. "One hundred and eleven..." I grinned and called trains part of our tribal heritage.

Well into the next town the train made its long, lonesome burp again. Want to know what's right and wrong about this country? I asked my now sleeping half. What's been good—and when? And what's wrong now? Take a look at the railroads. The whole story's there, if one knew how to read those iron wheels, big rusty boxcars, and gorged, yellowing timetables fifty years off-schedule. My sleeping self didn't answer. And pretty soon the rest of me, too, was all aboard the Sleep City Limited. *This train don't carry no gamblers...*

Chapter Four

Hermitage Decorator Antiques was in the phone book. The address was on Walnut Street in Shadyside. After checking my head, eyes and breathing machinery and finding them sore but OK, Charity and I drove over to Shadyside. Walnut Street was one of the main drags of what was an old part of Pittsburgh. I turned off Negley Avenue onto Walnut. At that end it was lined with small apartment buildings and single-family homes. The houses were all brick, all cheek by jowl, with only a few feet between them, an arrangement seen everywhere among those Pittsburgh homes built before World War II.

Closer to the business district came the artsy section—painters' studios, calligraphers, a stained-glass school, muddlers in biorhythms and horoscopes. On the edge of the high-rent district were shops and boutiques with unlikely commercial hopes: bathroom furnishings and bric-a-brac, owl goods, all-wood toys.

Just before the bank and pizza parlor I spotted Hermitage Decorator Antiques. It was housed in a single-story brick storefront, a display window on either side of the glass-paned door. I parked down the street. We walked back. Two undistinguished brocaded chairs stood in each window. The door blind was pulled down. A professionally lettered sign gave the hours as ten to four and by appointment. It was after ten, but Hermitage was closed.

Between the Hermitage building and the next one ran a narrow alley just delivery-truck wide. Charity hovered by Hermitage. I wandered down the alley and found a large four-bay garage with a second floor. It had been redesigned. A small warehouse had been made of two bays and the space above. The other two were a tool shop and what seemed to be a pottery kiln. A Plymouth Duster, a VW Rabbit and two paneled delivery trucks sat in the small parking lot. One truck was marked *Hermitage Decorator Antiques*. The other belonged to the business across the alley. *'sPots—Quality Handcrafted and Imported Ceramics,* its painted panels shouted to the world in Art Deco lettering.

The Walnut Street door of 'sPots was open for business. I followed Charity through the door. Ceramics stood on white plastic shelving. No knickknackery in 'sPots. Tureens were cast in lines that surprised—and delighted—the eye. Goblets *could* be made of clay and not look like they were brought home from third grade art class. Fish poachers, soufflé dishes, ramekins demanded to be bought. But not by everyone. That stuff was expensive.

A woman about twenty-eight wearing Big Smith bib overalls came up from the back of the store. She was tall, almost six feet, and solid. She wore her auburn hair in a long pigtail. Her nose turned up like Bob Hope's. She held out a large work-toughened hand to Charity. "Good morning. I'm Twiggy Twill. And you're someone special."

"I am?" Charity said.

"The first customer in Year Three of 'sPots."

"Oh, it's a *very* nice store. A little expensive for—"

"Tod's out back at the kiln. I'll buzz him up." She thumbed a desk button.

"I'm really just looking for—"

"Tod *loves* to talk to customers. Too bad there aren't more of you, that's all."

I waved at some of the pieces. "Tod made these? They look very elegant."

Twiggy pointed out a half dozen of the more audacious pieces. "These are his. They don't move too well.

42

But I think they're wonderful. Miles ahead of most con-temporary pottery. Some of these others are done by local potters. The rest are imports." Her heavy brows shot up. "The *best* imports."

I heard a distant voice. "Don't leave, customers. Don't leave! I'm on my way." The voice was husky and made me think of bass-baritones. It grew closer. The rear door opened and Tod appeared. He was broad and brown-bearded. He wore a heavy apron and a wedding band. He was about my age. "I'm the owner, Tod Buckcry. Which of you is the first customer of our third year?"

Charity said, "Well, I'm really not—"

Out on Walnut Street a revving heavy motorcycle drowned out all other sound. A huge Harley-Davidson piloted by a brute in leather and studs came bouncing over the curb onto the sidewalk—and straight into 'sPots store window. Wild female laughter followed the death rattle of forty square feet of display glass.

White arms released a leather-girded chest and a woman dismounted from behind the biker. He thumbed the reverse lever and backed off into the street. She blew him a kiss and shouted, "Keep on truckin', Steel-head." He gave the thumbs-up sign and *braaaated* away. She walked unsteadily to the door and came in.

She surveyed us, her eyes coming to rest on Tod. As they did, they saddened. "Might know you'd be right here in this damn store. *Know* you wouldn't be worried where *I* was. *Know* you wouldn't come looking for me." She was five eight, near thirty. Her hair, once permed into ringlets, was twisted and matted by long revelry. Her smooth right cheek carried the bluish smear of a bruise. Her designer jump suit was smeared and stained. It smelled faintly of vomit.

Tod made a calming gesture. "I couldn't have come looking for you. I didn't have any idea where you were, Selina."

"Bullshit!" Selina staggered. She was still drunk. "You dint drag your ass outta here because it's this pisshole's anniversary. Two years of never makin' ends meet." She twirled her vertical index finger by her ear. "Whooopeee, hubbee!" She wobbled toward him. "And me carryin' you all the way."

"You haven't been—"

"The hell I haven't!"

"Selina, you don't have to—"

"Damn you, Tod, for lovin' this store more than me—"

"I don't—"

She went for his face with nails curved to claws. He jumped backward to avoid her rush. His head hit the corner of a shelf and he staggered.

Outside, a police cruiser roared full tilt down Walnut Street, siren and lights working at max power.

"Hey!" Charity rushed over and grabbed Selina's shoulders from behind. Not a good idea. Selina whirled and went for Charity's face with her nails. "Stay outta this!" she shrieked. One of her nails caught the skin high on Charity's neck. She grabbed that hand, jammed it into her mouth and bit it. Selina shrieked. They stumbled into the stands of white shelving. Hundreds of dollars worth of ceramics tumbled to tinkling deaths. I moved forward to wrap Selina up before she killed Charity. With her free hand Selina scooped up a still intact pitcher by its shaft handle. I lunged at her as she swung it at Charity's head. I spoiled her aim, but Charity did a bad job of getting out of the way. It hit the side of her skull.

Her knees buckled. On the way to a Moslem prayer position, her head cleared a little. She grabbed Selina's ankle and foot and tried to pull her down. Selina was too strong. She elbowed me in the stomach, tore her left foot free and delivered a vicious but grazing kick to Charity's head.

I heard sirens and saw bright blue flashes. Police.

"Selina Buckcry, that's enough!" An authoritative woman's voice. Charging forward was a solid female officer flanked by a lantern-jawed partner holding a billy club. Selina turned away from Charity and flew at the uniformed woman. I didn't clearly see what happened then, but the lady officer shoved Selina's right arm up between her shoulder blades and ran her head on into the exposed brick wall.

Selina went down in a heap. The lady-in-blue straightened her out and rolled her face down on the small rug on which she had landed. The handcuffs made precision metal noises going around her wrists.

44

"This is one feisty lady, Charlie." She rolled Selina faceup. Blood ran down her forehead. The bruise on her cheek looked nastier than ever. "We want her cuffed in the cruiser?"

"For sure. Learned my lesson last time."

Twiggy Twill had got Tod sitting up and some of the color back into his face. She was lifting his midsection with one hand around his belt. With the other she was rubbing the beads of sweat from his forehead. She made soothing noises through pursed lips.

"He all right, Twiggy?" Charlie said.

"I've always been...a fast mender," Tod said.

"How about you, ma'am?" the lady officer said to Charity.

She stood up, took a couple of deep breaths. She felt the side of her head. A lump was springing up like a mushroom after a long damp spell, but the skull wasn't soft. Charity's fingertips to her neck came away sticky with blood. "I guess...I'm pretty much all right," she said.

"Why was she after you?"

"No reason except I tried to be a peacemaker. I've never been here before. I don't know her. We just stopped to ask about the place across the alley."

"I thought you both were customers," Twiggy Twill said. She helped Tod up. He shrugged off her helping arms and tottered to his desk chair. He flopped down, hands hanging to his ankles, and panted.

"You want to prefer charges?" the lady officer said to Charity.

She was still a little confused. She looked toward Tod. He frowned anxiously and gave a little "no" twitch of the head.

"No," she said.

"Selina's really opened a giant can of worms this time, Tod," Charlie said. He tipped his cap back. "Half the cops in the east boroughs been chasing her and her sweet friend, Steelhead Sweeney. He's a one-man gang of Hell's Angels East. And pound-for-pound she could fight with Sugar Ray Robinson. They been up to their necks in trouble, last two days. Evelyn here and me figured she might be partied out 'bout now. Ready to come home. Other car still chasin' Steelhead. They'll

45

get him, too. Time we write up all the charges, gonna be as many pages as *War and Peace*."

"What'd they do this time?" Tod said.

"Started up New Kensington way," Evelyn said. "Trashed damned near a whole bowling alley. Beat up folks. Came down Hulton Road to Oakmont and got boozed up at a roadhouse. Then tore *it* up. And five people went to the hospital. Two were woman. And Steelhead didn't lay a hand on them." She jerked her thumb at Selina. *"She did it."*

"Oh, God..."

Charlie had his notebook out. "Then they somehow got into an after-hours club in Verona. *Five* polack steelworkers put the two of them out. The damage: two busted arms, one lady with half her hair pulled out, and Selina grabbed an old man's cane and raked every bottle off the top shelf of the bar—"

"Oh, Christ, that's enough!"

"That's enough, all right. Last damage is this here plate glass window." Charlie wet his pencil point with his tongue and added to his notebook.

The ambulance came. A moaning Selina was stretchered and carried off. Tod asked Charity to put her name, address and phone number on a card. Then he rode with Selina after telling Twiggy to keep the store open.

We helped the big woman sweep up the broken pottery. "Selina used to be a pretty nice person, believe it or not," she said. "Used to really care about the store and what Tod was trying to do. Then about a year ago she found the money to hit the sauce and run off with one loser after another. Now she's driving Tod crazy, twisting the knife right in his heart."

"A drinking problem isn't a nice thing," Charity said.

"Think if you'd like to be yelled at the way she yells at him."

"I *did* hear some of it."

Twiggy's ruddy skin darkened with a blush. "None of those things are true about Tod. He's not like that at all."

I asked her why Hermitage Decorator Antiques wasn't open. She said they hadn't been keeping regular hours lately. Maybe we should take a walk and try again in a little while.

We walked out onto Walnut. I checked Charity's head in the sunlight. It seemed all right. "How you feel?" I said.

She took a deep breath and closed her eyes. "OK, I guess. Something about Felicia's doings seems to mean knocks on the head. You yesterday, me today. I hope that's the end of it."

"Probably just the beginning," I said. "Your skull bopper went to the hospital. Mine's still running around somewhere."

To help clear her head, I gave Charity the twenty-nine-cent tour of Shadyside. I hadn't been in the area for years. In my college days at Pitt the bars and coffee houses had eaten up my spare time. The Encore was still there, so was Taylor's, the most determined of neighborhood bars. More than once I had tottered tipsily out of one Shadyside bar or another with the uncertain hand of a date on my arm. Those beery evenings usually ended in the back seat of a car where she and I played out the victim-aggressor sexual rituals of the late fifties. No matter what happened within those steamed-up windows—and some strange things did—for me dissatisfaction and guilt were built in. I had never been much for letting loose. Now, staring forty-plus in the face, I wished I had loosened up more. A lot more. Life *was* short.

That part of my Shadyside was gone. Other, physical things were gone, too. The Shadyside Theater where twenty years ago I saw *Breathless* as a single student with pimples, and two years ago saw *If...* with Charity, as a divorced father-of-two, was now a small shopping arcade. So much was gone. That was endurable only if one replaced the old with worthwhile new.

My nostalgia might have run on all day, but we were interrupted. "Excuse me, are you the couple who were wondering about Hermitage?" She was about twenty-two with, what we, ignorant of orthodontics, had once called "buckteeth." Pity, because her eyes were bright blue and her cheekbones high and well shaped. "I'm June Gowell. I drive the truck for Tod and kind of help out around 'sPots. Twiggy said you wanted to know about Hermitage. I talked to Ruthie Spires. She's one of my roommates. She works for the count. She said they were doing some kind of bad news inventory. Going out of business, or something." June Gowell led us to a side entrance to the Hermitage building, which I had overlooked on my little tour down the alley. "They're in there," she said.

Charity and I walked up a half dozen stairs into an office. A redhead was sitting at a desk aswarm with papers. File cabinets sat with drawers protruding like metal tongues. Papers spilled from file folders were stacked on the floor in four-foot piles. The redhead scarcely glanced at us. "The auction is next week, folks," she said. "Wednesday, to be exact."

"What auction?"

"The 'Priceless Antiques Marked Down Auction.' What else? We're doing inventory, trying to figure out what we really have to sell."

"June Gowell said you were maybe going out of business."

"Maybe? Maybe the sun is going to come up tomorrow. It's that kind of maybe." She got up and went over to the office Mr. Coffee. She took it black and offered us some. "I'm afraid the old Hermitage is ready for the wrecker's ball."

A man came up the stairs. He had been back in the warehouse section of the converted garage. He carried a half dozen lists, two-hole punched and fixed in a vinyl binder. He was tall and pale. A single horizontal wrinkle divided his brow. A monocle magnified his right eye above a thick bristly mustache. He wore a peasant blouse. Black knickerlike trousers and mid-shin calfskin boots gave him a definite Russian look.

"Monsieur-dame, we are *pas ouvrier*."

"Not only that," the redhead said, "we're not open."

"Ruthie, see if you can find *any* record of those six Gold Coast wood statues," he said.

"I can't find *anything*. Only Felicia could ever make sense out of all this paper—"

"Felicia is with the greatest Bookkeeper of all." He had a slight Russian accent. "Which leaves me with *you*, Ruthie. A bit removed from the greatest. Find out something about the statues." He pulled a large silver flask from his back pocket and took a big snort.

"We've been at this *three* days, D-M. And every day

I wonder a little more about where you're going to get the dough to pay me for my time."

"You'll get your money. I promise."

She aimed a sour, green-eyed glare at him. "I know too much about your promises, Count. Life around you reminds me of one of those old fairy tales—everything is just over the next hill." She threw down her pencil. "You been asking a lot, and giving damn little. Maybe that's the Russian style, the Count Dromsky-Michaux style. OK for you. Not OK for Ruthie Spires here. I'm still hooked on the western Pennsylvania style—a tough, square deal." She stood up. Her coffee cup overturned, soaking papers. "What I'm getting from you is a screwing—both kinds. By the time you get done translating *that* into the six or eight languages you say you know, I will be *gone*." She snatched up a denim sack purse and headed for the door.

Count Dromsky-Michaux headed her off. He talked fast and hard. Her face was as unyielding as a mannikin's. He tried to put his arm over her shoulder. She went by him like Franco Harris breaking a tackle. She gave the front door a vicious slam. The glass broke. Wherever Charity and I went these days, I thought, things were breaking.

Count Dromsky-Michaux clenched his fists and took several deep breaths, eyes closed. Then he pulled out the flask again and took another big hit. Finally, he looked at me. "Not only are we closed, monsieur-dame, we are in dis-ar-ray. The management has been sleeping with the employees. This is not sound business practice." He managed a thin smile. "I understand the Harvard Business School is preparing a summer seminar on the topic..." I understood he had been at the flask all morning and was a little drunk.

"We came over here to ask about Felicia Semanova," I said.

"What's to ask? She used to keep books and manage the office here. Now she's dead. Of what interest is she to you?"

"I saw in the paper she was killed," Charity said. "I'm Charity Day, an old college friend of hers. This is my colleague, Yuri Nevsky. We live over in Marland Borough."

The count looked more interested. "I see." He tried fluent Russian on me. I answered him.

A black boy wearing a sweat-matted "Pirate Power" T-shirt came in the side door carrying a huge wood carving. It looked to me like a cross between a clipper ship's figurehead and a Muppet. "Mistah Mish-o, this is all there was in that storage room you said was fulla stuff."

The count groaned. He removed his monocle and rubbed his face with his palms. "Put it right there, Hugo. *Spasebo*."

The boy left. The count sat carefully in a folding chair. He kept his spine straight. "I can't believe Felicia's dead. A few days ago she was working at that desk where Ruthie was. And I mean *worked*, Ms. Day. And she knew what she was doing. It's clear, now that she's gone, how much we relied on her. I don't quite see why you're here, Ms. Day, Mr. Nevsky."

"She came to see us two weeks ago," Charity said.

He looked intently at us. He was handsome in an aristocratic Russian way. His thin lips were set in a horizontal line. I wondered for several moments if he was going to speak. "Two weeks ago?" he said.

"Something special about two weeks?" I said.

"Should it be special?"

Charity and I hadn't really thought much about how to find out about Felicia without revealing everything about her visit and bundle. But I had to try to muddle through. "I think she was in some kind of trouble," I said.

"What kind of trouble?"

"She wanted me to take care of something for her." Charity picked up my theme. "Keep it for her. For old time's sake. I decided it wasn't a good idea. I felt bad. As I said, we were college roommates. And I've always liked her, even though I hadn't seen her for years."

"I can understand. She had a very attractive personality. What did she want you to keep?"

Charity shrugged. "A funny-shaped package. Big. She brought it into the house, then came by later and picked it up."

"You don't know what it was?"

"She wouldn't tell me. When I saw in the *Post-*

Gazette she was dead in an accident I started wondering. Did she ever find anybody to keep her bundle? And maybe people should know about it. You know anything about it, Count Dromsky-Michaux?"

The count repeated his long moments of horizontal lip line and heavy thought. It occurred to me that a great deal was on his mind about Felicia. Perhaps he was deciding what we ought to hear. He rose slowly and began to pace. *"Nevozmozhno!* Impossible!" He scowled. "She was *in* on it. I would *never* have suspected."

"In on what? Suspected what?" I said.

He went for the flask again, then wiped his lips with a white handkerchief. He made himself comfortable. The booze made him want to talk. "All old scenario, Nevsky, Ms. Day. Played out yet again. And I've never thought of myself as an unwary person or a poor businessman."

"What happened?"

"The classic misadventure of partnership. One partner honest, the other...less so. Sergei Yelanov, my partner, and I worked hard to try to make Hermitage *the* quality decorator antique concern in western Pennsylvania. We were the ideal partners. Yin and Yang. My being a count—a real one, I assure you, with a European background and a sound fine arts education—was a great help. It allowed me to impress the corporate managers—and particularly their wives. When you deal with wealthy people who have no—or limited—taste, you're really selling trust and competence. The objets d'art transactions are almost secondary. And a certain élan. I can assure you, Ms. Day, in a dinner jacket among the wealthy, I am *formidable*.

"Sergei Yelanov specialized in acquisition. He had relations all over the Soviet Union and Europe. Many of them were in the fine arts and antique business, one way or the other. Sergei had the nuts-and-bolts of selection, purchase and transportation down cold. Even in such a volatile and competitive market as collectibles has become in these last years, he somehow found the very best bargains. Particularly in bronzes, with sound quality as well. For a while Hermitage was considered chic among the antique-minded trend setters. Those

51

who summer in Ligonier and winter in Palm Beach. We did well in those years."

"So what happened?"

"The economy turned down. Poor business climate. Poor steel business. Inflation. Hermitage became less trendy. We figured to hold on. We figured in a few years the economy would improve. Our old customers would remember we gave good value and come back. The last election was good for business. Things would have picked up. I think we might have made it."

"But...?"

The count hesitated. A light of caution shined briefly in his eyes. The booze put it out. "Sergei took off two weeks and a few days ago. Last saw him Thursday, May twenty-eighth. My loyal partner. The guy who sat here four weeks ago"—he pointed at a folding chair—"and told me Hermitage would make it—was selling and mortgaging just about everything we owned—for cash. He turned *everything* into cash except my gold inlays. The auditors have been here. They used fancy phrases, Nevsky. But the message was clear: I'm bankrupt. Thanks, Sergei Yelanov! Trusted partner! I can see now, Felicia would have *had* to help him clean us out. The books would have spelled it out. And she kept the books. She left sick, Friday at noon. Didn't come back to work till Thursday morning, June fourth. About then I began to think that Sergei hadn't gone fishing, or was fishing in the Seychelles or Aruba, or some infernal resort or other. One suitcase full of clothes— another with our money. When did Felicia visit you?"

"Wednesday, June second, very early morning," Charity said.

The count nodded. "I suppose it all fits. She just didn't seem the type to be a felon."

"She told me things weren't going well for her," Charity said. "That her life had...taken a downward turn."

"She was married, wasn't she? Never know it the way she and Sergei got on. Hot and heavy most of the time. I always thought of her as a person of quality. Possibly from one of the better families."

"She was."

The count offered us the flask. When we refused, he

drank deeply. He was committed to talking now. "Always imagined she could do better than Sergei, a married man." He turned a somber glance toward me. "Then I always thought I could do better than Ruthie Spires. But that was our foursome: Felicia and Sergei, Ruthie and me. We spent quite a few weekends together. When the business was good, we'd take the ladies to Vegas. They'd play the slots and we'd play baccarat. Once only once—we hit the bank big. We bought cham-pagne and co-caine and went up to the room. That was the only time we forgot which woman went with whom." His glance turned hollow. "Or what sex we were."

"So you think what she wanted me to keep was something from the business?" Charity said.

"I suppose so. Maybe one of our more valuable pieces. Everything's so mixed up, I don't know what's missing. Conceivably what she had was something Sergei had given her for helping clean me out." He nodded vigorously and began to pace again. "She had the upper hand in the relationship. Sergei was mad for fair women. She could make him do what she wanted, though she didn't push it. What she had was probably her share of *my* business."

"But now she's dead."

"Dead as Hermitage," the count said. "Just that Hermitage is still falling under the wrecker's ball." He pointed a slender finger at her. "Listen, Charity Day, anything Felicia Semanova was trying to cache belonged to the business. You find it, it belongs to me. Or more likely, to my creditors."

"If I find anything . . ."

He readjusted his pinch of snuff. "We oldest children of 1918 Russian emigrés are supposed to be the worldly and cynical ones. I was born in Paris in the mid-twenties. Grew up in a mad world of wealth and poverty side-by-side. My mother had a necklace with forty diamonds—and had to teach piano for one franc an hour. Before I was ten I knew intimately the meanings of suicide and prostitution. I knew other's despairs and broken hopes. I saw firsthand the sweet and the seamy. So I should have known about partnership. I should have saved money. Should have found myself a steady woman of good blood, instead of chasing giddy girls with butterfly tattoos near their nether parts. The ones who talked about the importance of the vibrator in sexual fulfillment. I should have bought Sergei out, cut back inventory. Should have...oh, *merde!*" Count Dromsky-Michaux held his aristocratic head in his long fingers.

"Now what?"

"Now I'm fifty-six years old. I liquidate everything. Creditors get it all, some percentage of what I really own. The customers who advanced payments for non-existent art, or for objects already sold..." He shrugged. "They'll take almost a full loss. And never *dream* of dealing with Hermitage again. I'll sell my condominium, my Jaguar, take my little nest egg out of the money market. Get a job in a shop. I've been broke before. I know how to learn a trade. I ran aground in Philadelphia awhile back. Earned myself a machinist's union card."

He almost bit into his palm. "That *bête* Sergei said he was taking the weekend and Monday off. Said he'd be back Tuesday morning and had a loan lined up that could see us through. No show Tuesday. Or Wednesday, Thursday. By Friday I was very nervous. More so when Mrs. P. Cranston Wilson called to inquire after the matched Muscovite enamel jewel cases scheduled for delivery two weeks earlier. We sold them two *months* ago. How many 1870 matched enamel cases did we stock, for God's sake? I called Anna, Sergei's wife. She said he was off fishing on Lake Erie somewhere. I called the Big E Marina where he keeps the *Stressless I.* They checked and said she was tied up and secured. By then, good people, I was a *most* alarmed man. I told Felicia to call the banks. She did. All the accounts were down to nickel-dime level. Right then I knew I'd been had. I phoned my attorney."

"But you didn't think Felicia had anything to do with it?" Charity said.

"Not till just now. When you said she was visiting you when she told me she had a bad case of the late-season flu. And that she wanted you to hold some goods for her. Sounds like she and Sergei were all tangled up together. She knew *everything.* Plus he would've eaten out of her hand. If she'd asked him. I guess her cut was a pretty big one. Enough to keep her quiet."

"Why did she want to have me hold whatever it was?"

"Maybe thought Sergei would change his mind. Maybe to get it out of the way for a while. Maybe she was worried I might catch on and check her possessions."

"It's hard for me to imagine my dear friend Felicia as a 'felon,' as you put it."

"Hard for *you?* She kept *my* books. If you can't trust your bookkeeper, who can you trust? And all the time she was finding new ways for Sergei to take cash out of my business. The rats were leaving the sinking Hermitage, but they were going first-class."

The black boy came crashing back up the stairs. "Hey, Mistah Mish-o, somethin' crazy going on. Got five wood cases back there. Labels say, 'Limoge, 1906.' But what's wrapped up in newspapers inside is nothin' but Coke bottles."

The count groaned again. He was really in a wash of self-pity. As he Magic Markered out a large Closed for Business sign to cover the hole recently filled by the door window glass, I understood he really wasn't a very gutsy man. He turned from his taping to look at me. "Remember, Ms. Day, Nevsky, any goods out loose belong to the business."

Neither Charity nor I answered. We walked back out onto Walnut. June Gowell, the cute bucktoothed girl, was taking the remaining shards of glass from the 'sPots front window frame.

I asked her if she knew Felicia. It turned out they used to live together, along with Ruthie Spires, Twiggy Twill and an Amanda Swale. They rented the second floor of one of the big old houses down Walnut. Amanda was probably Felicia's closest friend. They ran together, loaned each other money. Amanda was in her mid-twenties, hanging out with an older crowd. Felicia, being the oldest, was like a big sister to her. June gave me their house number, even though Felicia had since moved to "a fancier address."

June also told me that Felicia would be laid out at the Powers Funeral Home on Craig Street in Oakland. The burial would be Saturday, day after tomorrow at Calvary Cemetery in Hazelwood. The good news was that Winston Farrow III, her brother, had been contacted. He would be flying in from Boston for the funeral.

Charity said her head hurt. She wanted to go back to 138 and lie down. After that she had a phone call to make. "I'm glad Winston will be here," she said. "We can get the bundle off our backs."

"It's not all neat and clean, Charity. Like you said yesterday, there're strings everywhere. There's a Big Picture we're just beginning to see. It's not fair just to stick Winston with the bundle."

"It's his, no matter about strings," she said. "Felicia's orders. We'll tell him what we know. He'll just have to make some decisions. And they'll depend on what kind of character he has."

"We still have two days to find out more. Who knows what we might come up with?"

Charity winked. "Who knows, indeed."

Chapter Five

The Yelanovs lived in the Monroeville area east of Pittsburgh, part of the vast carpet of suburbs surrounding the smallish city proper. As long as the gas supply held out, this would be good living, I said to myself as I twisted up treed lanes abloom with new leaves, past enough Dutch doors, rampant eagles and garage-front basketball hoops to make a person think the American Dream was as alive and well as ever.

One of those stiff chain-supported mailboxes assured me that I had found the right place. The Yelanov house sat atop a rise in Woody Acres. That development was definitely inhabited by upper-middle managers and professionals, those not up to the income level of greedy doctors or corporate attorneys—but almost. All houses were split-levels, all designer originals. The bulldozers had left some big trees behind. Two grand oaks spread over the Yelanov lawn. The living area behind the brick and wood was generous. I saw no bikes, trikes, balls, skates or stilts. No babies cried or children fought. A lot of Yelanov space was going to waste.

The wide garage door was open. A Lincoln and a Nova filled the double bay. A blue Chrysler sat in the drive. From a vantage point in the early afternoon sun, a nicely clipped little poodle sounded the alarm. I called quietly to it and it came prancing up, puffy tail snapping back and forth. I petted it between the ears. It hopped straight up and down and kept its paws off my slacks.

It was a she. She licked my shoe and followed me up to the screen door. I pressed the doorbell. The door behind the screen was open. Within, chimes pealed the melody of "Come Back to Sorrento." I stood on the concrete square of porch and waited. From the house fifty feet to the right the TV sang the praises of smooth, shiny floors and determined homemaking. Two teenaged girls sailed by on 300-dollar ten-speeds. "Abba *sucks*," said one, and they traded what I would have bet were stainless-steel-and-wire grins. A few moments passed while the poodle and I kept company. I chimed again and hummed along. Tunes like that always made me think of Italian tenors with obesity problems. No one answered. In the depths of the house I heard voices. A man and a woman were arguing. I called out, but the voices continued, their tones slightly louder. I tried the screen door. It was open. I went in.

I stepped into a foyer. It led into a large living room furnished in Expensive Bland. Third-rate Russian sculptures hunched on pedestals looked like vultures about to fall on the first piece of untidiness. I was seeing dregs from the late collection of Hermitage Decorator Antiques. The drapes were drawn. A projector TV, sound dialed down, flashed a wall-sized color image of a box of tampons. The living room was quite dim. My eyes were drawn toward a lit room in the rear of the house. I was about to call out. A woman's curse froze my mouth open.

"Damn it, Vasya! I know whatever that Semanova woman had belonged to Sergei."

"You're awfully quick to believe Dromsky-Michaux, Anna."

"I believe him all right. Know why, Vasya? He's *never* called me in the morning before. And he's been partners with Sergei for more than five years. So *today*, ten minutes ago, he calls to say a couple was asking after the Semanova whore. And not to tell them anything if they come here. *Another* reason I believe him is that I had to pry out of the little weasel that the couple told him she was running all around the countryside a few weeks past trying to stash some kind of package. He didn't *want* to tell me that."

"I thought you shouldn't have pressured him," he said.

"Like hell, Vasya. He didn't *want* to tell me. That's why I bluffed, said I'd tell them anything they wanted to know if they ever came here. That opened the slimy little eel up. He was scared I would."

This was all too interesting to break up. I kept to the shadows while working my way around for a view of the vocal couple. I peered into a game room. Its knotty pine paneling carried Steeler, Pirate and Penguin posters, bowling trophies and framed 8 x 10's of a cabin cruiser. Probably the *Stressless I*. Not a bad-looking vessel.

Anna Yelanov had dark hair and a prominent nose. Her mouth was broad and generous. Below it swelled the first faint curves of a double chin. She wore a flowered muumuu tied at the waist. The dark ringlets of her hair were a bit disheveled. She was patting at them with her palm.

The man Vasya had been talking to her through the open door of a half bath. Comb in hand, he stepped out into the room. He raked the style back into a head of heavy jet black hair. He wore light tan trousers stretched tightly by the big muscles of his upper legs. His necktie drooped unfastened around his neck. Hanging on the belaying pin of a souvenir section of ship's rail was the jacket that went with the pants. I had a suit like it. I remembered being angry at how much it cost.

It dawned on me that these two had not long ago made love. I wouldn't have guessed it from the way they were going now.

"You're my attorney, Vasya. Why, then, may I ask, don't you want me to recover whatever the Semanova woman was trying to hide? I'm *sure* it was Sergei's property. He ran off. Now whatever he left behind belongs to me. I want it back."

"One frightened, confused phone call from your husband's partner? And I'm sure the count was half in the bag, as usual. Hardly reason to feel you've been cheated or defrauded, don't you think?" Vasya's voice was aimed at persuasion. Underneath, though, I heard the faint saw whine of rising irritation.

"The woman *had* something, the count said!" She moved closer to him, hand raised to make her points.

"That may be. I'm telling you to forget about it. There're more important—"

"Don't tell me what's important! Sergei made my life miserable doing it. Now he's split—and you're going to take over making me miserable?"

"Don't flatter yourself, Anna."

"Don't think you're so smart, and I'm so dumb."

The attorney frowned. His body stiffened. Anger, I guessed. "What's that supposed to mean?"

"Your attentions have been pretty sudden is all. Just like the count, now that I think about it. Sergei runs off a couple weeks ago and"—she snapped her fingers— "all of a sudden we're a couple. You're giving me a bit of a rush. Coming at me like I was a silver screen sexpot instead of a failed middle-aged opera singer. What are you up to?"

"That's enough!"

"Hit a nerve? Hit—"

He hit all right. He raised his flattened palm and brought the edge down on the side of her neck near where it joined the shoulder. Her mouth dropped open as her body stiffened. He did it again, harder. He watched her crumble. Her head hit the rug with a solid *thunk.* He looked down at her for a long moment, smiling. He picked her up—no easy feat considering her poundage—and stretched her out on the plaid spread of the daybed. He bent over her face and opened an eye with the side of his thumb. He trailed his fingertips across the olive planes of her brow and cheek. She moved and moaned. She'd be OK in a minute or two.

Time for me to end my little reconnaissance. I went back out onto the porch, closed the screen and knocked loudly on it. "Anybody home?" I shouted.

Vasya came to the door. "Yes?"

"This is Mrs. Yelanov's house?"

"Yes. She's lying down right now. You must be Tonio from the massage studio. She said she had an appointment." Vasya's dark brown eyes moved over me. I sensed he was the shrewd, nongullible type—good attorney.

"I didn't come from the massage studio," I said.

"Then—who are you? You *selling* something?"

"My name's Yuri Nevsky. I'm from Marland Borough. I'm a friend of a woman named Charity Day, who's a friend of Felicia Semanova."

"That's interesting, but..."

"Maybe if I could talk to Mrs. Yelanov?"

Anna's weak voice from the back of the house: "Who is it, Vasya?"

He hesitated then invited me in. He led me to the game room. Anna was sitting up and smiling thinly. She was a little pale. Eyes sullen, she joined in as we introduced ourselves. The attorney's name was Vasily Brunov. I mentioned Felicia's and Charity's friendship.

"Why come here? I heard Felicia's dead, Mr. Nevsky. My Sergei's hit the road for Alaska or Samarkand or some place. The two of them were..."—she made a rude gesture, fist jerked forward—"and I could care less."

"This morning Charity and I were over in Shadyside talking to a Count Dromsky-Michaux, your husband's partner. He said Hermitage Decorator Antiques is finished, bankrupt. And that Sergei liquidated everything behind his back and ran off with the money. That was a little more than two weeks ago, around June first. On the night of June second Felicia came to my house and asked my housemate, Charity, to keep something for her."

Vasya and Anna exchanged a quick glance that meant they connected me with the count's phone call of about a half an hour ago now.

"What did she leave?" Anna said.

"It was all wrapped up. It was pretty heavy. Anyhow..." I flexed my shoulders.

"Yes?" Vasily said.

Anna said, "You know, whatever it is, it was part of the business. With Sergei gone, whatever it is belongs to *me*." She turned to the attorney. "Vasya, explain to him how everything like that now belongs to me."

Brunov ignored her. "And are we to understand you have this...item?"

My eyes opened wide. "I didn't say my friend *had* anything. I said—"

61

"You said Felicia asked your friend to keep a big thing for her," Anna said.

"She told her she couldn't do it," I said. "She didn't want to get involved."

"What was it?" Anna said.

"I told you. It was all wrapped up. It was about five feet high." I spread my arms. "And about this wide."

Anna cursed and hit the heels of her hands together in vexation. "If she had something to hide, it must have been worth a *lot*. Damn it! I *know* what she had belonged to Sergei. *I* should get it."

Brunov said, "Who finally agreed to do the hiding for her?"

"Beats me. She drove off with it. That was the last I saw of it."

"Yuri, I think it would be useful to Mrs. Yelanov if you could pin down the time of Felicia's visit."

"She came about one o'clock in the morning. That was early Wednesday, June second. She left Wednesday after dinner."

"Why should she pick your friend? There were dozens of people she could have picked," Brunov said.

"They go way back together. They were roommates at Radcliffe. And best friends. She trusted Charity very much. I was sorry Charity couldn't help her."

Vasily's eyebrows were heavy but perfectly formed. His ears beneath styled ledges of hair were small and well shaped, almost dainty. Looks, style and voice made me want to trust him. "Just why are you visiting Mrs. Yelanov?" he said.

"I spent some of the morning talking to Mr. Yelanov's partner. He told me Mr. Yelanov was gone. I thought Felicia coming to Charity with the bundle might be connected to that. So I thought Mrs. Yelanov should know."

Anna looked accusingly at her attorney. *"See!* I said all along that semipro whore Semanova was hooked into it all. You kept saying no. I've known for years he was diddling her. He musta thought I was dumb as dough. But *I* knew. I—"

"Anna, *Anna*..."

"I've figured out what happened. He stripped the business and mortgaged everything he owned—this

62

house, for chrissake, his boat. *I* shoulda been loved like *it* was. He got all the cash together so he and the Semanova whore could run off together. Only she didn't want him. She probably had some young stud on the string with a dork a yard long. They grabbed his money and put a knife in his back and dumped him in the Ohio."

"That's *enough*, Anna." He moved over beside her. Her eyes showed fear spawned by his recent whacks. She took a half step back, away from him. "It might be better if I spoke to Yuri privately for a moment," the attorney said.

She said, "I don't see..." She swallowed. "That'll be fine, Vasya."

He led me out to the lifeless living room, snapped off the projector TV. "I'd like to get a focus on your role in all this, Nevsky."

"I explained. Felicia was my housemate Charity's roommate at Radcliffe—"

"Old Ivy League chums, eh?"

"As a matter of fact, yes."

His large brown eyes roamed my face. "Who is this Charity Day, really? One of those rich, idle women who live on investments and have nothing better to do than nose into other people's business? And who are you— her fancy man?"

I felt my face color. Vasily Brunov knew how to take a telling shot. An outburst on my part would teach him a lot about me. "Ms. Day happens to be a junior partner in a major Pittsburgh law firm. I'm her landlord."

"You do anything else except collect rent?"

"I garden and play the piano."

He nearly hid his contempt for Yuri Nevsky, the parasite. "And you wanted Mrs. Yelanov to know about the bundle?"

I flashed my dopiest smile. "Mrs. Day and I thought that would be the best way to help Felicia and her friends," I said.

"I see." He smiled disarmingly and his white teeth gleamed. "Being an attorney myself means I have the habit of looking deep to find motive—sometimes too deep. It's a hazard of the trade. I'm sure you understand. I'm sorry."

"It's OK."

"As a matter of fact, I'm interested in the fallout from Felicia's death myself. She was my client, you know."

"I didn't. She didn't mention you."

"I handled her will, some other minor matters." He walked with me to the door. "I found her an interesting person, Yuri. Just as I find you, by the way."

"Mrs. Day is more interesting than I am."

Vasily Brunov looked thoughtful. "I'm not so sure about that." His eyes snapped back to my face. "You're not what you seem, Nevsky. You're playing games with me."

"Come *on*." I opened the door. "You're imagining things."

"I'd like to spend some time with you both. Could I call you some time?"

"Take your chances," I said.

I walked toward my Datsun, the poodle dancing around my feet. I didn't look back. An oddly sterile place, the Yelanov house. Even the smell of sex and the abuse of the lady of the house failed to enrich the landscape. The shaggy, expensive wall-to-wall, the awkward Russian sculptures, and the projector TV formed a determinedly barren vista. Depressing, that was it. Not cheered in the least by Anna being used in some way by Brunov. A desperate woman. And he had called *me* a fancy man.

As I rolled down my window to let out the June afternoon heat, a car pulled up. A big black man was driving. He wore a white uniform. Tonio, no doubt. Knowing Anna's frame of mind, I guessed Tonio was in for a couple of tough hours. I gave him the thumbs up sign.

I drove to a payphone and called home to see how Charity was feeling. She was OK. I filled her in on events at *chez* Yelanov. We reached a general agreement. Amid the confusion and the interesting cast of characters emerged a theme: wealth in which a number of folks were really interested. Twining about that basic idea were related ones, like insolvency, bankruptcy, felony—and the distinct taint of greed.

"My mind was running that way all this morning,"

she said. "I called the McKees Rocks police headquarters. I said I wanted some information. Where were cars wrecked on West Carson Street taken?"

"Where?"

"The cop asked me registration number and driver's name. I gave them to him. He looked through his papers. He said he remembered that one: 'big truck, little car, hard pole.'"

"Ugh."

"Then I had to tell a little white lie."

"What insurance company are you representing *this* week?"

"Metropolitan National Casualty. It doesn't exist."

"Did it work?"

"They dragged the wagon—or what was left of it—over to a place called Smitty's Auto Parts." She gave me the address in Mount Oliver. I wrote it down.

"When we get a chance, one of us should pay a visit to Smitty's Auto Parts," she said.

"Looking for ...?"

"The worst."

I said good-bye. More was going on than we thought. More was at stake than we had first imagined. I was starting to feel my head bruises again and was getting grouchy. I looked at my watch. It was only a little after two. I was hungry. I found an Isaly's Dairy and ordered a chipped ham sandwich and a cup of coffee. I touched my head thoughtfully. My coughing had almost stopped. It was not nice to be Maced and conked with a gun butt. I *did* have a debt to pay. And Charity had one to pay—for her once best friend who had wanted to protect old memories of an earlier Felicia. Already we had found out she had been Sergei Yelanov's mistress. I had a feeling that was only the beginning.

My mind was definitely on Felicia. The way home took me through Oakland. I decided to pay my respects to her. I pulled into the parking lot at the Powers Funeral Home.

Inside, there was no directory. I took a wrong turn somewhere and found myself on the carpet outside a bank of small offices. I heard complaining.

"... I appreciate the cost of doing business these days, Mr. Powers. Just the same, these charges for preparation and burial are definitely out of line." The speaker had a well-modulated, persuasive voice. It sounded tones of good schools, old boys, summers in Maine, winters in Palm Beach. Whoever he was he had spent time around Eastern money.

Another man: "As you're Mrs. Semanova's next of kin, I assume you'll be bearing the full financial responsibility for our services."

"Well now, that's a matter open to a variety of interpretations. For example, my sister's husband is very much alive. I'm certain if you contact him—"

"No one's been able to locate him. I understand he's a Russian national. Half a world away. In a repressive society. You, on the other hand, are right here. Your quick arrival shows your sister meant a great deal to you. I raised the issue of compensation with you for that reason." The funeral director was smoother than a baby's ass. He went on. "Further, you're clearly a man of some breeding. I assumed you'd be able to deal with the financial side of this tragedy without the hysteria I've been the target of from so many of the bereaved..."

"To be sure, to be sure." There was a pause. Papers rustled under scrutiny. The man I understood was Winston, Felicia's brother, said, "Emotions aren't the issue here, Mr. Powers. I don't want to use the word *overcharge,* but we New Englanders are famous for our hard bargains. I would say these charges are too high. Something like...uh, a twenty-percent reduction would seem more equitable."

"I don't think that'll be possible."

The door of the funeral director's office opened. The knob was in the chubby hand of a balding man with heavy curls on the sides and back of his head. "To be honest, Mr. Powers, my liquidity isn't what it should be right now. My broker's advised me to commit myself heavily to certain electronics issues, some West Coast firms that promise exponential growth..." Winston had that tweedy, rumpled look that I always linked with folks whose income was organized, but whose lives never would be.

"Nonetheless, Mr. Farrow, these charges must be paid." Trailing Powers was a lean, hawk-eyed man with graying temples. He wore a dark blue suit. "I've delayed the embalming. I'll have to delay further. It's conceivable that the entire burial procedure will have to be...deferred. I'm sure you understand my position."

"My cash is tied up," Winston said.

The funeral director caught sight of me and lowered his voice. "Some phone calls I'm sure will correct that situation. Your sister, I'm sure, would want it that way." He glanced at a coin-thin watch. "Let's leave it that I'll hear from you by, say...three this afternoon. By then you should have your financial wheels turning."

"Well..."

"I'll need a substantial portion of the two thousand in cash or bank check. A notorized arrangement for the payment of the balance will be fine."

"I see. Of course. I'll...take care of it."

The two men shook hands. The funeral director went back into his office and closed the door. Winston stood unmoving.

I glanced at him out of the corner of my eye.

A tear ran down each of his cheeks.

Chapter Six

Winston groped vainly around his pockets. I pulled my handkerchief out. "Here."

"Thank you." He snorted into it and wiped his eyes. He took a good look at me for the first time.

"We never actually met, Win, but I'm Yuri Nevsky. I'm the housemate of your sister's good friend, Charity Day. She spent time in the summer years ago with Felicia at your place on the Connecticut shore."

His eyes brightened. "Yes, yes, I remember the name. Felicia mentioned her specifically, by name. She phoned me one night late several weeks ago. She ran on rather a lot." He sniffed, drew a deep breath, and put my handkerchief in his pocket. His blue eyes were now intently fixed on my face. "She said if anything happened to her, I should contact Charity. She said she was holding something she wanted me to have. Something ...valuable. She said you and Charity Day were very close." He drew me off into an alcove where a potted rubber plant kept company with a padded double bench. "I'll be frank, Mr. Nevsky. I rushed here ahead of schedule hoping to see your friend Charity. I wanted to phone her, but the phone doesn't seem to be listed in her name. I landed midmorning. A young woman, Miss Amanda Swale, who phoned the bad news to me in Boston, was kind enough to drive me to the Oakland Howard Johnson's. I walked over here to pay my re-

spects to Felicia and that bloodsucker fell on me..."
His voice tightened. For a second I thought he was going
to cry again. He fumbled in his inside jacket pocket and
pulled out a thick folded sheet of bond. On it were the
itemized charges: coffin, embalming, the whole dreary
lot. "I just don't know what to *do* with this." He turned
his oddly intense gaze on me and moved his face well
within my personal space. "To continue in the frank
tone I've set... My finances aren't as good as they once
were. Of course I'll right them soon." His eyes fell. "But
right now I'm...desperate. I wrote a bad check for my
round-trip airfare. I checked into Howard Johnson's with
an American Express card on which no more charges
are permitted until full payment is made." He cocked
his head. "Do you grasp my financial situation, Mr.
Nevsky?" The whiskey on his breath came at me in
pungent waves.

"Tap City," I said.

He nodded. "That's why as soon as possible I have
to have access to what my sister left me." He looked
still more sharply at me. "What is it? Jewels, money,
bonds? Possibly real estate deeds?"

I smiled. "I think you and I should go have a cup of
coffee," I said.

"It's very important that I—"

"It's very important that you pull yourself together.
You eaten anything?"

He shook his head.

"You should. It's on me."

There was a pizza joint right around the corner. Facing this sweaty, disheveled man, I sensed that his character—or lack of it—was going to send Felicia
Semanova's mystery off in an entirely new direction.
Winston Farrow III was clearly not in shape to give me
much direction. I was sure getting Felicia buried would
be Charity's first priority. "When can you raise the
money for the funeral?" I said.

"I can't." He stared down into his coffee.

"You must—"

"Yuri..." He looked up balefully. "For the last many
months I've lived first the life of a man looking for work.
I relied on the generosity of a few friends. Then somewhere during one of those many weeks I crossed the

line to freeloader, to parasite, to reprobate. I borrowed money I couldn't repay. I was generously invited into people's homes—and went out with some of their possessions in my pockets. I have no job, no fixed address." He drew a deep breath. "I *badly* need a break, a chance to tear out of a desperate downward spiral. I've trodden on a good family name. Now even that sound coin has been cheapened." He sipped his coffee and carefully put the cup down. "I am without resources. Without credit."

"I think it's time you met Charity Day," I said. "Finish up."

Charity tried to be social, offered coffee and a kitchen chair. Winston was too agitated about the chance for a big windfall to slow up. I pretended to misinterpret his excitement. "Winston's expected to pay for the funeral and he's broke," I said.

"It's Alexey Semanova who should be paying this bill, not me!" Winston muttered.

Charity and I exchanged glances. She was catching on quick to the essential Winston.

I explained what Felicia had said to Charity and me about her marriage having deteriorated into "a business relationship." "Even if Alexey could be found, he probably wouldn't foot the bill," I said. "It's up to you."

"I wish very much that I could do it. But I can't."

Charity got up and leaned against the sink counter. She folded her arms. "I'll tell you what, Winston. I'll lend you the two thousand. In a way, your sister left that amount with me." She explained about the five thousand.

"That's very kind of you, Charity."

"Felicia was an old, dear friend. She deserves to be buried decently and promptly."

Winston's baleful grin again. "My prospects for repayment aren't good. They hinge on her legacy to me. What did she leave with you?"

"A heavy bundle wrapped up in black plastic."

"You didn't open it?"

"We figured that was your job."

His eyes were bright. "It might be worth a fortune!"

"I have a feeling you shouldn't count a whole lot on that."

"Why?"

"Woman's intuition."

"I want to see it at once!"

"We'll take you to it in a little bit. But first there're some things you should know. It's not all tidy and clear," Charity said. "Your sister was mixed up in *something*. We don't know what."

"Her whole *life* was that way," he said dully. "Always in one kind of trouble or another. The pattern hasn't changed in twenty years."

"The point is, there's a man in Shadyside who feels Felicia helped to bankrupt him," Charity said. "Yesterday a man in a rubber mask Maced Yuri and forced his way in here. *He* wanted the bundle, too."

Winston's face turned pasty. "Well . . . the fact is you have it, and you'll give it to me, as Felicia asked. Right?"

We both nodded.

"There's one *more* thing," Charity said. "Maybe you better sit down for this one. Felicia said it was cursed. People who touch what's in the bundle *die*."

"I don't want—"

"Sit *down!*" I said. "You could make a corpse nervous."

Winston sat. He laughed weakly. "A curse I can shrug off. The 'strings' are another matter. I've already been exposed to the fallout of some of the complications," he said.

"Like what?" I said.

"Amanda was kind enough to take me over to Felicia's rather elegant apartment building." His watery blue eyes met mine. "Her suite, 14-C, was completely topsy-turvy. Wall-to-wall carpets had been pulled up, drawers emptied. Dishes were dumped on the floor. Kitchen cabinets' shelf paper was pulled off. That was the way Amanda found it. She wanted me to see the job I had in front of me. I'm expected to go through everything."

"How did Amanda know about the robbery?"

"She and a woman named Ruthie Spires—another good friend of Felicia—saw news coverage of her accident on the TV late news. They knew I was her only U.S. relation, and that Felicia didn't know where Alexey lived or how to get in touch with someone who lived in the Soviet Union. They knew I'd want to know.

Amanda had a key. So she and Ruthie went over to find my number in Felicia's phone index. Both women were in tears. The number my sister had was one belonging to a friend I had alienated. He wasn't too cooperative. It took them two hours in the middle of the night to locate me. Finally they got me and bawled out what happened." Winston leaned back and sighed. His thick-lidded eyes closed. "Charity, Yuri, I'll admit Felicia and I weren't close. We weren't even particularly fond of each other. Still, her death was a shock. I've been rather wrapped up in my own...difficulties. That my distant sister might have provided the means to turn my life around seems a most delightful irony."

"Did she have a will?"

"One was drawn up. It leaves everything to me. Amanda Swale's been a great help in all that. She reported the robbery, or whatever, to the police and the apartment manager, a fellow named O'Shea. And she also notified Felicia's attorney about the robbery and her being killed. The attorney asked Amanda to see if anything she knew about was missing. He's a rather efficient fellow, it seems." He reached into his soiled shirt's breast pocket. "Can't remember his name. Here it is." He pulled out a business card. "'Mr. Vasily Brunov, Esq.' Amanda told me he's straightened out the will. I suppose it was easy enough. This Brunov was official or unofficial attorney to Amanda, Ruthie, Felicia and some other women who once lived together."

"Did Felicia have any assets?" Charity said.

"Amanda said Brunov couldn't find any. Her car was about it. Some cheap furniture, only token balances in two savings accounts." He fastened his oddly intent gaze on my face. "That means *all* her assets were tied up in her legacy, Nevsky." He lunged to his feet. "I *must* see what she left me. Now."

"Not quite yet," Charity said. "I want to make sure your sister's buried right. And seeing as I'm financing the proceedings, I have *every* right to see to it. We'll swing by the funeral home so you can settle your accounts with Mr. Powers."

"Charity, I'm most anxious—"

"You will settle the funeral!" She didn't like Winston. I saw a painful, vexing ride coming up.

"I'll drive him over, Charity." I looked pointedly at her. "Give you time to get it out into the cellar."

She nodded. She knew how to work the electronic lock on the White Chamber.

"I think you should...use gloves." I felt a fool saying that.

"I was going to." We both laughed nervously.

On the round trip to the funeral home Winston sketched in his life for me. I read the evasions and half lies in his whiny litany. Altogether I heard a ragged fugue of false starts, unreasonable fantasies, self-deception and failures in character. Businesses financed by mother were mismanaged by son. Employment opportunities provided by a good family's connections were taken and frittered away. A steady decline in the quality of his jobs paralleled the fading class of his lady friends. None of his relationships worked. Sliding down to some kind of economic and emotional pit, he joined one of those organizations hovering somewhere between religion and panhandling. He wasn't up to the required commitment—or the discipline. He was tossed back into the rough seas with the rest of us. The waters could drown us all; those that destroyed him would be ninety proof. He finally tried straight Catholicism—without effect.

He asked me twice if I could stop at a state store so he could buy a bottle. With my money, yet. He could wait.

"I'm not worried about the strings attached to my legacy," he said. "I've decided how to handle them."

"Oh?"

"I'm taking it with me. And I'm leaving Pittsburgh soon after the funeral Saturday. I'm cutting away every string with that big silver bird to Boston."

I pulled into our driveway with a sense of relief. "The sooner you take it, the sooner we can relax. My head still hurts and my throat's still sore."

Charity was in the basement. We went right down. Winston was breathing heavily, not just from dragging his portly bulk up the rear porch stairs, either. He was panting with greed.

Charity was waiting at the foot of the stairs. She

74

still wore her gloves. Winston shoved past me. "Where is it?" he breathed, eyes probing.

She pointed to the irregular lines of the sheet she had draped over the black vinyl. She had dragged it out directly under a hanging 100-watt bulb.

"So big?" He sounded disappointed.

"Sorry. It's a little late to complain to Felicia," Charity said. "And you *better* not complain to the management."

He hurried forward, head lowered. He grabbed the hidden shape and tried to wrestle it upright. "Come, help me," he panted.

"No way. I'm not touching it without a pair of gloves," I said. I saw his look of irritation. "That's right, Winston. Another idiot. Afraid of some silly curse. Just because Felicia touched it and Felicia got her brain banged into pudding—"

"Shut up, then! Do *that* favor."

"You better watch your mouth." I knew he was puffed up with *nothing*. His anger was hollow. I felt sorry for him. He wasn't worth my vexation.

"I'm sorry. I'm sorry." His eyes were riveted on the sheet. He pulled it off and ran his hands over the vinyl like a blind man. The vinyl was held in place with lengths of green strapping tape. He tried to tear them away, but of course they wouldn't give. Each had to be peeled away. Winston was a nail-biter. He had to struggle. But he finally got the first sheet pulled free.

White paper lay between him and his sister's legacy. The paper carried the Hermitage Decorator Antiques logo.

My heart began to pound. I had done a masterful job of controlling my curiosity, but now it flooded out along with the sweat on my palms. The back of my neck itched with anticipation and not a little fear. Charity was leaning forward.

"What have you bequeathed me, dear sister mine?" Winston repeated over and over as he stripped off the last of the vinyl. Soon only paper stood between him and what had *really* brought him to Pittsburgh. "What have you bequeathed me, dear sister mine?"

He attacked the paper with frenzied hands. He tore

it savagely away. Without thinking of it, I was holding my breath.

I saw . . . bronze—pitted, polished ancient bronze.

As the first sheet came away I could put no recognizable shape on it. I saw only that it was all of a single piece. Then I saw! A figure lying horizontally. A sea of golden glow flowed about island darts of green and red jewels and glass. It was a bronze statue set with colored stones and gems!

Charity and I stepped closer. Our feet scraped on the cement. How old the bronze was! The polished metal was pitted and pocked in places. Most areas still gleamed. The light from the barely swinging bulb tossed a rainbow of reflections from the shower of handset stones.

Winston was cursing bitterly with disappointment. He grabbed the statue's head. With a heavy grunt he stood it up just behind the hanging bulb. It was a heavy, decorated male figure standing on a thin pedestal. He was barefooted but wore a single, long robelike garment. The garment was held in place by double cords around the waist and by a medallion in the center of the chest. From waist to ankle the bronze had been worked into a repeating pattern of palmettes and animals—elks, stags and goats. A heavy right arm held a malletlike hammer up behind the head. The left was poised to balance the coming savage blow.

My eyes passed quickly over the taut-looking body. When they found the pitted face they were seized, like a spider grabs a fly. The protruding eyes, the savage hook nose, the pointed beard and frame of eroded bronze curls—and above all the contorted, shrieking mouth—struck from my heart and soul, like a spark, a single oppressive sensation.

Menace.

My fear of the figure rose from far down in my being. Some ancient wizard bronze-worker had dived deep down to where we were vulnerable. He knew we dreaded the unseen beasts in the bush, the fatal blow struck from hiding, the darkness. He knew that the great earth was filled with terrors, and each of us alone was small, weak and bonded to primal fear.

Its power gripped Winston and Charity as well. The

three of us stood staring. The shivering light of a bulb stirred by unfelt air currents tossed rainbow darts about the cellar gloom. Had the hammer wielder stepped off his pedestal and started toward us, I would not have been surprised.

Finally Winston wet his lips and spoke in a hushed voice. "What in Christ's name am I going to do with *that?*" He waved his hand in disgust and shoved by on the way up the basement stairs. Charity and I followed him. I locked the basement door behind me.

He paced in the big living room. *"That's* my legacy? That's what's going to turn my life around?" He laughed bitterly.

"It has to be worth something," I said. "Maybe a lot. It's some kind of primitive masterpiece."

"I wanted something I could convert to cash right away." He turned his greedy glance to me. "I want to get out of Pittsburgh Saturday, remember? How can I possibly turn *that* into cash in time to catch the last flight out?"

"I have no idea. What I do know is that I want that thing *out* of here," Charity said in a quiet voice that surprised me. "I don't like it. I'm *afraid* of it."

He made an unconvincing sound, as though saying he hadn't been frightened. "I'll have to leave it here for now. I don't have any way to carry it." He scowled. "This all may be yet another of my dear sister's contemptible tricks played on me. Her 'legacy' to me. Some kind of ancient white elephant..."

I reminded him of our conversation with bankrupt Count Dromsky-Michaux. He felt anything belonging to Hermitage Decorator Antiques should be returned to him.

"He's not getting that bronze. It's mine now. Even though it won't be easy to convert to cash. Even if I want to slap my dead sister silly for playing her last— and best—trick on me."

"One last thing, Winston. Listen up, OK?" I raised my hand to make the point. "Nobody knows we have the ugly thing here at 138. I want to keep it that way until you get it out of here. You hear?"

"Sure. Sure. Remember, I'm going to cut all the strings—*fast.*"

"You do that," I said. "And in the meantime, keep your mouth *shut*."

After Winston's cab came, I made dinner. Asparagus omeletes, potato puffs and strawberry shortcake. Over coffee Charity and I had one of our talk-throughs. We tumbled around the last two days' new people and events. We touched on Tod Buckry of 'sPots and his drunken, violent wife, Selina. We speculated wildly on JFK's identity. Charity questioned me about lascivious Anna Yelanov, whose husband had been Felicia's weak balm against disillusion and failed marriage. We talked around Attorney Brunov, who treated his lover-clients rough. There was more to him than a soft voice and a talent for violence.

Like two apes we checked the lumps on each other's heads. Then, after returning the bronze to the White Chamber, we went to bed. At one-thirty in the morning I was still awake. It took little time for me to find the cause.

The bronze.

I slipped into my robe and looked out the window. Moonlight silvered the lawns around 138. I triggered the White Chamber lock in the back of my clock radio.

I padded quietly down to the kitchen, then down the stairs to the cellar. The ceiling light in the White Chamber went on when the door opened. The fluorescent tubes glared down on the bronze. Its shadow was thrown against the floor. Its colored glass and jewels gleamed dully at me like eyes of red, green, blue, yellow...

I wasn't sure why I had come downstairs. Maybe to make sure the metal figure hadn't moved. To make sure that savage, fang-gated mouth wasn't sounding the shriek it promised. Or that the mighty hammer blow hadn't fallen on an unwary mouse. No, it wouldn't fall on a mouse. Rather on a troubled human soul, crushing it in an act of dark, primal vengeance. Menace.

The face... Again it drew my eyes. I studied its lines, the message sent in pitted bronze down through the centuries. "No," I said aloud. "That's not true." We were better than that. *I* was better than that. I could not accept that dark, pitiless verdict about our species. It was worse than skepticism. It did away with all our wonders, our accomplishments. It sent us reeling, worse than worms, out to the indifferent stars.

And insistent, too... I found a bench and pulled it into the White Chamber. I smoothed the robe over my knees and settled in for a vigil. I stared into that enraged bronze face and imagined that the lifeless eyes stared back their message of implacable hatred of humanity. Though I knew the struggle was being fought in my mind, I felt no less determined to resist. I gathered my mental self and said aloud, "I am Yuri Nevsky. I am unique, important and irreplaceable!" It seemed necessary to say that. And a great deal more necessary to believe it. I said it again. "I am unique, important and irreplaceable." And so is every human being, I thought.

The next hour was a test of my inner strength. That strength was challenged, usually, under only extreme circumstances. I used that strength to deny the nihilist stance in bronze by not touching the embellished, rainbowed surface. Under the fluorescent glare it *did* demand to be touched. Worse, to my agitated wits it beckoned to be embraced with my arms—and my heart. In the back of my mind I kept reminding myself that *I* was doing all this, not the ugly bronze statue. That made the experience no less real. And, as I continued to sit and resist, no less valuable in shaping my vision of a worthwhile Yuri Nevsky living in a worthwhile world.

"Yuri."

Oh, did I jump! Charity stood in her robe right behind me. "Scared me stiff," I said.

"I couldn't sleep."

"Because of this?" I waved at the bronze.

"What else? Oh, Yuri, it's so...hideous."

I turned and she walked into my welcoming embrace. "It needs to be defied," I murmured into her hair.

"What?"

"You'll understand. Come sit beside me."

She did. After a while she said quietly, "I see." She put her arm around my waist. She shivered.

I put an arm around her. There we sat side by side, feet together, like two frightened children protecting one another against the unknowable shadows of the night.

Chapter Seven

The phone rang as I was putting breakfast on the table. Charity answered. The phone amplifier was on. The caller was Tod Buckry. His pleasant bass-baritone voice filled the Canadian-bacony air. "Is this a bad moment to call, Mrs. Day?"

"Charity, please," she said. "No, go ahead."

"I called to apologize for my wife's assaulting you yesterday morning. I'm very sorry it happened."

"De nada, Tod."

"It wasn't really *'de nada.'* It was dangerous for you and very embarrassing to me. Selina owes you a fistful of apologies. After I stand bail for her—again—I'm sure she'll want to apologize herself. I'm going to the hospital to see her this afternoon. I'm quite sure she'll feel miserable about what she did."

"She'd been drinking for about two days straight."

"It's getting easier to count the dry spells than when she's snockered. She never used to be that way. She used to be—ah, well, I guess I oughta keep family problems to myself."

"If you want to talk about it..."

"You're very kind, Charity." Tod was silent a moment. Then he said, "To show you how much I appreciate your not pressing charges and being so understanding, I'd like you to come back to the store soon and pick any piece you like. No charge. And I'd like to take you to lunch. The proverbial tokens of appreciation."

"I can't do that. Some of your stock is *very* expensive."

Tod laughed. "Hardly anyone buys it. Why not give it away? You'll come over?"

"To pick something small."

"Good. And don't forget the lunch. And if I can help *you* in any way at all, let me know, OK?"

"Sure."

"And thanks again, Charity. Thanks a lot."

Charity hung up and sat back down to her coffee.

"You're blushing," I said.

"Oh, I'm *not*." She blushed more.

"The potter has that *certain* something," I grinned. Charity was fun to tease. Her skin was very thin and, while it had color, it was the kind I associated with Ascot ladies under parasols and antebellum beauties riding canopied carriages. Reddish surges mounted her cheeks and the center of her forehead.

"He seemed...very nice. Not very well married, I didn't think."

"So you bit his wife."

"Yuri!" She giggled, then looked up sharply at me. "I wish I'd bitten her *harder*. A dreadful woman."

"I've always said women are the ruthless ones in love."

She sipped her coffee. "Somebody wise said we women are always at war."

"When do you launch your campaign against Fort Buckcry?" I said.

"There's something nice about Tod, all right," she said. "I'll have to think about what to do. It seems bad form to do anything while Selina's in the hospital." She turned a cool glance toward me. "I'd need a good excuse to do that."

"You'll have to find one, then."

She looked thoughtful. "Yes."

After breakfast she mounted her throne, a Harvard library circulation clerk's chair I had salvaged during my short career as a librarian. It was upholstered in an ugly institutional green vinyl and had a loose seat. Charity liked to roll the bottoms of her bare feet across the heavy tubular steel hoop welded above the foot pieces. She did her best thinking and planning on that chair, so we kept it in a corner of the kitchen.

"Battle plan for the day," she said.

I was glad the subject was changing from romance. I was always jealous when Charity talked about men. Probably because our own emotional connection was complex and clouded. Her refusal to marry me had been gracious but firm. I had settled down some since. Neither of us had again raised the issue.

"Yes, General Day?" I said, swallowing a definite ache.

"I think it would be a wonderful idea for the both of us to get *away* from our bronze friend sealed up below." She pointed down to the basement. "How long did we sit and shiver down there?"

"Till about four."

"So today we go out. Let Tuptim hang around to be spooked. You go to Smitty's Auto Parts, I'll go to check out Felicia's apartment. Winston's saying it was a lavish building is an interesting point. Not to mention her apartment was torn up. OK?"

"Sure. Where do we meet?"

"See you at the Union Oyster House, Market Square. About one-thirty. Oh, about our war chest..."

"Do we have one?"

"Felicia's money." She went to her purse and peeled some bills off the roll. "Here's six hundred for now. More if needed. I'll spend every penny I have to find out all about our bronze and bangled basement baby. How's *that* for alliteration?"

Once I was on the Parkway West, it took about forty minutes to get to Smitty's Auto Parts. It was a vast junkyard masked by shrubs, trees and high wood planking. The inner perimeter was measured off in Cyclone fencing. Red, white and blue wreckers came and went with six- and eight-thousand-dollar wrinkled cans of people's troubles.

A yellow brick building sat sixty yards from the main entrance. Emerging from the building's rear was a cinder block machine shop. I went up the three stairs and through the door marked Smitty's Auto Parts—Customer Service. Inside, car seats remodeled into chairs sat by low tables covered with auto racing magazines.

I went up to the long counter decorated with STP, Champion, and Goodyear stickers. Three men were handling customers. I picked the oldest one. He wore a Case Equipment baseball-style hat and had a walleye.

"Yes, sir?"

"I wonder if you could step outside a minute. I need you to look at my carb." I had parked my Datsun near the stairs and raised the hood.

We walked over to the car. I looked him in the good eye. "Forget the car. There're two things I'd like to ask you to do."

"Like what, pal?"

"There was a car towed in here last week. Towed off West Carson Street." I described Felicia's station wagon and gave him the plate number. "I'd like you to check and see if it's really here. Then come back and I'll tell you the second thing. There'll be some bucks in it for you right away." He hesitated. "It'll be worth your while, don't worry. And you can do the second thing on your own time."

He shrugged. "I'll check." He went back inside. I strolled around the rutty parking area. I saw his red and white hat bobbing out the machine shop door and through the rows of wrecked vehicles. In less than five minutes he was standing in front of me again.

"It's back there. Smashed to shit, pal."

"I'm Ernie. What's your name?" I said.

"Homer." He made a slight face. "They call me H.J."

I nodded. "H.J., do you know cars? I mean, you *really* know cars?"

"Does Howdy Doody have a wooden asshole?" H.J. grunted in pride. His bad eye darted around like a goldfish in a small bowl. "Beg your pardon, Ernie. But what I don't know about 'em ain't worth knowing."

A wisp of wind stirred my pant legs. I reached up and steadied my cheap straw brim hat, the one Charity said made me look like a professional gigolo. With the other hand I dug out my wallet. I came up with a hundred and a fifty. Felicia's money. I was sure she'd approve. "I want you to check that car over."

"Looking for what?" H.J. said.

"Anything unusual."

"Anything funny?"

84

"Maybe."

"You don't give a man much in the way of hints, Ernie."

"No. And don't ask questions. How long it take you to look it over?"

"Maybe I'll do it tomorrow, real early."

"I'll call you," I said.

H.J. slipped the bills into the breast pocket of his khaki shirt. "You didn't ask, Ernie, but I can have a really lousy memory, if I want to. This kind of cash makes my memory *real* bad."

I smiled. "That's nice to know. Call you tomorrow."

I got to the Union Oyster House a little early. The UOH was an Official City Landmark and had a plaque set into its front wall to prove it. Some towns put plaques where famous people shook hands or signed papers. Pittsburgh had the good sense to put this one up where several generations of good, hard-living people had gotten drunk out of their minds and stuffed their faces full. The UOH served spirits, beer and wines at low prices. Its success, though, lay in its fish sandwiches—several fried fillets of an unnamed whitefish on a large bun—and shucked oysters mixed into dough balls and deep fried. These Pittsburgh delicacies came crashing down from the kitchen above on a busy dumbwaiter. Four or five bartenders manned the single long bar before display six-packs of Union Oyster House Beer, the traditional shelf arrangement of spirits and framed photographs of presidents, poets and plungers at the UOH trough. The floor was made of small hexagonal china tiles. The furnishings were old stainless steel chairs and tables. UOH's decor was *no* decor.

I was midway through my second draft when Charity appeared. I was stunned! I had seen her not four hours ago in slacks and a paisley blouse. Now she wore an outrageously expensive spring suit. On her head was a scaled-down wide-brim straw hat of such simplicity and elegance I knew it had to be one of just a few. She also wore designer heels I had never seen and carried a fawn shoulder bag. She whipped off her hat. Her hair had been cut, an entirely new style. Layered and shaped blonde hair framed her face in a "summer look." Heads turned when this lovely, classy lady strode to my table. "Boy, do I have some things to tell *you*," she said.

She had gone to Felicia's address, a building called Mount Royal Apartments. She was surprised. It turned out to be one of the new prestige Pittsburgh addresses. Two doormen in the near distance were whisking tanned, middle-aged executives, blue-haired matrons, and glamor girls in and out of Continentals and snappy sports cars. The lobby had a guard, gilt mirrors and period furniture. She had the feeling the lobby rug was so thick that tenants needed snowshoes to cross it.

The fifteen-story building reared up elegantly from the edge of a stony bluff. Below, to the south, was a rolling green tangle of sumacs, second growth oaks and maples and the meandering silver thread of Ninemile Run on its way to the Monongahela. Not a great view, but one saw no steel plants and but a few rooftops. Mount Royal Apartments were only a sprint down the Penn Lincoln Parkway to the Golden Triangle. She was for sure standing in a high-rent region.

For that reason she retreated. She had planned to just walk in and see what she could. That wouldn't work, dressed as she was. She drove right over to Squirrel Hill, found a parking spot on Forbes, and headed straight for Trendsetters, the most elegant shop in town. An hour and a half later she walked out in her new outfit. Her other identity was in a shopping bag handed her by Shatell Millstein, her "clothing consultant," who made a face as though she were handing over doggie doo.

Next Charity went to the Cutting Board and bribed her way to an instant appointment. As Miss Vicki snipped and chirped over her she decided she had been working hard and needed an early summer bit of self-indulgence. An emotionally healthy decision, she was sure. And one that used Felicia's money as intended, even if a little indirectly.

"Then, *then* I was *really* inspired," she bubbled. "This outfit was great, but it wasn't enough."

"You bought a mink."

"I rented a *limousine*," she said.

"You *what?*"

The rental agency was right down the street from

the Cutting Board. Forty-five minutes later she was driven to the portals of Mount Royal Apartments in a long black limo, driver in front, privacy partition, the works. Her driver waited.

Both doormen tipped their braided caps to her. She told the lobby guard she was there to see Mr. O'Shea, the manager. While the guard was calling upstairs she studied the tenant roster book open at the phone desk. There weren't as many names listed as she had expected. Mount Royal Apartments had fifteen floors with maybe five chichi apartment suites on a floor. That made around seventy-five total. She guessed at fifty-odd names. The Mount Royal Apartments were one-third vacant.

Mr. O'Shea was at one of the other two complexes, the guard told her. His secretary said Charity could go up and wait.

Manager O'Shea's secretary, Lily, was a blonde. Her breasts were large and round, her velour jersey tight. Charity guessed her typing rate—if she could find the machine—at between six and eight words per minute. She had a toothy smile and liked to talk. She worked for Frank "Boothie" O'Shea and he worked for Condaco Corporation. Condaco also owned Imperial Towers in Monroeville and the Sewickley in Sewickley Heights. All had been built within the last four years, all were true luxury apartments, many with additional rooms for live-in servants. Rents started at $800 a month.

Lily said that kind of price tag kept out the riff-raff. She described Mount Royal Apartments' tenants. Charity got a quick, clear picture. Solid money lay in a lot of backgrounds. Old money rode the elevators along with corporate executive vice-presidents. Tables were set with lead crystal and Royal Doulton china flanked by brocaded chairs resting on Bidjar and Isfahan rugs. Mood music and Mozart from Luxman amplifiers piped into Bose speaker systems. Coffee tables groaned under $450 art books. There was much vacationing and going to and fro with the seasons to Las Vegas, Cozumel, northern Canada fishing, with occasional visits to glassed-in private boxes at Three Rivers Stadium to see the Pirates and Steelers.

Lily went out of her way to make a point about the

life styles she so clearly envied and admired. They weren't renting to fat, slow old moneybags. Just about everyone in Condaco buildings was under fifty and liked a good time. Nobody sweated the rules too much. Charity asked her what she meant by that. She said the tenants wrote their own rules.

"I asked her, 'rules about what?' and she got a little hesitant," Charity said. "I had a feeling a thought was trying to work its way up through a head full of disco tunes and Robert Redford fantasies. She asked me why I wanted to see Mr. O'Shea. I said I was an insurance adjuster."

Relaxed by that, Lily went on to say that she meant that class of people knew how to have a good time. They liked to get laid and get high. And money was no object.

"Then Boothie walked in and things got *really* interesting." Charity took a break to test-gnaw at a fish sandwich. I knew she was fairly restrained and not inclined to be reckless. But she *did* lather on the hot sauce.

"He took me into his office. Lily had told him I was insurance. I had given her a fake name: Kitty Welles. The minute I said I wasn't insurance, he got really uptight. Very suspicious. Then I said I wanted a rental. He said I should go over to Condaco Rentals, McKnight Road, South Hills. He also lied. He said there were big waiting lists for all three units. Would-be tenants needed personal references, extensive credit ratings... blah... blah.

"Knowing he was lying gave me a psychological edge. I kind of sat back and studied his act."

"What's he look like?" I said.

"Boothie O'Shea is burly, bald and very tense. He's in love with the rich. He oils his way around them trying to keep up a class front for Condaco. I saw him angling for crumbs from the rich, a stock tip here, a couple of extra tickets there, gifts and commissions the IRS will never know about."

She went back to her sandwich and I went to the bar for two more drafts. When I got back Charity was licking the hot sauce off her fingers and ignoring the equally hot glances of a would-be admirer at the next table.

She picked it up again. "I looked Boothie right in the

eye and told him I understood that Felicia's apartment was available. He gave me a big spiel about how sorry everyone was about her accident, what a great person she was and all. I said she and I were old friends. I said I knew she had lived there about three months, but couldn't really see how she could afford it." She looked coyly at me over the top of her glass. "Did *he* have any idea how she could afford it? I said."

"And...?"

"He got more nervous still. Started to sweat a bit. Asked me if I was a cop."

"Guilty conscience, sounds like."

"Ummm. Then I asked him if he knew why anybody would search Felicia's apartment. That really got him. He stood up and paced, looking at me as if I were going to explode. Then he blurted out a bunch of questions. Who was I? What did I want? So on. I said I was just a friend of Felicia Semanova who wanted to rent her apartment. He said he didn't think so. I asked to see the apartment. He tried to refuse. I said I'd file a discrimination suit against Condaco. Single woman being given unfair treatment. He wouldn't buy that. I thought I had taken him as far as I could..." Charity sipped her beer. "Then I thought of something. I said Condaco couldn't afford a scandal with only a two-thirds occupancy rate. That got him! You'd think I'd hit him over the head with a stick.

"Then he rushed at me. I thought he was going to smack me, but instead he said—exact words, OK: 'If you're friends of Felicia's friends, too, take them a message for me. Tell them I'm the one hung up. Tell them I had nothing to do with anything...' Mmmm...Let me make sure I get it right. Then he shouted: 'Tell them that unless things get back to normal, my ass is grass. And that there's *no* way they'll be able to do business the old way.'"

"Very interesting."

"I tried to pump him for more. But he clammed up and showed me Felicia's trashed apartment."

"See anything there?"

"Not really. He said the police had been there. The place was a mess. Everything torn up, rugs ripped up, drawers dumped. Yuri, it was on the fourteenth floor. Next to the top. It had *five* big rooms and two baths."

"The furniture?"

"Was junk. Stuff Felicia dragged over from Shadyside. One more thing: Boothie lived in the next apartment." Charity made a sour face. "Oh, he's a *scummy* man! When I said it was odd the two of them were side-by-side, he smirked and said was I asking him if he and Felicia made it. Well, they did. Plenty. He said she was pushing forty like me. And women our age couldn't be choosy, could we?" Her face reddened above clenched teeth. "Felicia crawling into bed with that third-rater. Some of us are so... vulnerable."

I nodded, waiting for her to center herself.

"About then I had had enough of whatever role I was playing," Charity said. "On the way out Boothie grabbed my arm and told me not to forget his message to my 'friends.' When I said I didn't know what he was talking about, he called me filthy names. I kept my temper. I wanted to leave with the advantage. I waved good-bye from the back of the limo."

I sat back in my chair with some awe. I applauded quietly. "A magnificent performance."

"It was... fun being the elegant Kitty Welles."

On the way back to 138 Charity and I kicked around our new information. Felicia in *that* building. Somebody was paying her rent. Sergei Yelanov was her great love. But he was no Daddy Warbucks, that was for sure. Another tenant? The owner? Condaco? I wondered who the Condaco officers were. So did Charity. She would make some calls about that to people in her firm.

And there were strings. "Friends of friends," indeed! Boothie was doing some kind of business that wasn't in the manager's job description. Felicia was in on it as well, I guessed. Strings, strings. Winston would be wise to cut the bronze free after Saturday's funeral. How many other people, places and things were linked by those strings? They were looking less like a few strands and more like a web. The more Charity and I gathered in our fingers, the more fascinating things were becoming. It had taken some nasty knocks on my bald head and a nick-of-time rescue by Charity to get me up to her level of commitment. But there I was. *There I was.*

I had just put the eggplant Parmesan for the evening's dinner in the oven when a battered Land Rover pulled into the drive and stopped by the garage. Through one of the kitchen windows I saw our visitor was a big woman in bib overalls—Twiggy Twill. She wore heavy waffle stompers, a light vest and a blue and white bicycle racer's hat. Her heavy auburn pigtail dangled down behind it.

Charity went up to let her in. They came down to the big living room. "Beer or tea?" I said.

"Tea. I'm kind of a health freak, Mr. Nevsky." She followed me out into the kitchen and sniffed the air. "Ummm!"

"Join us? Eggplant Parmesan, ziti with oil-and-garlic sauce."

"Sounds great! Specially for a veggie like me." She smiled sheepishly. "You...have enough? I didn't have any lunch."

"And you're a good-sized young lady. We'll fill you up, don't worry." We wandered back to join Charity.

"I grew up wanting to be Audrey Hepburn. It died hard." She held out her solid hands. "Nothing gamin about *these*."

"Lot more practical, though," Charity said.

"And now I do daredevil things sometimes, like swim in the Allegheny on New Year's Day and climb the sides of buildings. Got my name in the paper a couple times. Audrey wouldn't do those things, but Twiggy did."

We sipped our tea. "You probably wonder why I came over," Twiggy said. For the first time I noticed lines of melancholy etched into her wide forehead and around her blue eyes. "I'm down and I didn't feel like talking to my housemates. I remembered you, Mrs. Day, and your name was on that card. I won't hurt your feelings, will I, if I say you seemed a nice motherly type?"

"A good mother is hard to find, Twiggy. Thanks. I once had three children." Charity sipped her Twinings. "What's bothering you?"

She looked questioningly at me. "I—I'm glad you're here too, Mr. Nevsky. Even if I don't quite understand..."

"We're housemates and good friends," Charity said. She grinned. "He can be a comforting person to talk to, too."

Twiggy nodded. "I need to run over what happened in the store the other day. So I can maybe talk to him, make him feel not so bad."

"You mean Tod? Mr. Buckcry?" Charity said.

"He's such a great guy. We should have all grabbed Selina and held her till she cooled off. That kinda stuff's happened before. We shoulda been ready for it. The three of us should have grabbed her when she came at you, Mrs. Day." Her eyes scanned our faces. "Mrs. Day, Mr. Nevsky, did Selina get a bad smack on the head that you remember?"

"I bit her. We went crashing into the shelves," Charity said. "I don't remember hitting her head."

"The lady cop rammed her head into the wall pretty hard," I said.

"That's *right*. While I was trying to give Tod a hand with his cramps. That could have done it—screwed up Selina's nerves, her brain some way. You two think that could have happened? What they call it? Brain damage?"

"I suppose so," I said. "But what do I know? What's all the talk about brain damage now?"

"Tod was over at the hospital this afternoon visiting. Selina was sitting up and happy as a clam, talking about coming home in a day or so. He said she was apologizing like she always does. He went out for a Big Mac. When he got back, there were about ten doctors and nurses sticking needles and tubes in her. All pretending they weren't panicking. Selina was already dead, I guess. She just up and...died."

Charity gasped. I felt that morbid distant tug at the loss of a known member of the tribe.

"There's gonna be an autopsy. Probably show it was boozing and fooling around that killed her."

"What about Tod?" Charity said. Earnest concern in her voice. Her interest in that potter was sincere.

"Not shook up *too* bad. He's over at their apartment. The doc's got him on tranquilizers. The count from across the alley's holding his hand." She shook her head, close to tears. "Poor guy. Poor *nice* guy."

Charity touched the sore spot on her head, dropped her hand to the fresh scabs on her neck: painful souvenirs of Selina Buckcry's drunken attack. I guessed what she was thinking—that dead was forever, unless you were a believer. She wasn't. Good-bye, Selina....

With Twiggy as guest, there weren't any leftovers. With permission she cleaned off the sides of the plundered casserole with pieces of Italian bread. She talked about Selina and Tod. "I was with them from the day 'sPots opened. I was the first person they hired. Selina had been in a car accident and collected big. They used that money and some Tod inherited to start the business. That was about two years ago. Back then Selina was OK. Just high-spirited. Then about a year ago she started to really drink and carry on. Found the money somewhere. Just the same, up to a little bit ago, she wouldn't touch booze when something was coming up that needed her sober. Like crewing for Sergei Yelanov on his *Stressless I*."

"Sergei Yelanov!" I said.

Twiggy put down the casserole dish with a puzzled smile. Her large hands hovered uncertainly over the last pieces of bread. "I didn't think you knew Sergei."

"We don't. We heard he flew the coop with a whole lot of Hermitage's money."

"So people are saying."

Charity frowned. "But that's not what you're saying?"

"No. 'Cause I heard he didn't."

"Who from?" Charity said.

"A good friend of his." Twiggy picked up the casserole dish, bread in one hand, and looked for missed morsels.

I guessed. "Felicia Semanova," I said.

Twiggy gasped. The dish went crashing down onto the table and bounced to the rug. It didn't break. Apologizing, she put it back on the table and sat back. "Mr. Nevsky, how could you *know* that?"

"I've been Felicia's friend for years," Charity said. "Yuri knows both of us. If she said Sergei didn't run off, did she say what *did* happen to him?"

Twiggy shook her head.

"Felicia and I were college roommates," Charity said. "I talked to her last about two weeks ago. My late husband and I went to visit Moscow on our honeymoon. Felicia and her husband were wonderful hosts."

"That's right. Her husband was Russian. Alexey. I met him."

"That's a surprise. She told me her marriage had pretty much dissolved. She hardly ever saw him."

"Well, he was here, visiting. He spent most of his time hanging around Hermitage and 'sPots while Felicia and I worked. He was sort of handsome-going-to-seed. Curly hair with a bald spot in back. Bad teeth. My health magazines say that comes from the bad Russian diet." Twiggy wrinkled her ski-jump nose. "I didn't have to understand him to know he was sort of a slob. You know, B.O., dirty shirts, bad breath. Like he didn't give much of a poop. You know. What a bad match! Felicia always seemed to have class. Why'd she pick him?"

"A friend of mine who plays chess says: move in haste, repent in leisure," I said.

"I've heard about *Russian* men. Well, he was one, all right." She grimaced. "One time while he was here he, Felicia and I were sitting out back of 'sPots. It was summer, two years ago, right after Tod opened the store. Anyhow, we got started talking about going swimming. Alexey didn't have a suit. He said he wasn't like Americans: he didn't have everything. He was drinking vodka with ice cubes in it. The more he drank, the more he knocked the country. Felicia, who was translating, kept saying it was a love-hate relationship. I didn't care what it was. He was pissing me off. After a while he sent Felicia off to buy him a swimsuit. I went back in 'sPots to the fridge for more orange juice. There weren't any customers—as usual. It was dark and cool in the back of the store. I'm bending over to reach into the fridge—all of a sudden he's shoving up against me from behind. And his greasy hands are trying to untie my halter. He's whispering all these *-nitchkas* and *-notchkas*. Oooo! I was so *pissed!*" Twiggy rammed her sizable elbow backward. "I caught him right in his babka-bloated belly. He doubled over. His chin was right close to my knee. Who could resist? You could hear his teeth click together all the way to Fifth Avenue. Scumbag lech! He fell over backwards with a little nosebleed and rolled around like I had stabbed him or something. He touched every inch of his face to see if anything was broken. When his hand came away with a little red on it, he started to cry. 'Tvigee!' he kept bawling. 'Tvigee!' When Felicia came back with the suit I didn't say anything. So as not to shame her, not *him*. He had to leave for Russia the next day."

"That the only time you saw him?"

"The only time he saw *me*. But I saw *him* again. It was early last summer. Just about a year ago." Twiggy got up and paced the dining room. "You know, you two, lots of nights I have trouble sleeping. I'm what they call 'a nocturnal' a lot of the time. I usually go out and walk around Shadyside. Sometimes I walk all the way to Oakland and find an all-night coffee shop. Sometimes I go back to 'sPots and do a little paperwork. Last summer one night I walked back to the store and down the alley. It was a hot spell and Hermitage's side door was open. I heard people talking inside. The light was on and I recognized Sergei Yelanov's voice. So I knew everything was OK. He was talking to Felicia and somebody else, a guy. At first I didn't recognize the voice. Then I heard they were all talking Russian. I realized it was Alexey. I didn't know he was back in the country. I walked back into the yard by the back of 'sPots. There's an angle where you can see through the side door into Hermitage. It *was* Alexey. I don't know Russian, but I could tell the two guys were trying to get Felicia to agree to something. She was resisting pretty good. Every once in a while they'd stop yammering at her. She'd say 'no,' and they'd be at her again."

"Any idea what it was all about?" Charity said.

"Huh-uh. In the end, though, Felicia gave in. Through the door I could see Alexey give her a hug—more than he'd bothered to do during his whole visit last summer. They all walked out laughing." Twiggy sat back down. "You going to the funeral Saturday?"

"Uh-huh. I want to talk to Felicia's brother," I said.

"I met him this morning. A boozer."

"A good man is hard to find," Charity said. "By the way, did you ever see Sergei's boat?"

"Once. He keeps it up at Erie. I don't know much about boats, but it was big. Had a couple of bunks and like a pilothouse on it. He took everybody from 'sPots and Hermitage out on it one weekend. He loved playing the big spender. He used to sit in a deck chair with a bottle of vodka in a bucket of ice and bellow at everybody—'Eat! Drink!'"

"Who was at the helm?"

"Huh?"

"Who was being captain?"

"Oh, Felicia, usually. She really knew a lot about boats. Sometimes Selina took over. She was raised on the Gulf in Louisiana and did all right. Next to as good as Felicia, Sergei used to say."

"What did he use the *Stressless I* for?" I said.

"Fishing mostly. Way out where the pollution is clearing. He always went after the big ones out there. He'd go out weekends, sometimes for a long weekend. Sometimes he'd take Felicia and Selina along. They ran the boat, I guess, while he fished."

Charity gathered up some dishes and silver. "When was the last time they all went fishing?"

Twiggy looked at the ceiling, closed her eyes. "It was...ah, a couple weeks and a little ago. First weekend in June. They were gone Friday. Supposed to be back at work Tuesday morning, but nobody showed till Wednesday morning. At least Selina showed. She looked beat, but she was there. I didn't see Felicia over at Hermitage till Thursday morning."

"How about Sergei?"

"No show. Then or later. About a week later cops came around and talked to Selina and Felicia. Where'd they fish? Catch anything? When did they last see Sergei? What was he wearing? Was anything bothering him? So on. They went at it quite awhile, at two different times. Then they went away and didn't come back. And neither did Sergei."

"So what do *you* think happened to him?" Charity said.

"I have a guess," Twiggy said.

"So tell us."

"I really didn't tell you the truth a little bit ago. I did get something out of Felicia. I talked to her and Selina together. I told them I'd noticed something different about the last trip and wanted them to level with me."

"What was different?" I said.

"The cars. Every other time they went, they used Sergei's car. I remembered seeing it in the Yelanov garage. A big Lincoln."

"Maybe they took one of the girl's cars," Charity said.

"Huh-uh. All of them were parked behind 'sPots the whole time they were gone."

"Maybe they took a bus," I said.

"Sergei never took a bus in his life. His car sat behind the store till his wife came and drove it away." She leaned forward, enjoying our great interest. "Felicia and Selina told me Sergei's friend drove them all up to Erie. He went out on his boat while Sergei and the girls went out on the *Stressless I*. All four started back in the friend's car. They said Sergei asked to be dropped off at the Erie bus station, and that was the last anybody saw of him. I don't believe that. I think he's hiding with the friend somewhere in Pittsburgh."

"Felicia and Selina tell the police the same thing?" I said.

"Almost. They left out the friend. It was easier that way. They said Sergei drove to Erie, got on a bus, and told them to leave the car at 'sPots when they got back to Pittsburgh."

"Who was the friend?"

"I asked them. But they said they didn't want to get him involved. He was just a guy who did them a favor." Twiggy looked at her Cookie Monster watch, then went to get her vest to go.

Charity and I saw her to the door. "Maybe we could talk about that night some more sometime," I said.

She tossed off a shrug and a grin. "Sure. Anytime. Just feed me and I'll tell you my life history. Well, goodnight Mrs. Day, Mr. Nevsky. See you at the funeral."

Tomorrow Winston Farrow III was going to take the statue. When he did we wanted to make sure he took all the strands we had gathered up in the last few days. That was the fair thing. We wanted him to know what went along with our ugly, sparkling friend with the hammer.

What *was* going on? Charity and I turned our attentions to that matter out on the porch. We sat on the top step, watched skateboarders and pedestrians, and chatted. The *Stressless I* fit right in somewhere. And so did the fishing trips into the middle of Lake Erie. I had spent some summer weekends at Erie before the heavy pollution poured in from each end and had sickened that great water. The city of Erie was about 130 miles north of Pittsburgh. North northeast of the city, jutting out into the lake, was Long Point Park. That was Canada, only thirty-five more miles away....

We recalled how tired Felicia had been when she got to 138. How wet her sneakers had been. She had come off the *Stressless I* not too long before, we guessed. For the first time we thought about the weather in the hours before she had come. There had been long and violent rainstorms! The smell of gasoline on her clothes would go along with bucking a lake storm and perhaps cranky engines acting up in heavy seas. Charity imagined Sergei puking sick while Selina and Felicia manned the craft. "Stand up, Sergei!" she had cried out in her sleep. Probably screaming for all the help she could get out of a seasick lover. Lake storms were no joke. They were altogether dangerous business. The only reason people would sail in weather like that was...profit.

There were lots of ways to make a big profit quick. Considering what we had to go on—the characters and the circumstances, and that monster in my White Chamber—Sergei, Selina and Felicia were bringing art objects into the country illegally and selling them dear through Hermitage. Art treasures that Alexey Semanova was somehow providing. Valuable ones indeed if just the one we had was enough for Felicia to "retire" on.

Then we talked over Boothie O'Shea shouting about not being able to do business any more. Was that business reselling smuggled art to the rich in his three luxury complexes? We thought it was. But we'd have to find out more about the statue and about art smuggling in this part of the country.

One thing we hadn't found out that niggled at me

like the beginnings of a mouth ulcer: where *was* Sergei Yelanov? Quite possibly he had touched the statue....

At seven in the morning I called Smitty's Auto Parts. H. J. took my call in a deserted office. "That Fairlane was smashed up pretty good..." He paused. "But not good enough, Ernie. Folks see cars totaled on TV, think there ain't nothin' much left. Thing is there's plenty."

"Like what?"

"The brakes was OK. I got the wheels off. The lines what was busted, busted in the accident. The steering, though, that was something else. Might've missed it, if there wasn't some shine on a couple bolts shouldna been shining. Somebody took a wrench to them."

"Yes?" My heart thudded.

"I pulled off some plate to get at the bottom end of the steering column. That there steel rod had been sawed damn near through. I mean *damn* near. I could see what little metal was left to fatigue break. No tellin' where or when it would go. You *know* when it went."

"You're sure?"

"Does Howdy Doody—yes, sir, I'm sure. One thing more. It took some work to cut that rod near through. Had to be pulled out, sawed, and you're talking maybe three-quarter-inch *steel* rod. Took some time, and the murderin' sumbitch knew what he was doing. Am I out of line, Ernie?"

"You are *right on*. And you're already forgetting, aren't you, H. J.?"

"For sure."

"Thanks." I hung up with a grimace. I remembered that morning Charity had showed me the article about Felicia's accident. How cynical we had been! So often it seemed our worst suspicions were confirmed.

The phone rang. It was Winston Farrow III. His voice was pinched with fear. "Nevsky, I've changed my mind about the statue."

"What do you mean?"

"I don't want it. It's too much—trouble. It's too dangerous." His voice rose. "I never want to see it again!"

"Winston, what are we supposed to do with it?"

"I don't care. *I* don't want it."

"What happened? Why you talking like this?"

"Never mind!" His voice stretched to panic. "I'll give

you some advice. Don't tell anybody you have it. That thing is *terrible* trouble with the law."

"Winston, Charity and I have to talk to you. We have plenty to tell you. You ought to know—your sister was murdered—"

He cried out sharply, like a wounded animal. The sound pierced my ear. I jerked the receiver away. When I put it cautiously back, the line was dead.

I started smiling. I paced a few steps, then jumped up with pure exhilaration.

Now things were *really* getting interesting.

Chapter Eight

I was still grinning when Charity came into the kitchen. "Winston's decided he doesn't want the bronze."

"What?"

"And Felicia was murdered," I said. "Somebody sawed her steering column nearly through. It gave out on Carson Street."

Charity's jaw went slack. Her eyes flashed. "Then what are you *laughing* about, for Christ's sake?"

"Selfish grin. About a nice juicy puzzle on our hands. I'm sorry."

She waved away my apology. "She *was* murdered. My dear friend . . . Yuri, I'm *very* much involved now."

"I'm there myself."

"She wasn't *your* best friend. You never looked out a dorm-room window with her at the first snowfall. Or crewed for her when she outsailed a yacht club archsnob." She snatched a bagel out of the fridge and slammed it into the toaster oven. "So for me this is different than all our other problems. It's not just 'information' this time. It's not justice I want either. It's *vengeance.*"

"I see."

She turned her pale glance toward me. "Men don't own the need for revenge, you know."

"I don't remember saying we did."

She put on the kettle. "I'd love to deal out harsh justice in this situation, Yuri."

"If I were one of your clients, counselor, you'd advise me *not* to do any such thing."

"I'm not talking law. I'm talking heart and passion and anger."

"And taking the law into your own hands, as they say."

"Maybe I'd like to. Maybe I'm a little crazy over Felicia's being murdered." She slid onto a kitchen chair and touched my forearm. "Maybe I'm something else, too."

"Like what?"

"Half scared by that thing in the White Chamber. It stinks of death and menace. And it's *cursed.*"

"It's Winston's. I'll see to it he gets it out of here after the funeral this afternoon. No matter that he says he doesn't want it."

"It can't be too soon for me. I feel death seeping out of there like gas. It's going to choke *all* of us. At the same time...I'm fascinated by it. And I'm going to find out more about it."

"How?"

"Listen."

She dialed Tod Buckcry. The potter's voice sank leadenly out of the phone amp. "You feel up to talking, Tod?" Charity said.

"Yes. I need to. It's good for me."

Charity offered her sympathies for Selina's death, then asked how he was holding up. No mistaking the sympathy in her voice. The potter really meant something to her. I swallowed my envy.

"Are you seeing people?" she said.

"Like you? I'd see you, Charity."

"I don't want to intrude on your grief."

"It needs to be intruded on," Tod said. "It's not a long way from self-pity."

"You offered to do me a favor a little while back. I'd like to take you up on it over lunch today. I'll buy."

"Where and when?"

"The Gazebo down the street from 'sPots. Say about noon."

102

"Can I get a sneak preview of what kind of favor you need?"

"Looking for information. About art smuggling in western Pennsylvania. I wondered if you might know something about it."

"That's a touchy subject."

"You *do* know something about it then?"

"I've heard things. There're lots of rumors." He had a mellow, unhurried voice. I had to admit Tod Buckcry was a pleasant, laid-back guy. "You know, Charity, getting out of here will do me good. Felicia's funeral today, Selina's Monday..." His voice caught. "There's so much death in the air. I need a little *life* now..."

Charity loaded her Polaroid Swinger and took a picture of the bronze. She dressed for the funeral. She said she was going to spend the rest of the morning at Chatwin and Burke, her law firm, nosing into Condaco. She'd see me at the funeral.

Five minutes after she left, Judy Larkin dropped in. A year ago she had moved into the big house next door. She had three boys under ten and a workaholic husband. She dropped over frequently Saturday mornings to talk to Charity, usually bearing hot muffins, coffee cakes or doughnuts. Today it was an apple crisp. I told her Charity wasn't home. "This came out of the oven a gift, Yuri. Now I guess it's a bribe. Jed was in a hurry to get to the office today, so he took my car. *His* doesn't have enough gas in it to go *any*where. He keeps *doing* that. Before I can start my shopping and errands, I have to crawl to the nearest gas station like a Legionnaire to an oasis. I suppose I ought to scream and shout instead of quietly complaining..." She tossed off a small shrug. "Not my style, I guess."

Judy had wide green eyes and straw-colored hair. She often wore it as she did today, tied up with a scarf that caught some of that deep green iris. Sweat shirts, loose slacks, Pendleton shirts and tattered sneakers made up most of the rest of her wardrobe. She had an easy way of moving—peppy and graceful. I had never talked to her for more than five minutes. "I'll get the keys," I said. "By the time you get back, I'll have the coffee ready."

I'd fill in for Charity in the role of safety valve and

confessor. The coffee klatch and beer-out-with-the-girls were the suburban housewife's low-cost therapy. Levels of confession could run high. Charity told me Judy was a bright lady with the frequent feminine burdens of poor self-image and lack of assertiveness. "But she's a real *jewel*," Charity said. "One day she'll wake up and—wham! Who knows what'll happen?"

Judy Larkin came back with toddler Louis and a plastic net playpen. He napped in the dining room while she and I sat over coffee and crisp in the kitchen. The complaints and spousely sniping that I expected never came. My strange, masculine presence put her off stride. There were several minutes when we both groped for shareables. Her green glance lit only briefly on my face at first, then darted off—and back—like a butterfly homing in on a blossom.

Despite us, the conversation got rolling. Judy was no sedate talker. She bounced on her chair, waved her hands, giggled, applauded and swayed. We talked about children, marriage, her volunteering at a retirement village, her stained-glass work, her four years at three colleges, my five years at two, Pittsburgh events, Pittsburgh sports...

I spotted two trodden paths in the lush forest of her conversation. Charity was right—she really didn't think as much of herself as she ought to. And her husband helped her to keep feeling that way. I had met Jed several times, made neighborly conversation. He lived his life in a three-piece suit. About forty, a bit thick in middle and jowl he was, with a clear idea of his role and Judy's—I hunt and gather; you mind hearth and child. Patented 30,000 B.C. I didn't think it worked even then.

"Oh, my God, it's twelve-thirty!" She sprang up. "Yuri, we talked for two-and-a-half hours!"

I grinned. "We'll have to do it again sometime. You're good company." I helped her fold up Louis's playpen. I noticed her red face. Dealing with gabby Russians made her nervous. In her haste to leave me—and her embarrassment—she nearly dropped Louis on his head. I opened the screen door for her. "Thanks for the use of your car, Yuri," she tossed over her shoulder. "I just *have* to talk to Jed about leaving mine empty." Off she went, almost at a run, crib bottom bumping with every fourth stride.

I was midway through dressing for Felicia's funeral when the phone rang. Judy Larkin. "I want to apologize for running off," she blurted.

"Don't bother. Not necessary."

"You complimented me, Yuri. I don't get many compliments. I'm not used to handling them. It's like—like trying to hit a change when you only see fastballs. I'm sorry."

I knew that "sorry" was a key part of Judy's vocabulary. Her being sorry extended past anything she did or was responsible for, to things like the weather and the price of gold on the London market. She was deep down sorry for being Judy Larkin. A bum rap for a surprisingly lively lady. "Let's make a deal, Judy," I said.

"What deal?"

"I'll trade you another super chat for your promise not to say you're sorry again in my presence."

"I don't get it."

"As stated. No more sorries from your ruby lips."

"Do I say it *that* often?"

"And you have *nothing* to be sorry for, Judy. Really. Is it a deal?"

"That's an...odd thing to ask."

"I'm an odd person," I said.

"But what's the *point* of it?" She was half laughing.

"To get you thinking...."

"You don't want to do that." Her voice was thin, edged. "That wouldn't be smart at all." She hung up....

Calvary Cemetery was Catholic. I remembered Charity saying Felicia was an Anglican. I sensed Winston's clumsy hand. He had told me he had, at the tail end of his efforts to find himself, accepted Catholicism. Now Felicia's remains were going to accept it, too. Why object? Mother Earth would open to take back her daughter, no matter the words and gestures of the living.

I got out of my car in the mortuary chapel parking lot. I went into the chapel. Four people were being buried that sunny Saturday afternoon. The coffins bore discreet Dymo Marker occupant names. I walked out and around the small garden. I found Charity and Tod Buckcry deep in conversation. I heard Tod say "I'm excited by all this. I really *am*. Tell me where that photo of the bronze was taken."

"See what you can find out, Tod. Then we'll talk about it," Charity said.

"I want to *see* it. I want to touch that metal." His eyes were very bright. "I know it's worth a small fortune."

I stepped closer. Charity reintroduced us. We shook hands. Tod dropped the bronze as a topic and began to talk about Selina, his wife—how she had been when things were good, the way her life had slid down over the last two years. She had been a trial for him and the business. He talked about 'sPots. It was a lifelong dream, that ceramics shop. He had poured all his energies and resources into it. "When you pass forty, Nevsky, I think you'll agree you're pretty much past the worst illusions. You want to *do* something, *leave* something for others. You're into the business of building small monuments. My small monument is 'sPots." The last month, he went on to say, was the toughest with Selina, and so the hardest on the business. Thank God for Twiggy. She had come in early and worked late. Now with Selina gone, she was already beginning to take over the bookkeeping, sorting things out that had been ignored over the last weeks.

Mourners were gathering. The hearse led the way up the winding asphalt road to the cemetery's high ground. Calvary was on a high hill in Hazelwood, well above the Monongahela where it bent south before swinging up and around to the southeast. The day was clear, with a light breeze. I could see the Glenwood and Homestead High Level bridges and the U.S. Steel Homestead Works, gray and quiet in the valley. Behind them lay the city sprawl of Homestead, Munhall, Whitaker and West Mifflin patched with the growing green of early June.

I parked behind a limousine and trooped with Charity and Tod to the grave site. I saw Count Dromsky-Michaux and Ruthie Spires, who had walked out on him, at least for the day. June Gowell, 'sPots's squirrel-

toothed-odds-and-ends girl, stood by Twiggy Twill and
a pipe-thin girl I guessed was Amanda Swale, their
roommate. All three leaked tears. And there was Winston! He who with suspicious speed had claimed to have
lost interest in the bronze. Beside him stood Brunov,
the attorney, tightly woven summer straw hat in hand.
On his other side stood a heavyset, plain woman I didn't
know at first. Then I recognized her: Evelyn, the lady
cop who had stunned Selina and handcuffed her.

The coffin hung above the grave on its strap mechanism. The priest stood off to the side. A gust of breeze
stirred his cassock as he walked into the group. He wore
gold-wire glasses and looked very pale and Irish. When
the time came he opened his little book and read the
words. Winston, head down, threw a handful of dirt on
the just-lowered coffin. As he turned away I expected
to see the shine of tears in his eyes. They were dry. The
ceremony was over in what seemed a very short time.

I stayed close to him, hoping to get in private words
about why he didn't want the statue and what the hell
happened. First Brunov was at his side. Then it was
thin Amanda Swale, who had picked him up at Greater
Pittsburgh International. She rallied the little group
of mourners and played subdued cheerleader. "Hey,
everybody, we need a little wake. Winston needs a little
wake, huh?" She threw a comradely arm around the
heavy man's neck. "They have wakes in old New England, Winston?"

"Well, not...my people. But the Irish..."

"Yeah! You can be an honorary Irishman for a few
hours." We were all well away from the grave site.
Amanda ran ahead and backed down the slope. She had
a pixie haircut that the breeze stirred on her brow, and
an athletic, long-legged lope. "Hey, everybody, we're
going to Sanborn's for a few. And every one of you better
come!" She ran back and took Winston's arm. "Especially *you!*" she said.

By the time all the cars sorted themselves out of the
cemetery, I was bringing up the rear. I was last into
Sanborn's. The lounge was on the edge of Oakland, so
it got a lot of the University of Pittsburgh crowd. Board-
game boxes were stacked on shelves in a large room off
the bar. I had often been there. I had never found a

game with all the pieces in one box. Friday nights it was packed with myopic prof types seducing coeds with dying left-wing coals fanned to a flame for the occasion, and undergraduate men bent on grapy oblivion.

On Saturday about one o'clock Sanborn's was nearly empty. The mourners were packed around two tables. I couldn't get to Winston. I ended up at a table by myself. Charity and Tod were at his table, but it wasn't the time or place for serious discussions. We started buying rounds. That suited Winston, I was sure.

The liquor started to work on the man from Massachusetts. The sour expression I had caught at grave site now deepened, dragging his face down into a pout. After an hour or so, he began to talk to no one in particular over the half dozen ongoing conversations. I leaned toward him, worried about what he might say. Charity had her eyes only on Tod. He was trying to nibble her ear. She was putting on a feeble act of resistance—to whet his appetite, I was sure.

"...my sister's gone," Winston was saying. "Gone, gone...I'm feeling sad. She shoulda amounted to something. S'pose I shoulda, too. Good family. We had a good family, my dear 'Licia and I. Went all the way back to Emerson—blood, by God. We just never got the breaks..."

Cheerleader Amanda sat beside him, the two of them the thick and thin of it. Brunov was on his other side, sipping a glass of white wine. She stroked Winston's hair where it curved above his collar. Under the fringe of her pixie cut, her brow was dotted with the sweat from the effects of the four Seven-and-Sevens she had downed. Her skin was white and smooth and young. "It's tough," she said. "Life is tough." I guessed she didn't know how tough.

"...no breaks. Me, I drink a bit too much. And I'm... not a brave man. Felicia was a bit too...easy for men. She had talent, but it sifted away...sand through her fingers...life through her fingers. So many promises she made...so few she kept—to mom, dad, me..." He pressed palms to his face. Pale Amanda whispered comfortingly. He raised his voice then, the bitterness loosened by a half dozen martinis. "Still, I kept believing

108

in her to the end. Believed in her legacy to me. Her damned legacy!" Heads turned toward him.

OK, Winston, I thought. That's enough.

He rambled on. "I thought blood would tell. Thought my sister was gonna turn my life around. I'm afraid it was one cripple leading another." He looked around at the circling, attentive faces. His failure to focus told me he was quite drunk. "All she had for me was a cold bronze statue. Ugly, dangerous statue. An' a pale beauty an' her bearded friend watching it for her." He pointed an unsteady finger at Charity and then me. "Joke is on me, good people. The hideous work isn't worth anything to me."

He covered his face again and shuddered. Amanda said he'd maybe had enough. She was about twenty minutes too late. The harm had been done. The news was out: bronze at 138. I frowned in puzzlement for the benefit of the gullible. "What's this bronze he's talking about?" I said.

"I don't *know*," Charity said on cue.

Winston babbled on, by now well into his old-New-England-family-bred-out litany. I headed for the men's room. I wasn't in there long, but when I came back out Winston's seat was empty. I aimed an accusing look at Charity. She never saw it. She was kissing Tod, both of them awkwardly craning in their seats.

On my way to the door I shouted, "Charity, Winston's gone!" Then I plunged outside. Winston was drawing deep breaths standing at the curb by a row of parked cars. I rushed up to him. "Winston, you better tell me what's going on, now that you've told the world Charity and I have the statue."

The bright afternoon sun bared his drunkenness and self-pity.

"Get rid of it, Yuri. It's trouble." His eyes were red and the fumes of downed martinis sailed his breath like yawls.

I grabbed his shoulder. "It's *yours*. Sister's orders."

"I don't want it. I'm going to straighten out with Mr. Brunov what little else was left to me. Then I'm going back to New England and find some other way to recover my life." His slurred words and steadying hand on the hood of a late-model Ford told me he was even drunker than I thought. The booze had stripped away some of his New England reserve, too. I saw clearly how afraid he was.

"What's happened to you, Winston? Who you been talking to?"

"Been warned to forget about the statue. Here's some free advice from a man who's in no position to give things away. Get rid of it. It's trouble. Sell it to the Junior League bazaar, give it to the Little Sisters of the Poor. Whatever."

"Who's threatening you?"

"Never mind, Nevsky." He threw himself toward me, both hands raised. He slammed me in the chest. As I staggered back my legs tangled. I took a hard seat on the sidewalk. Winston staggered down the line of cars. I caught him as he tried to scramble into one of them. I grabbed his shoulders and straightened him up, held him against the side of the car. "Listen, *Mr.* Farrow, your sister was murdered. You and that bronze are all of a sudden right in the middle of it. I want some answers out of you. And I want them *now.*"

Winston's eyes darted about, looking for help. Damned if he didn't find some.

"I suggest you release my client, Nevsky." The soft voice of Attorney Brunov. He had just that moment hurried up.

"I will when I find out what I want," I said.

"What you're doing is assault, Nevsky. By the glint in your eyes I'd guess battery is next. And a lawsuit to follow, I assure you."

I looked over at him. "Stay out of this, Brunov. This is a private discussion."

"I should have figured you for a strong-arm artist the other day at the Yelanov home," Brunov said. "Trying to cut yourself in on a piece of action that's none of your affair."

"Make him...let me go, Brunov," Winston whined.

"Let him go, Nevsky."

"Stay out of this!" I said.

He was big and quicker than he looked. His first shot—a left hook—headed for my right kidney. I spun, but not fast enough to slip the punch completely. A wash of kidney pain brought cold sweat to my brow and

discomfort to stomach and anus. I got my hands up—
and he drove a lowered shoulder into my belly. He
slammed me back against the side of a car. Nearly drove
all the breath out of me. Now I had kidney and wind
to worry me. Serious worries. He set himself up, feet
wide on the sidewalk, and started throwing left and
right hooks at my head and chest. I got my chin down
and kept my hands up. My little "rest" cost me a solid
thump in the left ribs and a grazing dazzler to my forehead. Stars danced as kidney eased and wind came back.

My lack of offense and my nonstance gave him confidence. The rain of meaty punches fell on the best parts
of my forearms and the top of my head. I got onto his
pace and rhythm and he did no more real damage. Still,
he wasn't in bad condition and kept on heaving and
pounding away. In time his breath came a bit shorter.
He caught on that I was riding him out. He straightened
up and tried the upright stance. All of a sudden he was
a classic boxer. His layered haircut was askew. Sweat
had sprung out on his brow. There was a faint light of
hesitation in his brown eyes. Then he came shuffling
at me, ringwise and crafty.

I wasn't that kind of fighter. I have no offense. I'm
a Pandora's box of counters. Leave me alone and I'm
benign. Come at me, though, and I'm trouble. Come at
me hard, and I'm *big* trouble. I let one of the head shots
come grazing through. It edged my cheek and chin. I
tottered and bent over in a fake stagger. Sure enough,
he stepped up to dig a destroyer into my gut. I nailed
his instep with the best angle of the heel of my go-to-
funeral dress shoe. I followed that with four rigid
knuckles jammed into his windpipe. I grabbed his right
ear with the palm and fingers of my left hand and jerked
just hard enough to loosen a little cartilage. I lashed
the back of my right hand across his left eye. Before he
could stagger back to regroup, I rammed the heel of my
left hand into his nose. Bone and tissue ground under
flesh. I knew it hurt, and I knew it would bleed. Nothing's as distracting as the pain from even one slightly
damaged sense organ. I had hit three. To finish the job
I waded forward for one lone left hook into his unpro-
tected stomach. I borrowed a trick from Evelyn the lady
cop. I grabbed his arm, swung it around behind his back

and ran him two steps headfirst into the side of a car. His head whuunked loudly. He went down on hands and knees. I kept my eyes on him while I checked my ribs and drew a half dozen deep breaths. I felt strong, in condition and effective. I was so busy gloating I forgot for a short while why we were brawling.

When I spun around, Winston was gone.

Charity came trudging sheepishly back from the far curb. "I went after him. Chased him across the street. Would have caught him, but he jumped in a cab and off he went. Gonzo!"

"Necking on the job."

She looked at the sidewalk. "I don't often let us down. Glands is what it was."

I scowled. The gathering was breaking up. The former mourners were getting into their cars. Curious eyes fell on Brunov as he got up on shaky legs and dusted off his clothes. His nose was oozing. He touched his tender ear. The first step he took brought a dart of pain from his instep. He motioned me toward him.

I went warily.

"That was asinine," he croaked. He swallowed and touched his Adam's apple. "Damn you. You bruised my golden throat." He managed a believeable smile. "I suggest that if we deal with . . . each other in the future, we do it like adults."

"Right on," I said.

"Shake on it?" Even with a bloody nose, his face told me he ought to be trusted. We shook hands. I studied his face further and read only conciliation amid sweat and swelling nose. After a few more gentle words and pleas for reason in the future, he went his way.

Chapter Nine

Tod hurried up, asking if everyone was all right. We said sure. Drinking seemed to have sparked grief at his own wife's death, and probably guilt over nuzzling Charity. "I'll call you," he said. "About the art research..." He was going to say more, but tears began to well. He shook his head and turned toward Twiggy's Land Rover, where she waited to drive him home.

"Me first." Charity faced me and brushed off my suit. Her thin white hands straightened my tie. "What were you brawling over *this* time?"

"I wanted to get some straight answers out of Winston. Brunov thought I got too rough."

"So he got rougher."

"He thought I was thin, weak and easy."

She got a tissue out of her purse and daubed my cheek and chin. The sting told me the skin was broken. "A lot of people make that mistake. They really ought to *look* at you close first. Just the same, you're bleeding a little." She put away her tissue and took my arm. "You men are such violent beasts. We women are, of course, above admiring your silly, bloody victories. Did you make an enemy?"

"We shook hands."

"Maybe because he got what he wanted?"

"Huh?"

"Well, you never *did* get a single answer out of Winston, did you? And I couldn't catch him."

"You figure Brunov could afford to make nice. I'll talk to Winston later. Call him at his hotel." I touched my aching ribs. I took a deep breath. Sore, but no clicks or sharp pain to tell me any were cracked. "I hope you did better with Tod Buckcry—if you managed to talk between smooches."

"I did—before the funeral, smarty. He was the right one to ask, all right. He met a lot of art types through 'sPots—the potters and crafts people, the customers. Second, he holds an adjunct lectureship in Carnegie-Mellon's art department. It's part time and low pay. But he knows the faculty. At one event or another he also got to know most of the art patrons in the tri-state area. He knows what's happening around here in painting, plastic arts, fabric, the lot."

"And?"

"If I'd come around two years ago and asked about art smuggling, he'd have laughed. But the last two years there's been 'talk.'"

"About...?"

"Tod said a piece of smuggled art is like masturbation. Everybody publicly goes 'tsk-tsk!'—but in private it's another matter. If a person is a serious collector and has a chance at a really great bargain...or if the potential buyer is a real novice who likes pretty things...it can go."

"And it's going?"

Charity nodded. "No names are mentioned. But over the last two years there's been a supply. Bronze statuary exclusively has been changing hands. Very old stuff. And Tod understood it was very good. Prices are reasonably high—*high,* but not gouging."

"Where's it come from?"

"Eastern Europe, southern Russia. Somehow it gets into the country, into western Pennsylvania."

"Stolen stuff?"

"Tod said it was probably removed illegally. Stolen? He didn't think so. Art thefts get very good publicity in the right circles. Stolen art gets *hot* like nothing else. From what I've heard, we're talking about second- and third-rate stuff. But still valuable. No name pieces of

114

any kind. That means they might have been in private collections. Tod said maybe they're being smuggled out and sold by owners to dodge taxes and government regulations. Governments—particularly Third World ones—now won't let what they consider national treasures leave the country. At the same time customs and border control are weak. Smuggling's very tempting—and easy."

"What about hard data?" I said. "Number of pieces coming into this part of the state? The routes they travel?"

"He said there wasn't much. There haven't been many pieces—maybe a dozen-odd. They tend to show up a few at a time. Then for a long while, nothing. So he heard, anyway."

"He heard what kind of money?"

"He said it depended on the piece." She giggled. "Then I showed him the Polaroid. His eyes got wide as a kid's mouth at a pie eating contest. He asked me if it was a piece of smuggled art. I said maybe. Then he took a *long* look at the photo." She stopped walking and spun on the pavement to get my attention. "Yuri, he said he thought it was worth well into *six figures*."

"My God! Small wonder Felicia called it her 'retirement'! What kind of bronze is it? Where did it come from?"

"He wasn't positive because of the gems and other shinies. But he thought it was Sarmatian."

"My Art 101 didn't cover that. What's that? What's 'Sarmatian'?"

"Sarmatians were nomadic rulers of southern Russia at the time of the birth of Christ."

"That bronze is *2000 years old?*"

"Ummm. Give or take. He wanted to take the photo to help him with his research. I made him make a sketch. He's going to try to find out *what* it is. Maybe why it's so ugly and threatening."

"He didn't want to see it?"

Charity frowned. "Oh, he *did*. I wanted to let him see it. But"—her skeptical glance passed coolly over my face—"I didn't think you'd like the idea."

"You were right."

Ruthie Spires, who had been hovering outside Sanborn's, approached us. She wore a cloche hat with a bit of veil. Green-eyed, red-haired and curvy, she was a foxy young lady full of pep and sass. "Everybody's got it tough, huh?" she said.

"I *guess,*" Charity said.

"Felicia's brother, you, me, my ex-boss, Count D-M." She fell into step with us. "I remember you two from Hermitage a little while back—when I told D-M to shove it all. A grim scene today. And what's-his-name?—Winston—made it worse."

"Drunk."

"For sure. How'd you two end up here today?"

"I'm an old friend of Felicia's. We were college roommates." Charity wriggled my arm. "This is my housemate and landlord."

Ruthie smiled. "College roommates . . . I always wondered what happened to coeds when they got to be middle-aged ladies."

"Same things that happen to noncoeds: some good, some bad."

"If I hadda guess, I'd say Felicia had hit a little 'bad.'"

Charity snapped at her. "You think her funeral was *funny?*"

Ruthie Spires frowned right back. I sensed a redhead's temper stirring under the pale skin. "I *don't* think it was funny. And it's rotten of you to think I do, Charity Day. I worked a couple of years with Felicia. She helped make Hermitage go as well as it did. I got to like her *plenty.*"

"Sorry. The last few days have been kind of rough for Yuri and me. One of those cases of my not engaging brain before starting mouth. Sorry."

Ruthie's charmer's smile was back. "You're OK, Charity. Can I talk to you two before you leave?"

"Sure."

"You and Felicia ever sail together?" Ruthie asked Charity. The question surprised me.

"A long time ago, in the summer. Over on the Connecticut shore."

"Not since then?"

"No."

"How about you, Nevsky?"

"My middle name is Mal-de-Mer."

There was a big Cadillac at curbside. Ruthie boosted herself onto it's hood in a swirl of dark skirt. She smoothed it over her knees and patted the spaces on either side. "Both of you stand right here in front of me for a minute, OK?" We stood and she looked us over. She chucked Charity's chin. She tilted her head back slightly and studied it. Her fingertips brushed the corners of Charity's eyes, the lines in her neck. "You've been around, haven't you, lady? Seen a few things?"

"Guilty as charged. Wife, mother, widow, career woman."

Ruthie studied me. "You got brains to go with that body?" she said.

"I can count with my shoes on, if that's what you mean."

"If I hadda guess, I'd say you both have some smarts. So I'm gonna say some things, and I don't think you'll get the wrong idea. When I said I was sorry Felicia was dead, I meant it. But—you know what they say—life belongs to the living. And the days keep coming at you in waves. You get swept along, you're not careful. Maybe you find yourself like Felicia and me, behind a couple beat-up desks in a place like Hermitage—or you name it. Working for small money and screwing guys like Sergei and the count, the way we were. I mean...the count never took off his monocle. Not even when—well, the hell with *that* kind of life! Felicia saw what was happening, did something about it. She tried to break out by...branching out, you might say."

"You mean by being Sergei Yelanov's lover?"

"Just partly. I mean what she was doing *extra*."

"Which was what?" Charity said.

"Come on, Charity, Nevsky. I could hear Brother Winston as well as you could. You're holding. Holding all kinds of stuff right now. He called you two on it. Stuff for Felicia." She looked at each of us in turn. "I been asking around after you both. I started at 'sPots and went from there. I found out Charity's a lawyer with some big law firm downtown. A nice front. And you, Nevsky? *You*. You don't work at *all*."

"I'm an information specialist. It's up and down work."

"Up and down, my tushy," Ruthie said. "Don't forget, I used to live with Felicia. Me, Amanda Swale, Twiggy

Twill and Squirrely Gowell. So she moved out a while back, but she was on Walnut Street with us for over, say, two years."

"So what's that have to do with us?" Charity said.

"I'm coming to that. Don't worry. Here's what would happen. About every four or five weeks when the weather was good, she'd flash a little extra money. Nothing big, get it. But she'd, like, spring for a gallon of Baskin-Robbins double chocolate for the house and a couple of new dresses for herself. I mean nice stuff from Sachs. An we'd say, hey, who's your sugar daddy? But she wouldn't let on what was up. Then about three months ago, all of a sudden she had a lot of bucks. She bought a big Sony color TV and a nice little used station wagon. And she was passing out cocaine. She had a little Miracle Whip jar full of it. We were all snorting our heads off—except for Twiggy, of course."

Ruthie paused. She slid off the hood and curved a hand around one each of our elbows.

"And when Amanda and I went to her fancy apartment the night she died, it was all trashed. Something was going on for sure. What more do I have to say?" Ruthie said. "You all hit some kind of trouble, right? Things got rough or something. Now you have to build it up again. And this time I want to be on the team. Like I said, Felicia's gone. But here comes Ruthie Spires! Strong back, doesn't get seasick, works hard, knows how to put two and two together."

"Ruthie, you are *not* putting two and two together right," I said.

"*I* think I've spotted the moment you both can change my life." Her eyes bloomed like green flowers as she leaned closer to me. "With you both right here, I can't make it any plainer: I want in."

"What do you think we're in?" Charity said.

"Look, Charity, we've already said you're a smart lady. Don't play dumb with me. You and your bold brigadier on my right. You're both with the people who spread it around after it comes in."

"After what comes in?" I said.

"The *coke.*"

"I see," Charity said. From her frown I knew she didn't see at all.

118

"I don't want any part of spreading it around," Ruthie said. "You can have it. I want to work with the people who bring it in. I know it's risky. I told Felicia she should stick to hot art. Who gives a shit about some moldy old Russky statues. Now here I am wanting maybe to take her place. By the way, what did happen to Sergei Yelanov?"

"Felicia didn't tell you?" Charity said.

"She said he took off scared and rich."

"Nobody knows where Sergei is," I said. "Did Count Dromsky-Michaux know about the art smuggling?"

"The count was so happy over the low prices and the high markup that it never entered his mind that the goods were 'duty free' and probably hot. The count kept up the front; Sergei was the man who dug in the mud, got the antiques and art stuff one way or the other. How come you came to Hermitage anyhow?"

"To ask about Felicia," Charity said.

"To ask what?"

"You can put two and two together—right, Ruthie?" I said.

"For sure."

I had an idea, but no real understanding of where it would take me. Something like keeping Ruthie hoping till I found out all she knew. Behind that I had the distant goal of helping Charity find out who murdered Felicia. I moved my head forward till our foreheads nearly touched. "We were trying to get a lead on who sawed Felicia's steering wheel column nearly through."

"Who..." Ruthie's face paled till her eyes greened to round emeralds. "That's...a terrible joke."

"Who's joking? She was murdered. Probably because she was mixed up smuggling art or...cocaine." The word stuck in my throat. I didn't like dope. It ruined people. It chewed them up with nasty chemical teeth and spat them out used up, like so much gristle.

Ruthie's eyes were still very round and green. "Who would...?"

"Maybe rivals. Maybe some heavy hitters from out of town."

Ruthie looked down at her heels. "I want some time to think things over. Can I call you later today?"

"Come over for dinner," Charity said. She gave her our address.

Charity wanted to go back to the cemetery. She had left the grave without enough thought for her dead friend. Poor Felicia, I thought. She was dead because somebody sawed through the steering column of her car. That happened because she had been smuggling art and something went wrong. She probably needed money or wanted to help her lover's business. She had a lover because her marriage had dissolved. It was all so complicated, so tangled. Life had been like a juggernaut bowling her over, rolling her along ahead of it awhile, then crushing her. I heard her voice again: *Nobody ever told me how hard life was.*

I stood surveying marker and monument. Back turned to the grave, I once again savored the lovely June day. The Monongahela Valley stretched out below, the twist of gray river, railroad cars strung along the southern banks, houses following the rolls of the land.

Tears came quickly to Charity's eyes. The breeze stirred, cooling the thin rivulets on her cheeks. I gave her my handkerchief. She had a good old-fashioned cry while I looked on with burning eyes. When she was finished, she said, "That made me feel clean and decent, and a good friend after all." She picked up a handful of dirt and sprinkled it over the mounded grave. It made a light rainlike sound. She gave my handkerchief back and we turned away from Felicia Farrow Semanova for the last time.

Ruthie Spires arrived early—single girl, lots of energy, ready to go somewhere, never ready to wait. She lugged in two six-packs of Beck's Special Dark Beer. She wore peach-colored slacks, a light V-cut blouse. A Vera handkerchief was knotted neatly to keep her red hair off the neck.

While Charity gave her the grand tour, I worked to get the chicken curry to the simmer stage. I opened three beers and waited for the ladies in the large living room.

Ruthie came giggling and swaying in, heels dangling from her index finger by the straps. "Your house is *terrific,* Yuri. And Charity is great fun to talk to. Like Felicia was. That's probably why I told Mr. Riding Boots to shove it. It wasn't fun there anymore without her. I thought it would be fun to start doing what she was..." She looked warily at me. "But I changed my mind. I'm *real* attached to life."

"Well, we're not what you thought we were anyhow," Charity said.

"I kinda caught on when I saw the house and life style."

I passed the beer around. Charity and I told her some of the circumstances that had brought Felicia to us. She hid her face, giggled, looked away. She was embarrassed about her wild assumptions. While she blushed I told her we had "got rid" of the bronze.

"That must be one hell of a valuable hunk of metal—if Felicia was going to retire on it."

"Something happened that scared her," Charity said. "That's why it didn't go right through Hermitage to a waiting customer. I bet she was waiting for things to cool down. After a while she probably planned to sell it and keep whatever money for herself."

"Only she never made it. Somebody sawed her steering column." Ruthie took a deep slug of beer. "Somebody really wanted her dead. What's in running a little art that would get anybody excited? Course if they were running coke, too..."

"Felicia ever say just how they did it?" Charity said.

"Not really. I'm pretty sure they used Sergei's boat, the *Stressless I*. Went out on Lake Erie. Maybe they went all the way to the Canadian side. Lots of open shorelines on both sides."

"Anybody in the house on Walnut ever ask her where she got the extra money or about the time she had the cocaine?" I said.

"Amanda used to. Felicia would say she hit the state lottery for a few hundred, or Sergei had a good night at the poker table and felt generous. Or she finally broke her piggy bank. Something like that. That time she had the coke was a *trip*. Charity, you know what coke is like?"

"Me? The only kind of Coke I've ever used is the kind you put ice cubes in."

"Straight as you look, huh? Nevsky?"

"I grew up predope," I said.

"It's such a nice high. A nice clean buzz, you know? Sky high, but not falling down like from booze. Or stinking up the place like pot. No sore throats the next day. Never forget that night she had the jar full. Amanda, Felicia, June and I—the four of us. We invited over a couple of guys. One of them brought an electric piano. We all got high, sat around and listened to the music. Then Felicia sprang for a Chinese dinner. About ten courses and all delivered. Everything tastes so good on a coke high. Everything you see so sharp. Every smell is separate. You think *grand* thoughts. You really oughta get some and try it."

"How much does it cost?" Charity said.

"Well, there *is* that." She took a solid swallow of her Beck's. "Depends on how good, where you get it. Somewhere between two and three hundred an ounce. More if it's super pure. Keeps on going right on up with inflation, like everything else."

We broke for dinner, then went back to the beers. Something about Ruthie's free-spirit style and down-to-earth gutsiness kept Charity and I tippling right along with her. "You two have me spotted for what I am, don't you?" She giggled. "A fun lady. I know already I'll never have any of what you two have." She lowered her shoulder to take in all of 138.

Charity began: "Ruthie—"

"Guys know I'm strictly a good-time girl. I couldn't cook an egg if I lived in a microwave oven. It shows."

"Men aren't necessarily the only way to get somewhere in life," Charity said. "I've had it both ways. Dependency is ugly. In every one of us there's a little voice that wants to shout: I did it myself! It's *mine. Mine* is a basically healthy word that's out of fashion."

"So you're a woman's libber," Ruthie said.

"She's a wise human being is what she is." I saw that Ruthie wasn't one who learned through theory and instruction. She learned only in Ben Franklin's dear school: experience. Trouble with that was few of us lived luckily enough to make quick sense of what was happening in our lives. Charity didn't realize she was talking into a deaf ear. I changed the subject.

"Why'd Felicia move out of the Walnut Street house?"
I said.

"She sort of hinted it had something to do with where
she got the extra money. She said the rent was being
taken care of by 'a friend.'"

"Who?"

"Didn't say. Did say she missed the high times in
Shadyside. Said a view wasn't everything unless you
were ninety-five years old."

We finished the Beck's and a half dozen Rolling Rocks
from the bar refrigerator. Just the same I wasn't quite
through with informative Ruthie. "You're not hitting
the road unless we get some coffee into you. Papa's
orders." I put the percolator on low so the coffee wouldn't
be ready too soon. Casually I asked her if she knew
Anna Yelanov, Sergei's wife.

"Madame Yelanov." Ruthie stuck out her chest and
inflated her cheeks. "I found out about her from Felicia,
who got it from Sergei. She used to be an opera singer,
a few years back. She was OK for Pittsburgh. Once she
even sang with the symphony when they used to play
at Syria Mosque. She was that big fish in the little pond.
When she saw she wasn't going to make it big, she
married Sergei. Then she spent years blaming him for
her failed career. How much she gave up for him! What
she could have done! They never had any kids. Pretty
soon they had one of those famous arrangements you
hear so much about. She'd screw anybody who could
get by her load of blubber. Sergei was more particular.
He liked younger women, but with an eye on marriage.
His style was the home, the family, the loving wife. He
just never got lucky."

"You know anybody Anna slept with?" I caught
Charity's puzzled stare. She wondered where I was going
with it.

"Me?" Ruthie frowned, trying to remember after six
beers. "Don't think so."

"How about one being Vasily Brunov?"

"Vasily? Impossible! Vasily's an Important Person
in Pittsburgh. He wouldn't bother with her. He's a big
attorney in town. He's also the lawyer for Hermitage—
or what's left of it. He was Sergei's lawyer, too, before
he took off. And I'm sure he's on a retainer from Count

D-M, too. God knows he needs an attorney. Going bankrupt is tough to do on your own."

I told her about my visit to the Yelanov home. She tittered and looked shocked. "I can't *believe* it."

"I heard he was Felicia's lawyer, too," I said.

"Yeah. She met him at Hermitage. She needed her will changed. She decided she didn't want to leave her stuff to her Russky husband. That had pretty much fallen apart. Everything was to go to her brother." Ruthie threw up her hands. "If Winston, the way he acted today, is her idea of a deserving heir—Jesus! What was Alexey like?"

"I met him a long time ago. He wasn't so hot then," Charity said. "And Felicia and Twiggy said he got worse."

"What do you think of Vasily Brunov, Charity?" Ruthie winked.

My housemate blushed. "Tell you the truth, I liked him. Nice smile. Soft voice. Even though he and Yuri brawled, he seemed like a gentle guy. Probably has a temper is all."

"Crazy as it seems, even *I* like him. He's a charmer," I said.

"Charmer on the way up, too. Last election he got voted into some kind of small office in Allegheny County," Ruthie said. "Not bad for a guy his age. He's got a good practice going. He's making good money." Her eyes brightened. "About the election...Brunov was very much the underdog. Probably would have lost. But there was some mudslinging during the campaign."

"About what?"

"About his uncle, Misha Brunov. He's an old Russky who lives up on Russian Slope. People say he's kind of a small-town godfather. He's been in trouble over the years, but he's never spent a day in jail."

"So?"

"Brunov's opponent was a Polack pol who had a nasty streak. He started saying—in code, of course—that Brunov had contact with the mob."

"Anything to it?"

"Nothing. Nothing. Brunov opened up all his records and tax returns to reporters. And if *they* couldn't find anything—"

"When was this?"

"Oh, about three-and-a-half, four years ago. Anyhow, he came out smelling so good the whole deal backlashed on the Polack. He got buried in the election. And that gave Brunov his start in politics. Since then things have looked better and better for him. He came from some money, you know."

"I didn't."

"His father owns Willow Grove."

Willow Grove was Pittsburgh's biggest amusement park. The biggest in Pennsylvania, for sixty years the place to go for thrill rides. Nearly every Pittsburgh high school had its spring picnic there. I loved it, particularly the three big roller coasters. Most of all I loved the biggest of the three, the Hurricane. Pittsburgh families poured through Willow Grove gates like lemmings in search of a cliff. Tens of thousands of families, more couples, and armies of singles paid ten dollars each for ride-all-day tickets—never mind the concessions. Willow Grove was a gold mine.

"I think Ivan Brunov, Vasily's father, is pretty much retired—but everybody knows he still controls every penny," Ruthie said. "They have a good general manager. That lets Vasily run the place with his left hand. But he's making it on his own in law and politics. And maybe real estate, too. I think he owns some property. That's the way he wants to make it—*on his own.* His marriage plans won't hurt him either."

"Who's he going to marry?" Charity said.

"Trishie Widemann. I saw the announcement in the *Post Gazette.*"

"Duke Widemann's daughter?" Charity said.

"The same."

Duke Widemann was one of Pittsburgh's modern self-made industrialists. The Carnegies, Fricks, Schwabs and Mellons did it in heavy industry and banking. Duke had made it in plastics and electronics. His public image was one of a no-nonsense sports-minded freewheeler, art collector and patron of community theater. Reports of his bighorn-sheep-hunting jaunts to Montana or fishing trips to the Gulf for tarpon were often on TV. At Christmas he opened up Poplars, his sprawling mansion near the Fox Chapel Hunt Club, to inner city kids for a day of music, food and games. Word was that what they broke cost more than what they ate and got. Duke didn't mind. "What's Trishie like?" I said.

"Plain as a post. And Vasily could've had *me!*" Ruthie dug her fingers into her red mane and heaved up her breasts. "Look! All this. Thirty-six C and I screw like a mink."

"But what about your stock portfolio?" I said.

"Huh?"

"Time to break up the party, I think," Charity said. "I sense the conversation sinking."

"I guess. Hey, listen, Nevsky, Charity. We've been thinking of having a party for Tod the night of Selina's funeral. Gonna try and bring him up and out of the glooms. You should come."

"We'd like to. Just let us know." Charity showed her to the door.

I staggered to bed and lay awake only a few minutes. The soft fingers of sleep were at once tugging at my mind. I still had time to sum up the day. Charity and I now had one big problem in our lap—the Sarmatian statue. Now I knew how it had come to us—but not *why*. Curious, too, how a single person seemed to know or work for just about everyone we had met in the last few days: an attorney named Vasily Brunov. He fit in somewhere. I knew it.

Chapter Ten

I had just poured Charity's coffee into her Gothic *C* cup sitting by the *New York Times* crossword puzzle when the phone rang. I picked it up. A man's voice, dark and muffled. "Yuri Nevsky?"

"Yes." I hit the amplifier button. The heavy voice filled the kitchen.

"Listen carefully to what you hear next."

"Who is this?"

"Never mind. Just listen." There was a soft thumping on the line. The unmistakable voice of Winston Farrow III came bleating into my ear. "Nevsky, this is Winston. This is no joke! Believe me, this is no joke!" The words tumbled down the line with scarcely a pause between. Winston was totally terrified. Charity and I exchanged frowns. "I'm in a phone booth. Somebody's here with me. Nevsky, there's a pistol barrel against my throat. Hear me? A pistol. A *loaded pistol*."

"Christ..." I felt some of his terror leak down the line.

"I—I've told the person all about the bronze statue. How you got it. What it looks like. *Everything*. I've told this person it's in your house."

I began to deny it.

"Listen, Nevsky, these people *want* it. They want you and your housemate out of there in one hour. They want the bronze in plain view—"

127

"We don't have it any more. We got rid of it."

"I doubt that," Winston said. "I doubt it very much. There's nobody to take that thing."

"Well, it's gone just—"

"Leave the side door unlocked—"

"It's not here!"

"I—I don't believe you." There were muffled whispers I couldn't understand. "We know it's there," Winston said. "You're lying. No one would buy it. It's still somewhere in your basement."

"Winston—"

"Get out of the house one hour from now. Or they'll kill you both!" More muffled thumpings, as though from a struggle. "No! Don't!" Two shots!

They slammed into my ears as the slugs must have slammed into Winston's flabby body. The line went dead. I stared at my trembling knuckles on the receiver. My mind flashed the bronze statue's vicious face, the nihilist message in that undelivered hammer blow. "No," I said. "No!"

Charity paled as she rose to stand beside me. "The...statue. You were thinking of that ugly thing, too, weren't you?"

I nodded.

"Do you think Winston's...?"

"The bronze seems to bring death with it, doesn't it?"

"And he touched it..."

"Coincidence," I said. "But it shakes me up just the same. Anyway, I think they shot him."

Charity paced. "They want us out of the house."

"That'll be the day."

We both toured the house making sure all doors and windows were firmly shut. We checked our various caches of weapons. I uncloseted the sawed-off shotgun loaded with rock salt and stood it in a kitchen corner. Charity got her derringer out of her purse and checked both cartridges. "I think whoever they are, they're bluffing."

"We'll see."

An hour came and went as we paced about and stared stupidly at each other. It did seem a bluff or a war of nerves. Charity decided to do the dishes. I looked on from a nearby chair facing the sink. Midway through the breakfast china, a cup squirmed free of her rubber-gloved hand. She bent over quickly to try to catch it. At that moment the window in front of the sink cracked into a spider's web around a finger-wide hole. Hot, nasty lead churned up flinders of floor tile. I dove off the chair like an interior lineman and took her legs out from under her. We had only begun to fall in a tangle when the vinyl back of my chair was punctured. The chair flew over, KO'ed by a lead fist.

Above us the kitchen counter corner caught one, two, three—five slugs from the silenced weapon. I heard shouting from the garage side, the direction from which the silent fire had come. Judy Larkin's voice. No more shots.

I scrambled over and grabbed the shotgun. I waited for more shots. There were none. I looked over at Charity scrambling away from the window area. Her face was bleeding. Cuts from flying glass. Head down, I worked the faucet lever to wet a towel. She sat up. "Sit still." I dabbed off the blood. Two bits of glass came out with some delicate thumb-and-forefinger work. The two or three left would require tweezers to get out. "Not bad. You're still the beautiful Wonder Widow."

"I'm *very* lucky."

We slunk away from the shattered window into the dining room. We kept out of sight of other windows. "They want to kill us both," she said in a shaky voice. "Why?"

"The Sarmatian statue. Kill us quiet, then search the house later."

"Why not just search the house when we're gone?" she said.

"Good point. Maybe getting us came first. If they found the bronze, too, so much the better."

"Then they're *very* reckless. If we died, they'd *never* find the White Chamber."

"One thing's for sure: JFK and the sniper aren't on the same team," I said. "The sniper thought maybe he could walk past our bleeding corpses and find the bronze in a closet."

Charity clutched the back of a dining-room chair. Her knuckles showed white. "If I hadn't just ... dropped that cup ..."

"And I hadn't moved to knock you down. I didn't have time to think the next shot was for me."

Charity looked at the floor, toward the basement where the statue stood sealed away, but no less potent. "I must be really...jumpy, Yuri. I feel like we both just *postponed* dying." She began to shudder. Her face twisted with anxiety and fear.

The door chimes rang. I peeked into the porch mirror. Police.

"I think this is a *wonderful* time to play dumb blonde." Charity stretched out on the living-room couch and pressed a damp towel against her face. I let the cops in. We were honored by a visit from the chief, as well as the expected officers, Slapko and two others. "Got a call from a Mrs. Judy Larkin," the chief growled. "Man up on your garage roof taking pot shots at your house with a silenced rifle. We didn't see him. He musta beat it."

Chief Koneski had been a Green Beret early in the Viet Nam War, when it was still glamorous and Barry Sadler was singing about it instead of being in trouble. Koneski had become a small-town cop, had been promoted fast and ended up chief, whipping Marland's small force into shape. His computerized reporting and record keeping system, the *East Boroughs Eagle* said, was a model for small boroughs in the state. It was his non-electronic curiosity, though, that had brought him to our living room. He carried in a straight-backed chair and sat by Charity. His spine was straight and his hair butch cut. Chief Koneski, I thought, at ease! Charity said, "Yuri, could I have a mirror, please?"

Despite my information business I had managed to stay clear of the local police. No. 138's having been owned by the same family for forty-odd years tended to relax the locals. On my way to get a hand mirror, I agreed with Charity's idea to play dumb.

She examined her nicks and small gashes, jabbering and chirping nonstop about would her face be ruined, who could have done such a thing, blah, blah. She was playing the blonde simp well enough to win a New York Drama Critics Circle Award.

Chief Koneski, who was nobody's fool, was taken in just the same. He turned away from her, glance raised ceilingward. Officer Slapko of the pocked, mustached face came out of the kitchen. He reported number of shots and damage. He had one of the slugs in the middle of a handkerchief. "Thirty-thirty," he said.

"Maybe a deer hunter took the wrong fork," I said.

"What the hell is this?" Koneski said. "You sound like you like being shot at, Mr. Nevsky."

In the middle of Charity's and my don't-know-nothing spiel, Judy Larkin came pushing in past the cop at the door. "I'm the woman who called the police," she said. She burst into the living room almost at a run. Her eyes searched for, and fell, on me. There was no mistaking the relief in her green eyes or in her smile of delight—followed by a blush worthy of a 104-degree fever victim. Levered up by her relief, she gave Chief Koneski a full description of what she had seen and done—complete with the gestures, voice tones and body movements that had so charmed me during our Saturday morning coffee klatch.

What it boiled down to was that she had glanced out a window facing 138. She saw a bearded man in jeans and a dark turtleneck up on my garage roof. He was aiming a rifle at my kitchen window. She tore open the sash and shouted at him just before he fired. Before he shot again she was running for the phone to call the police.

Just as she finished, my phone rang. It was Jed, her husband. Her conversation was short. She came back to the living room apologizing. Jed wanted her back home to watch the kids. It was time for him to leave for his golf game. She went rushing off. Her straw-colored hair danced over her shoulders as she nodded to Koneski's request to make a witness statement later.

The chief's officers finished their counting, measuring and note taking. Charity and I signed some papers. A vaguely dissatisfied Chief Koneski got ready to leave. He paused at the front door. "Mr. Nevsky, Ms. Day, you say you don't have any enemies, you don't have any legal or family problems, you aren't mixed up in anything funny..." He snorted. "Then, by God, you have some *damned* odd friends."

After restudying her face in the mirror Charity felt better. She found the small Band Aids and covered her cuts. The phone rang and she answered. Her eyes lit up. I knew it was Tod Buckcry even before she started to pull the Band Aids off. "He'll be here in fifteen minutes," she said. "He's found out more about the Sarmatian bronze." She eyed her Sunday morning slacks and blouse. "I better change."

"Don't you need some time to get over being shot at?"

She looked startled. "Oh! I guess not." She hurried off to her side of the house. I swallowed my faint surge of jealousy and grimaced.

How much we all wanted love and attention! The lucky ones of us admitted it. We hurried for our combs and mirrors. We polished our teeth and our wit. We dared to look for others to share some parts of our small lives. The meek bit the bullet of their own loneliness. They filled their lives with diversions, turned to stamps, cooking, cameras, summer cottages. Like the princess's pea, though, that great need niggled on. Better to take the risk of search than settle for that timid life of swallowed longing.

Tod arrived bubbling with information and curiosity. We three sat around a cleared dining-room table. "Let's talk about the Sarmatians!" he said. He made Charity get her Polaroid of the bronze. "I found material on the Sarmatians, and"—he slapped the photo—"this is a *very* unusual piece." He turned a sour glance at her. "And while we're talking about it, *Ms*. Day, I have to tell you you really disappointed—and hurt me."

Charity was startled. "Me?"

"When you wouldn't tell me before the funeral *you* had the bronze. You and Nevsky here. And I was trying to *help* you."

"I—I just—"

"Winston was wrong," I cut in. "We had it, but it's not here any more." Tod looked very doubtful.

Charity's face was red. "What have you got to say about the statue, Tod?" she said.

Tod glowered at me. I wasn't having any of that. I let him know in nasty tones what had happened that morning. I took him out to the kitchen, showed him the shattered window, the splintered counters and the furrowed floor. "How does *that* compare with your hurt feelings?" I said. "And you were so keyed up about the bronze, you didn't notice the nicks in your lady love's face."

"Yuri..." Charity's try at hiding her irritation failed badly.

I knew I was being an ass. It felt good. I should have been an ass more often. It was an interesting way of asserting myself.

"Look, Nevsky, I don't have to do either of you any favors—"

"Will you two please *stop?*" Charity grabbed our arms and led us back to the table. She sat between us.

Tod avoided my eyes. He dug into his file folder and spread out his papers and Xeroxes. "As I mentioned to Charity earlier, the Sarmatians replaced the Scythians as rulers of southern Russia about 200 B.C. They were nomads and traders. They dealt a lot with the Greeks of the Black Sea. It was the Greeks who ran the towns and ports. The Sarmatian artists did their work and the Greeks served as middlemen." He spread out a half dozen photocopies of utensils, costume jewelry, arms and weapons. "There's no color in these, but if there were you could see how the Sarmatians developed the art of combining precious metals with colored gems. Their favorite was gold or bronze with red stones like garnets and red chalcedony."

Charity frowned. "But look at the bronze." She touched the Polaroid. "It's *covered* with stones."

"That's the big contribution of Sarmatian art. They didn't use precious stones just to adorn objects. They did something more interesting. They used stones and enamels to encrust the metal surfaces. That's how I can explain these patterns on the bronze. There's more." He touched all the Xeroxes and photostats. "Notice? Animals and monsters only. This one here is the Iranian winged griffin—a lion's head here, a curved eagle's beak there."

"No human figures," I said.

"No! And that's the point, Nevsky. This bronze *isn't* part of the mainstream." With a smile of anticipation he took another smaller envelope out of his leather purse pouch. "I found *these* in a book printed in Russia

133

around 1750. It was in the rare books room." He slid out four small photostats. "Look at these medallions."

The first was an angry-looking woman with stag's horns. Tod looked at his notes. "Some kind of fury," he said. The second was an icy-eyed lady being mounted by a goat. "An early obscenity," he said. The third was a spear-wielding horror of a man. "These were the demons thought to torture and punish the Sarmatian dead around 200 B.C. These medallions were found in tumuli—grave mounds—in the bend of the Dnieper River near Alexandropol. And there's the ugliest one of all."

Charity gasped. I didn't want to touch it. It was too much like the bronze statue. The figure was raised. I saw the same hooked nose and bestial, enraged face that had whispered seductively to the shadow sides of our hearts.

"A nameless demon," Tod said.

"Sarmatian Demon," Charity said softly.

"Two hundred B.C.!" Tod's eyes widened with the thought. "Rome was consolidating control over Italy. Christ wasn't even *born* yet."

"Twenty-two hundred years old!" I said.

"Imagine how much it's worth!" Tod said.

"Enough to kill for," I said. Charity and I filled him in on Winston's anguished phone call and possible murder. That, on top of the shooting, I thought, would cool his excitement over a bronze he seemed to have taken to heart.

He stacked up his photocopies and notes with businesslike efficiency. The corners of his brown eyes crinkled above his beard and smile. "Well, let's see it."

"The bronze?" I said.

"Of course."

"It's not here," I said. "I told you."

"Look, Yuri, I did a lot of work for you—"

"For Charity," I said.

He flushed. "So? I still don't deserve the runaround." He turned to Charity. "Is it here, or isn't it?"

"N-No," she said. She was blushing. My poised and polished partner was fast losing her composure. Emotions made fools—and angels—of all of us.

"I don't believe either of you!" Tod growled. "You lied to me once, Charity, now you're lying to me again.

I don't like it! And I won't put up with it!" He scooped up his papers and jammed them angrily into his envelope. "I've taken time from *grieving* to help you. And I get my thanks in *lies!*"

I saw that woman-guilt at work in Charity's heart— even in her, a strong, confident woman. She swallowed. "I...thank you for all you've done, Tod."

"Fine. You're welcome. I guess I'll be on my way." He jumped up from his chair.

Charity got up, too, and held his forearm in both hands. "No, don't go." Her tone was sincere. "Stay the afternoon. You've done for me. Let me do for you for the rest of the day."

He hesitated. I thought he might shake off her hands. Instead the anger drained out of him. His mood changed so quickly his face seemed to dissolve and shift like a turned kaleidoscope. His features now reflected grief and loss.

"I feel...odd about that. Selina...I should feel... more. Be sadder."

Sensing softness, Charity waged womanly war. She put her arms around him and pressed her face against the upper colored squares of his Mondrian sweatshirt. "Please...walk with me. Let's go for a walk."

I watched them amble down Morlande Street, arms around one another's waists. How merciless women could be in pursuit of what they thought they wanted. We men could be merciless, too, but ours was a rougher strike of that coin, alloyed of shove and punch and push. We worked on the surface of things; we had our fragile rules. But for women at war there were no rules. The point of attack was diffused, the target the softer, more vulnerable sides of our souls. Men fought with iron. Women used sweet poison. Altogether we were all of us a lethal lot...

I went to the baby grand in the music room and practiced my exercises, chasing mellowness across the curving hills of *legato*. I wasn't sure what I found among my halting notes. Whatever, when Charity asked if I would cook dinner for Tod, too, I said yes. I said it would be no trouble. I didn't know if I lied or told the truth. I had a very hard time sorting out my feelings where Charity was involved.

One thing, though, was clear. The tender glances and simpering smiles Charity and Tod traded with the zeal of Arabs in a soon-to-close bazaar were damned annoying. I felt sunk to butler and cook serving the willfulness of a spoiled lady upstairs. After dinner when they went up the staircase to her side of the house, clearly bent on enjoyment at close quarters, I sunk lower—to bordello lackey.

I wasn't quite sure what I thought or how long it took me to get there, but I found myself on the Larkin's doorstep about seven o'clock. I knocked and Jed Larkin answered. In the background kids were screaming with determined prebed intensity. I saw from the lines set in his closely shaven face that domesticity wasn't his strong suit.

"I came over to beg a neighborly cup of coffee," I said.

Judy waved from the kitchen with a high chair under one arm. "Hi, Yuri! C'mon in."

"You want *into* this bedlam?" Jed shook his head.

"One man's bedlam is another man's family," I said.

Jed grunted and followed me toward the kitchen. We sat amid the debris of three young kids' dinner hour. Eight-year-old Jimmy was on a stool by the kitchen counter banging glasses filled to different levels with water. He was accompanying himself singing "Oh, Susannah!" off key. Bobby, the six-year-old, was bawling and screwing little fists into leaking eyes. Little Louis, now under Judy's other arm, had spilled a pitcher of milk down his front. A large yellow cat and a spaniel lapped at the puddle on the linoleum.

"Stop that *singing*, Jimmy!" Jed shouted.

"I'll hold Louis for a minute," I said to Judy.

I helped restore the scene to the standard controlled chaos of a small-children family just before bedtime. During a lull in the action Judy turned on the burner under the percolator. "I am going to *love* sitting down," she said.

"I just came over for coffee and gossip," I said.

"Well, I'm in the mood for that," Judy said. "What a day you've had! I told Jed about the mess your kitchen was in and about the police."

"Umm. I'm trying to forget about it. Let's talk about something else."

"Just killing time, Nevsky?" Jed said. He had heavy brows and the beginnings of jowls. He had worked on his glance and style. Along with middle age they brought him, at last, the wished-for air of Authority.

"More or less."

"That's a luxury I can't afford. Judy was after me to sit around here with her and do nothing tonight." He dried his hands on a dish towel.

Judy's head rose, fearfully attentive, like a deer disturbed at grazing. "Jed, you said—"

"I said I'd stay home because you wanted company. I told you the Manguson account is causing big trouble. And *I* have to ride herd on it. And I *was* willing to stay here with you."

"'Was'?"

"Well, Nevsky seems to have time to chat. I don't." He looked at his watch. "I can get in three good hours at the office."

"If you have to..." Judy's voice was too calm and resigned. The edging of her facial muscles and a slight coloring told me I was sitting across the table from one angry, resentful lady. "Will you wait to kiss the kids good night?"

"I'll kiss them now," he said.

She nodded, teeth working her lower lip. "What time will you be home?"

"Before eleven."

"I've learned to add an hour by now. Twelve, right?"

Jed turned his cool gray eyes on me. "Judy's never understood that money doesn't grow on trees. Or what kind of commitment I have to make to let her live the easy life she has. It's not easy to be an effective middle manager. Possibly you don't understand either, Nevsky. You don't seem a busy man."

"I pace myself. Right now my pace is slow."

"Fine. Then you have an evening to waste with Judy. I don't."

Judy closed her eyes and drew a deep breath. Jed hurried off to gather up his papers.

"He's...crazy." She kept her head down. "Work's all he *does*. He sees to it he's home as little as possible. He doesn't like his kids. I don't even know if he likes *me*." She finally looked up at me. Her face trembled in its frame of sandy hair. I read the tenacity, the resentment, the feeling of betrayal, and the sincere doubts about just how she was living her life. I knew, without a word, just what Charity had been hearing in her informal counseling sessions.

In time Judy got the kids to bed and came back downstairs. She had shaken the heaviness in her voice and movement. Now she was the vivacious, almost giddy woman with whom I had spent a cheerful two hours chattering.

We took our coffee into the living room. The dog and cat followed us. The furniture was expensive, the wall-to-wall nicely shaggy. I sat on the brocaded couch. She sat on an easy chair.

"Your friend Charity has a visitor," she said.

"You don't miss much," I said.

Judy held her knees together and rested her saucer on them. "Ever since that awful shooting I've found myself looking out that little window. I saw a big guy with a beard go into your place." She shrugged. "His car's still here. So's hers. And you're here. It wasn't very hard to figure out." She sipped her coffee. Then she said, "Yuri, what's Charity mean to you?"

I told her I wasn't sure. I explained a bit of our history: Charity the sudden widow, moving in as a rent-paying house sharer. I didn't mention that she often helped me chase down information. Nor did I tell her I had proposed marriage not long ago, and Charity had refused me. The spaniel rubbed against my shanks. I scratched its floppy ears and delivered my monologue. How Judy processed that long flow of information I couldn't guess. Across the room her green eyes mirrored no more than polite interest.

The spaniel followed us out to the kitchen. "Flops likes a lot of attention." She poured second cups. "Like all the rest of us, I guess."

Back in the living room I sat on the couch where I had been. She sat at the other end. We talked. Sometime later Flops hopped up to fill the space between us. Sorrowful spaniel eyes turned to me for petting. So I stroked the thick curls on his back. Judy, leaning forward, did the same.

Shortly our hands touched, then touched again. My

thumb and forefinger closed around her index finger. I opened my hand. Hers moved to lie on my palm. I enfolded now her whole hand. I looked across at her face. Her eyes were luminous, fixed unblinkingly on mine. I leaned over and pressed my face into the hair above her ear. It smelled of domesticity: the evening's fried peppers, the faint sweet musk of Dawn detergent and spilled milk. No scents by Guerlain or Lanvin could have stirred me more. I nibbled the vulnerable curves of her ear. I raised my hand to caress her face. She pressed it to her cheek. I kissed her brow, her eyes. I ran my tongue over the fetching arches of her brows. I tried her pretty lips. Her mouth tasted of discreetly discarded Trident Sugarless.

My heart thumped those hard knocks on the opening door of desire. How could this be happening? I asked. This lovely, mad woman in my arms. And her arms now around me, tightly stretched springs across the broad span of my back. "Hold your mouth like *this*," she breathed. "I want it shaped like *this*." Her voice rasped in naked hunger.

Oh, how the world was filled with wonders!

Flops bounded away from being squashed in our tangle of arms and pressing torsos. After a long while we came up for air. Her eyes glinted with the tears of upended emotions. "Oh, God, how much I wanted you to touch me!"

"I'm very...surprised," I said.

"So am I!" Her mouth was on mine again. Under her loose blouse and jeans my caressing hands found enough curves and softness to satisfy the worst lecher—never mind an amateur like me. When my spread fingers took the slow measure of her breasts, she grabbed my wrists and pulled my hands away. She got up on shaky legs. "I—I don't *do* this. I wasn't raised this way." Her face was set in lines of bewilderment that edged toward grief. "But...but I *want* you." She pulled me up, hugged me with all her strength. Her kisses were voracious. Her silent, squirming lips said, "Starved...starved... *starved*."

I grabbed her soft rear and pulled her against me. Her breath, with her mouth sealed with mine, hissed warm and damp from her flared nostrils. She broke away again. There was no mistaking her willingness and her desperate hunger. Nor her guilt. She held me at arm's length and began to tremble with inner conflict.

I held her and stroked her cheeks and forehead. "It's all right," I said. "Whatever you want is all right with me, Judy."

She sighed and slumped against me. The shuddering passed off like a dying fever. "Not here. Not now."

"But you want to."

She nodded. "I apologize for behaving this way. I'm s—"

"Don't say you're sorry to me! Remember our deal."

She looked up at me and smiled. "Sure. I remember. Doing this . . . isn't like me. It's against the way I've been raised. It's not easy to go against the way you're raised." She glanced at the expensive reproduction grandfather clock. "Anyhow, it's late now. Jed could be home any minute."

She led me to the door. Her good-bye was a long, ardent kiss that stirred my desire like a paddle of flame. I stopped and my gaping mouth worked against her clothed breasts.

"Oh, God," she sighed. "You wanta give Jed lessons?"

I was too busy to talk.

Hands on my shoulders she shoved me away. Her face was flushed and her breathing heavy and fast. "Later. We'll talk."

Then I was outside. The June night air cooled my sweaty forehead and my tumescence. Judy? I asked myself. Judy Larkin? My *neighbor?* Judy was starved for love. Judy was pert, pretty and curvy. What more did I want. Yes, we men were fools. We rushed to our destiny, casting the warning words of the wise aside like so many gum wrappers. So fools were made devils, and devils fools. And there were no real rules for any of it.

Chapter Eleven

My falling-asleep thoughts should have been about the Sarmatian Demon lurking in the White Chamber, about terrified—and maybe dead—Winston Farrow, about the five shots slamming through my kitchen window. Connections, relationships should have clamped my consciousness. Instead I ran memory's film of my three hours in the Larkin home with the care of a producer at a first screening. I drifted to sleep with the slowly closing shutter of my leaden mind filled with dear Judy teetering between caution and desire....

I slept poorly and got up about six. The kitchen was drafty, thanks to the smashed window. I made a pot of coffee and waited for the *Post-Gazette*. When it came I read it slowly and carefully—a dying luxury for those of us born before the epidemic tube addiction.

Over a second cup of coffee I savored reports of Sunday's sports. The Pirates had bonged the Mets in a double-header at Shea. I wallowed in the box scores. It was important to know who got the hits and the win.

I heated up two Waldorf's Bakery cheese pockets, ate them, and finished the paper. Still no signs of Charity and Tod. The phone rang. Judy. "Yuri, Jed just went to work. We have to talk. Come over. Please." Her voice was husky, either from early morning or anticipation. It started my heart thumping. I felt the color rise in my face.

"I have to talk to Charity first. Don't you have to get your kids off to school?"

"Y-Yes." She giggled huskily. "I couldn't wait that long to talk to you."

"I'll be over. Hang on."

"You haven't had ... second thoughts, have you?" she asked.

"I don't think I ever had first thoughts. You swept me right off my feet."

"I'm blaming Flops for it all."

"Dangerous beast."

"Yes, you are. Grrrr! See you *soon*." She hung up.

Before the second pot of coffee was ready Charity and Tod came down for breakfast. They didn't look all that well rested. Tod had dark smudges under his eyes. Charity's eyelids were at half mast. Her face was puffy and her lips slightly swollen. Above the pale blue cotton collar of her robe, a mouth-shaped bruise purpled her slender neck. We exchanged good mornings. Charity's eyes avoided mine. They played over Tod, caressing him like fingers. She poured them both coffee. Finally she looked at me. "Any breakfast this morning?"

"I already ate," I said. I didn't move. She could screw him, she could cook for him. So I was jealous. So I wasn't a very grand personality. So be it.

"Never fear, good lady," Tod said. "You have on hand one of the truly accomplished omelette chefs on the face of the earth."

"Well, isn't *that* nice," she said.

I wandered off in some kind of unreasonable sulk. I didn't face Charity until she had finished her long good-byes to her guest. I found her standing by the big front window staring down Morlande after Tod's long-gone car.

"Pleasant night?" I said.

She turned to me and I saw the dreamy smile on her face. "He's a very tender and considerate man."

"Find out anything more about our bronze friend in the White Chamber?"

"Well, I'm not sure. We did actually do some talking." Her face crinkled up with delight. She followed that with a most un-Charity-like giggle, a near bellow. "Tod really *wanted* to talk about the Demon. Mostly about how much it was worth. And he certainly wanted to know where it was."

"You didn't tell him."

"Well..." Her eyes slid away. "Not exactly."

"What's that mean?"

"I didn't tell him *where* in the house it was."

My poorly hidden irritation bubbled up. "Now that was a dumb and dangerous thing to do! That puts *him* in trouble. If somebody twists his arm, that puts *us* in trouble. Nobody was absolutely *sure* we had it. We managed to fog that up a *little* anyway. Now you had to go blow it."

"Yuri—"

"I know there aren't any rules for us working together in this crazy information business. We use a lot of common sense. Telling Tod where the bronze was *wasn't* common sense."

"Yuri, we owe him a lot."

"*You* owe him a lot. He didn't sleep with me."

"You *do* have a nasty side, don't you?"

"Look, Charity, I got Maced and you almost got your little blonde head exploded like a tossed cantaloupe because of the bronze. It was *stupid* to blab to Tod that it's in the house. Even if he did screw you silly."

"Stop it!" Red danger spots bloomed in her pale cheeks. "What's wrong with you anyway? You're... *crazy.*" She turned away. "Get away from me!"

I grabbed her shoulders and spun her around. "Felicia Farrow was *your* friend. I'm doing you a bigger favor than *he* is. Her problem, her bronze is *ours* to figure out. Not Tod Buckcry's. If you don't watch your mouth, you two can handle it—"

"And if you don't watch *yours*, I can handle it *alone.*" She broke away and hurried toward her side of the house. I walked around inside, then went out and circled the block.

Cooled, I knocked on Judy Larkin's door. She let me in. "I thought you'd *never* come," she said. Her loose orange blouse was unbuttoned to the waist. Soft, white flesh shifted in the narrow gap. She took my hand. Her skin was warm. Her nails felt thin and sharp against my palm. She led me into her living room.

"Where's little Louis?" I said.

"I took him to the sitter for the morning." Her nails dug further into my palm. "There's no one here but *us.*" She led me to a pile of large colored pillows arranged in the center of the floor. "Here," she said. "Here's where I want to be. And I want music. Do you want music, Yuri?"

"You're what I want," I said. My voice was husky. Yuri Nevsky, forever the panting adolescent.

She went to her turntable. Schubert. A woman of taste. There was no stereotyping housewives nowadays. She came into my arms, eyes closed. I hugged her. "Oh, Yuri, Yuri, I want to be loved so much!"

So I loved her. It was certainly no hardship. She was willing, wet and grateful. She asked often, what was I *do*ing? In time she figured it out. It was all unfamiliar ground for her. Rigid muscles, trembling, moaning and delighted whimpers came to her as completely unexpected as her mounting delight. Her willingness, her openness and total vulnerability spurred me to new heights of tenderness and control. Our desires quenched themselves, at least for the moment. We lay in a sweaty, panting tangle.

She lay very still, her face turned away. Her straw-colored hair was matted to the back of her neck. After a while I noticed she was trembling. "Cold?" I said.

"No!" She blurted and turned to me.

I saw she was crying.

"Those happy tears?" I said.

She nodded. Face contorted with the weeping of sweet release, she turned back to me to be loved again. Success is a powerful aphrodisiac. I loved her again—and even again, the last a long, grinding marathon like the last movement of Schubert's "Great" Ninth Symphony showering over us for the tenth, twentieth or hundredth time.

"How . . . how can you *do* that?" she asked amid fresh tears.

"Takes two. Me *and* you. You . . . you . . . Judy-Judy. What a pleasure you are! Like a kid with a sweet tooth on her first visit to the candy store."

She sat up adribble with sweat. Her brown-tipped breasts, even after being plundered by my hands and mouth, needed touching yet again. They filled my spread

144

fingers. She leaned against me and tongued the twists and turns of my ear. "I think you're addictive, Yuri Nevsky. I hope you're not dangerous to my health."

"I *added* two years to my life just now, Judy. I don't know about you."

She gathered up our clothes from the four corners of the room where they had landed during our frantic shedding. "The panties with the pink pansies are mine, right?"

"Let's swap for the smell."

"*Stop* it! You have time to crawl out to the kitchen with me for a cup of coffee?"

We had our coffee. At the door she clung to me, forehead pressed to my chest. "This is adultery, Yuri Nevsky."

"Yes, Judy Larkin."

"So many people talk against it, I *knew* it would be great. They want to save it for themselves."

I hugged her good-bye. Judy, my bundle of sweat and female odors, matted sandy hair and soft curves, wasted on the barren desert island of indifferent marriage. Another kindred refugee from that never-never land of The Way Things Ought to Be.

"Again, yes?" she said.

"*Now?*"

"You'd have to say 'Shazam!' first, I think. I'll call you."

Light of foot and abloom with grin, I trotted briskly back to 138. Briskly because the June day now at eleven in the morning blazed with summer heat made for the day's adventure I had planned. Briskly, too, to outstrip the inevitable Slavic Guilt limping along determinedly somewhere behind me.

I found Charity on the phone to Tod. When she hung up, I assaulted her with Judy-driven grins and Yuri apologies. It wasn't long before we were nearly friends again.

"We need a change of scene," I said. "The sun's out, the day smells like deep summer. Good day to be by big water."

"Yeah!"

"A trip to Lake Erie."

"Should I take my bathing suit?" Charity said.

"Your notebook might be better..."

We stopped for takeout Big Boys at the Eat 'n' Park on the way to Route 79 north. Traffic was light and I drove fast to the City of Erie. In just a bit over two hours I pulled into a gas station and asked the gas jockey where the Big E Marina was. I went into the rest room with my best suit in a garment bag and came out looking like a colleague of Jed Larkin. I picked my attaché case out of the trunk.

I dropped off Charity and her notebook at the local library to do her research. Five minutes later I was pulling into the Big E parking lot. The marina was tucked into a small natural bay guarded by a solid concrete breakwater. The stones marking the spaces were freshly whitewashed. So were the fences lining the gravel walks leading toward the water.

I helloed the office. The door was open. No one was inside. A speaker by the door was angled to blast hard rock toward the moorings. I went out on the boardwalk and headed toward the water.

The marina was early season shipshape. Fixtures had been shined. Hoses and pipes were firmly clamped in place. Cables climbing into electrical hookups gleamed like shiny snakes in their waterproof casings. About a third of the slips held crafts. There was space for at least a hundred. Three Exxon pumps and a frame shack stood on a float buoyed by a half dozen oil drums. To landlubber me, Big E Marina passed inspection by a mile.

I found a kid in a denim jacket and yachting cap. He was cutting lengths of rope woven from plastic strands and melting the tips with a bottled gas torch so they wouldn't unravel.

"I wonder if you could help me?"

He eyed me. My suit did its job. "Yes, sir."

I held out my hand. "I'm Charlie Welles. East Coast Marine Insurance. I'm an adjuster. We have a claim on a vessel...."

"Which one, sir?"

"Stressless I. Owned by a Mr. Sergei Yelanov—"

"Sure enough." He smiled. "Glad to be of help. Right over here, sir." He led me to the far end of the floating

146

walkway. A thirty-foot cabin cruiser battened down with plastic and canvas tarps bobbed in the slip.

"Mr. Yelanov hasn't been out in over two weeks," the kid said. "You marine adjusters must be as slow as the car ones." He laughed.

"We do our best."

"Need any help?"

I smiled icily. "I'll call you if I do."

"Yes, sir." He wandered away.

I didn't know what I was looking for. A good place to start was to pull off the tarps. They masked the gunwales and had been rigged on cables to also hide the sides of the high cabin. Thin cord held the thick plastic to cleats. Some of the knots had worked loose. I guessed that to be results of haste and sudden departure. Two plastic panels flapped in the light breeze.

As the plastic came away I saw the signs of a bad battering in heavy weather—twisted metalwork, sprung boards and split seams. Amidships I tugged loose a large square of canvas makeshift tarp. I grunted. Inside the gunwale by the cabin were jagged holes. There were four holes in a random pattern on the starboard cabin wall. The holes were about as big around as my index finger. The cabin door was ajar. I opened it and looked in. The holes inside were splintery like the ones inside the gunwales. No doubt about it. They were bullet holes.

Water still puddled the cabin floor. Evaporation had been at work, but I saw the sediment and the white walk of mold along the flood line. Yellow oilskins lay heaped on the cabin deck. All were signs of high seas.

I opened the rear hold, swung up the hatch and looked down at nearly a foot of water. In the square of light falling on the bilge water I saw the cruiser's portable winch. It had been rigged, used and tumbled down into the hold. Used for what? To get the Sarmatian Demon in his crate on board and off, I'd bet.

All signs were of wild, desperate haste to get ashore with the bronze. Yet there could have been no shooting here, on this shore. No suspicions of any kind had existed, or the vessel would have been sealed and impounded. Whatever happened took place somewhere else. Either out on the lake—or on the Canadian side.

Then I remembered the matchbook in Felicia's pants

pocket from an Erie diner. She had been here, all right. On the way to Canada they had time to stop for a meal.

I battened down the *Stressless I,* thanked the kid with a tip, and went to pick up Charity. On the way to the library I imagined what that night on the lake must have been like for Felicia, Selina, Sergei and—if Twiggy's tale of the cars was right—the "friend" who might well have been another passenger. In storm and fog high seas had crashed over the craft, flooding the cabin, bludgeoning into the hatches. I remembered the smell of gasoline on Felicia. Probably the engines had been doused. The two women had struggled to restart them, terrified every moment of capsizing or foundering, and probably badly seasick, too. I remembered as well Felicia shouting from the terror of her nightmare: "Stand up, Sergei. Stand up, *for the love of God!"* She had come to 138 at the tail end of that night of horrid weather, high seas—and violence.

I went into the library. The librarian was an elderly lady with swollen ankles and a twinkling smile. She told me Charity had looked through the papers but hadn't found what she wanted. "She said it was about something that may have happened on the lake. So I sent her off in a cab to call on Captain Tighe."

"Captain Tighe?"

"He's retired. Got a big old house on the high land—not that it's that high—on the edge of town. He's a collector. Collects things that have to do with Lake Erie. He used to be a pilot on the big ore carriers. The ones that came all the way down from Duluth bringing the ore to the steel plants."

"He saves newspapers?"

"Does clippings, if they're about the lake. Sinkings, accidents, drownings, just everything." Her twinkling blue eyes turned motherly. "Your friend was looking so *sad.* I just had to help her. She said for me to tell you the way..."

Captain Tighe's house had a widow's walk. The captain was lantern-jawed and lean. His face carried a web of wrinkles gathered like sacks around eyes that had scanned 100,000 watery horizons. Charity came out of the den clutching a sheet of yellow note paper. She folded it as she thanked the captain.

"Find what you wanted?" he croaked.

"Just about."

Outside, I said, "What'd you get?"

"Something good."

"Like?"

"Cost you a dinner."

"That good?"

"Ummm..."

When she ordered cheesecake after a three-course diner meal I knew she *really* had something. She smothered a ladylike belch, unfolded her yellow sheet, and shoved it across the table. I devoured it with more appetite than I had shown for my greasy meal. She had copied a news article from a Canadian paper, the *Gasden Gadfly*.

MAN DEAD IN
SHIP-TO-SHORE FIRE FIGHT

June 2. One man was shot to death and another believed wounded by on-shore Canadian Mounted Police and government agents last night in a Chicago-style shoot-out with the passengers and crew of an unidentified cruiser at a deserted cove on the south shore of Long Point. Fog and heavy weather allowed the 30-foot vessel to slip out into the lake and elude pursuit.

Dead was Mr. Alexey Semanova, a Russian national and an alleged conspirator with the crew of the renegade vessel. Police alleged Mr. Semanova had helped transfer contraband from his rented truck to the deck of the craft. He brandished, then fired an automatic rifle at the approaching officers. They returned his fire and that of the vessel's crew. The dead man was struck by a half dozen heavy-caliber bullets. Captain Donald DePierre of Gasden barracks reported that another smuggler on board was possibly wounded. Rain and deliberate masking of registration numbers by tarpaulins made identification of the vessel impossible.

Inspector Machlin of the Southeast Canada

Border Security Unit, newly formed to combat a reported rise in north-to-south drug traffic, described elsewhere as "The Montreal Connection," issued a brief statement through his office. He identified the late Mr. Semanova as "An opportunist in the gray areas of international commerce," with no drug-connected offenses on his record. The Security Unit was withholding further information which could aid the escaped smugglers.

The incident was the first this year at the west-central lake shore, though arrests and violence have been common on the Buffalo-area shores where drug smuggling has been linked with organized crime.

My heart thudded. "More pieces for our puzzle. Alexey dead..."

"He touched the Demon," Charity said softly.

"You don't think—"

"Felicia said it was *cursed,* Yuri. The stink of death is all through 138. All through our *lives.*"

I opened my mouth to disagree. I shut it. The bronze's spell couldn't be done away with by a glib denial. "So who could have been wounded?"

"Sergei maybe?"

"If it was, where's he hiding? Where was he treated?"

Charity clutched my hand. "Remember! What Felicia said that night she came to 138 when it all started? She said: 'Two people who meant a lot to me are *dead* because they touched it...' One was Alexey. The other...likely Sergei."

"I'm not so sure about that."

We chewed on it all during the ride south to Pittsburgh. A lot of still-missing pieces were needed to clear up what had happened after the *Stressless I* landed in Erie before Felicia brought the Sarmatian Demon to 138.

The early-June night had marked the last trip the *Stressless I* had made to Canada. There had been others, but that last one was different. First, they had been gone an extra day, not counting the storm delay. Second, a "friend" had driven them to Erie, and likely was a passenger. Selina, Sergei and Felicia had been running a long weekend cruise. For whom? And why?

Chapter Twelve

Tuesday morning at eight-thirty the phone rang. It was a call for Charity from a Gordon Rightfall. She had contacted him Saturday morning while looking into Condaco. She hit the phone amplifier switch.

"What's Condaco to you, Charity Day?" Gordon Rightfall's voice told me he was a Down Easter.

"Why ask? All I wanted was information."

"Thinkin' of investin'?"

"With what? Come *on,* Gordon. What or *who* is Condaco?"

"You know, I been in and around law in Pittsburgh mebbe twenty ye-ahs," he said. "Afteh so long, know what happens? Fella get a...nose for things. It goes past readin' between the lines. It gets to readin' between lines that ain't even they-ah."

"So?"

"So you shouldn't get involved—if you-ah thinkin' of it—with Condaco people."

"I see."

"*Were* you goin' to get mixed up with them?"

"Not really, Gordon, you miserable Maine-iac. Will you get to the point!"

"Gettin' they-ah. Said don't get involved 'cause ...well..."

"*Explain.*"

"Condaco's officers were three Russian fellas. That's fine. Lots of fine Russians in Pittsburgh. I'm godfathah to two wonderful Russian girls myself. And the guys who were officers seemed OK." I heard the distant squeal of Gordon's desk chair's hinges. "Had some time on my hands. Old Maine attorney just sleepin' in the sun..."

"Sure, Gordon." Charity covered the mouthpiece and said to me, "He has a small law practice. Sensitive cases. He's a shrewd old man. Nobody's fool."

"...so I made some calls to good friends in the right places. Condaco built three buildings back three, foah years ago. I checked up on the contractors, the fellas who built them. Found out at different times Total Circuit Electricians, Universal Plumbin' and Smolonov Construction have been in trouble with the law."

"For what?"

"Different things. Underneath it all's what my deah mothah used to call 'the rackets.' Nice fellas or not, Condaco's tainted, or so my instincts say."

"I see."

"A good attorney keeps his fellow attorneys out of trouble," he said.

Charity laughed. "Where's a good attorney end—and an old busybody start?" Gordon began to bluster, but she cut him off. "You *still* haven't told me what I asked you. Who runs Condaco?"

"Used to be three men. All of them clean. A Petyr Melanova."

"Spell it."

He did and I wrote it down in my Harvard Coop notebook.

"Yevgeny Rodonosky."

"Ummm..."

"And Vasily Brunov."

My pencil point snapped.

"Now only one fella owns it. Brunov bought the others out about a year ago."

Charity thanked Gordon and said good-bye.

A knock at the kitchen door—Judy Larkin with a plate of hot rolls and hot glances for me. I felt my eyes hood before the memory of our sweet carryings-on of yesterday morning.

"I thought you were working for a living, Charity," Judy said.

"Vacation."

"Oh." Judy did a poor job of hiding her disappointment. She thought I was alone. Slow-on-the-uptake Yuri saw that the only roll she was really interested in was another one in the hay with me. That made two of us. "Well..." Judy began.

Charity tried to find the familiar rut of small talk which she had shared with Judy. I knew she was waiting for the complaints about Jed, his golf, his working hours. Judy fussed with her coffee, ate the soft insides of half a sweet roll, and looked slightly bewildered.

"You OK, Judy?" Charity said.

A leering grin. *"Never* been better." A sidelong glance at me. "Really great summer coming up."

"Going away?" Charity said.

"No. Staying *home.*" The last word Judy caressed in speaking with the awed affection usually saved for Heaven and Salvation.

The phone rang. Charity picked it up. The amplifier was turned on from her call from Gordon. A muffled man's voice—not the one that had threatened us before the rifle shots. "Ms. Day?"

"Yes?"

"Get rid of the bronze statue. Or the next time you *will* die!" The line went dead.

"What was *that?*" Judy said. "Your weird friends?"

Charity shook her head. She had paled. The scabs of the cuts made by the shattering of the kitchen window stood out on her face like measles. "I don't *like* that!" she said.

"'Bronze statue'?" Judy glanced at the shattered kitchen window. A bright lady, she began to make associations. *"What* is going on here? People shooting at you...I *wondered* what was happening. It wasn't just some crazy. You're mixed up in something..." Her eyes fell on me. Her expression told me she felt that newly joined lovers had the obligation to be open about themselves. "Somebody going to *explain* that call?"

Charity looked pointedly at me. She was too upset to deal with our neighbor.

"Judy, come on out to the living room," I said. She

155

followed me. Once there, I turned and she lunged into my arms. "Kiss me, kiss me!" she whispered. Then her mouth was on mine. I savored crumbs of yesterday's feast. "What else have I done since yesterday but think about yesterday?" Her chin was on my chest, head tilted back to devour me with her eyes.

"Nothing succeeds like a little excess," I said.

"I can't *wait* to be excessed again." Her face clouded. "But I don't really know about you. What are you? Some kind of mystery man?"

I sat her down and told her about the information business. It was a capsule summary, but the idea got across. Her green eyes grew rounder and rounder. "You're some kind of *detective,*" she said. "You and Charity."

"Well, not exactly..."

"Oh, that's—*wonderful.*" She hugged me wildly.

Her passion and abandon of yesterday, her wild enthusiasm now... My goodness! I had found a romantic woman. Being a bit of a romantic myself, I decided we were a natural match.

Knee-to-knee, she said, "I want to know *more.* I want to know all about your different 'capers'—is that the word?" She bounced up and down on the couch in her excitement. I was very conscious of her body close to mine. Its heft, its surprising curves and softness reminded me of the wetness and hunger of her surrenders. My mind retasted the sweat I had licked from her forehead and the deep valley between her breasts. My mind wasn't on talk. It was turning down a carnal path.

I kissed her. Good old Slavic Lust flared up. We groped and fumbled for several intense minutes. Judy broke our clutch, panting and sheepish. "I left Louis alone in his playpen." I sat up. "Not a good idea." She touched my face. "Can you come over?"

Before I could say yes, Charity called out from the kitchen, "Yuri, you and I had better talk about things *right now.*" That phone call had shaken her.

"Enter realities," Judy whispered.

"Usually I'm not one to let reality intrude on a really *solid* fantasy."

"See you soon." A little kiss and she was gone to her son. One of her three sons. All sired by her husband.

Face it, she was a solidly married woman by most acceptable standards. Slavic Lust, as so often happened, was now followed by Slavic Guilt. What was I doing turning the head of a happy-enough housewife? Sons, husband and hearth were like so many fleas under the heavy boot of my desire. Nor was the source of that desire very grand—my jealousy of Tod Buckcry and my own glands' pressures. I was tampering with her life; no messages were more clearly heard than those sent through the loins.

Such bleak thoughts, and others bleaker still, seized most of my attention over the next forty-five minutes. The remainder was occupied with half listening to Charity summarize and analyze where we were with the Sarmatian Demon. I followed her general lines of thought, agreed with her decisions. When she finished I was standing with the phone in my hand. I woke like a sleepwalker, ready to take what we hoped would be a big step in unraveling bronze mysteries.

I dialed the number for the law offices of Vasily Brunov. A moment later the handsome attorney was on the line. "Nevsky, a pleasure to hear from you. I still feel some embarrassment about our boozy scuffle."

"Let's forget it. You heard anything from Winston Farrow lately?"

"Haven't seen him since that Saturday afternoon." Brunov had a good phone voice, a low vibrato. I wanted to believe him. "Why? Some kind of problem?"

"Maybe."

"That all you need?" the attorney said.

"No. What I wanted to know was would you have lunch with Charity Day and me tomorrow?"

He hesitated. "Well, I have an engagement. I was planning to spend the noon hour with my fiancée."

"Oh, well—"

"I'd have to ask what's on your mind," he said.

"It's about your late client, Felicia Semanova...." I paused.

"What about her?"

"It's not so much her as what she was doing and what she left behind."

"I'm not sure I understand you."

"I need two things from you, Vasily—information and advice."

"Is this a legal matter?"

"Not exactly."

"You mentioned advice. About what?"

"I think Felicia was smuggling art into this country. I think she might have been smuggling cocaine, too."

Vasily was silent for several heartbeats. "I see," he said.

"You knew that?"

"Of course not. So I don't see how I can be counted on for advice. As for information—"

"Remember when I met you at Anna Yelanov's house? I mentioned a bundle that Felicia wanted to leave with Charity Day. Well, I know where it is."

"Was that the bronze statue Winston mentioned at the funeral?"

"Yes."

"He said you and Ms. Day had it."

"We had it briefly. It's not here any more."

"Where is it?"

"I'd rather not talk about it on the phone, Vasily. I don't want to ask for trouble. Someone's already shot at Charity and me with a rifle. Damn near killed both of us."

"My God! Well, the cocaine then? Where did you get *that* idea?"

"Ruthie Spires. You know her?"

"Not well. She works for one of my clients, Count Dromsky-Michaux. I'm not sure how much of a reliable personality she is."

"Charity and I think some of the other people from Hermitage and 'sPots might be involved. I understood you knew most of them. I wondered if you could fill us in on them. That's what I meant by information."

"I see. Yes, I think lunch might be possible."

We set the time for tomorrow and the place. I smiled. Charity felt that cash flow and his apartments were part of the riddle. His practice touched all the key people. He had been very possessive with Winston. Likely he knew something or was trying to hide juicy facts.

Maybe she and I could charm, bluff or lie them out of him. Worth a try.

The second step of our offensive: I booked a Cadillac from the rental agency Charity had used to visit apartment manager Boothie O'Shea. I went upstairs to change into my best suit. When I got downstairs Charity was just hanging up the phone. She shook her head. "That was Tod. He's so down over Selina's funeral that he doesn't know whether or not to settle for a cremation. Says he doesn't know if he can face that hole in the ground. He also reminded me of the party Twiggy and Ruthie are organizing for him tonight. He wants us both to come. Beer and wine there, or BYO. Starts about eight-thirty or nine."

"I'll think about it," I said. Maybe Jed would lend me Judy to be my date for the evening. Dream, I thought. Go ahead, mess around with married women....

On the way out, I touched the light-switch wall fixture by the front door. It was a dummy. A good spring swung it aside. The .32 snub nose waited, butt toward my hand. I kept it handy in case I needed more than words to keep an unwelcome foot out of the door. I hadn't had a chance to grab it before getting Maced. I dropped it into my pocket. Its trim design scarcely disturbed the line of the suit jacket.

I parked around the corner from the Cadillac dealer. In ten minutes I was getting out of a limo with the help of one of the Mount Royal Apartments doormen. I told the driver to wait.

I marched past the lobby guard. "I have an appointment with Mr. O'Shea," I said in my most solid-citizen voice. "He's expecting me."

I went up the elevator and walked into O'Shea's outer office without knocking. It was a toss-up who should be more embarrassed. Maybe Lily, Boothie's secretary, whom Charity had described. She sat on the edge of the desk, naked to the waist. Or maybe Boothie himself, whose head seemed from my angle to be nearly buried between Lily's sizeable pillows of pink and pearl flesh. She shrieked while trying to shove nuzzling Boothie away and hide herself at the same time. I realized I had quite a psychological advantage. I pushed it. Boothie rushed toward me foaming with curses. "Get rid of her!"

159

I shouted into the wind of his obscenities. "I'm going to talk to you."

"You come busting in here"—Lily squealed—"like some kinda *king*. She scooped up her bra and jersey and fled for the safety of her boss's private office.

Boothie rushed at me with raised fist.

"I'm one of Kitty Welles's friends. Touch me and you're dead."

"Kitty's friends!" His heavy face was bright red with sexual arousal.

I feared for his heart. He stared at his fist as though it were as strange as a fossil but finally dropped his hands to his sides. "They're not the friends I thought they were. *She's* not what I thought she was. I heard from *my* friends. Now who the hell are *you?*"

"Get rid of her." I waved toward the closed door. He glowered at me. "You made one mistake just now," I said. "You want to make another worse one right away? You one of the people who never learn?"

He knocked on the door. "Take the rest of the morning off, Lil. OK? And take a long lunch."

"On what?" Lily's voice was muffled, but there was no mistaking her vexation. "You were s'posed to take me *out*. It's my birthday, remember?"

Boothie shook his head and reached for his wallet. The office door opened and Lily returned, still stashing away her fleshy glories. He gave her a bill. "Go buy yourself a present."

"*Fifty* bucks?" She held the bill up between thumb and forefinger and let it dangle. "And I thought Rockefeller *died.*"

Lily breezed by Boothie, but she had a word for me on her way out. "When you louse up something, buddy, you do a *hell* of a job."

Boothie turned sullen eyes to me. "You and Kitty weren't with the Semanova woman, the rest of them."

"No, we weren't."

"Where the hell's Kitty? And who are you?" Boothie walked around behind his desk. He sat down and waved me toward the chair. "I'm not happy to see you, pal. Nobody knows where you and your group fit in."

"Who's nobody?"

Boothie made a vague gesture. "With the Semanova

woman out of the picture I was high, dry and nervous. I got a call. A new contact who was with her bunch. He said to sit tight."

I tried to keep him off-balance. "Find out who searched Felicia's apartment?"

He shook his head. He was wary. "You got a name, pal?"

"Jim Smith. OK? If you could figure out who searched the apartment, you'd be in a better position, Boothie."

"To do what, Jim?"

"Get your hands on the big art shipment you were expecting."

He looked puzzled. "Art? Oh, yeah. The art shipment. Yeah, art." He chuckled.

Charity and I thought he was hustling smuggled art to the ritzy tenants. I saw with that idea I had just swung and missed. We were wrong. His face told me. In this guesser's ballgame, two strikes were all you got. I had used up one already. "You don't take a joke very well," I said.

"Was that a joke?"

"Yeah." I drew a deep breath and hoped Ruthie Spires had her head together. "You were distributing all right. Maybe it started with art, huh?"

"Maybe." Boothie's face was closed up tight, guarded like a Norman castle.

"But it ended up with cocaine."

"It shit!"

"Felicia Semanova brought it to you, and you sold it to all the beautiful people in your three apartment houses. All those rich people, all that expensive cocaine."

"I'm not admitting anything. I don't know who you are."

I took the chair facing the desk. "You must have figured out Kitty and I aren't the law."

"I know who you're *not*, Jim. It's who you *are* that's got me hung up."

"How could you afford to put the Semanova woman in that apartment next to yours?"

"I didn't. She was put there by a friend of mine. Sergei Yelanov asked if she could move in."

"He was half owner of a business doing bad," I said.

161

"Real bad. He could hardly pay the mortgage on his own place."

Boothie shrugged and leaned back. "The rent got paid every month. The cash came in an envelope addressed to me. Why should I ask questions about who paid?"

Everything between us hung in the balance. I had made one wrong guess and one right one. I was dealing with a chiseler. He nibbled around the edges of things like a little mouse. Here a percentage for selling Felicia's cocaine. There a daytime wallow amid Lily's bouncing bounty. He had a good setup here at Mount Royal Apartments. He didn't want it upset. So I would upset him *now*. I wanted to scare him good and pump out what he knew. Making him nervous wasn't enough. The only thing I really had to work with was Charity's and my membership in a bogus, shadowy group dealing in you-name-it.

"You afraid of me, Boothie?"

He laughed a little too loudly. A good sign. "Why should I be afraid of you, Smith?"

I got a crazy, wonderful idea. "Because people I don't like end up dead," I said.

He frowned. "What you talking about?"

"Or they end up beaten so bad they just"—I giggled because it sounded grotesque—"give up and die. Like Selina Buckcry, for example."

"Who's that?"

"One lady who helped Sergei Yelanov run his boat when they brought over art and cocaine from Canada. I forgot: they kept you in the dark, didn't they? Felicia was your only contact." A guess.

"You're lying. There's no such woman."

I giggled again and got up slowly. *"Sure* I am. She's being buried right about now. You can call her husband and check. You can look at the death notice in day before yesterday's *Press*."

Boothie muttered weakly under his breath.

I walked over beside him. "You don't think Felicia died by accident either, do you? We fixed her car."

"What the *hell* . . . ?"

I put my hand on his shoulder. "Seen your friend Sergei recently, Boothie?"

He shook his head. "I called his wife. She got no idea where he is." He twisted his neck to look up at me. His once florid face was the color of raw pie dough. "You got him, too, huh?" He believed!

"We got him, too. And we are not above getting *you*, too, if we need to."

"*What?*" He tried to get up. With both hands on his shoulders I held him in the chair. "Just *sit*." I had talked enough. It was time for a serious threat. I pulled the .32 automatic out of my pocket. I made sure the safety was on. Then I held it out where he could see it, just out of arm's length.

"Holy-Mary-Mother-of-God!" he said. I saw sweat begin to leak from his pores. "Please, *don't*." His eyes were riveted on the O of the automatic's barrel.

"I think we should talk," I said in a chatty tone. "Just Boothie and Jim, right *now*." I backed up and locked the door from the inside. I didn't want him to move around, maybe try something. I pointed to the carpet. I want you to lie face up right here," I said.

He groaned. He was still pale and his hands shook. His knees popped as he knelt.

"Your outfit killed *three* people?" he said.

"We might stop there if you cooperate."

"Whadaya want?"

I improvised on the theme Ruthie Spires had given me. "There's a new ball game. The old people had trouble. The old people are gone. New people want to move in. I want to know the details of how you got started and how you used to work it."

Sweat poured from his forehead and upper lip. I pulled a handkerchief from my pocket and let it flutter down on his face. He wiped the sweat away and started to talk. And did he talk! I felt like a priest hearing the confession of a man fifteen years away from the Church.

It all *had* started with art. Tenants in the three apartments were forever looking for art objects to pretty up their personal surroundings—including their other homes. They had enough money to be able to be capricious. They would buy a piece and, a month or two later, get rid of it and buy another. They took substantial losses doing so, but it was all pin money to them. Boothie was looking for an angle to cut himself in on each exchange for a small percentage. It didn't seem possible.

Then he met Sergei on the street in Shadyside about three years ago. They had gone to Peabody High School together. They brought each other up to date on their lives. It didn't take them long to figure out they had an area of common interest—money. They quickly worked out a deal: Boothie would provide the contacts, Hermitage the art. It was all legal and everybody made clean money.

After about a year the supply of quality legitimate art that Sergei could collect from his network dried up. About that time—it was summer—he said he had a new Russian contact who could get his hands on some quality merchandise. Problem was, it was taken out of churches and ill-guarded provincial museums. There were some paintings and pottery. Most of it, though, was bronzes. They would have to be smuggled in. Was that OK with Boothie?

It was. Boothie didn't nose into just how Sergei managed the smuggling, and vice versa with the sales end. I saw how Sergei did it. Alexey Semanova brought the art out of Russia somehow and into Canada. He'd truck it down to Lake Erie and arrange the time and place of pickup through Felicia. Always on a weekend, of course, when Sergei could go "fishing" with his two-woman crew. That was the "business arrangement" Felicia said was all that was left of her marriage.

About a year ago, though, trade with the rich fell off to one or two items a month. They had enough expensive art. Maybe collecting became less trendy. Maybe bronzes were out and welded auto-part sculptures in. No matter. Sergei had a foolproof pipeline and nothing to pump through it—until he met an "old friend" whose name Boothie didn't know. The old friend suggested he could arrange for a small shipment of cocaine to be picked up by Alexey in Montreal. It could be brought south along with the art. A little bundle among the heavy art crates. Question was: could Boothie drum up some trade with the beautiful people in the three apartments? Boothie could—and did.

It all worked out well. The lion's share of the profits—well into five figures—went to Sergei's friend. It

164

would go even smoother the second time: Sergei found a way to move Felicia into Mount Royal Apartments. To make the next delivery, all she had to do was go home after the voyage toting the bundle of cocaine. Sergei's friend was very anxious that the whole deal have a very low profile. Moving Felicia helped that.

Boothie had expected to continue doing the same thing over and over again as they had with the art— the whole scheme very controlled, very private. So did Sergei. He was upset when he came to talk to Boothie about the second run. His friend needed a large amount of cash fairly quickly. Complicated arrangements were being made that involved up-front money—a lot of it. Boothie solicited up and down the three apartments. Word had spread about what high-quality cocaine made up the first shipment, so he had no trouble gathering more than $45,000. Sergei raised an additional amount. And Sergei's friend more yet.

When the shipment arrived, Boothie was to take out his share. Sergei's friend would sell the rest to another party. He and Sergei would divide the profits. The markup on the sales amounted to nearly five hundred percent. That explained why Sergei had mortgaged everything and promised the count that a "loan" was coming through to save their business. The deal was to go through the weekend of May 29 through June 1.

The shipment never arrived.

"But you saw Felicia, didn't you?" I said. "She came back to her apartment here?"

"Can I sit up?" Boothie said.

"Yeah, but don't get up."

With a grunt he heaved up. "*Sure* I saw her. I just about jumped on her Wednesday night when she finally got back. She said there'd been trouble. That things were on hold. I asked her what the hell *that* meant?"

"What did it mean?"

"She said it meant I shouldn't worry. She said the shipment was delayed, but it would be along."

"Delayed how long?"

Boothie shrugged. "I tried to pin her down later. I never got anywhere. She avoided meeting me. Folks started wanting their coke. All those folks who upfronted the bucks. I was—and still am—in a *very* bad position."

"Did she say whether they brought the coke in from Canada?"

"Didn't say nothing."

If they did bring it in, I guessed there were two possibilities. It was with wounded Sergei wherever he was healing. Or, more likely...the *Stressless I*'s passenger had it—that mysterious person who had driven the group to Erie. "You talk to Felicia enough to find out anything more about your silent partner?"

"Nothing. And before I knew it she was dead." He turned frightened eyes on me. "You people killed her."

"We know everything about your little social group—except the name of that one person. And I think he's the one who took the coke and stood the rest of you up."

"You forgot, Jim. I got a call two days ago from somebody who maybe was that friend. He said the coke would be along soon. You haven't killed everybody—yet."

"We're working on it. Maybe we'll get to him before he gets to you with the stuff." After my false start I had made up ground with a vengeance. My bald and frightened friend had cued me. I had fallen on those cues like an inspired actor. Out of his whole cloth of fear Charity and I had cut a pattern of threatening identities and phantom hoodlums.

He sat cowed and sweating at my feet. He was just a small-time chiseler who had taken a chance on some coke. It had seemed an easy, simple deal. Now "Kitty Welles" and "Jim Smith" were threatening all he had built up for himself. Charity came with veiled threats. I came with word of murder and death. The eggshell on which his life was built was crumbling. He and all he had could be blown away. I saw in his puzzled frowns and anxiety that he had no more resistance.

"When Felicia brought you the first shipment, how was it packed?"

He shrugged. "Nothing special. Heavy glassine bag, all wrapped nice and tight, tape around it. It was in a bag from Sergei's store."

"A Hermitage bag?"

"I guess. Building silhouette on the paper." Boothie's voice was strained with anguish. He raised pleading hands. "Smith, for the love of God, *what do you want with me? I've told you everything I know.*" He began to blubber—choking chicken noises.

His misery made me more audacious. I needed one more grand bluff to pave the way for my exit. I found it.

"You owe a lot of people a lot of money, Boothie," I said.

"The stuff's coming through."

"So somebody told you. How you know the call didn't come from one of our people."

"Huh? *Why?*"

"To make you stall longer, get you in worse trouble."

"Holy Mary..." He hid his face and trembled.

"Boothie!" I pinched his upper arm. "Listen up!"

He whimpered and cringed. His baggy eyes dribbled tears.

"You're in deep, but there's a way out for you," I said.

"I don't want any more trouble!"

"Trouble's the last thing you'll get from us. There's not much left of your little ma-and-pa system. You're about it. You have it worked out in your three apartments. You do a lot of business with these rich people. You can work for us."

"For...you?" His tear-smeared face was ashen.

"We'll provide the coke. Good stuff, as good as what you've been selling. You keep your low profile. You stay safe. We supply as much as you need."

"W-What would I have to do?"

"Come on cool and classy for all your beautiful people. Pretend it's all so clean and nice it ought to be legalized. Build up trade as much as you can. We'll take care of getting the stuff to you. We'll watch out for the cops. If you behave yourself, we'll let you handle everything yourself. You pay us for the coke, but you can charge whatever they'll pay and keep the difference."

"I'm...not sure. I haven't liked any of this, Smith."

I scowled. "Take it or leave it. We're leaving you *something* that way instead of nothing. And you're the one who owes money to your tenants. A *lot* of money."

He began to stammer. I cut him off. "You think about it. I'll call you." I put the .32 in my pocket. Boothie sat cross-legged on the floor, listing heavily to the right. Fat and balding, he looked like a third-rate actor starring in the *Life of Buddha*.

Back in my Datsun heading home I realized how lucky I had been, bursting in on bountiful Lily and compromised Boothie. He had been off-balance from the go. I had played the part of Syndicate Sam to the hilt. I had been inspired. I had worked hard for all the information I got.

Seven miles from 138 the Datsun's engine quit. It gave out a grinding thump that meant the end of expensive bearing metal parts. Trying to start it brought only weak, farting backfires, then nothing. I walked to the phone and called the tow truck. I gave the dispatcher the name of my favorite garage. I went into the nearest bar and ordered a double brandy. I figured I had earned it.

Chapter Thirteen

By the time I had my car towed, talked to the mechanic, and had dinner, it was after seven. Taking time to brief Charity on my profitable session with Boothie made it nearly nine o'clock. We got dressed for Tod's party. Charity went out to the garage to get her car.

Five minutes later she came back. "Goddamned cars! It won't start!" I went out and gave it a try. Turned over and over, but wouldn't catch. I didn't feel like getting greased up by groping in weak light. I reported failure. Charity called Tod at 'sPots on the kitchen phone. Through the amplifier I heard early-party buzz, mumble and music. Could Twiggy or June come and get us?

"I'll find somebody, don't worry." He lowered his voice. "I love you, Charity Day!" he murmured.

"Shame on you, Tod! Cooing sweet nothings with Selina just six feet under."

Charity, Charity, you're mad, I thought. Shoving dead Selina at him, warring with the dead. What had she said about women always at war? Surely it was the kind of war that took no emotional prisoners and left only the scorched earth of broken spirits.

"She wasn't a happy woman," Tod said. "It wasn't a good marriage. I'm trying to pick my life up again. I don't just mean by partying tonight. I very much want you to help me do it."

"Getting us a ride would be a great way to start," Charity said.

When she hung up, I said, "You *tease* him? About his wife dying and his feelings for you? I can't believe it."

She looked astonished. "Oh, was I teasing him? Must have been trying to increase sexual tension. Make him *angry* at me. He's a *real* tiger then." She made a faintly feline face and growled at me. She wandered off to her side of the house.

A knock on the kitchen door. Judy! She slid in with a wink and a leer. "Jimmy's across the borough. I pick him up around ten. Louis and Bobby are *sound* asleep. Jed's at work—*toujours*. I have about forty-five minutes!"

"I'm not sure I have even *that* much time."

"We'll *really* hurry then."

I grabbed her hand and we went thundering and tripping up the big staircase like two farm kids on the way to the hayloft. We littered the long hall with clothes. Judy was a smear of pink lace, white skin and sandy hair as we tumbled onto my bed in the dying light. Her mouth and hands were voracious. I was quickly witless with desire. She grabbed my neck. Her nails were needles above my spinal cord. Her lips jammed my cheek, misshaped her words. But I understood. "Do anything you want to me. All I want is for you to come inside me!..."

Less than half an hour later I heard Charity's voice. Ruthie Spires had just pulled up. Judy and I hurried shaky-kneed out of bed, retrieving our clothes like two silent-film comedians in a backward-running movie. I let her out the upstairs door. "Perfect timing. I have to go pick up Jimmy." My heart was still thudding. I smelled the sweet scent of sex on my hands.

I took my time composing myself and walked downstairs. Ruthie Spires was in the living room. She had that flush-faced, bright-eyed party glow. "The whole *gang's* there! There's plenty of booze, and some grass showed up." Her eyes widened. "Yuri, Charity, this is a *party*. Ummm... before we go, could I use your john?"

While she was upstairs, there was an angry knocking on the kitchen door. I peeked out through the little window. Judy again.

"That damn Jed! He left my car on *empty* again. Can I borrow a car from you? I have to go pick up Jimmy. And I'm already late." She lowered her voice. "And I wanted one more look at you, Yuri."

"Well, you'll get half of what you want, at least. My car's in the shop. Charity's won't start."

Ruthie and Charity came into the kitchen. When the redhead heard Judy's problem she offered her car for the ten minutes it would take to run a mother's errand.

It was a warm night, so we all went out the back door and up the walk to where Ruthie's Ford sat in front of the garage. "I'll show you how to start it. You drive a stick?" Ruthie said. "It's a piece of cake."

The three-quarter moon was riding high. The sweet, warm night breeze that meant summer-at-last was stirring the leaves of the old horse chestnuts by the street.

Judy slid into the driver's seat with Ruthie's key in her hand. The redhead gave her a quick lecture on how to operate the car. She leaned closer to the window. "You really just turn the key. If you can do that—"

The world split in half. For an instant I thought the soaring moon had come plummeting at me—a white flash, the slam of a fist of air against my body. Another crunched against my head. I whirled down in a speeding spire, arms outstretched, but no grip anywhere....

Even before I opened my eyes, I knew the smells. I was in a hospital. I was afraid. My eyes shot open. I saw a whitish ceiling. Cream walls carried a high ridge of molding. June sunlight poured in below a raised window shade. I heard a noise, a steady high-pitched whine. Sounded like a light motor. In an instant of panic I thought it was some kind of life-support machinery. In time I realized my ears were ringing nonstop. There were two empty chairs against the wall by the foot of the bed. A low table sat by a reading lamp that had a shade with a puppy-dog design. I saw the back of the chart that held the squiggles telling the medical world how and what Yuri Nevsky was doing.

I hadn't moved my head. I turned it very slowly toward the right. It turned, but something was awkward. I saw a bedside table and an insulated water pitcher. I sent down a signal to where my right hand ought to be. I told it to come up and feel my head. There was movement. My hand, looking very white and clean, nosed out like a mouse from under the sheet. It went on up to my head. There I felt a turban of bandages. Uh-oh. Not good. I moved each limb in turn. Each time, I dreaded one not being there. Abruptly I was *so* tired. Nothing mattered except sleep....

I woke to a shadowed room. Somewhere behind me an indirect light cast a horse-shaped shadow on the ceiling. The ringing machinery in my ears was operating at a lower level. I rolled my turbaned head to the left. I saw an IV stand supporting a bottle. Tubes ran into my forearm. They were held in place by stout-looking surgical tape. A buzzer stuck out like a black nipple from its can-shaped mechanism. The black cord ran up to the head of the bed and out of sight. I buzzed.

Fast action. A nurse with a small head and a big behind crepe-soled in with jinnilike speed. *"Well,* good to have *you* back with us, Mr. Nevsky!"

Her voice *clanngged* into my ears. She said something else, but the ringing drowned it out.

"I'm not hearing right." I realized I was nearly shouting. The tone-level adjustment in my head was out of kilter.

"That was the dynamite. The car blowing up," she said.

"Dynamite..."

She smiled down at me, hands on hips, and shook her head. "You're a lucky lout. One more day out cold and they were going to open your head up and look for short circuits. Not surprising you're a little out of it."

"I am?"

"Doctor will be by soon."

"Where is he?"

"Maybe off sharpening his bone saw." She winked. "He'll be *real* disappointed."

Dr. Milberry didn't show till noon the next day. Found out later he was one under par at the fourteenth hole at Oakmont when a message came out from the club-house that I was conscious. Patients had regained consciousness before. Never had he been one under par on Oakmont's fourteenth. I also found out that a Mr. Schlomo Stein wanted a chance to chat, too.

Dr. Milberry had a golf course tan and a smile that would have warmed the heart of Pedro the Cruel. It wasn't fair that some guys should be so armed. There was no disliking him or others in that clan. I had been working up a big mean against him for the delay. It faded with that big *caring* grin. Right behind him came a man in his late fifties. He wore an immaculate dark business suit and vest and carried a gray Homburg hat and an attaché case. His lined face was olive and heavy-boned.

Dr. Milberry came right to my bedside. "Mr. Nevsky, it may be wisest for you to call your attorney right away. Before Captain Stein—"

"Barry, Barry, that's *quite* unnecessary. It isn't that kind of situation." Schlomo Stein's voice carried faint tones of the educated over which years of police work had laid a harsh edge. He turned his bright eyes to me. "Mr. Nevsky, I'm Captain Schlomo Stein. I was only wondering if you're willing to answer a few questions about the deaths of Miss Ruth Spires and Mrs. Judy Larkin, your neighbor."

I blinked and stared. "Miss Spires. Mrs. Larkin..."

"I don't think he's quite ready for questions, Schlomo." Dr. Milberry's voice took on a sharp edge. It said patient's health was more important than captain's questions. I just *had* to like him.

He had a look at my pupils. "Tell me your name."

I did. I added that I was an employee of the Harvard University Library. Something was wrong. I hadn't worked there in fifteen years.

"That's wrong," I said. "That was years ago."

"Try something that happened this week," Dr. Milberry said.

I frowned. "The...garden. My garden in Murrysville. I was there...a little while ago."

"What's the last thing you remember, Mr. Nevsky?"

"I pretended I was a mobster." What did *that* mean?

The doctor cleared his throat and snapped a quick glance at Captain Stein.

"Where am I?" I said.

173

"You're in Columbia Hospital. You came to us in an ambulance. You had a bad concussion. Something had dug a trench in the outside of your skull."

"I have a housemate!" I shouted weakly. "Charity Day!" Panic! "My *housemate*."

"You'll find she's fine, Mr. Nevsky," Schlomo Stein said. "She's resting at home. A fellow named Buckcry is taking *very* good care of her."

Dr. Milberry sent Schlomo Stein out of the room. He took the tubes out of my arm. Then he did the catheter.

"Arise and walk!" he said.

"What?"

"Try it."

I sat on the edge of the bed. He slid a strong golf-hardened arm around my shoulder and helped me stand. I leaned against him and tottered a few steps. I understood why so many women read doctor-nurse romances. Light-headedness made me feel the doc was all-powerful. Across the room and back and my heart was pounding amid winded lungs.

On his way out, Dr. Milberry said I didn't have to talk to Captain Stein any longer than I wanted.

Captain Stein lifted a chair and carried it to the head of my bed. He sat, crossed his legs and folded his hands on his lap. He looked like a banker or stockbroker hoping to close a deal. I had no idea what he was going to say. "You don't look like someone who's mixed up with the mob," he said.

I looked at him blankly. "I've got a lot of empty stretches in my memory, Captain. But I don't think any of them are big enough to hold *that* one. How about filling in some blanks for me. You said two women were killed..."

"One was your neighbor, Judy Larkin. The other was a woman named Ruth Anne Spires. The bomb squad spent a long time scraping around 138 Morlande Street. What they found was that the Spires car had had the latest Sicilian auto accessory attached."

"I don't follow you."

"A bomb was wired to the ignition. Not the regular kind where somebody turns the key and everything goes boom. This was a 'smart' bomb. Type that first showed up in New York. Then Philly. Moving west, I guess." Stein was all business now, full of tough talk and cop smarts. "Anyhow, from what I pieced together, you, Mrs. Day and the Spires woman were at your house when Mrs. Larkin came over and asked to borrow a car. Seeing as yours was gone and Mrs. Day's was missing a distributor rotor, Miss Spires agreed to let Mrs. Larkin use her car. Both died real quick and probably painlessly. Mrs. Larkin was paste and pieces. Spires ended up a rag doll in the next yard—about seventy feet away. You were far enough away so you only got blown off your feet. Your head hit one of those curving metal S's that decorate your wrought iron fence. Your housemate, Mrs. Day, was knocked out. Nothing worse."

Two women dead...Spires and Larkin. No matter my shaky memory, sadness flooded in. I groped to place them, to center my grief where it belonged.

"Spires," I whispered. "Tell me about Spires, Stein. Who was she?"

He looked at me with his head cocked quizzically. Then he got out his notebook and read off what he had on Ruth Anne Spires. I listened and little connections clicked into place. Not all of them, I knew, but enough...

Stein read my face. "She didn't feel a thing, Nevsky. There was too much dynamite and it happened too fast."

"She was...young. She hadn't had time to...focus her life." I wasn't sure what I meant. Damn my memory.

"She didn't leave anybody, near as I could find out," Stein said. "There wasn't that kind of ugly fallout at least."

That didn't help my unfocused grief. I wanted to shake my head in dismay, but it hurt too much. "Go over that business about the car, the neighbor..."

He did. Judy Larkin...Judy Larkin. My mind tried to wander back to just who she was, like a newly blinded man groping desperately in his own house. A flash of memory struck, as punishing as lightning. We had been lovers! I groaned.

"Nevsky!" Stein was reaching for the nurse button.

"It's all right." I had remembered only a little, but it was enough. I was crying, nasty choking sobs that made my pillow sticky.

Stein tried changing the subject. "I'm...sorry about

the women. I know that doesn't help." He walked over to the window. "You want to hear about damage to your property?"

"I suppose. Big deal."

"The house and garage are being fixed. They're working on the glass and the wooden siding that got blown off."

"Who's working?"

"Couple women from a place called 'sPots in Shadyside. They work for that Tod Buckcry who's been taking care of Mrs. Day. He's all upset over the bomb. He seems to think if he had come to pick you two up, instead of the Spires woman, it wouldn't have happened. I doubt it."

"Why?"

"I think it was *you* they were after. Because of the bomb. I told you it was the 'smart' kind. The dynamite—all four sticks—and the detonation contacts were the usual mob work. Attached to all that was a counter a killer could set so that the detonation would take place anywhere from the first through the tenth start. That way the person to be hit might be miles and days away from the people who *really* didn't like him." Schlomo's heavy face twisted into a mask of distaste. "People who use bombs to do their dirty work ought to be drummed out of the human race. And have their mothers tied to the business ends of eighteen-inch guns. Anyhow, whoever hooked up the bomb figured the little counter would be blown to tomorrow. It *was* banged up bad. But the bomb squad found it." Schlomo's bright eyes met mine. "It was set at two. If it was the Spires woman they were after, they'd have set it at one." He shrugged. "Or maybe they were after her *and* you *and* Mrs. Day. I don't know. She left from a party in that pottery shop. That 'sPots place. There were a lot of people there. I thought I better talk to you before I talk to any of them."

"Just who are you?" I said.

"Captain Schlomo Stein."

"Captain of what? Where?"

He adjusted his conservative tie into a still more perfect knot. "I'm with the Allegheny Inter-County Police. It's a new cooperative setup to handle problems that cross borough, city and township lines. I used to be with the Squirrel Hill police. Forty-five years I've been in law enforcement. Now I'm rather a specialized investigator working out of the AICP. I've been in the system so long I come and go as I please. To a large extent I work on the cases that interest me."

"Sounds too easy."

"The commissioner was smart. He knew what compulsive workers *do* when they're left on their own. With no regular hours to work, we work *all* the time. I buried my wife four years ago. Cancer. My boys are in Denver and L.A. So I work. Give me an unknown like Yuri Nevsky, and I'm likely to take the five days he's been lying in the hospital to nose around about him. Seems like you're unemployed, divorced. Did some kind of hush-hush in D.C. Came back to Pittsburgh from Massachusetts...."

"That's me...even with the memory holes."

"I was all through your house. Found nothing much. Decided you're not in the rackets. Checked your bank accounts. They could use a transfusion. You're damn near broke."

"Still sounds like your essential Yuri Nevsky."

"It does...so I don't really think you're mixed up in the growing cocaine racket in the tri-state area."

"Good." I half remembered a conversation with a fat, bald man....

"That's going to be a big league ball game when they finally play it, Nevsky. A lot of other car bombs are going to go off—the fancy radio-controlled ones built by MIT dropouts at five K a shot. Little people will get stomped, big people will set themselves up for life—or die trying. It'll be Godzilla versus King Kong. And it *will* happen." Schlomo got up and stepped closer to the bed. He looked down at me. "But *you're* not going to have anything to do with it. No matter how many crazy-head visits you pay to Boothie O'Shea in his rich-only apartment house."

"Oh." A lot of memories of my visit to Boothie came flooding back. I played dumbish. "Why not?"

"Because you're not nearly nasty enough. The cocaine business is very tough, as I said. Everybody's organized up to here. No one has any morals. Consciences are put in cold storage with the floozies' minks. The lucky folks get their forearms broken with sash weights. The unlucky ones end up like your friend and your neighbor. Cops with twenty years of clean service get bought. Society ladies and Smith debutantes with nice skin and horse-show ribbons touch the tar baby of coke running and turn their lives to ashes."

"You seem to know an awful lot about it."

"I do."

"Why you talking to me, Captain Stein?"

Schlomo snorted and rubbed his large nose. "The reason depends on who you talk to. Count Dromsky-Michaux says one thing. Anna Yelanov says another. I might have heard a third tale from Winston Farrow III, the brother of the Semanova woman who seemed to be your housemate's friend. But he was found shot to death, half buried in a vacant lot in the Hill District. You wouldn't know anything about that, would you?"

I shook my head. That name . . . it floated at the edges of my memory.

"Far as I can tell, you first came nosing around asking about the Semanova woman. Then maybe you got the idea she was mixed up with drugs. You should have ceased and desisted at that point. The police get paid to take chances for you. You pay taxes instead. It's easier."

"I see."

"I don't." Schlomo paced around the three sides of the bed. "I don't know how you get from—where is it?— 138 Morlande Street to a small-time coke dealer named Boothie O'Shea."

"How did you find out he was a dealer?"

"A lot of rich people are conservative. Some of them have conservative ideas about what's right and wrong. One of them turned him in. We were hoping for bigger fish, so we staked out Mount Royal Apartments. . . ."

"You were watching him?"

"Taking pictures of people who went in and out."

"Since when?"

"Day or so before we saw you pull up in your chauffeured Cadillac." Schlomo's grin gave way to light laughter. "What the *hell* were you doing? What do you know?"

I closed my eyes and took a few deep breaths. I thought of begging off, of getting him out of there. I really wasn't well. But that wasn't the way to go. "Maybe we should...trade information, Captain Stein."

"Trade already happened, Nevsky. What I did for you was *not* have you booked. You been holding out information that the police ought to know. That's called obstructing justice. You were carrying on some kind of trade with a suspected felon—"

"Did you talk to Boothie about me?"

"We talked at *great* length to him. We wanted to know who the flashy bearded hood was who had visited him in the mile-long limo. And we showed him your picture, made from one of our movies."

"Movies?"

"Everybody going in or out. He told us this incredible story about you pulling a gun and trying to put him into *your* cocaine network." The captain scowled. "Only we didn't know it was you. We thought you *were* the lead to the big leagues we wanted. Then when I got a look at you while you were gone sleepies...I mean, what the hell is going on?"

"How'd you know I was bombed?"

"Your chief of police has a great information system. Too bad he doesn't run one for the whole county. Maybe he'd tell me what you were up to."

He was confused. That encouraged me. "You first," I said.

"First what?"

"To share some information to trade."

He sighed and folded his hands on his lap. "All right, I'll humor you. Let's give it a try. I started with the Spires woman. That led me back to Hermitage Decorator Antiques and to Anna, Yelanov's wife. She said he's disappeared. The Buckcry woman who used to crew for him—"

"Selina. She died in the hospital." I remembered *that*.

"She was murdered in the hospital."

"Murdered?"

"We've been keeping that quiet. She was hooked up to a bunch of vital-sign monitors. Consoles were out by the nurse's station. Nobody paying much attention because she wasn't a critical case. And they were short a

nurse that night. Won't bother you with the details.
But when they put the charts and tapes together...Dr.
Greenlaw guesses she was smothered to death with a
pillow. She got bumped on the head pretty good, so at
first everybody figured something was wrong with her
head. It was a lot simpler than that: she couldn't get
any air."

"What about her husband, Tod?"

"He was around the hospital. Said he was out getting
a Big Mac when she had her 'seizure.' Some other people
were around. Well-wishers. We'll keep quiet about the
autopsy and see if anyone tips his hand." Schlomo sat
back. "Your turn now."

"Some of what I know you know, too."

"Probably. Go ahead anyway, Nevsky."

"This is what I found out. I mean this is what I
remember. Might be more knocked loose. The last weekend of May a cabin cruiser called the *Stressless I* sailed
from the Big E Marina, Erie shore. Aboard were its
owner, Sergei Yelanov, Selina Buckcry and Felicia Semanova. And someone else. I don't know who. Don't ask
me. They met Alexey Semanova, Felicia's husband,
somewhere on the southwest shore of Long Point Park,
in Canada. They were shot at by Mounted Police and
narcotics officers. Alexey was killed. Maybe somebody
else on the *Stressless I* was hit. But they got away in
a storm with a smuggled bronze statue and I think a
big shipment of cocaine, probably in a heavy plastic
bag. The cocaine was never delivered. Felicia came to
my house that night. She wanted her old friend Charity,
my housemate, to hide the bronze for her. Turned out
it's worth a medium-sized fortune. Charity wouldn't do
it. I think either the fourth party or Sergei has the
cocaine."

"Where's Sergei?"

"Nobody knows. Selina and Felicia maybe knew, but
they're dead. Maybe the passenger knows."

"What else?"

"I don't know what happened after they moored back
at the Big E Marina. But Felicia showed up at one-
thirty in the morning with the statue. According to the
plan I scared out of Boothie, she was supposed to make
a delivery to him earlier that night. The delivery was

never made. And Boothie couldn't get out of her what had happened. Beside 'trouble.' My memory's getting a lot better."

"I still have a feeling you left some things out."

"Captain—"

"But you've given me lots of stuff I can use. I can check with Canadian folks. I can nose around in different directions now." He leaned back in his chair, calm as ever. "You sure *did* louse up things with Boothie. We're letting him off the hook. No charges. No time in the slammer. Maybe he'll still draw some attention."

"I don't remember much more about talking to him. Maybe later my memory will come back about that. Got any more data to trade, Captain?"

"Just about the bomb. And I already sort of told you. It's a mob special. Some very nasty people wanted you dead. And—if you're not holding out on me—I can't guess why. I can't guess why they'd want the Spires woman dead. From what you said, she was one of the few *not* involved with smuggling anything."

I decided the captain was basically OK, so I told him what I knew about the art smuggling. Valuable Russian items had been coming in via Alexey.

He shrugged his fashionably padded shoulders. "I think we've gotten to the bottom of the barrel, Nevsky. Nobody gives a fart in a hurricane over art, one way or the other."

"You have anything more for me?"

He shook his head.

"I'm going to put you in my debt, then." I had thought it over and decided Captain Schlomo Stein was a good cop doing a good job. He might come in handy later. I told him about the sawed steering column on Felicia's station wagon.

He cursed in Yiddish. "Maybe I should have thought of that. Maybe I *would* have after hearing your little piece. Maybe not." He looked at the soundproof ceiling tiles for a long moment. "Interesting. And it gives me a bit to pass back to you in partial repayment."

"Oh?"

"That was an amateur murderer's trick. I might even say a nonconfronter's trick. No guarantee at all of success. Who could guess when it would let go? Maybe turning into a driveway.

"Seems like we're traded out for a while."

Schlomo Stein got up and stood very straight. He looked like a prosperous grandfather about to lecture his giddy grandson. "I can't imagine what's in your head, Nevsky. The whole concept of you baiting Boothie O'Shea in his den, posing as a syndicate front man, was a *zany*, to use a polite word. When I found you don't work and are just about broke, I didn't know what the hell. I figured you for a nut. I figured you for the tail end of a bred-out line of postrevolutionary Russian emigrés. No good at any damn thing."

"You met me. Now what do you figure?"

He shook his head. "Maybe you blundered into all this and are trying to play narc."

"Maybe." I smiled.

"I'm working toward some advice, my good man. My gut feeling is that you have some kind of deep personal investment in the death of the Semanova woman. My advice is—drop it, put it aside."

I opened my mouth to protest, but he kept talking.

"Two reasons. Both good ones. First, let police do police work. Second, I count five murders—up to now: Judy Larkin, Ruth Anne Spires, Selina Buckcry, Winston Farrow III and Felicia Semanova. You fool around, you could be number six." He picked up his Homburg from the low table and put it dead flat on his head.

"You're not going to arrest me?" I said.

He stared coldly at me. "There is nothing funny about murder and running cocaine, Mr. Nevsky. Jails aren't used to keep people from making fatal fools of themselves. Alas." At the door he turned back. "Don't touch the candle flame. Take my word for it: it's *hot*." He touched his hat brim. "Good day."

Chapter Fourteen

Less than a minute later another head leaned in the room doorway. This one was decorated with blonde summer-cut hair. Charity!

"Welcome to the land of the awakened!" she said. "I called every day to see if you were conscious."

"Thanks. It's good to be back. Except I seem to have left parts behind. My memory's shaky."

She sat down and held my hand, then kissed it. Her grin connected her ears. "Having you here, in danger and away, did *not* sit well with me. Life's less fun with no Yuri Nevsky to kick around." She leaned over and kissed my lips. I got my arms free of the sheets and gave her a shaky hug that hurt my head.

"I want to know about the women who were killed. I want you to tell me who they were and what they meant to us."

Her eyes told me she hadn't thought my memory had been that badly damaged. She sat in the bedside chair. She told me everything. She catalyzed my recall. In my remembering, the sense of loss was overpowering.

I wasn't so macho over the next couple of hours. Judy's death was the worst of the two, of course, but Ruthie had been so . . . alive, too. I wept again. I carried on. Charity did her best to calm me, but I wouldn't calm. She finally called a nurse. She called the doctor. He used a needle.

I slept for a while. Charity came back from a light dinner. The dead women were off limits for conversation. The house was a safe topic.

"I found your homeowners' insurance policy," she said. "You were covered for explosion. Adjuster's been there. June and Twiggy are already working like beavers putting back the glass and siding. Tod's doing the heavy stuff. Everything's OK."

Everything wasn't OK. Dear Judy and red-haired Ruthie were gone. Crushed, blown to bits. Winston had been shot. Selina and he had both touched the Sarmatian Demon. Judy and Ruthie were innocent of those gleaming lethal curves. They had never seen the hawkish face or dreaded the hammer blows. Still the Death I imagined oozed up from the pitted bronze had found them, too.

Charity told me nothing had happened to solve the riddle of the bronze or the murders in the five days I had lain there deciding to avoid brain surgery.

She told me about Selina's funeral. Despite the bad stunning she had got from the bomb, she had insisted on going. She wanted to give Tod all the emotional support she could. "It rained. That's supposed to be right for the dead." Her eyes turned blank, revealing nothing of how she had felt about being a hasty successor to the deceased. "The coffin was cheap. Neither Selina nor Tod had any religion. He found a friend to chant mantras. We all stood around in a circle and listened while the rain ran down off our noses."

"Charity..."

She continued in a leaden voice. "About halfway through, Steelhead Sweeney and three of his biker buddies came roaring up. He was out on bail. They were pretty drunk. Steelhead told everybody he didn't know which Selina was better at—fighting or fucking. Then his pals made Hunlike passes at Twiggy, June and me. They wouldn't take no for an answer. June got hysterical and Twiggy broke one of their thumbs with some kind of Far Eastern self-defense trick. They roared off cursing..."

I closed my eyes. Thoughts of the legendary Forces of Evil and Death flitted like bats through the gray cathedral of my damaged brain. Selina's funeral joined the parade of those dark hosts. A potent backdrop to a nightmare.

Thursday before noon Dr. Milberry took off my large bandage and with a mirror gave me a look at a ragged terrain of shaved skull and longish stitched wound. "We'll take off the fortune teller's hat and give you the fancy Band-Aid." He flashed his light into my eyes. He made me stand on one shaky leg with my arms out and eyes closed.

"How's your hearing?"

"Down to a continuous dial tone. Much better than the alarm bells I started out with."

He grunted. "Head ache?"

"A little. Seems like now and then."

He wrote out a prescription. "For 'then,'" he said. He put away his doctor's tools. "I'm sure you're on the mend. Spend time sitting and lying down. Don't overdo. Your memory's what I can't tell about. Maybe you'll get it all back. Maybe eighty percent. Who knows? One thing's for sure." He closed his black bag with a snap. "You win the Dr. Barry Milberry Lucky Lout of the Year Award. I'm sorry your lady friends weren't lucky at all. Pay the hospital on your way out. I'll send you a bill."

Pay the hospital? How? I was broke. I went into the bathroom and took a careful shower. When I came out, a candy striper was just coming in with my street clothes. She gave me a sheet of paper.

"What's this?"

"A receipt from the cashier."

I looked at it. Charity had paid my bill. Her scrawled note said she had used the last of Felicia's five thousand dollars.

She and Tod were waiting out in the hall. My abused memory reported I had been angry and jealous about Charity's feelings for him. How small I seemed now before her generosity. Walking across the parking lot, their steadying hands on my elbows, made me light-headed. I stopped and took a few deep breaths. I said I was OK and we went on to her car.

After so many hours asleep my senses were now hypersensitive. Sharp vision! The trees in full, mid-June flower, the glint of sun off car chrome, the dazzling white of tennis dresses on the rust-colored clay courts in the park, the old red brick and woodwork of the Second Congregational Church. And odors—gasoline, hot seat covers, Charity's talc. Life thrust at me with the strength of my long rested senses. The fresh air charged my brain with energy. I saw how much life lay before me. What a feast had been spread!

On the way home Charity filled me in on what a great help Tod had been. Not only had he been foreman of his two-woman work crew, but he had been an errand boy and light nurse for her.

We pulled into the drive leading to the garage. My poor house! All its garage-facing eyes had been put out and its skin of wood siding had been gouged away in patches. Light, fresh boards and the stickered new glass marked repairs. There was a foot-deep crater as wide as I was tall in the asphalt of the driveway. The garage windows had yet to be reglazed.

I took a stroll through the first floor of 138 and decided that was the limit of my energy. I went to bed. Charity brought me a cup of soup and a liverwurst on rye. I left half of each and felt stuffed—and a little sleepy. Still, I couldn't sleep without thanking her for paying my hospital bill, telling her how much I owed her.

She heard my gratitude politely while blushing. She was full of such odd surprises. Unflappable at law, a skilled actress in court, she was a valuable partner—more than a match for the Boothie O'Sheas of life. Yet, once in a while, little girl peeked through. To place the final brick in the repaired wall of our friendship, I asked her how things were going with Tod.

Her blush deepened. "Oh, Yuri, we love each other *very* much. He was *so* much help when I was on the mend. He came over and stayed. We played house together. He waited on me hand and foot. He drove me to Judy's funeral. He read me all the newspapers and went down to the firm and picked up my mail. Those four days together were *wonderful*." Her dreamy smile backed up her words. "He mentioned marriage."

"A *proposal?*"

"Not exactly. Just as something that would come along in time."

"Make you happy?"

"Very. I'm feeling all the throb-throb giddiness of being in love. I know it's a grand passion; I'm starting to believe even the worst love-song lyrics."

I squeezed her hand. Drowsiness washed over me in heavy waves. "Don't run off with him before I wake up," I mumbled.

My nap lasted through the night. The next morning I felt much stronger. The noise in my head was down to a faint recording-tape hiss. My balance was better. I dragged a lawn chair out back by the garage and sat by a bush in the sun. Beyond my ruined windows and damaged brick rose the Larkin home.

My mending memory, like a burst dam, flooded me with sudden thoughts of Judy. I heard her voice swiftly shrill with giddy wit. I felt again her gentle touch, the hunger of her wet surrender, the pebbles of her brown nipples lying in the tender centers of my palms. I smelled and tasted her mouth, the fleshy channel above her spine, the hairy tangle and glistening folds of her sex. Memories slammed at me like fists.

I sat slack in the bright dazzle of the early morning sun. I marveled how the conjurer's show of life misdirected us. What seemed like Judy's and my future had disappeared like an illusionist's colored handkerchief. The promising prologue of our tale of friendship and intimacy proved to be the whole story. My determined Slavic Guilt seemed ludicrous now. What were scant indiscretions before the awesome finality of death. If anything, our brief pleasures were affirmations in the face of that finality. No, there was no *knowing* about anything. We were all defenseless before the grinding road machinery of destiny.

There was no stopping the tears. They poured down my cheeks—cool tracks under the sun's heat.

I heard the rattle of the latch on the Larkins' front door and a woman's bright metallic laughter. Out the door she came, in heels and an inappropriate Persian lamb coat. Beside her came Jed Larkin, so recently Judy's husband. I wasn't particularly noticeable by my bush. The woman reached out and goosed him good. He chortled and briefly groped for her breasts within the curly pelt. I saw their hands join with easy familiarity—

then part, to maintain the thin veneer of a widower's bogus grief.

In an instant, with comic-strip-light-bulb brilliance and certainty, I understood all about Jed. His "business" commitment had been this flashy dish all along. She had been his golf date, his late accounts, his sales meetings, his financial closing, and who knew what else. He had cheated Judy of all the things that mattered: time, attention and love. Probably he had never liked her, as he hadn't liked the home she made for him. What a cruel edge that gave it all! Another conjurer's silk ripped away, another level of meaning exposed—another dare for Yuri Nevsky to look further into the riddle of being human. A dare of my emotion wouldn't let me take.

It was all, all beyond prediction, understanding, beyond any sense. How clearly were marked the limits of reason!

The shrill woman laughed again beyond my now closed eyes. I could more easily have stopped my own heartbeat than my tears. They burned their way between my lids. I opened them to the dazzle brightened by the droplets. I asked myself whom I wept for this sunny morning abloom with heat and irises, deception and impenetrable mysteries.

I wept for all of us. All of us!

I sat streaming and wiping for ten minutes. I drew some deep, damp breaths and reminded myself I wasn't quite whole yet. Not that being a little stronger would fix me up enough to sort everything out. All of us forever groped about blindfolded in the fun house of our days.

Twiggy Twill and June Gowell came wheeling up in Twiggy's Land Rover. I wiped my face. They piled out and rushed up wreathed in smiles. Twiggy wore her usual Big Smith overalls, June a yellow Pirates cap and a carpenter's apron. She also wore a shiner around her left eye.

"You look wonderful, Mr. Nevsky!" Twiggy said.

"And so does my house and garage, you two. I didn't know you both had cards in the carpenter's union. Thanks much."

"The worst job was vacuuming and sweeping up the

glass from inside the house," June said. "It was *every-where.*"

"Today should do it, too. We're right on schedule." Twiggy hurried for the garage and June followed. Their tools were waiting where they had left them. In seconds they were pounding away on the damaged boards. The sun soothed and warmed my face. I dozed a bit then went inside to make the girls some iced tea. When it was ready I strolled back out, tray in hands, and surveyed their glazing operation. June was fitting the last three small panes into the wooden frames and tapping in the glazing tacks. Twiggy, following with putty and knife, said she had just run out of putty.

"Tea before you go to the hardware store?" I said.

They dragged some lawn chairs up from the basement and set them up on the patio on the other side of the garage. We sipped the tea. I looked around and saw that neither of them were smiling. I knew why. They were both thinking about the bomb. They had roomed with Ruthie Spires.

"I keep seeing it over and over," I said. "And feeling the blast hit me like a locomotive." I touched the large economy-size Band-Aid atop my head.

"Some of the parts of the car trimmed the hedges flying through. Some of them stuck in the siding in front of the garage," June said. "Tod had to use a sledge hammer to knock them out."

"What're they saying about the bomb?" I said. "Who put it in Ruthie's car?"

"I saw on TV the police think it was gangs. And they made a mistake. Put the bomb in the wrong car," Twiggy said. "Ruthie for sure didn't have anything to do with— mobsters."

"Were either of you at the party when Charity called Tod and asked for a ride?"

They exchanged glances. "I guess we both were."

"What happened after the call?"

They mulled it over. "Tod was a little high, so he shouted. 'Charity Day and Yuri Nevsky need a ride. Who'll go get them?'" June said.

"Ruthie, Tod and I were the only ones who knew where you lived," Twiggy said. "And I was heavy into playing hostess. I organized everything and had to make sure it went off OK. With no hassle for Tod. He was the guest of honor, so he couldn't go. That left Ruthie. She had already had a few rum-and-cokes and had got down to some heavy boogying with a guy from Shadyside. She shouted she'd go for you in a little bit."

"How long before she went out and drove off?" I said.

Twiggy shrugged her hefty shoulders. "About ten, fifteen minutes, I guess. Not any longer."

I was working with something Schlomo Stein had given me. Someone had attached the "smart" bomb when Ruthie's car had been parked behind s'Pots. Had to be, because there would have been no stops between 'sPots and 138 or the car and Ruthie would have never made it. "Who was at the party when Ruthie left?" I said.

June made a face and looked more squirrelish than ever. "A lot of people. A real mob. Twiggy invited everybody."

"How about naming the people who knew Ruthie that I might know?" I said.

"Why?" June said.

"Maybe one of them hooked up the bomb."

"Oh..." Twiggy's blue eyes opened wide. "I thought it was somebody off the street who snuck down by the garages—"

"Maybe it was. But I'd still like to know who was there."

June said, "Well, Twiggy and me. Tod, Count Dromsky-Michaux from Hermitage, some people Ruthie knew from C-M University, the Langelles. He's bought from Hermitage. Some of the Shadyside crowd—'Deacon' Dan Green; Orrstein; Selina's attorney, Brunov; his fiancée, rich Trishie Widemann." She muttered something.

"What?" I said.

"Nothing." She looked at Twiggy and forced a grin. "I forgot the count's girlfriend." I had a feeling she was somehow changing the subject.

"Oh, yeah. She musta been all of about eighteen. With her dress cut down to here and so tight across her ass I thought it was gonna bust open and take about half the people with it."

"I think the count is self-destructing."

"Anna Yelanov, Sergei's wife was there. *Madame* Yelanov. She *can* sing still," June said. "She sang a part of some classical requiem for Selina later that night. She started to cry. I could tell she wasn't crying over Selina. Something else. Just the same everybody started crying right along with her."

Twiggy got up. "Our roomie Amanda Swale was on piano." She shrugged. "That was about it for people you know who knew Ruthie, Yuri. Hey, I gotta go get the putty for the garage windows. June, why don't you stick here with the invalid. Be back in twenty."

June drank more iced tea. The glass by her face made me notice her eye again. "How'd you get the shiner?" I said.

Her smooth cheeks colored. "Guy hit me."

"Anybody I know?"

"Somebody who should know better—from a legal point of view anyhow. Vasily Brunov."

Vasily! I remembered the whack he had given Anna Yelanov. Seemed he enjoyed hitting women. "Why'd he hit you?"

"It's a long story."

"We have at least twenty minutes."

June's frown above her buckteeth gave her a worried-chipmunk look. "I wasn't supposed to say anything. He lost his temper. He apologized. Then he gave me some money 'to buy a steak for it.'"

"Oh? How much?"

"Two hundred dollars." She adjusted the bill of her Pirates cap with nervous fingers. "The idea was for me not to let it get around he had bonged me. His rep, you know."

I grunted. "I wonder if you could tell me what you were talking about?"

June sipped her tea. "I shouldn't tell you. But I don't *like* getting hit. It was about Selina, I guess. That's how it started. Selina and Felicia. Felicia used to live with us, you know."

"Till she moved out to Mount Royal Apartments."

The bucktoothed girl nodded. "He asked me if I was, you know, good friends with the two of them. I said not particularly. Selina was either off running around or with Tod in their apartment. And, hey, let's face it, Felicia was a *lot* older than me. Ruthie ran with her,

191

not me. Oh, he wanted to know if Ruthie and I were close, too. I said not."

"For that he hit you?"

June giggled and shook her head. "Here's what happened. He called 'sPots and asked for me. He invited me to the Gazebo for lunch. I figured he wanted to talk to me about something legal, you know. And...I like to eat. So I went. After I said I wasn't real close with either Felicia or Selina, he gave me this big smile that said he was gonna enjoy lunch. Then he started with the questions. When Selina and Felicia went off in Sergei's boat, where did I think they went? I said they went fishing out in the middle of Lake Erie somewhere. I knew Felicia and Sergei had a thing going. I'm sure they made Selina drive the boat while they went at it down on those bunks it had."

"What did Vasily say to that?"

"Nothing. He didn't say much to any of my answers."

"He asked more questions?"

"Yeah. I kept waiting for him to get to the point. He *did* finally say it had to do with wills and insurance policies."

I thought for a long moment. "When was that?"

"While you were in the hospital."

"What else did he ask you?"

"If Felicia or Selina ever spent a lot of money, like throwing it around."

I remembered what Ruthie had said about Felicia splurging from time to time. I held my breath.

"I said no." I saw she wasn't as sharp as Ruthie. She hadn't put her former roommate's little flings together with Brunov's questions. "I thought that was kind of an off-the-wall question. None of us ever had much money or we wouldn't have been living four-on-a-floor.

"Then he asked me if Amanda Swale or poor Ruthie had ever mentioned Felicia or Selina having money to burn. I told him no. I wasn't that close to Ruthie. She was always with Felicia. And Amanda's so spacy..." June put down her empty glass. She kept one ice cube behind her gopher teeth to suck. "Then Mr. Brunov said he was going to take me into his confidence. He said he wanted to make sure I wasn't an 'accessory' to anything Sergei Yelanov might have been doing. He wanted

192

to make sure Amanda and Twiggy weren't accessories either. He said that while looking after Mrs. Yelanov's interests he got the idea Sergei might've been up to something funny. He wanted to protect us all. *Was* I being honest? he asked me." She looked at me with innocent eyes. "Of *course* I was being honest."

"That's always the best way to be."

"You don't happen to know what Sergei and them *were* doing, do you, Mr. Nevsky?" The ice cube rattled against her teeth.

Smuggling art and cocaine, I thought. I would never tell June. It had dawned on me that that was dangerous information for anyone to have.

"I had the feeling Mr. Brunov was pretty much involved with what we were talking about. Taking it real serious. I knew it was big legal stuff. He seemed to know so much about the *Stressless I* and all. So I thought I'd ask him. So out on the street I did."

"Asked him what?"

"The question everybody's been asking around Hermitage and 'sPots for the last two weeks and some—where's Sergei Yelanov?"

"What'd he say?"

"He looked kind of grouchy and said he didn't know. Nobody knew. Then I told him *my* theory," June said brightly.

"*Your* theory..."

"Well, it all seemed pretty *obvious* to me. They all started out together—Selina, Felicia and Sergei. I told Mr. Brunov I thought only the two women came back. I thought Sergei fell overboard." He said that was absurd. I wish I had noticed how upset he was getting. Instead I rushed right on. I said *I* didn't think it was absurd. And the police didn't either because *they* had talked to Selina and Felicia—twice. Maybe they were all drunk or stoned or something and didn't want to admit he went splash. I said to him, 'Mr. Brunov, I don't care what you think. Sergei slipped overboard and *drowned!*'" She paused.

"And that's when he hit you."

"Yep. He was really mad, but he cooled down fast. He said I was running my mouth in ways that could confuse and mislead people who were really trying to find out where Sergei had gone. When he cooled down all the way he gave me the money...."

That gave me some more mulling material. In the early afternoon I sat in the sun like an old dog nipping at the fleas of my guesses. My first conclusion was that Charity and I had been marked for death the night of the party, well before Ruthie arrived. The tip-off was the missing distributor rotor from Charity's car. Sometime that afternoon someone had slipped into the garage and removed it.

So we would come in one car.

Then one bomb would get us both—after the party. So the bomber was a party guest. No help, though. Before the do, the guest list had been no secret. During, all of Tod's friends and acquaintances were there. When word spread that we needed a ride and Ruthie would provide it, the bomber slipped outside and did his dirty work on her car. Fate had dished out her cruelty elsewhere that night: Ruthie and Judy had died, not Charity and I. We couldn't count on being spared again.

More than before I sensed that Death was stalking us—a Death summoned by the ancient bronze demon only a few dozen yards from where I sat. That hideous Demon leaked evil. It had killed Ruthie and Judy, my so newly launched love. It had killed Alexey, Winston, Selina, Felicia. I sensed it had killed Sergei, too. And was not content....

I tried to shake my foreboding by going back over the events connected with the Demon. The gaps in my memory made that hard. After two hours in the sun my ears started to ring again. Nap time.

I woke scarcely rested. Phantoms cast in flesh in the mold of the bronze had run lumpishly after me across the arid plains of my dreams.

Tod fixed dinner and we three ate together. I had little appetite. It was made worse by the intense lover's stare my housemate riveted on the potter as he went about dinner chores. How could she have time for that when Death and evil seeped up through the boards under our feet?

I supposed I was feverish. My head throbbed and the

ringing had picked up. I tottered away from dessert like a man of eighty while Charity and Tod, oblivious, played footsie. I fell into a restless, sweaty sleep. Hours or minutes later I started awake.

I had heard a woman scream—in the house. I scrambled to sit up on the edge of the bed before realizing what I had heard. Through several thick walls and many cubic feet of heavy June night air I had heard Charity's wails of pleasure.

Gloom, depression and fear of Death swirled around me like wraiths. The darkness of my bedroom seemed to heave and pitch with threatening shapes. Among them lunged the hideous pitted face of the Sarmatian Demon. I whimpered and raised my hands to ward off his hammer blow. No matter which way I turned my defenses he was always behind me. His fanged mouth hungered for my flesh and his hammer for my soul— to crack it like a nut. To crack it as he had cracked those five other. Judy, the last loss, was the most dreadful of all. I blubbered, awash in weakness, that her messy death had left *me* alone. Yes, her sons in the end would be hurt worse. Tonight, though, I was not being strong. Tonight I felt sorry for myself.

Streaming tears, I wandered to my upstairs phone. I fumbled with my phone index. I picked up the receiver and dialed...Boston.

Ann's number. Ann, my ex-wife.

It rang once, twice, three times. I sniffled, then drew deep breaths in a try for control.

The receiver was picked up. A man's voice. "Good evening. May ah help you?" A Southern accent!

"Is...Ann Nevsky there?"

"May ah tell her who's callin'?"

"Yuri. Yuri, her...ex-husband."

He did a poor job of muffling the receiver. I heard him laugh. I heard Ann say something, then more laughter.

Very slowly I hung up.

I went back to bed. I lay face up, covers pulled to my chin like a frightened child in a creaky house. My skull throbbed with every heartbeat. In time I groaned up into the darkness aswarm with the bronze's demon kin. Half asleep, in my feverish fantasy I thought they screamed at me in fiendish voices of all tones asking me again and again, where was their Sarmatian king?

fall asleep. In my feverish fantasy I thought they crackled in all our Croatian voices of all time, again and again and again, where was their Carnatian fog.

Chapter Fifteen

I woke up late. My fever was gone. I felt spent, but much stronger. After Tod left for 'sPots Charity joined me by my chair in the sun. She told me about Judy Larkin's funeral. Tod had driven her to the cemetery right from the hospital. Three bewildered little boys were wholly in the hands of their stranger father for the first time ever. Well-meaning relations buffered his parental incompetence. On the near outskirts of it all moved a flashily dressed woman who had tone coordinated her funeral blacks. She and Jed Larkin exchanged encouraging glances. She was asked to fill in in a motherly role on two occasions, both of which she botched. Neither her presence nor her relationship to the deceased was explained.

"I saw her goose him yesterday," I said. "She's his mistress. Has been for a long time."

We glowered at each other. "It doesn't look good for the three boys," she said.

We sat facing the Larkin house. It was rather a nice house—three high stories, old stained-glass half-windows, a skylight studio. As it turned out, though, it really didn't mean much. Like so many of our possessions, it was a trapping, almost a mask for the essential human business going on within. When that business was going well, the trappings made it more fun. When it wasn't, they only added a spice of irony to the bitter stew.

Sitting in our separate sun-splashed reveries, we were both surprised when a long silver chauffeur-driven Rolls nosed into the driveway. Riding behind the panel was a single figure. I had a very strong feeling I wasn't looking at a rental vehicle this time.

The engine made so little sound I thought it had stalled. I wondered what a poshmobile like that was doing around modest Marland Borough.

The chauffeur eased out with stately speed and opened the rear door. A woman about twenty-five in a blue sundress and low white heels got out. She had piano legs—straight down from knee to foot. She was wide-hipped and small-breasted. I got up. She walked toward us. Her eyes were blue and rather close-set. Her styled hair was the color of dust under a bed.

"Mr. Nevsky? Ms. Day?" she said.

We nodded. I asked her what we could do for her.

"It's not for me. It's for my father." She held out her hand to Charity first, then to me. I saw she bit her nails. "I'm Patricia Widemann. I'm Duke Widemann's daughter. They call me Trishie."

This drab creature was Vasily Brunov's fiancée? The wonders money worked! "Nice to meet you."

"I don't know your father, Trishie," Charity said. "I can't imagine what we could do for *him.*"

"Talk to him. Come out to Poplars and talk to him."

I knew why Charity was hesitating. Duke Widemann was a billionaire with personal investments in a score of countries—a man of power and influence. "Talk...about what?" she said.

"I don't know."

"When?"

"Now. I came in the car for you both."

I surveyed Trishie's pale face with its thin lips and uneven nose. She had good skin at least. How had Ruthie described her? "Plain as a post!" So she was.

"He said it would only take an hour at most," she said eagerly. She wanted to please her father, this Trishie Widemann. I marveled at how far the Sarmatian Demon's evil net had been cast. Whatever Duke had to say to Charity and me would be about the bronze—

198

some way. He wasn't going to invite us to a polo match, that was certain.

Charity and I traded nods. "OK," I said. We started toward the big silver car.

"Mrs. Day, Mr. Nevsky!" Trishie's long jaw dropped. "You're not *dressed*."

"You don't count cutoff jeans?" Charity said, looking down at dimpled knees.

"Father feels *very* strongly about dress."

Charity kept walking. "He sent for us like some kind of Pooh-Bah wanting to talk to a subject. He'll have to take us as we are."

"Mrs. Day, he will be *angry*."

"I'm not invited for a dinner party, am I?"

"No."

"Or for shooting or sailing or running foxes?"

"N-No."

"For a *chat*, right?"

She nodded, biting her lip. Here was a girl not at all used to hearing a woman say no.

"Well, these are my *chatting* clothes. Let's go!"

We tried conversation in the back of the Rolls. The seat would have held three more of us with no hips touching. Charity had put Trishie off with her loose dress code. The younger woman nibbled her lower lip and wrung her hands. Her anxiety was over her fear of her father's reaction. What a little mouse she was! All gray and scared. Vasily the cat would gobble her up.

"Why'd your father send *you?*" I said.

"So you'd both know it wasn't business, that it was family..."

Poplars had a big stone-and-wrought-iron gate at the entrance to its main road. In a large matching stone kiosk two guards waved us on. The road wound up and around through maintained woods that finally gave way to lawns, gardens and fountains. Blue-and-white-striped summer awnings fluttered like sails on the gray seas of the main house's building stone. Beyond that sprawling palace other smaller buildings housed horses, servants, guests and equipment. The lawns reminded me of the English ones rolled every day for three hundred years.

199

Sculptures reared up at appropriate spots on the way to the front entrance. We got out. A butler opened the door. His hair was black and plastered down. He eyed Charity's bare legs. No reaction whatever. Likely he was worth his salary.

"Edmund, please tell Father that Mrs. Day and Mr. Nevsky are here," Trishie said.

Edmund came back and said Mr. Widemann was unexpectedly in conference. He looked at Trishie. "He suggests you might want to show your guests around the first floor."

The first floor, long as a par five, was stunning. Hardwood floors and paneling, Indian and Persian carpets, tapestries, and furniture from a half dozen periods all integrated elegantly into individual rooms and areas. We saw the main living room, the dining room, the smoking room, the library, the breakfast room.... In widely separated spots four staircases—marble, hardwood, wrought iron and stone—curved up toward more, unseen wonders.

Trishie paused before two tall, gleaming teak veneer doors. She grasped one brass pull in each hand. "This is Father's Russian room."

She led us in onto a marble floor. A wealth of furniture and art objects glowed under lighting varied to represent the vast Russian regions—harsh cold light for the far north, golden for Samarkand and the Black Sea. "One of Father's favorite places in the whole world is this room," Trishie said. She led us forward. Pedestals held Muscovite statuettes in perfect condition. Alternating with floor-to-ceiling windows were three alcoves. In the ceiling of each was a spotlight shining down on a centered prized object. The first held a man-sized Kazakh vase. Painted figures danced endlessly between gray, tan and yellow bands. The second was a heavy iron shield, gleaming survivor of wars with corrosion. The third...

Charity smothered a scream into a short yelp.

"Yes, it *is* ugly," Trishie said. "*Really* ugly. But father *loves* it."

I stood staring. The hair on the back of my head stirred like grain before an evil wind.

On the pedestal stood the Sarmatian Demon!

200

Gleaming bronze and glittering red and blue en-crustations fouled the room's beauty.

Trishie moved on, but Charity and I didn't. "W-What do you know about this? How long's it been here?" Charity said.

"Oh, about a year."

"A year!"

"Um-huh. I remember the day they brought it here—"

"They?" I said.

"The two guys who sold it to Father"—Trishie touched her forehead to spur memory—"from, ah, that place in Shadyside."

"Hermitage! Hermitage Decorator Antiques," Charity said.

"Oh, you know it? Anyway, the two of them tried to carry it in from the truck. They were so *funny!* Panting and sweating and *everything.* It was too heavy for them and they didn't know how far it *was.*" She tittered. "Edmund had to send for a little flat cart with wheels."

I leaned close to this Sarmatian Demon, as I had leaned close to ours. I studied its chest. I remembered a pattern in the multi-colored checkerboard encrusta-tion. I looked for the seven rough squares of red chal-cedony in the alignment of the Big Dipper. They were there! I walked around the bronze, studying the angle of the lethal hammer. I stared again into the nest of fangs that was its mouth. I could not forget the angles of those teeth. They were the same. On ours a large gouge arched across the kneecap of the left leg. I peered at the irregular channel in this bronze. My nose was less than a foot from the damage. It, too, mirrored our White Chambered monster. This encrusted bronze also oozed cold and Death.

I stepped back. I looked at Charity. Her face was ashen, her eyes large. I sensed the fear rising in both of us.

What was going on here?

"Mr. Widemann will see you now." I started. Ed-mund *was* quiet on his feet.

I was glad the house was so large. I had time to get myself halfway together. I still felt cold and knew my face was nearly as pale as Charity's.

Duke Widemann was in the small den he used as an at-home office. The small den was the size of 138's large living room. Edmund announced Charity and me. He closed the door behind him.

The industrialist sat behind a solid antique desk holding four telephones and a golden double swan-quill-pen inkwell. Period. The rest of the desk was a single gleaming mahogany expanse. He wore a white suit with a blue handkerchief in the breast pocket. His large hands and face were suntanned. His graying hair was styled short. His eyes were bright blue and shrewd. I sensed the power in him.

He got up and came around the desk. He had big shoulders. He gripped Charity's hand in both his. "So kind of you to come." He shook my hand. His grip was firm and dry.

"Please sit on the couch." We eased down onto an antique of curving maple and blue brocade. He drew up a chair to face us. His shrewd eyes sized us up.

"Your clothes send me a message, Ms. Day," he said.

"Trishie said you were clothes conscious." Charity looked him dead in the eye. "What message am I sending?"

"You're not in awe of Duke Widemann," he said.

"Should I be?"

He smiled. "This is social, not business."

"Trishie was worried about my cutoffs."

"Trishie worries a lot about nothing. She has to be managed. She needs some of your I-don't-give-a-damn-ness, Ms. Day."

"I learned that through experience. If you'll pardon me, Mr. Widemann, I don't think she's had any."

"Trishie said you wanted to chat, Mr. Widemann," I said. "About what?"

The industrialist leaned forward, put white elbows on white knees. "Investments," he said.

I frowned. "That sounds like business."

"Investments I've made in a certain young man. Investments I expect to profit from in the future—as I do with all my investments."

It took me a brief moment to catch on. "You're talking about your son-in-law-to-be, Vasily Brunov."

Duke's eyes narrowed slightly. "You're one *fast* fellow, Mr. Nevsky. Yes, I've invested in Vasily. I like his style. I like his independence. I admired the way he didn't turn to his family's amusement park resources and take the easy way through life. I like his taking risks by going into debt to build valuable real estate properties."

"Those three apartment houses." I named them.

"He used to be a one-third partner in Condaco, Inc.," Charity added. "Now he *is* Condaco."

"Damn! How do you two know all that?"

"I'm an attorney. I know how to ask around."

"I'm just nosy."

Duke sat back. Whatever he had expected us to be, we weren't. About twenty seconds passed before he leaned forward again. "Vasily came to my attention three, four years back. He won an election he wasn't supposed to. I imagine you two know about that, too."

We nodded.

"I invited him out here to the Poplars for dinner. As I said, I was impressed enough to begin investing in him. I became his adviser, you might say. I became his mentor. Better than that, I opened political and legal-practice doors for him. From time to time we sit down for little chats. He airs his problems and I give advice or try to help him out. One of his recent problems was the unexpected death of a woman named Felicia Semanova. But his stickiest problem these days seems to be you two."

"Oh?"

Duke nodded. "Seems you got wedged into the middle of some old business that's pretty much wound down. Now, Nevsky, Ms. Day, I like a man who's willing to take a risk to get himself out of a tight spot. No risk, no gain. Right? Now awhile back Vasily found himself a bit strapped in the cash flow department. He didn't come asking for favors—from his father, who's doing just fine in coin of the realm, or from me. He decided to take a big risk. An older man might've found a safer risk, of course. But Vasily picked his own risk and took it."

A few pieces slid together. "He needed the money because his three chichi apartments didn't fill up as fast as he figured. He couldn't make payments on his loans," I said.

Duke's head cocked stiffly and the muscles under his tanned skin shifted his expression. I couldn't read it. "Possibly," he said.

"What risk did he take?" Charity said.

"Why embarrass him all the more by talking about it?" Duke said.

"Let me guess, then," I said. "I'll guess he found some people who had set up a system to smuggle art into this part of the country. The system worked. Vasily talked them into trying to bring a little something extra as a test—a little bag of cocaine. *That* went so well I'll guess he brought in a *big* bag—"

"You don't want to spread that kind of dangerous nonsense around, Nevsky. Not *at all*. If you were to noise that trash about, there'd be no way we could reach an agreement."

"Agreement? About what. What's to agree with?" Charity's arms were folded.

Duke's unreadable expression shifted to a tight smile. "Let's take a look at things from my perspective. I've found myself a bright, up-and-coming young attorney with a very good reputation and a knack for getting votes. He knows how to handle himself. He's ambitious. By working hard he's managed to be identified with the right kind of political currents running in this country today. He's the man I and my colleagues want to see in Harrisburg. The man who'll fight for our interests through legislation and any other way he can. Now, he won't take financial help. But when he marries Patricia all that'll change. He won't have to take any more silly risks. Just so you know: Trishie's mother set her up with a generous, comprehensive portfolio."

"We can't all be lucky," Charity said.

"After the wedding, look at what we've got," Duke went on. "A solid man with old, solid money behind him. A man who can charm in person or on TV. You've talked to him. You know what I mean. You even scuffled with him, Nevsky, and came out friends."

"I admit that, but—"

"Then you see! You see what an unusual man he is. You see how much is at stake." He reached out and touched my knee with his index finger. "Too much to be muddied up by some crazy talk you maybe heard from a dead two-bit tramp and her buddies."

"Felicia Semanova was an old, dear friend from a good family." Charity's voice was cold. "I think, deep down, she was made of better stuff than your Vasily. Or if you meant Ruthie—"

"I don't want to debate those unessential points." Duke's face reassumed its flexed, unreadable expression. "What I do want is to be assured that my investment in Vasily's image isn't in danger."

"If it is, it was Vasily who put it there, not us," I said.

"A man shouldn't suffer a lifetime of penalty for one foolish act. Not a man with a future like his."

I stood up and paced over the thick carpet. I didn't want to be close to Duke Widemann when I said: "I think you made a bad investment. You thought you were buying Exxon and it turned out to be Wild-Eyed Speculative Uranium Mines."

"What's that mean?"

"You made a mistake," Charity said. "Vasily's not a nice person. He beats women."

"So?" Duke glared at Charity. "Some of you *need* beating. Some of you like it."

"Oh, that's *rotten*, Mr. Widemann. That's not worthy of you."

"You've been hearing from the kind of women who don't understand high spirits in a man. The kind who think every whack comes out of anger—instead of desire."

"What're you going to say when your daughter turns black and blue? 'High spirits' going to be OK then? *Huh?*" Charity was nearly snarling.

Duke Widemann looked baffled—and angry. "What kind of crazy people are you two? To come here and try to get under my skin? You, Mrs. Day. You're *nothing*, just another unlucky woman trying to push your way into the man's profession of law. You, Nevsky, you don't even have a *job*. Neither of you has any power, any money. How can you stand here in *my* house and be so... *difficult?* You have everything to lose and nothing to gain."

I swallowed my anger. Charity's cheeks showed her red rage spots. "You invited us out here," she said. "If you wanted a weak woman patsy to push around, you should've ordered one. If you want to get mad at somebody, get mad at Vasily." She stared into Duke's blue eyes. "Because I'll tell you something, Mr. Widemann. Vasily Brunov's way past slap-on-the-hand bad-boy misbehavior!"

"What do you mean?"

I chimed in. "Felicia Semanova wasn't the only person to die who was mixed up in smuggling cocaine—or got caught where it was dangerous to be. I count five more right now. And another really strong maybe."

"What are you saying!"

"That people are getting killed and maybe Vasily's killing them."

"Watch your mouth!" Duke's tan lightened as blood left his face.

Charity headed for the door. Staying around for more insults seemed a bad idea to me, too. I moved to follow her.

"Wait! You can't believe that Vasily..."

"We do 'believe that Vasily...'" Charity said. "We don't know *why* exactly, but..."

"Don't leave quite yet. Please." He smiled and held out a hand to her. Hesitantly she took it. He led her back to the couch. "I believe you two are wrong. Very wrong. I have great faith in my powers to discriminate, in my knowledge of what makes a man tick."

"We all have opinions," I said.

"Nevsky, you know anything about poker?"

"Something."

He nodded. "When you play poker with no limit, there comes a time in the game when bets get bigger. Winners want to be big winners. Losers want to cut their losses. The bets rise, and so does the ante. I've bet heavily on Vasily." He fixed his blue eyes on me. "And it's late in the game. We're playing out a big hand. To stretch the metaphor a bit more, Nevsky, you two are pushing hard with a handful of wild cards. I want you out of the game. I want you to throw in your hand."

"I see."

"How much will it cost me? No, let me rephrase that."

He looked at Charity. "I can read a woman's face as well as a man's. I see you are both people of...principle."

"Sticklers," Charity said.

"Exactly. Offering you money is useless. But what I would like to offer you are...jobs."

"Jobs?"

"Pick any one of my companies, one of their divisions, Mrs. Day. I'll guarantee there're slots for bright women attorneys like yourself. Ones that have real challenge and pay well. After you pick one, you're on your own. Stand or fall. I won't interfere. You'll never hear from me again. You, Nevsky. You have the look of a man who knows people. You can be an executive. I'll slide you in so high you'll spend your days at meetings or making decisions." His eyes bored into mine. "And neither Vasily—nor anyone else—will ever hear about his indiscretion from either of you."

"I couldn't do that. It's the cheap way out for Vasily," Charity said. "I'm an old-style person. I think folks should own up to what they do."

"Ditto," I said.

"*Would* money do it?"

"No."

"No."

"Not even say...six figures? You have responsibilities. There'll be retirement."

We stood silent.

"No tax to worry about. All at once if you want it that way. Into a Swiss account..."

We told him we weren't interested.

"You're not right about Vasily, Mrs. Day, Nevsky. I swear it. All I'm doing by offering to make you rich is covering a distant long shot. You might say I want to stop someone from drawing the king and queen of spades—you two—to fill an inside royal straight flush that beats Vasily. It wouldn't happen anyway. But I want to make *absolutely sure.*"

Charity looked him full in the face. Her voice was firm. "The queen of spades stays in the game," she said.

He jerked his head impatiently. "Vasily's not a killer. Are you a crazy enough lady to be looking for wild vengeance for Felicia Semanova's death?"

"Our neighbor died, too. Our friend Ruthie Spires is

dead." Charity pointed to the bandage nestling in my hair. "And he was almost a vegetable. You probably know a bomb went off in Ruthie's car. I don't think people should go around killing other people."

Widemann growled. "You're not the law. You're not the bringers of justice. What do you two *really* want, woman?"

"In the long run? Who knows?"

"You want a philosophical summary?" I said.

"I think I have more of a philosophy than either of you," Widemann said. "Relax and I'll tell you about it."

I sank down on the couch beside Charity. "Vasily Brunov will be heard from," Duke said. "He'll be a rep from Allegheny County. He'll ride the political tide like a surfer. He'll go to Harrisburg and he'll vote right. But that won't be the end of it, you two. He'll come back home and run for Congress next time. And he'll win, because we'll *back* him. He'll become a *force* in Washington. And all the time he'll keep the interests of western Pennsylvania, the tri-state area, right up in front the whole time. He will *serve the people,* all of us. He'll be one of the ones who brings muscle to what God knows has been a flabby Congress for so many years. *I know it.* In my heart I'm asking you to see it, too. I'm asking you to see my philosophy—working for the good of the people of western Pennsylvania." He was in his chair again, white knees on white elbows. *"Do you share my philosophy?"*

"No," we chorused. I didn't doubt his sincerity, his principles. It was Vasily I doubted.

He sprang up vexed. "Then you've got to sit down and talk all this through with Vasily."

"We were going to have lunch—the three of us. We were going to talk about art and cocaine. The bomb went off the night before our date," I said.

"You ought to watch your mouth, Nevsky. Just out of common sense. Saying nasty things you can't prove is libel." He rose. Our "chat" was nearly over. "Will you talk to him today?"

"I'm still a little shaky. I just got out of the hospital. Have him get in touch with us tomorrow."

He saw us out. His face carried that unreadable expression. Trishie was waiting. She led us to the Rolls.

We were soon on our way. We rode in silence. After a while I noticed she was staring at Charity.

"Is my nose running?" my housemate said.

Trishie blushed and raised a nail-nibbled hand to her cheek. "You...stood up to him." Awe dripped from every word.

"I guess I did. We both did," Charity said. "How'd you know?"

"So rarely I see that *look* on his face. When a real big deal falls through or some other way he doesn't get what he wants. What was it about?"

"Never mind."

She studied Charity. Drab Trishie, attractive Charity. "I envy you," she blurted.

"For saying no?"

She nodded. "I want to say no a lot, but I *can't*. He's my *father*."

"And pretty soon Vasily Brunov will be your husband," I said. "Then *he'll* tell you what to do."

"Yes," she said almost eagerly.

"You oughta do something about that," I said.

"Oh...oh, I...*couldn't*. What I'd like to do is...be Mrs. Day."

I couldn't believe it. She wasn't smiling, not even a twitch of grin. She was *serious*. The billionaire's daughter. Be Charity...

"You say what you want. You do what you want," Trishie said.

"So could you. You have everything going for you," Charity said. She shifted in the seat to get a better look at Trishie's face. "I don't have to tell you how much you have."

"I'm not very brave."

"Just the same..."

Trishie's face wrinkled, the misery muscles lunging out of hiding. "So much has been done for me, I can't do for myself."

As we stared over at her she dissolved into tears. Instead of sympathy I felt a jolt of anger. Couldn't she get hold of her life? Couldn't she stand up for herself?

"Trishie Widemann, you are a *wimp*," Charity said.

"I—I *know*." She bawled louder.

"Oh, Christ!" I thumped the window between us and

the driver. "Drive faster!" I shouted. "I want to get home."

While Trishie wept on in her seizure of self-pity, I gathered my rattled nerves and looked out the window. The confrontation with Duke Widemann had been a strain. Before it had come a worse one: the second—or was it the first?—Sarmatian Demon! What did it mean? How did it fit in?

I saw that the duplicate was somehow the main strand of the Demon's spider web. The murders lay strung along it like the drained carcasses of victim insects. The strand of Duke's encrusted bronze was something else. It closed the perimeter of the problem. Now I sensed I knew all the major facts. The final answers would be found in connecting them all.

I asked myself if that was my job. Officially it was Schlomo Stein's. Unofficially Charity and I had both willingly and unwillingly richly invested time, money, health and emotions in the mystery. Judy Larkin's ugly death had ended any chance I might have had of backing out of my housemate's search for revenge for her old friend's murder.

I had made a full commitment.

We were driving by the edge of Shadyside. Charity asked the driver to swing by 'sPots. She wanted to pick Tod up. At 'sPots Twiggy said Tod left long ago for 138. About then I lost my taste for home. Let Charity and her lover have the run of the house. I didn't want to sit and watch them swap steaming glances. I got out.

I sent them on their way. My last look at the air-conditioned Rolls featured Trishie's doughy face pressed against the closed side window, a sad little girl looking out on the long rainy afternoon of her life.

The door to 'sPots yawned invitingly. I stuck my head in. Nobody was in the display area. "Anybody here? Twiggy, where'd you go?"

There was a small alcove made of shelving and filing cabinets. Twiggy's head popped up from within. "Oh, Mr. Nevsky. I thought you went off with Mrs. Day."

I saw that her wide, usually ruddy face was pale. Her cheeks were silvered with the smears of newly brushed away tears. I walked around behind the filing cabinets. Ledgers and account books were spread out

under a gooseneck lamp. A six-inch pile of opened envelopes lay under a ceramic paperweight. "You OK?"
I said.

"No—yes, I mean...oh, *shit*..."

"Twiggy, what's wrong?"

"*Every*thing."

That this solid young lady could be rattled seemed
unlikely. "Sounds like a job for tea and sympathy," I
said. "Where's the hot plate?"

"On the shelf there. Hey, I should be doing for *you*.
You're the one who was in the hospital."

"I'm on the mend. A cup of tea will taste good. I need
a chance to sit down. I've had a tough afternoon."

Twiggy had a look at my large economy-size Band-
Aid. "You're not bleeding or anything. Tod told me you're
lucky to be alive."

I drew a deep breath. "Yeah." I looked at her over
the top of the tea bag canister. "You know, Twiggy,
whoever put that bomb in Ruthie's car did do it at the
party for Tod."

"That's what you said before."

I added the stuff about the smart bomb. "No doubt
at all: Charity, I—and maybe Ruthie—were the targets.
I know you don't drink or do dope, Twiggy. You were
probably the only person at the party who was totally
in command, you might say. I asked you before...but
this time think real hard, try to remember. You see
anybody fooling with the cars?"

"You know I did go out on the back porch to get some
air. I heard a noise out by the garage"—I saw the faint-
est shift of expression, the gate going down—"and I
shouted. 'You better get away from there!' Then I didn't
hear anything else. And I went back in."

"You're *sure?*" I said.

She nodded.

"I don't think you're telling the truth, Twiggy Twill."
I tried a jolly smile.

"Well, I *am.*"

"I have a friend who's a captain in the Allegheny
Inter-County Police—AICP—who's accused me of obstructing justice."

Twiggy's blue eyes grew very large. "Obstructing..."

"When he thought I wasn't being honest with him

211

he said that. And we weren't talking about anything nearly as important as *two* murders. If you know anything and aren't saying, you're obstructing justice. And that's a crime."

"You're not police, Mr. Nevsky."

"No. And call me Yuri. I'm just saying if you know something important, you could tell me and I could speak to Captain Schlomo Stein—"

"Captain Schlomo Stein—"

"I'm sure he'd make sure you stayed out of trouble." Right then I wished Twiggy were a wimp like Trishie. But she was made of sterner stuff.

"Well, I *don't* know anything interesting about people putting bombs in cars," she said.

And that was that. The idea niggled that she knew something....

She blew on her mug of tea. "Tod's been spending time with your housemate, Mrs. Day."

I nodded. "Quite a bit of time. All of a sudden they're hot and heavy."

"You like the idea?"

"Charity's a grownup. She does what she wants."

She leaned forward, suddenly intent. "What kind of person is she? I mean for Tod?"

I told her something of Charity. That she was an attorney, widowed, a complex personality. Twiggy's wandering eyes told me that wasn't what she wanted to hear. "I mean—is she *good* for Tod?"

"They seem to enjoy each other."

"After Selina he needs someone good. And she seems to make him happy."

"I'm glad."

"Because I'm here so much now, I sort of know when he comes and goes. And sometimes where." She looked sharply at me. "He's spent the night with her."

"Yep."

Her frown was deep as a scowl. "She's not—you know...fooling around with his emotions, is she? I mean he's a real great guy. An artist. He's different. His wife and life have been tough on him. He needs somebody to be good to him, for once."

"If anybody knows how to be good to somebody, it's Charity."

"Like I said, Tod seemed happy—until this morning."

I put down my cup. "So what happened this morning?"

Twiggy waved at the open ledgers. "It's a long story, all in numbers. You know anything about bookkeeping?"

"Something."

She shoved a ledger toward me. "Take a look then." She talked on as I studied debits and credits. "I suppose you know 'sPots has never done all that well as a business."

"So I gathered."

"One reason it's stayed open was because Selina didn't get a salary. And I had a little money put away, so I could miss paychecks. At least up to about now. Squirrely Gowell has another job. So I figured each of us was trying to pull Tod through hard times. There was always some way most of the bills got paid." Twiggy got the tea pot and refilled our cups. "When Selina died, somebody had to take care of the books. I volunteered. Tod's an idiot about numbers. I looked in all the books since the place opened. One thing was plain right away."

"What?"

"'sPots was never a going concern. I mean as far as sales went."

I was puzzled. "How'd you keep the door open, then?"

"There were savings books in with the accounts. The first six months after 'sPots opened it lived off the rest of Selina's insurance settlement. There was a little flurry of sales after that. Some rich lady in Squirrel Hill got into one of our imported lines. That didn't last long. And pretty soon the place was easing down to bankruptcy. That was about two years ago. 'sPots was really in the red in early April. Looked like somebody had hemorrhaged on the books. But then that changed."

"How could it if business was bad?"

"Selina started making deposits of a few hundred bucks every other week all through the summer and the first half of the fall."

"I see." Her share of the art smuggling money! She kept the store afloat. She paid for that in resentment. I remembered her angry words to Tod after her long, wild biker revelry. She ran around—even as she helped—because Tod loved the store more than her.

"Six months of sliding into the red. Then six months of deposits used to pay 'sPots's bills. It started up again this year, too. The last deposit was different. It was bigger. Coupla thousand. That was about two months ago." She looked baffled. "I can't imagine where she got the money."

I knew. The big one was the first trial cocaine run. "Did Tod know about the deposits?"

Twiggy shook her head. Her wide, handsome face shaded with sadness. "Since then there haven't been any more deposits." She walked to the desk and snatched up the stack of envelopes in her big hands. "These are all unpaid bills. I added them up. And I added in the debts on the books. Yuri, 'sPots owes more than *eight thousand* dollars! I talked to Tod this morning about it. I told him he was worse than broke. And while we stood talking about it the mailman came. He brought a letter from the rental agency. It was an eviction notice. Nobody paid the rent in *three months*." She threw down the bills. "'sPots is *bankrupt*."

"My God. How's Tod taking it?"

"He ran out of here this morning after we got the eviction notice. He drove off in the truck. He said he was going to your place. I haven't seen him since." She sank down in a chair. "I'm worried sick. 'sPots is everything to him. In a way it's *my* whole life, too. I'm afraid he'll do something crazy to try and save it. Something *real* crazy. And ruin all of us."

Chapter Sixteen

I got out of the store fast. I turned down toward the Casbah Lounge where there was a cab stand. I began by walking quickly. Half a block later I was in a loping run. My legs felt good. I was stronger, more fit than I realized. I scrambled into a Checker and told the driver where 138 was. "You go fast, I pay the tickets," I said. "Get me there in ten minutes."

He cranked the cab up and lowered his meter flag. "So your wife's playing around while the pot roast cooks," he drawled. "Be *cool,* man. It's happenin' all *acrost* the City of Pittsburgh."

"*Go!* . . ."

On that wild ride, pitching around the back seat, I kept telling myself that I was unreasonably suspicious, probably vindictive, certainly unfair and very likely dead wrong. Just the same, suspicion was more than merely nibbling when I rushed in a side entrance to 138. "Charity! Tod!" I shouted. "You here?"

Silence.

I hurried out to the kitchen. It was empty. The door to the basement was open. Hair stood on the back of my neck. They were here. I had seen Charity's car and Tod's 'sPots truck in the driveway by the garage. I called out again.

I started down the stairs to the basement. I should have taken time to grab some kind of weapon. Too late now. I reached the cement floor and peered around the corner.

The White Chamber door was ajar! Fluorescent fixtures within cast the only light in the wide, dim cellar. I squinted and scanned the deep shadows. My eyes passed over screens, furniture, the dead Gas King Supreme.

I saw the bronze. It had been moved over beside the door leading to the hatchway. Its metal and semiprecious stones shone dully in the weak white light. It looked like an idol overseeing an ancient crypt.

I moved out into the center of the main cellar area. I was up on the balls of my feet, like a boxer, ready to go any direction. The damn shadows! I had just started back to the light switch when I caught a glimpse of fabric behind a dusty armchair—and a figure to give it shape. Charity! I leaped toward her sprawled, motionless figure. My surge of misguided concern short-circuited all my trained caution.

That's when Tod came running at me with the shovel.

He had been in the White Chamber, pressed flat against one of the near inner walls. He swung the shovel with the blade parallel to the floor. The low ceiling kept him from a good overhead shot to my head—so it saved my life. The heavy metal edge slammed into my left side and did damage. Some wind went out of me. Blooming stars, I was staggered. I shook it off and lunged toward him. I got inside the arc of the shovel blade before I stumbled. I wrapped my arms around his thighs and pulled him back. I sucked in air as he cursed me.

He got a knee loose and gave it to me right in the face. My large nose caught part of his knee cap. I heard the tissue creak and give. My eyes poured water. The searing pain juiced my nerves like electric current. My body told me it was working at about eighty per cent of full strength. I hoped that would be good enough.

He grunted with the effort of swinging the shovel. The blade slammed my back like a dull axe. Missed my spine by inches. I scrambled to my feet and retreated. My head was clearing and my wind coming back.

He stalked me. His eyes blazed above his bushy beard. He breathed in short explosive gasps. He had the shovel cocked like a ball bat, hands together on the handle.

I kept my eyes on the blade. He feinted, shifted, feinted again. I reacted and realized he had done me a favor. Showed me that my reflexes weren't as sharp as usual. Thank the bomb blast. My head was improved but not back to normal yet. That told me a lot about what I couldn't get away with during the next minutes.

The shovel blade came to me again, *whummming* the air on the way to my neck. I jumped back, then closed with the burly potter before he could swing back to recock his arms. A surge of rage told me it was about time I dished something out. I chopped at his throat with the meat of my palm. I went for his eyes with fingers curved into hooks. He dropped the shovel and got his arms up to knock my hands away.

He waded at me swinging his heavy arms with explosive grunts. His thick fists thudded into my sides and belly. I smelled his sweat in the cool basement air. His energy and strength seemed boundless. I knew their roots lay in his desire to save 'sPots. The money he got for selling the bronze would bail him out forever.

In the face of his charge I retreated, chin tucked down, hands up. My forearms collected wild punches. More than a dozen left them numb and heavy. In time his breath came in racing gasps. Adrenaline had pumped him along. Now it was fading and he had to do his best on stamina. I continued my circling retreat. He kept lunging forward, swinging and kicking at me. The sound of our shoes scraping on the concrete and our panting grunts echoed in the stillness.

I waited for the moment he lowered his arms just a bit, the moment he slackened his repeated rushes. The desperate violence in him hadn't yet been spent. Violence without pace and plan.

He launched another flurry of wild punches. He hurt me, covered up or not. I saw stars and the whistling started again in my head. When I weaved and bobbed away, I glimpsed the Sarmatian Demon glowing and glinting in the distant dim white light. It stared impassively at us, a metal mammon reigning over its disciples. And so we did practice the dark art of greed—and hurting.

In time Tod's breathing told me what his hands didn't—that his reserves were waning. I straightened up and jabbed stiffened fingers into his stomach. The air whooshed out of him and sweat sprayed from his face onto mine. His mouth yawned in the dense bush of his beard. He bent over gasping. I got my hands locked together. I swung up from the deck and hit him flush on his tangly jaw. He straightened up, tottered, turned half way around like a square dancer. He took three shaky steps toward the Sarmatian Demon and went down. That surprised me. He had seemed a lot tougher to put down than that. I knew something was wrong with him.

I bent over, panting and dizzy. The lights went on! A surge of panic made me start awkwardly. I looked toward the switch.

Charity stood with her hand still on the toggle. She had regained consciousness and crawled over. Blood matted her hair and ran down onto the center of her forehead. A half dozen thin scarlet trickles branched like river delta channels across her brow.

Her face was contorted, as ugly at that moment as the Sarmatian Demon's.

"You OK?" I panted, hands on knees.

She didn't answer. She walked toward sprawled Tod. He stirred, began to sit up. Her shriek drilled my ears. She flew at him. For an instant I thought she was going to offer comfort. Instead she kicked him in the ribs with all her strength. "You bastard!" she howled. She kicked him again. Not hurting him enough, she swept over and scooped up the shovel. Her white fingers curled around the hickory shaft. "I didn't mean a thing to you! That *thing* was what you wanted!" She glanced at the leering bronze by the hatchway door.

With the shovel she hit Tod a glancing head blow. He groaned and tried again to sit up. Impatient with her awkwardness, she flung down the tool. Before the blade ended its concrete clatter she was on her knees beside him. She howled in hurt and rage and began to claw his face.

"Charity!" I shouted.

She paid no attention. She was trying to tear his eyes out. He waved his arms weakly trying to defend himself. She was screaming and weeping hysterically. Her nails dripped blood.

"Charity!"

She kept up her work. Clumsy with exhaustion, I grabbed her shoulder and dragged her off. I was dizzy and weak. My goddamned head! She lashed at me, stinging slaps to my neck and face. "Let me kill him! Let me *blind* him!"

"You can't—"

"You stay out of it!" she screamed. Her spit hit my face. Her features were a bloody, contorted mask. She lashed at my eyes. In her hysteria and my weakness, she seemed all muscle, like a cat. I wrapped my arms around her, pinning her forearms. She twisted and lunged. "Let me *go!* Let me kill him! I'll kill *you.* Yuri, I *will.*"

While we struggled, balanced between her hysteria's wild strength and my weight, Tod stirred again and sat up. He rose to one knee. His face leaked blood from the scratches around his eyes. He stared at us like a man hypnotized. His mouth opened slowly. "'sPots..." he said. A sudden convulsion shook his body. His hands flew to his chest. His chin jerked against his collarbone in the grinding vice of what seemed a heart attack. From his throat came a low, tense whine of agony.

Charity clawed at my face. When I protected my eyes, she broke away and again kicked Tod in the ribs. "Die, you horrid bastard!" she shouted. "You *used* me..."

I lunged across the concrete, ready to deck her if I had to. She was arched above him, back curved like a working bow. Abruptly the tension leaked out of her. Her shoulders fell and her weeping sank from the shrill heights of hysteria to the steady heaves of an aching soul.

I rested my hands on her shoulders. She spun and knocked them away. Her face was blood and tears. "I am just so stupid!" she spat. She urged me away. "Go call the ambulance. He's having some kind of seizure." I hesitated. "Go ahead! I'm all right. I won't hurt him. Even though I *should* kill him...."

When I came back down to the basement I froze. Tod lay moaning alone on the cold concrete. Charity stood about six feet from the Sarmatian Demon. She squarely faced the savage bronze face. She was speaking softly to it.

"...it's you behind all this death and misery, isn't it? Behind my blood and my tears. Behind Tod's lies of love. Behind the murders and the shooting and the bomb..."

"Charity..." I moved across the basement floor toward her.

"...you—or what you stand for—take lives and souls, too. You're the evil, dark side of all our hearts..." She took two steps toward the demon. "Who can resist you? Saints? Aesthetes? The deaf, mute and blind?" She stepped within range of that deadly cocked hammer. Raised against the human race two thousand years ago, that blow had surely never seemed more ready to fall and crush a soul than it did at this moment. And few souls had been more primed to accept the blow and its deliverer than Charity Day at this single moment of one of the darker days of her life.

She raised both hands, fingers spread, toward the snarling bronze head. She leaned forward from the waist like a high school freshman ready to bestow her first goodnight kiss....

I got to her—fast—when her lips were inches from the tangle-toothed pit of the mouth. I wrestled her to the floor. We lay tangled up at the statue's feet, spent and spiritless. She wept on, wrapped in my arms. Never, though, had we seemed more distant.

In a wailing rush the ambulance arrived. They found only Tod, Charity and I. The bronze was back in the White Chamber. Of course I had used gloves. One of the two medics glanced at the gory delta smearing Charity's forehead. "You need to come with us, too?" Her short headshake freed him to plunge back into the legitimate medical emergency of Tod's heart attack. The two knew what they were doing. He exited, stretchered but alive, in a wash of sirens and blue flashes.

Charity plodded upstairs. She said she didn't want me around. Her face was drawn, aged. Before she went to her bedroom I insisted on cleaning and checking out her head wound. In a heavy voice she told me what had happened.

Tod had been waiting for her. He had brought up the subject of the Sarmatian Demon and tried to jolly her into telling him where in the house it was. He came on casually and she nearly told him. She would have if he hadn't been nervous and harried behind his apparent indifference. I understood why. Added to the pressure of possibly losing his store was the problem of an essentially straight guy being forced into a dishonest game. The potter had no habits of familiar callousness and deceit to oil his way. So Charity smelled his play in that stranger's game.

After her first refusals, he got desperate. He hit her with the shovel to force her to tell him how to open the White Chamber. While wrestling the statue toward the hatchway he admitted to making the phone call I overheard that threatened her. But he hadn't shot at her or Maced me. While knocking her down again, he denied the horror of the car bomb. He knew she wouldn't go to the police over the statue because that would mean trouble for me. He just wanted the bronze to save his store. He didn't want to hurt anybody. Just the same he had to knock her out....

Charity let me walk her to her bedroom. I saw tension set in her shoulders. Her every year was molded into the weary mask of her face. I knew she'd never sleep. I knew she'd gnaw the bones of betrayal and heartbreak like a starving dog. I rummaged through her medicine cabinet and found the old childproof bottle of what she called "Dr. Bender's Mind Menders." The prescription dated from the early days of her widowhood. It was Dr. Bender's special concoction, a chemical answer to anguish. Charity had weaned herself away from them. But this afternoon I figured a little backsliding was in order. She gulped two down with half a glass of water. "Thanks." She looked at me with heavy, cold eyes. "Leave now. Don't come back up here. I'll come down when I'm ready."

I cleaned up the basement and took a shower. The bruises and scrapes of my struggle with Tod were making themselves felt. My nose was swollen; no air passed through my nostrils. I had badly overdone it and so was probably in some danger. I closed up the shop of activities. I sat in the sun for the rest of the afternoon, pondering the pieces Tod had fitted into the puzzle. Near as I could tell, they didn't fill in all that much. Tod's 'sPots truck sat in the driveway, its rear bay doors yawning, waiting for the Sarmatian Demon that would never come. Those doors reminded me of the big unanswered questions still surrounding the hideous bronze.

That evening I was playing the piano when a visitor arrived. Schlomo Stein. The captain wore his Homburg and a three-piece suit. He carried a violin case. He looked like a concertmaster on his way to a symphony orchestra date. "I've engaged a consultant to help me deal with you, Nevsky." He gave me his Homburg and went into the living room. "I often use the same consultant in difficult cases."

"Oh?"

He put down the violin case and opened it. It held a gleaming instrument. Its honey-colored wood shown in the light of a floor lamp. "Meet my consultant," he said. "The only lady detective we have. I find she stimulates thinking, as do most beautiful shes. My thinking, of course. And often that of others who hear her persuasive arguments." He looked around. "Your housemate, Mrs. Day, is...?"

"Upstairs. Asleep. She's a little under the weather."

He nodded. "I had hoped to play for her, too. To stimulate *her* thinking as well."

"She may be down. Don't know."

He began to tune his instrument. "Nevsky, do you know Bach's three violin partitas?"

"What brings you here, Captain Stein?"

"You didn't answer my question."

"I like him, but I can't play him. Left hand too busy for this amateur pianist."

Schlomo's eyes brightened. "Ah, you *play,* Nevsky. We'll have to think of a duet. I suspected you were a man of some talent. I'm so sorry you find Bach difficult. Through long practice I've been able to make a good try at the first partita, G minor." His voice was softer with the violin in his hands. What little tough-cop argot he used was gone. "I'll play and you think."

"About what, Captain Stein?"

He looked at me down the neck of the violin. "About your borough police chief's cooperation. How he didn't forget the little chat I had with him. I asked him to kind of keep an eye on what happened around this big old house—"

"Police surveillance, you mean?"

Stein rosined his bow. "Nevsky, you know Marland Borough has only a handful of officers. No way they could spare one for surveillance. I just asked him to let me know if anything at all unusual happened at this address. You forgot to mention you were shot at a while ago. I didn't notice when I was here. The bomb had blown your kitchen windows completely out."

"But nothing's happened since," I said.

He raised graying eyebrows. "Ambulance call early this afternoon. Routine notification of the police. Followed by notification of me. So I see you as having *plenty* to think about, Nevsky. Think about the guy hauled out of here being Tod Buckcry. Now according to what you told me in the hospital, Selina Buckcry was mixed up in coke smuggling. Now her husband pays you a visit."

"He and Charity are lovers. You saw him here after the bomb explosion looking after things while she and I were mending."

"Maybe half true. But I got myself over to the hospital earlier today. I couldn't see the man. He was in intensive cardiac care and the docs said forget talking to him. All I had to work with was the medical data." He looked sharply at me. "He had bruises and lacerations around his eyes, Nevsky. Fresh ones. And your nose is now the large economy size...."

"I don't know anything about his cuts," I said. "Charity and he had a fight and he just keeled over. I walked into a door in the dark."

"Sure. And Charity Day just happens to be 'indisposed,' like Dame Nellie Melba. Listen to me, Nevsky! You're right on the edge of trouble with the law. You *have* things to think about. Things maybe I should know. You think, I'll think. Then we'll compare notes."

"If you say so."

He played. Leave it to a tough Jewish cop to play like an angel. Even in my large living room the instrument sounded loud and commanding. Bach's orderly notes spilled out through screened windows into summer night.

I did do some thinking while he played. I thought how lucky I had been when Tod slammed me in the side with the shovel. That blow, between the ribs instead of across them, had only badly bruised cartilage instead of cracking bones. I ran through a check list of recent and not so recent memories. Poor Judy Larkin, dying before she had ever been thoroughly loved. Felicia Semanova crushed by the rolling boulder of her sinking life. Others recently dead...I edged my way back to Nicholas Markov's mystery and how my search for him had also been a search for myself and my cultural identity. I remembered clearly, then, my days in Washington working for a nameless agency specializing in the most private activities. I strolled the memory stacks of my stint in the Harvard libraries. My memory had come back in full!

The music wove in and around my thoughts. It dipped down in my ragged emotions, my disappointments, the warts on the skin of my life. It led me on an invigorating tour back around to...the Sarmatian Demon. With Tod's role clarified and him eliminated, the puzzle of the bronze for the first time seemed manageable. I was certain now the boundaries around it had been drawn. Charity and I would have to work things out within those limits.

The final note died. I had closed my eyes and took my time opening them. When I did I saw Schlomo's had yet to open. "You play the varnish right off that thing," I said.

"That it sounds good is proof of Bach's genius, not mine." He put the violin and bow on his lap. "Did you find it stimulating to your thinking?"

"In a way. How about to yours? I've heard from Schlomo the violinist. How about Schlomo the cop?"

"You've already heard some of what I think. And I suppose you should be talking instead of me." He shrugged. "So what? Truth is, I can't get anywhere on the bomb, Nevsky. I can't get anywhere on the cocaine smuggling. I can't get anywhere on the sawed steering column—or on the woman smothered with the pillow. Maybe I'm getting old. I *know* Winston Farrow III was murdered, that robbery had nothing to do with it. But I don't know who did it, or why. This case for me is like one of those big knots with all the string ends hanging out. The trick is finding the one to pull that makes the whole thing come apart. I've been asking around, trying to find out what string it is. I think it's that bronze statue people talk about. The consensus is you have it."

"You're wrong, Stein. You searched the place cop-thorough while I was in the hospital. You know Charity and I don't have it."

"Registry of deeds says you own a place out near Murrysville. Maybe you buried it out there, on one of your thirty-six acres. Maybe it's somewhere else. How about telling me where it is?"

I saw then that I needed time. Time to maybe get Charity back on track. Time to talk to Vasily Brunov and figure out how deep he was in it all. Stein had been easy on me all along. He was being easy on me now. No doubt the suave old cop could make things tough. He could harrass Charity and me. He could have us grilled. So it wasn't fair to lie outright to him. But I couldn't level. Judy's death and Charity's friendship with Felicia had committed us to unraveling the De-mon's puzzle ourselves. Revenge, plain and simple.

"I saw it the night the Semanova woman tried to leave it, Captain Stein," I said. "And I saw it again this morning."

"Where?" His sidelong gaze was sharp.

"At the Poplars. Duke Widemann's mansion."

Stein stopped putting away his violin. "*You* were at Duke Widemann's place?"

"That's what I said."

"Doing what?"

"Talking to him about some of his private business. And don't—"

"I *won't* ask. Believe me." He stowed away his bow. "And you saw the bronze statue out there? How'd it get there?"

"Beats me. It was in his 'Russian Room,' first floor."

"That's not the best news I've heard today."

"Why not?"

"Because Duke Widemann is Duke Widemann. He's so big and strong in western Pennsylvania he's just about above the law. With one phone call and three sentences he could ruin—or make—either of us. I stay clear of the Duke Widemanns of this world. No way I'll

225

go out there and bug him about the statue. This old hebe's too smart to try and turn over *that* rock."

"What am I hearing, then, Captain Stein? You giving up on the whole business?"

He turned his eyes to my face. "Give up on five connected murders? Huh—uh!"

"You said the statue was the key. And you said pulling Widemann's chain was a no-no. So what do you have to work on?"

The captain picked up his violin case. "I'll check your story about the statue being out there. On the quiet. To make sure you aren't trying to do a trick on me." He followed me out to get his Homburg. "After I talked to you in the hospital, Nevsky, I thought whatever had been going on had *stopped* going on. That all I had to do was figure out what had happened and who done it. But things *keep on* happening. A minute ago I thought it was the statue that made things happen. Now I'm starting to understand it's something else."

"What?"

"*You,* Nevsky."

"Me."

He nodded. "I warned you in the hospital. I'll warn you again. You're just a little out-of-work guy trying to be Don Quixote. Your windmills are big-time coke dealers and one or two hard-assed murderers. I don't know if Duke Widemann is tangled in all this in some way. If he is, he's the biggest windmill of all." He opened the screen door. "You're gonna get knocked on your ass like the old don! Only hard enough maybe you're *never* going to get up."

He put down his violin case on the front porch and raised a hand to my shoulder. His intense gaze hinted at the wisdom of a long life. "I'm an old cop, Nevsky. I know how these deals work out—where folks try to be their own law. They end up getting killed—and that breaks open the case for the folks with the badges. I'd like there to be an easier way this time through. I don't want you and maybe the classy lady upstairs to cash in so Captain Schlomo Stein can get all the credit. Level with me, Nevsky. I mean *all* the way."

"You know everything I know."

"I'm going to talk to Buckcry when he's out of intensive. Maybe tomorrow. I have a feeling his story and yours won't jibe."

"You do that." That would do it for my lies. But the potter was still a pretty sick man. I had bought some time. When that time was up, this good cop would be my enemy.

"Good-bye, Nevsky. I hope you live for me to see you again."

"Thanks for the concert."

"You practice hard, we'll play a duet."

Chapter Seventeen

The phone rang as Schlomo pulled away from the curb. I answered it and heard the soft voice of Vasily Brunov. We exchanged greetings. He said he had heard about the bomb blast, asked how I was. Said it was all terrible and ugly. He knew we had had our differences, but hell, life and death—that was a different matter. After we went around with that for a while he said, "You remember our lunch date? You, Charity Day and I?"

"Sure."

"I spoke with Mr. Widemann earlier today. He said you're up and around and mending. So I'd like to make good that offer of lunch. Tomorrow, noonish, same trio. Could you come to Willow Grove? My office is in the administration building tower. I'll have a nice meal sent up."

I told him I'd call him back early tomorrow morning. Charity was a little under the weather today....

I didn't do anything about Charity that evening. The next morning early I put a pot of coffee on and waited. I had no idea if she'd come down today, tomorrow, by the weekend... She came down at quarter to ten in slippers. "I'll take it black. No food." Her voice was husky and her eyes red from long weeping. She had done nothing with her hair. Her recent layering-for-summer was an uncombed tangle. There was still some blood caked in the silvery strands near the crown of her head. Smudges lay like burns under her eyes. Every line in her face showed. She adjusted the lapels of her light-blue robe as I set the coffee down in front of her.

There were so many things I could say. I had to pick the right one. Her emotions were a mass of bruises. The wrong line could send her down a long, tear-filled dead end. I needed an ally, not a re-creation of yesterday's beaten creature. "Vasily Brunov called. He wants us both for lunch around noon."

"What'd you tell him?" She looked up from her coffee. I saw behind the pain in her pale eyes a spark of interest.

"I said I'd let him know after I talked to you."

She nodded and looked back down. "If I don't go?"

"I don't go without you. Not on this one."

She ran hands through matted hair. "Yuri, Yuri, I feel so...drained."

"That won't end today. Probably not for a long time. You were kicked crazy."

"I'm numb. I just can't deal with Tod being..."

"Vasily Brunov. Think about him. Focus, Charity, focus."

"If I go...I won't be much good."

"I want you there." I sat across the table from her. I reached toward her wrist, thought better of it. "Christ, Day, I *need* you. After all—*you* started all this."

She nodded. "In a way, I did. Got to finish it, I suppose."

She covered her face with shaking hands. "Oh, I don't know...I don't *know*." She turned her tired eyes toward me. They seemed transparent gates through which I could see her asking the essential question of why she or any of us lived. I knew: we threw our own individual meanings like trivial flotsam into the vast sea of the Void. So I understood when, after several minutes, she said, "What else *is* there? OK, I'll go. I'll need the two hours to get myself together. Don't count on me for much is all..."

The full summer amusement park season was still a few days away. Then the city schools were dismissed and vacation travel began. Just the same, cars were pouring into the parking lot and the ladies with striped coats were guiding them into parking slots sardine close.

I wore a lightweight summer suit. Charity wore a blue dress and white heels. She had used makeup, unusual for her. She nearly looked herself. Her step was a bit listless. Aside from that she looked whole to all but the most experienced Day watcher.

We went in the business entrance. A secretary pointed the way up to Brunov's office. The door was open. The office was circular. Windows reached from the ceiling to waist-high woodwork. Brunov was looking out over the amusement park. His back was to us. He wore a light tan suit and woven straw loafers.

"Trying to pick your favorite ride?" I said.

He turned and smiled at us. He had good teeth and color. He looked ruddy, healthy and trustworthy. "You know, I've never ridden *one* of them." He motioned us up beside him. His handshake was solid. He kissed Charity's hand. I felt vaguely ashamed I had knocked him down during our big boys' brawl. I noticed his nose, like mine, was swollen.

We looked out at Willow Grove. From the tower we could see all the rides. "I've been on them all, man and boy," I said. I pointed. "The Auto Race, the Old Mill, the Swiss Sleigh Ride, the bumper cars, the Log Jam, the loop coaster and all the rest. 'Specially the roller coasters. How could you *not* ride the coasters, Vasily?"

"Pop said they were for the suckers. Said they were a waste of money. I wanted to be like him in those days. Now it's got to be a habit, or maybe a matter of a kind of oddball pride."

"Not even the Hurricane?" I pointed off to the pale plank parabolas of the famous old coaster off in a corner of the park.

He shook his head. "It's all been more Pop's than mine. I've headed in other directions."

"Headed *up,* Duke Widemann said," Charity murmured.

He turned away from the window. His smile had thinned out, but was no less sincere. I sensed he was analyzing, thinking of changing his opinion of us. At Anna Yelanov's and at Felicia's funeral, hostility had been my posture. Now he wanted to know more about me. Charity was a complete unknown. So he got right to it.

"From what Mr. Widemann told me, you two seem to want to make trouble for me."

"We're not *after* you, if that's what you mean," Charity said. "It's just there're some facts—"

"Mr. Widemann felt you *were* after me. He said you were making some real crazy charges. He also said if you two 'ran your mouths on Main Street,' you possibly could cause me some embarrassment."

I smiled. "I think we could."

He shrugged casually. "I really don't think so. That business about you thinking I was mixed up in running a load of cocaine—"

"A couple of loads," Charity said. "First a small one, then a *big* one."

Vasily's eyes narrowed. "I'm feeling outnumbered all of a sudden. So, two loads. What difference? Take just a minute to think, Mrs. Day. If you intend to tell the world about your wild theories, I'd deny them rather convincingly. You must realize there's no evidence whatever. All the people involved in that completely passed business are either dead or have disappeared." He led us away from the windows. "Maybe you're not convinced. Maybe you both still want to talk, say, to newspapers. I've already announced for the state legislature this fall. There'll be some real weight behind me. It wouldn't be hard to make you look like an out-of-work publicity seeker, Nevsky. Maybe Mrs. Day, who I understand is an attorney, could be painted as someone with political ambitions of her own. Or possibly as a gadfly feminist. Both of you paid puppets of my opponent. It's happened before."

"What would your voters think if some angry women got together notorized statements from Anna Yelanov and June Gowell, saying you had beaten them?" Charity said.

"You said you're not after me, Mrs. Day. That sounds rather the opposite."

"I don't like men who beat women." Charity's voice was grave with sincerity and rising emotions. "It's ... poor form. I have a hunch Anna and June aren't the only women you've beaten. I think you *like* beating us."

His tan darkened, but he got back on the track quickly. "Having it advertised that you're not afraid to use your strength to persuade a woman could prove to be a vote *getter*. A backlash against women's lib."

"That's sick!" Charity hissed.

Vasily walked over to the windows and surveyed the amusement park. He spoke with his back to us. "Mrs. Day, we're educated people, the three of us. We know something about the relationship between men and women. Surely we all know that we men, deep in our souls, are afraid of you women. Afraid of your power over the creation of life. Afraid of your immersion in the emotions, your nurturing, your sacrifices, your commitment to the *human* side of life." I expected a tone of sarcasm, but didn't hear it. "So we men devalue those strengths, those powers, those qualities. We call you bitches, witches and sorceresses. We do *all we can* to keep you down. And even though you're also programmed by society to accept our abuse and eat our shit—we're *still* afraid of you." He turned and faced us. "If I got known as a man who had sometimes struck a woman, I'm telling you many men—and many women, too—would vote *for* me on that basis."

"What *kind* of men and women?" I said. "Men with no foreheads, women with the self-images of galley slaves. All-American Kinks Incorporated?"

Vasily raised solid-looking hands. "I suggest we change the subject. Let's all be less...feisty." He walked to us and touched each of our shoulders. "This lunch is my way of asking both of you to understand."

"Understand *what?*" Charity said. Her tone was nasty. I caught the briefest flicker of a far nastier glance across Brunov's eyes.

"That attorneys with bad tempers, who should know better, can do things they later regret." He spread his hands. "I'm going to level with you. You know I was the attorney for Hermitage Decorator Antiques. Also Count Dromsky-Michaux's and Sergei Yelanov's personal attorney. I knew a couple of years back Hermitage was going downhill, but that Sergei was keeping it afloat by selling Russian bronzes at high prices. It took me a while to figure out he was smuggling them in across Lake Erie. As his attorney I advised him against it. He ignored me. *And he kept getting away with it.*

"About six months ago I got into a tight financial

spot. I'd invested heavily to build Condaco's operation. Rentals were down but loans had to be paid. I was getting desperate. I have an unbending policy never to turn to my father for money. One day Sergei and I were talking. I said he ought to smuggle something worthwhile, like cocaine. Before you knew it we had worked out a trial run. I used my uncle's connections in Buffalo. Alexey Semanova passed through Canada north of Buffalo with the hot art shipment on a truck. He picked up the cocaine in a heavy plastic bag. He just passed it over the deck rail of the *Stressless I* along with the art. My apartment manager organized the sale.

"The next trip we all invested very heavily. Special arrangements had to be made—"

"By you?" I said.

"Yes. I want you to understand that all along, that second run was to be it. We were going to make our bundle and call it quits. But things didn't go right."

I swallowed. I felt the tension clamping down on my innards. "So what happened?"

"Tell us who went out on the *Stressless I* that weekend," Charity said.

"The usual—the three of them. Selina, Felicia, Sergei. I waited for them in a motel in Erie. I had to make and receive several phone calls all that weekend to and from Canada, to make sure things happened on schedule. It took an extra day over there, which we had planned on. Then that goddamned storm blew up and I nearly went crazy when they didn't get back to the marina on time. Hours went by. I had turned most of my assets into cash. Every *one* of us was in hock up to here—me; O'Shea, my manager; Sergei. Selina had taken some money out of 'sPots—God knew where she found it. Felicia sank every penny she could raise in it. I was going *nuts!*

"When they finally got back, things weren't all that much better. Canadian narcs had done some snooping. They came out shooting and killed Alexey and nicked Sergei. A furrow across his belly. Nothing serious. The *Stressless I* barely got out of there. I helped them unload a crated antique bronze statue that Sergei had promised to someone. He was carrying the big plastic bag of coke in a duffel bag. There was that much of it.

234

"We tied the crate to the roof rack of my Lincoln. Sergei had the coke duffel bag between his legs. On the ride south to Pittsburgh we decided not to deliver the dope. Trouble from narcs at one end might mean worse trouble at our end. We decided to hold the dope for a week or two, till we could see if a bust was in the wind. We decided Sergei should hold it. We all trusted him. Besides, you can't dispose of a duffel bag of coke without street channels. Through my uncle I controlled those. My manager, O'Shea, controlled the distribution in the apartments. So we felt safe letting Sergei hold the goods."

"How did Felicia behave during all this?" Charity said.

"Your old Radcliffe roommate? Scared shitless. She kept saying she was *through with all this,* over and over. And bawling because her husband, who she couldn't stand, had been killed."

"What happened when you got back to Pittsburgh?" I said. "Where'd you go?"

"To Hermitage. I got out of there fast. So did Sergei. We left the two women and the statue in the store. I never saw either alive again."

"What happened to Sergei?"

"Gone. I tried to reach him the next week. No dice. I have an idea what happened to him though," Brunov said. "Want to hear it?"

"Sure," Charity said.

"I think Pittsburgh's been on the coke pros' list for a while. They heard a little dealing had started up before they were ready to move in big. I think they got to Sergei right after he went off to stash the dope. They scared him real bad. Then they paid him a pittance for the coke and told him to take a long vacation someplace warm."

"Where'd that leave you, though?" I said. "You had a big piece of the dope. You couldn't turn it over for profit. All your assets were tied up. What'd you do?"

"I had to borrow."

I studied his face closely. I was sure some of what he said was lies. "Who'd you borrow from?" I said.

"Mr. Widemann, of course."

Charity said, "What about Count Dromsky-Michaux? He catch on to any of this?"

Vasily shook his thick, groomed mane. "Now he's paying for Sergei's scam. He's holding the proverbial bag. He's a coward, and not too bright on top of it. He was dozing in Hermitage when Selina and Felicia went in with the crated statue. I'm sure he figured it was just another one of his partner's bargain acquisitions arriving at an unusual hour. It had happened often enough before."

From our vantage point by the windows we saw a restaurant delivery truck pull up. "For you two, a catered affair," Brunov said. "Believe it or not, you're both very important people to me."

I frowned. "I don't get that. We're here giving you an inquisition, making nasty accusations. I'd say we're both thorns in your side."

"Not seriously so." He gently held Charity's wrist and led her away from the table set up in the center of the tower room. "I think Mrs. Day the attorney knows why."

"There's no evidence at all," she said. Her flat tone of voice told me she was sure of it.

"Precisely. There are no witnesses to anything that went on that weekend so long as Sergei stays wherever he is. Just the same, I've been honest and told you more than I should have. Because I trust you both." His heavy brows arched questioningly. "And I have an offer to make to you over lunch."

Lunch arrived in the hands of two women owners of an Italian restaurant in McKeesport. The hot food was packed into Styrofoam carriers. They bustled around the table. We stood aside while they laid the linen cloth, silverware and china. They uncovered the spread: chicken broth and egg soup, grilled marinated fish, veal with a Parmesan cheese sauce. Dessert was crispy pastry horns filled with sweet cream. Two bottles of Segesta white wine rounded out the feast.

I had cooked many a meal. I knew good food when it was in front of me. I knew what to do with it, too. Charity only nibbled, so Vasily and I packed most of it away. The sun sang through the fields of glass, the yellow-tinted wine sparkled in the stemware and a breeze through a screened opening stirred the loaned linen cloth. It was a fine lunch.

After the food and wine, Vasily poured us each an icy vodka thick as crankcase oil from his own refrigerator. He apologized to Charity for the meal she didn't seem to like. He was quite gracious, and Charity saw the need to apologize in return. "I *would* like some more vodka," she said. He poured it and for a moment their eyes met over the proper rubble of a decent meal. I thought Charity was too numb to be romanced. Yet Vasily Brunov's winning smile brought a little sun to her solemn face.

I studied the attorney's handsome features. Ruthie had said he had his pick of women. And he had picked that timid wimp, Trishie Widemann. I sensed that if the world were allowed to turn a few times, he could have Charity on any terms he wanted. I knew when I was in a room with a man to whom women were vulnerable. "You said you had an offer for us," I said.

Brunov leaned forward and rested his spread hands against the white table linen. "I want to talk politics for just a moment."

We told him to go ahead.

"You're a bright couple, a very bright couple. I don't have to lecture you on the pendulum in politics and nature. Back and forth it goes. We knew where it was in the fifties, to the right, then it went to the left for twenty years, now it's swinging back again. You're both Pittsburghers. You know what's happened to our city, to the tri-state area, in those twenty years. We've gone sliding down a lot. Not as much as in other parts of the country, but enough to hurt. The country turned a corner with the last national and local elections. A new political power system is 'abuilding. And it's a system I'm betting is going to be in place for the next twenty years. Following me?"

Charity sipped her vodka and nodded. Whatever his message, Brunov was deadly serious.

"Pittsburgh, western Pennsylvania, must have a voice in that new political power system, a voice that's heard. There are too many fine people and great traditions here to be forgotten. The people need first-rate representation." His frank glance moved from my face to

Charity's in turn. "Destiny is pushing me to be that representative. Destiny, Duke Widemann and his associates. They've made me realize my abilities, my aptitude for public life. I've done a lot of thinking, you two. In my mind I've gone to where Duke and his group are. The old style conservatism won't do in this age. We have to get rid of the weary polemics against the Communist phalanx, the abuses of human services and big government. We need to move down to bedrock. From there we need to build up a new way of doing things in this country.

"My job over the next five to eight years is to get into a position where I can do what needs to be done. I'm neither so vain nor so naive as to think I can get to Washington—and stay there—on my own. I'll need help. I'll need a staff. First a campaign staff for the fall election. Then a larger staff in Harrisburg. Finally, Washington." He reached out and covered Charity's hand. "Charity, I want your help. I want you working for me—on my staff. Name your salary. We'll work out the details later." He turned to me. "You, Nevsky, same kind of offer. Hell, man, you're not even *working* now."

I was convinced. I believed he would do the things he said. I also understood Duke Widemann's enthusiasm about his promising soon-to-be son-in-law. There was just one word to describe his overall effect on both of us: *charisma.* From Charity, the woman, there was that leaking out of tender emotion toward him. From Yuri Nevsky came a grudging admiration.

"What do you think of my life plan?"

"It sounds...unselfish," Charity said.

He smiled. "Thank you. And what do you think of your part in it?" He moved around the table. Charity stood up as he came forward.

"W-What do you want from us in exchange?" she asked. He was standing very close to her. "You must know there've been murders connected with your smuggling."

"*Murders?*" He looked convincingly startled. "You mean the bomb in the Spires woman's car?"

"Felicia was murdered, too," Charity said.

He closed his eyes for a long moment. "Who did it?"

"We don't know. And Winston Farrow III was shot to death in the Hill District," I said. "You know that?"

He shook his head. "This is...*dreadful.*"

I didn't tell him about Selina being smothered. That was Captain Schlomo Stein's little secret. "Those people were mixed up in the smuggling. So were you," I said. "So a person couldn't be blamed for thinking you had something to do with the murders."

"And Sergei Yelanov is missing," Charity said. "With the cocaine."

Brunov looked troubled. "It's important you understand *I* didn't murder anyone. Nor do I know what happened to Sergei and the dope. I made some mistakes, but nothing like murder. My mistakes are past. Please believe me." He sat down smiling. "I'm cheered by the improvement in the climate among the three of us. I can use your brains in my future. And in exchange I can *give* you both a future."

"You want us to quit being paddles stirring up all the mud," Charity said.

He shrugged. "Not really. There's really nothing that important I have to hide...."

"So then what do you want to trade?" I said. "Suppose we get on your bandwagon just as it starts rolling. What's the ticket cost us?"

Vasily got up and put both hands lightly on my shoulders. His glance was level and sincere. "I want the bronze statue," he said.

"Why?"

"Because it's the last loose end to my folly. As long as it's out there somewhere it could crop up months or years from now and cause me political embarrassment. I want to destroy it."

"You know it's really not worth very much."

He frowned questioningly.

"It's a copy," Charity said. "There's one just like it at Poplars. Maybe *that* one's a copy, too. We saw it yesterday."

His face *did* pale slightly. "I see. Just the same, I don't want it around." His hand fell lightly on Charity's waist. Gently he drew her closer. "Why keep it, Charity? You said yourself it's not worth much."

"I don't—"

"Don't ruin the frankness, the *promise* among the three of us by dragging out the tired lie that you don't have it."

"We *don't* have it." She looked up into his warm eyes. "But I know where it is."

Right away I got very angry. Charity was a bright woman who usually learned from her mistakes. Telling Tod Buckcry the statue was at 138 had nearly cost her her life. We were *both* carrying the lumps for that folly. Now here she was doing it *again!*

"I have some things to straighten out," Charity said. "Some personal, some emotional. When I get it together I'll tell you where the Sarmatian Demon is."

I bit my teeth. I knew my face was getting red. What was she *doing?*

Brunov nodded impatiently. "When will that be?"

"A day, maybe two."

"No longer, please, Charity. I'm uneasy about it. And I need you both to help me lay political plans."

"I'm not absolutely promising—"

"We have to leave," I said. I slipped a quick scowl in Charity's direction. We offered thanks and exchanged farewells. I was boiling. Brunov insisted on walking us downstairs to the entrance. We said we'd soon be in touch. The sun, the blue sky and his big grin all dizzied my wits. I was bubbling over with sexist what-am-I-doing-working-with-this-broad ravings. I was about to dump them right in Charity's pink ear. She said, "I did that to keep him off balance, Yuri. Because I *know* he's a live one. I *know* he has all the answers and blood all over his hands."

"I *doubt* that. I think he half seduced you. I think if I hadn't been there, you'd have given him the statue and everything else you have—"

"Yuri Nevsky!"

Before we could get into it, a familiar face loomed beyond the business gate. "What're you frowning about, Nevsky?" Captain Schlomo Stein said.

"What're you doing following us around?" I said. "Playing gumshoe instead of police captain?"

He tipped his hat to Charity. He had traded his Homburg for a summer straw. "Now and then I do."

"Discover anything interesting?" she said.

240

"Not a thing, young lady."

"I don't like being spied on." Charity's made-up face was plundered by the merciless sunlight.

Schlomo decided to change his approach. He pointed toward the park entrance. "Let's go in. This old Jew feels the need to sit in the sun and talk a while."

We found an empty bench between the frozen custard stand and the small stage set under the cantilever of the Space Odyssey, a monster of taut cables and twirling silver rockets. We watched the Willow Grove crowd go by. The clientele hadn't changed much in my twenty-five years of patronage. Sauntering by were the familiar undernourished-looking adolescent girls brandishing their cigarettes like white staffs of independence. Classic, scrubbed American families. Mom-and-Dad-plus-two, moved along before us. Teenage blacks with hair picks in their back pockets performed for the world. Sexpots with swelling hips and breasts like the business ends of artillery shells strained shirts and halters to their limits. Old folks with canes and hearing aids filled benches soaking up sun, gossip and a little youth.

Schlomo took off his straw. "Got some things to tell you. How close to you was Tod Buckcry, Mrs. Day? I've been around long enough to know how to read a woman's face. Yours says 'unhappy.' I guess he's behind it, one way or the other." He raised a palm in question.

"He was a great disappointment. He lied to me. He tried to hurt me. I never want to see him again." Her voice was tight, clipped.

He nodded. "I visited the hospital again this morning. I wanted to talk to him about what happened in your house, Nevsky. I had nosed around a little and found out his business just went bankrupt."

"'sPots."

"Yep. Sheriff's gonna get his poster up before long. Going to be an auction of all that pretty glass and china nobody had the good taste to buy." He waved to summon an ice-cream vendor. "I said to myself, that being the case, he must have really needed money. I think he was trying to get it out of you. Now I know you don't *have* any money, Mrs. Day. And I know all about Nevsky's bank balances—Tap City. I figure it was the *statue* he wanted from you. As I said, I went to the hospital to talk to him, to get to the bottom of all this statue business. Couldn't see him, though."

"Why not?"

"He had just had a second heart attack. He's dead."

"Oh, *no*." Charity bent over slowly and pressed her knuckles against her cheek. Tears leaked. "Oh, I'm... *mad* to cry for *him*."

The captain looked sorrowful. "Celebrate the human heart," he said softly. "We can't make it reason. We must thank God for that." He put his arm around her shoulders. "I'm sorry. You mustn't think anything you did had anything to do with his dying. Docs said it wasn't the lumps he had taken..." He scowled meaningfully at me for my lying. "He had a heart condition for some years. What finished him was hearing his 'sPots was going up on the block." He paid the vendor for the ice-cream bar.

I nodded. "That *would* do it. But how'd he find out?"

"A big girl in overalls with a ponytail told him. She said she was 'family' so she was allowed five minutes with him."

"Twiggy Twill," Charity sniffled.

"That was her. She was still there when I left, pacing the halls like an Olympic walker. Bawling and mumbling to herself about how stupid she had been to tell him. Half crazy with real grief. Nevsky, she and Buckcry have a thing going?"

I had never thought about it. "He didn't. Maybe she did, but it would have to be from a distance."

He grunted and unwrapped his ice-cream bar. "Another piece of news might interest you... big federal drug bust at all three Condaco apartments. You know we had your pal Boothie under surveillance. Well, the feds got a tip. They notified us that they were going in. I was invited along as a 'local law enforcement observer.' It was quite a show. Right at dawn. Just like I remembered it at Normandy Beach. Not *quite* as big a show. Maybe a dozen unmarked cars and two dozen serious-looking guys in conservative suits. They had a stack of warrants up to here." He held his hand shoulder high. "They went into some *important* people's apartments. I was at Mount Royal, so I know they busted into Boothie's pad, too. He was sleeping off a tryst with his 'secretary' named Lily—"

"We met her."

"Officers unable to discipline their minds totally to law enforcement reported she belonged on a *Playboy* gatefold instead of Boothie's leaky waterbed." Schlomo attacked his ice-cream bar with an oddly tentative nibble. "Agents found a half pound of coke and five grand cash in plastic bags inside the back of his toilet. He broke into tears while Lily looked not very hard for something to put on. Decided on a bath mat for the nonce.

"A lot of important folks were found to have a stash. They had been hoarding it because the shipment they expected hadn't come in. As I said, important people were woken out of sound sleeps. Quite a parade of 'social leaders' and upper-level managers and their ladies. The fed and state flack-catchers are going to have a busy day handling calls from influential people and their influential friends and shysters. I went down to the booking station. Pretty soon there were more attorneys running around than in that AT&T versus the government case. A lot of people were making plans to pay off their leases and move out. Scandal is the *only* thing those type people *can't* afford. Those three apartments are going to have a bad name for years."

"I don't quite understand what happened," I said. "You had scared Boothie, questioned him, set him out as bait. Why'd he get involved by buying more coke?"

"He was under heavy pressure from the people who had paid up-front. He needed a score to give them at least part of what they ordered. They were losing faith in him. If he lost what little leverage he had as a small-time operator, they'd freeze him out of their lives."

"No more little tax-free deals and free tickets. His whole life style was on the line, wasn't it, Stein?"

"Sure. So when the real pros laid plans to move into Pittsburgh, he was one of the small-timers who had to be put out of business. With his record with us, and now the coke in his toilet, he's headed for jail."

"Who turned him in?"

Schlomo shrugged. "Big-timers from the East, New York, Buffalo. This is just the beginning. For the next six, eight months they'll be finding people in the trunks of cars in Brentwood and Sharpsburg suffering from an attack of lead worms."

Charity made a face.

"Maybe they've been at it longer than I thought. Maybe those out-of-town boys did in your friend Felicia Semanova."

"You said sawing her steering wheel column was an amateur's trick."

"It was. But the job got done." He nibbled his ice cream. "I've been thinking a lot about all these cocaine goings-on. All the folks bringing the coke in are gone. Two are dead. Selina Buckcry and Felicia Semanova were murdered. Sergei Yelanov, the mystery man, I think is dead, too. I think somebody put him into a pair of cement overshoes and dumped him in the Ohio...."

Schlomo rattled on through his theory. I found myself tuning him out. What he had just said rang a distant bell. When I had visited Anna Yelanov's house Vasily had rabbit punched her for saying something like that. Near as I could remember, she said "...they grabbed his money and put a knife in his back. Dumped him in the Ohio..." And June! June Gowell had been smacked around for the same reason. My mind made a leap that, once taken, seemed so obvious I couldn't imagine why I hadn't made it days ago. Sergei hadn't been stabbed and dumped in the Ohio. He had been shot in Canada by the police and dumped later in Lake Erie. Felicia shouting "Get up, Sergei! Get up for the love of God!" was her plea to her lover to stay alive. But he couldn't get up because he was either shot in the spine or otherwise seriously wounded. He couldn't be treated for gunshot wounds without raising embarrassing questions. I knew Felicia was made of tougher stuff, too loyal by miles to drown the man she loved, even to save herself from jail. She had been forced to allow it to happen.

Sergei Yelanov's was the first murder.

With that piece in place, it wasn't hard to see that Vasily had lied to Charity and me. He hadn't stayed in the Erie motel and made phone calls. He had sailed with the others. He had taken that extra day to pick up the coke and rendezvous with Alexey. He had demanded that the wounded Sergei be dumped into the storm-churned lake. Probably he had had to threaten the two women. He had probably waited till they had navigated the *Stressless I* to maybe a mile from shore, so they couldn't use their seamanship as a lever to save the man.

And once accomplices, neither Selina nor Felicia dared turn Vasily in. It would likely mean jail for them. That ruled out blackmail, too. I was sailing right along in my little ship of discoveries. Then I ran aground.

Why then would Vasily want to kill either woman? And who killed poor Winston Farrow, and why?

I came up for air and found a sniffling Charity telling the captain about our chat with Brunov. When she paused to blow her nose, he said, "Man like that can talk the fillings right out of your teeth. Talk about a born politician. That fellow's going places. He made you two a proposition? You oughta take it."

"We went to have lunch with him and shove his face into some nasty ideas we had about him," Charity said. "I left half in love with him."

"I wanted to be his friend. And I wanted to trust him," I said.

"That's one kind of power the man has. The other's the kind Duke Widemann and his pals are piling up to put behind him next November. By the time campaign time's here they'll all be so ready I don't think even John Kennedy could beat him."

"He wants us to help him run his campaign."

"Like I said, you oughta take him up on it."

"He dumped wounded Sergei Yelanov into the middle of Lake Erie," I said matter-of-factly. "Sergei was shot in Canada. Vasily had to drown him to keep their little smuggling business a secret."

Schlomo stared at me and swallowed several times. "You can prove that?"

"No. But with your help maybe we could dig at it and—"

"Time out! Time out, Nevsky." He shielded his eyes against the midday glare. "You have to learn to look at that kind of *dangerous* statement from an old county employee's point of view. Remember what I said about Duke Widemann having the statue? I mean, suppose

Brunov did no such thing, and word got out that some old Jew cop on the edge of retirement is trying to get the goods on Pittsburgh's Political Gentile Hope."

"But he—"

"You think I'd ever see *one* retirement check, never mind maybe fifteen, twenty years of them? No way. Think I'd ever see that nice little retirement condo I put a little deposit on, west coast of Florida? Crazy cops who get bugs up funny places about important people lose their jobs. I lose my job *now*, I lose a lot of my retirement. No condo, no piña coladas and sunsets over the ocean. No chance to share brave-cop fables with sweet young things in bikinis."

"I don't suppose your rage for law and order would rear up if I told you Vasily admitted to us he was running cocaine with the others," Charity said.

"He said that? Trying to win you over, he was. Giving you ten percent of the truth to bury the other ninety." Schlomo smiled slowly and fanned himself with his hat. "Too bad you told me that. It tends to fit in with the way *I'd* analyzed our young hopeful's character. Oh, the outside package is nice, as we agreed. Tall, dark and handsome, more than a bit of the old chutzpah. He'll fit the husband's role in the picture Miss Trishie has in what I hear is her largely empty head. And he'll help her spend her money, sure enough. Just the same, if I was Duke Widemann, I wouldn't want my daughter getting hooked up with a man with the kind of mean streak he has. Maybe worse than mean. Lethal.

"Maybe four, five years back our friend Vasily was smack in the middle of some hushed-up trouble. Something like he picked up what turned out to be a decent girl at the Hop 'n' Scotch downtown. He took her to his apartment and beat on her. Her family raised a stink real bad. Finally some *real* money changed hands and the girl moved out of town and went to try and buy herself a new face."

"I saw him take some whacks at Anna Yelanov," I said. "And he got rough with June Gowell, the delivery girl at 'sPots."

"That's not the worst of it, I don't guess." He went on to ask us if we knew about the attorney's first stint in politics. About the Polack who had said he was linked with the rackets. We said we had. "Bet you didn't know what happened about eighteen months later."

"No. What?" Charity said.

"The Polack left the city. First time in twenty-three years. Went to Philadelphia to a VFW convention. Somebody got into his hotel room and waited for him. Tied him up and put a .22 slug in the back of his neck."

"Not *more* death..." Charity said numbly.

"Our friend Vasily?"

"He was conspicuously in public in Pittsburgh all weekend," Schlomo said. "I always figured it was a mob hit man. Brunov waited a year and a half to get 'em."

"Just the same, he's on his way up, up, up," I said.

"No stopping him. At least none of us is going to stop him. He's off to Harrisburg and points south."

"I fear for the Republic," Charity said.

"Amen," Schlomo and I chorused....

Charity and I drove slowly to 138. We were restless and depressed. We wandered around the big house, crossing paths again and again. It took us till the cocktail hour to discover neither of us wanted to be alone. We decided to have a drink together.

And that started it.

What it was was some kind of mutual catharsis. We poured out all the turmoil and terrors we had been bagging away since the night the Sarmatian Demon had entered our lives. Neither of us was a big drinker. Just the same, we sipped away on rye and Chablis. I heard from her, in a steadily rising rush of words, thoughts clustered to the core of her personality. She started with her dead family, moved to Felicia and then to Tod. She told me about him, the ways he had shown her he loved her. She told me how she had felt falling in love again. She spilled out the agony of her betrayal, the bitterness. She quivered when she remembered her rage—and the errant guilt she felt over his death. In turn she shouted and wept. She paced and waved her arms. She pounded her white fists against the small bar. Finally she slumped into panting silence.

While she performed I steadily sipped rye on the rocks. Then it was my turn. I watched her face as I told her how I had felt about Judy Larkin, about the insanity—and utter rightness—of what we had done. I saw shock in her puffed features, then sorrow and tenderness. "Yuri, I never...you should have *said*." I went from Judy backward, blurted out confessions, exposed my life's open sores. I didn't leave out my former wife or my distant children. I stirred into my maudlin stew loves and opportunities lost through stupidity, miscalculation, cowardice or death.

Thoughts of death turned my emotional stream a different way. Since the Demon had come into the house, I went on, death had leaked like cancer into all our lives. The bronze had to go. We gave ourselves three days to clear the whole affair up—even though we were utterly stymied. If we didn't crack it open, the statue was going anyway. We tried to shake hands on it. By then we were so loaded we needed three tries to make contact. We stared into one another's tear-streaked faces and fell into a heavy hug. We bawled. Life had never seemed more perilous, our wounds deeper, our skills and talents smaller. The bronze Demon and the dark forces we had linked with it swelled in our drunken imaginations with power and menace. Nameless, unfocused threat poured up from the basement, flooding our brains with fear of the shadow side of our souls.

We toppled to the hardwood floor, arms locked around one another. There was nothing of desire in our tangling. We were a primitive, panicked Everycouple clutching warm flesh for meager comfort against the vast unmeasurable Darkness beyond our campfire.

Chapter Eighteen

Somewhere in the wee hours we untangled from our drunken sleep. Achy-boned, mouths filled with the sour ashes of hangover, we crept off to our beds.

Late morning we woke. It was a typical late-June day. High humidity and bright sunlight. We stirred around enough to make coffee. I carried the rest of the lawn furniture out to the patio by the garage. I raised the big orange and white beach umbrella. Charity crept under it behind a pair of sunglasses. I joined her for coffee. We looked at each other and traded sheepish smiles. Last night's boozy confessions and lowering of defenses had purged the anger and bitterness from our relationship. I took several deep breaths and lounged back with closed eyes. We each had our physical and emotional wounds left, but this day of blue skies and rich green lawns rubbed a little balm into those sores. We would survive. No, better than that—we would prosper!

We were having a light lunch when the phone rang. Trishie Widemann wanted to talk to Charity. I hit the amplifier switch and gave her the phone. Trishie wanted to have dinner with her at the Top of the Triangle, the restaurant atop the towering U.S. Steel Building. Charity hesitated. *"Please,"* Trishie said. "It's important. I want to talk to you *tonight*. My father doesn't know I'm doing this."

That, from Trishie Widemann, was the clincher. Charity agreed. It took her five minutes to persuade Trishie to include me.

It seemed a good evening to wear our best. I did the three-piece suit and tie. Charity walked into one of her closets and emerged in a blue dinner dress. When she chose she could dress as thin-and-rich as any central Connecticut shopping mall matron.

Trishie hadn't hesitated to exercise her family's privileges. As a substantial stockholder in U.S. Steel she could reserve one of the private dining rooms. The small one she chose had a table set with linen, silver and candelabra. The outer wall was made entirely of insulated glass; the drapes were open. From there, atop the tallest building in the City of Pittsburgh, we looked out northwest across the green lawns of Point State Park, the West End Bridge, Brunot Island, and beyond to McKees Rocks, Stowe Township and Neville Island.

The soft light of the mid-June evening was fading. Great gray boulders of clouds were rolling in from Ohio. They were lit by sudden white winks of distant lightning. A storm was gathering on the far horizon.

Trishie wore an expensive tan dress with a subdued flower print. It was too conservative for her. Better suited to someone twice her age.

We sat on a low couch and drank sherry, our glasses on a round marble coffee table. Charity and I looked out over the city. Trishie's eyes clung to Charity. I saw muscles trembling in her heavy face. She was anxious and tense. I hadn't noticed the shadows under her eyes. "I...had to talk to you, Charity. I want to know what you two and my father talked about day before yesterday. It was...Vasya, wasn't it? My fiancé?"

Charity nodded.

"What did you say that made my father so upset?"

"He was upset?" I said. "He didn't show it."

Trishie's gray eyes widened. "Well, he *was*. Even worse than I told you on the way home. And I think it was Vasya he was angry with—not you. I'm... *distraught* about all of it. I love Vasily Brunov. I want to help him any way I can. I have to find out why father's so—I don't know—*testy* about him all of a sudden. Please tell me whatever went on among you three that morning."

Charity and I took turns exchanging glances and taking tiny sips of sherry. We hesitated because we didn't know how much to say or how she'd take it. Well, she was a grownup—at least as far as the calendar went. I crunched the bit. "We talked about...Vasily maybe not being such a good guy."

"Father surely didn't think—"

"Your father thought he should be President—tomorrow, if not sooner," Charity said.

Trishie made a good try at suddenly looking sullen and hostile. "What've you got against my Vasya?"

"Nothing we can prove, so don't go and worry," I said acidly.

Charity added, "Just a few *teeeny-tiny* things about him bother me."

"Like *what?*" Trishie was ready to rise mightily to his defense.

"Like smuggling cocaine and murdering people," Charity said.

Trishie stared blankly. Her heavy jaw descended, leaving her mouth open wide enough to admit Charity's fist. *"No!"* she said.

"Well, *that's* what we talked about—like it or not. And at the time your father did *not* seem to be having any of our weirder theories." Charity put down her glass. "Well, maybe not so weird. Yesterday Vasily admitted to the smuggling. He'll deny it, of course, if you ask him—"

"I don't *believe* this."

"I also think he murdered my friend Felicia Semanova. That he *didn't* admit to."

"And I think he put a bomb in Ruthie Spires's car that killed her and my neighbor, the mother of three," I said. "And about did it for me, too."

Trishie was really shaken. Just then the waitress came in and asked if we wanted another drink or to order. Trishie said yes to both. When we had second sherries in our hands, she led us to the window. The storm was moving quickly toward us from the west. White twigs of lightning branched through the looming thunderheads.

251

"If Father's upset with Vasya, there won't be a *wedding*," she said. "I *want* to be his wife. I don't believe any of these wretched tales you're telling. Vasya agreed with you about the smuggling as some kind of joke, I'm sure."

I didn't follow her reasoning—or what passed for it. It was tough to come down hard on such an ineffective personality. I felt the need to pad the blow. "Maybe your father's not angry with Vasily's shady doings. Maybe it's the big loan he made him that's making him uneasy."

"Loan?"

"The loan to tide him over until after the wedding," Charity said.

Trishie shook her head, and looked for an instant like her financially serious father—stiff and honorable. "Vasya has *never* come to our family for financial assistance. Not *one* penny has he ever asked of us. He's much too self-reliant a personality to *dream* of borrowing from us. It's one of the best things about him, Father says. *Self-reliant.* And I know for a fact he has never taken a penny from *his* father either. And Willow Grove is *very* profitable."

Charity's expression grew distant, thoughtful. "You're *sure* about no loan of any kind?"

"Positive."

I knew what Charity was thinking. Vasily Brunov had borrowed heavily to finance his share of the cocaine purchase. Also, he had his hefty mortgage payments on the three chichi apartment houses. The situation there was worse than ever. Since the bust folks were moving out. Money was in shorter supply. He had told us he had borrowed from Widemann. But evidently he hadn't. He had borrowed from someone else. It could only be from one person. Vasily didn't want to be in his debt. He would want to pay him off as fast as possible, and put it all behind him.

His uncle! Who had links with organized crime.

Trishie intruded on my thoughts. "You said ...murders, plural, Yuri. Who else do you imagine Vasya killed?"

I picked one. "Selina Buckcry. While she was in the hospital. She was the last witness to the smuggling."

She smiled and looked relieved. "Your imaginations *are* working overtime," she said. "Vasya *was* there the night she died..."

"He *was?*"

"...but I was with him the *entire* time. I had no idea why he wanted to visit the Buckcry woman. We were on our way to a dinner party. He insisted. She and her husband were his clients, he said. He wanted to wish her well. When we got there Selina was awake and we chatted. Then she said she wanted to watch TV. We were only there a short time, a few minutes. She was awake and alert when we left."

"You sure you were with him every minute?" Charity said.

"Absolutely."

I was disappointed. "Did you maybe *see* anything funny there?"

"There was something—"

The waitress wheeled in a cart carrying our dinner. Lobster, rack of lamb and wines. It went down on my list as one of the least noticed, most timidly picked at meals of my life. Charity and I were too excited and charged up with new possibilities to pay much attention to the food. Trishie was on edge, first because of her father's annoyance with her fiancé, now over our accusations—and over one more thing.

The storm.

It was still some distance off. She kept turning her head toward the glass wall and making small ticlike grimaces. Charity asked her what she saw at the hospital that was peculiar.

"Just a person crossing the hall is all," Trishie said. "Vasya and I had walked down the hall toward the elevator. I remember thinking how odd it was at that moment that the hall of a busy hospital should be empty. Of course it was just a coincidence, Charity. But I looked back over my shoulder just for a moment to see if I could spot anybody. Well I did see somebody cross the hall. I just caught a glimpse, you see. But it looked like the person was headed in the direction of Selina's room. Then the elevator came and we both got in."

"What was peculiar?" Charity's voice was hushed.

"The way the woman was dressed. She was wearing

bib overalls. That wasn't the sort of outfit either hospital people or visitors wore." A distant rumble of thunder made Trishie start.

No doubt about it. She had seen Twiggy Twill!

Now the storm was closer and it grabbed Trishie's attention. She rose from the table and turned toward the glass wall. Her expression was strained but unfocused. She moved like a Grade B movie zombie. "I never was frightened of thunderstorms until...recently." Seeing from a height a storm lashing downtown Pittsburgh would be quite a spectacle. We followed the timid heiress to the glass wall, stood on either side of her.

"There was a storm like this better than two weeks ago," she said softly, as though to herself. "Remember it? Up to then I kind of liked them. All that crashing and banging and the rain coming down in sheets." A distant roll of thunder made her flinch. "Now look at me."

"What happened?" Charity said.

Trishie didn't answer. She stared out at the approaching storm. Below, above the streets and smaller buildings, bits of discarded paper soared and darted like gulls in the rising prestorm wind. When Trishie spoke, her voice carried a trancelike monotone. "The storm two weeks ago. It was on Tuesday night. I had wanted to see Vasya the weekend before. He said he had to go to New York on business. I missed him so much. He said he'd be back late Tuesday afternoon. He promised he'd call me. When he didn't call, I started worrying." Her bovine face turned to each of us in turn. On it showed determined adoration for Vasily Brunov. "I started really missing him, too. I called his apartment and his office. His secretary said he wasn't back yet. I had Jason drive me in to his apartment from Poplars. It had already started to rain. There were storms off and on all that day. I had a key and let myself in and"— I couldn't believe it, she was blushing—"I got into Vasya's bed. His apartment was on the ninth floor and it looked out over the Ohio. The storms kept coming. I could see them building and breaking over the city like waves, one after the other. It was awesome. About eleven I finally heard Vasya's key in the door. It was right at that time the last big storm was right over the city. The thunder was crashing and there was lightning..."

The storm we were watching from the Top of the Triangle was about at its peak, too. Clouds boiled over a midnight-dark forest of steel and concrete.

"...I called out to him, but I guess he didn't hear me over the thunder. He walked right into the bedroom. There was a long white lightning flash. He was standing in the middle of the room turned toward the bed. The center of his light shirt had a big black-looking, smeared stain in the middle. I called to him and he heard me. I snapped on the light. He told me to turn it off. I did. He went out of the room and came back in his shorts. I asked him what he had done with his clothes and what had been on his shirt—"

A mighty crash of thunder shook the whole U.S. Steel Building. Trishie gave a weak yelp and swayed against me. I got a comforting arm around her. She smelled of expensive perfume and fear. She whimpered.

Charity hurried to the table and snatched up a wine glass. She forced some wine down Trishie's throat, the glass chattering against her teeth. "Go ahead," she said softly. "What was on the shirt?"

Trishie straightened a bit, taking some of her weight off me. "I—I said it looked like blood. He said it wasn't. He said it was grease. He said he had had a car breakdown. I said I smelled damp on him. Was he all wet? He...told me to stop asking questions. What he was doing was none of my business—" There was another mighty roll of thunder. "It was thundering just *like that!*" she shouted. "Just like that when—when..."

"When what?" Charity whispered.

"When he—he *beat* me. When he beat *meeee*..."

It took half an hour to stop her hysterical weeping and hear the rest of her story of abuse and repression. He had beaten her on the torso where it wouldn't show. The thunder drowned out most of her screams. He had then persuaded her to forget about everything—his being wet, the shirt, his abusing her. He explained that it was her fault—coming uninvited to his apartment and bed as she had, being inquisitive, overimaginative and too suspicious. What kind of a wife would she make? Maybe she was a nag and needed it beaten out of her.

255

We took another twenty minutes to try to persuade her to file a formal complaint. If she did, it might help bring some other nasty things about him to light. She dismissed the idea angrily. Speak up against the man she loved? Never.

Another dead end. Damn the man! He was knee-deep in ugly slop—and his feet stayed dry.

Charity and I put it together on the ride back to 138. We both saw wounded Sergei Yelanov lying bleeding but alive on the deck of the *Stressless I*. The lake storm was mounting. Selina and Felicia were battling to navigate the vessel. Brunov was a little ahead of them, wondering what would happen if they safely reached the U.S. side. We imagined the *Stressless I* tossing and pitching around, Brunov holding on or doing what the two frightened women told him. In sight of shore, with survival a certainty, there had probably been a powwow. Brunov said Sergei was to go overboard, or they'd spend the rest of their days in jail. Selina was probably readily convinced. Not Felicia. No one was throwing her lover over the side, no matter what happened. Then Brunov either knocked her down or pulled a weapon. Either way he had Felicia back off long enough to wrap his arms around gory Sergei and get him up over the rail and overboard. Once done, the women were accessories. It paid them to fall into line. It was hard to be moral and upright over a *fait accompli* when it meant time in jail. Felicia had made her own decision: get what she could out of the death and disarray—the bronze statue. Sell it for a small fortune somewhere else in the country.

"And no evidence of *any* of it," Charity said. "Only the monster in the White Chamber. Remember, if we don't settle it all by day after tomorrow, we're just gonna dump that thing in the river of our choice."

"You forgot. There's one thread left. We've got to pull it out and see where it leads."

"What's that?"

"Twiggy Twill," I said. "She murdered Selina. As an anonymous 'favor' to Tod."

The next morning I drove over to 'sPots. An auction was in progress. Shelving had been hastily moved aside. Folding chairs were set up. A dozen-odd people were bidding on the store's stock and scanty equipment. The auctioneer in a red vest, waving a Groucho-sized cigar, touted every lot as a princely treasure. The audience was unconvinced. Bids came slowly. I scanned the crowd for Twiggy. Didn't see her.

June Gowell was standing off to the back of the room. She looked tired and disappointed. I gestured at the proceedings. "This is pretty fast going. Tod's hardly cold yet."

She nodded. Her buckteeth and solemn expression made her look like a starving rodent. She needed a smile to light up her vivacity. "Twiggy figured we could get more in a private auction this way. I mean Tod's 'estate' would get more than from a sheriff's sale. I'm not sure how legal it is. Anyhow, these people are mostly dealers and know ceramics. There've been a few good sales. Twiggy got the idea from Count D-M next door. It worked pretty good for him last week."

"Where is Twiggy?" I said.

"Gone."

"Gone where?"

June shrugged. "She was all messed up over Tod dying. I mean *all* messed up." She turned her large blue eyes on me. "I don't think anybody knew how much he meant to her. I mean even *she* didn't know." She raised the edge of her hand to the bridge of her nose. "Like, you know, about this deep in love. It made sense, you know, how she had worked free for the store. Living off her savings and all. And then doing the dumb thing she did, wanting to keep him up to date and all."

"What was that?"

"Telling him the store was finished. What else, Mr. Nevsky? Since then she's been walking around lower than a worm's instep. She kept saying she killed him. I told her that was silly. He was a sick man. His time came. That was it. She wouldn't listen. She said she 'stank of death...'"

My mind spun back for a moment to the Sarmatian bronze seeping death and suffering. More death and, I guessed, still more to come.

"...and she said she had to get away and start over again. Maybe she'd go to L.A. or Atlanta. Everything she had here was gone, she said. Two weeks was all it took for everything in her life to be blown away."

I led June Gowell outside the store. "Can this auction run for a little while by itself?"

"Well, I'm kinda in charge. Sort of 'sPots's Gunga Din. Last one left, y'know?"

"Could you spare maybe half an hour?"

"To do what?"

"Take me to your house on Walnut and show me Twiggy's clothes and stuff."

"How come?"

"To see if she really left."

"She left all right. But—OK, it's not far."

We walked. It took five minutes. Twiggy's room was next to June's. It was an odd blend of feminine and jock. The mattress on the floor had a frilly spread. A bull-worker exercise machine was propped in the corner with a baton. A barbell loaded to 150 pounds lay among stuffed toy monkeys and piggies.

"She entertain guys?" I said.

June shook her head. "She had offers, but—now that I see it—she wanted Tod."

I sat down on a chair. June sat cross-legged on Twiggy's mattress. "She left what wasn't light and portable." June waved around the still furnished room. "Most of it I don't want. I'm not the jock she was."

"That wasn't an act, then?"

"No *way,* Mr. Nevsky. She used to swim in the Allegheny River on New Year's Day. And do the shot put for a track club. And there was that time she tried to climb the Heights of Ignorance—the Cathedral of Learning. She would've made it, but some cops dragged her in through a window."

"What else do you know about her?" I said.

June frowned and folded her arms. "Why all the questions? Is there a law against deciding to start a new life?"

I got up and started to have a look at Twiggy's leavings. Didn't see any personal effects. "There's been a *lot* of trouble around 'sPots the last month. The bomb you cleaned up after was just part of it, June."

"Oh." Her round eyes grew rounder. "I'm sorry if I—"

258

"Forget it. What might have happened was Twiggy did something super stupid thinking she was helping Tod. Maybe deep down she was trying to help herself."

"Did what?"

"Don't worry about it. I'd like to find her if I could. It would be a big help in trying to find out who planted the bomb, and maybe some other things. If I don't find her, then I don't think we'll ever know who killed your roommate Ruthie."

"Ruthie *was* murdered, wasn't she? For sure." I had June's full attention now. "Are you *police,* Mr. Nevsky? Like, a *plainclothesman?*"

I shook my head and grinned. "Just friends with some of the dead people. Some of them were your friends, too. So anything you can tell me about Twiggy leaving would be a help."

She really tried to help. She screwed up her little squirrel face and dredged up every trivial fact in her head that even remotely touched Twiggy. After twenty minutes I asked her to stop. The only thing I got out of her that meant anything was an odd statement the big girl made when June asked her where was she going to find getaway money. 'sPots had eaten up all her savings.

Twiggy had looked at her with her familiar determined, jaw-out glower. "I'm going to get it from somebody really nasty," she said.

And that was it.

I walked June back to 'sPots. She had no idea which direction Twiggy had gone or when she actually left. She had seen her early last night. She was packing up her knapsack. After that she went out. June didn't check the big girl's bed so didn't know if she ever came back. The Land Rover was still in its parking place.

Dead end, I thought. Schlomo's last thread had been pulled right out and the knot was still there.

I didn't drive back to 138. I turned my Datsun toward my farm cottage in Murrysville. I wanted to think it all through, start to finish.

I had always been a lousy loser.

Chapter Nineteen

I slept poorly and woke up early with the birds. I took my black coffee out to the little porch and studied the banners of mist unfurled over the valley. I sat on the steps, cup in hand. I knew why I was up at dawn. My mind was trying to sort it all out, churning and chugging in the back room of the subconscious.

I performed an amateur's medical exam. I pressed my head below my large Band-Aid. The skull was only slightly sore under the comforting crust of a heavy scab. With cautious fingers I explored the left side of my rib cage where the edge of Tod Buckcry's shovel had struck. My last few nights' tosses and turns told me one rib was maybe cracked after all. Just the same, I was lucky, lucky, lucky....

As the sun inched up and the gray faded, I tested my recovered memory by running through the events since the night Felicia had dragged the bronze horror into 138. My mental computer was running smoothly. Some of the memories were painful. Judy Larkin's face floated up to stab my breast like a stiletto. I saw her pert features aligned in her giddy grin. I saw her green eyes lit with love for little Louis in her arms. I remembered the taste of her good coffee.... She hadn't lived to play the face cards out of the deck of her life. It had been all weak suits and little pips. And there had been some cheating at her table as well....

I got a brief call from Charity. She couldn't sleep either. Yesterday she had phoned Anna Yelanov, then paid her a visit. The former *diva* had been drinking and gabby. Once the subject of Vasily Brunov came up, she gave way to the dramatic. Their love had been torrid but fleeting.... Charity said it all boiled down to the attorney making love to her to find out how much she knew—if anything—about Sergei's smuggling. She knew nothing. At the 'sPots party she had wept to see Trishie on Vasily's arm.... So he had checked with friends *and* spouses of the crew members to make sure no one knew about the *Stressless I*'s illegal journeys. Interesting and typical Brunov. But it wasn't really evidence.

I turned my attention back to the Sarmatian Demon and its web of death. I kept it there all morning. A rabbit had infiltrated my sturdy garden fence. While I reseeded the beans I kept turning over recent events. Around two in the afternoon I was still idly puttering and sweating. Then I caught on.

I was missing something.

There was at least one connection I wasn't making. I tried to jiggle it free. I found more chores—whitewash the foundation stones, feed the compost pile, find the wicked rabbit's entrance. The more the connection eluded me, the more I kept after it.

I nibbled some cheese around four o'clock. I was too bored for more chores, but restless just the same. It was about three miles to the center of the small town of Murrysville. I decided to walk off the last of my energy in the cause of buying the early edition of the *Pittsburgh Press*.

I got back to the cottage about six. I opened an Iron City beer, thereby realizing a mirage that danced over the last dusty uphill mile. I poured the brew into a tall glass and sank into a porch chair in the shade. I sipped and read the paper. The Iron City was cold and sweet in my mouth.

Until I got to page three.

My thirst died and nameless insects strolled my upper spine. The headline read: Woman Daredevil Dies in Coaster Fall. The article went on to say that the body of Samantha "Twiggy" Twill had been found by Willow

262

Grove Amusement Park employees under low bushes inside the Hurricane roller coaster enclosure. She had fallen from the coaster's highest point, evidently in an attempt to scale the famous ride structure. The medical examiner had established the time of death as late last evening, well after the park closed.

The article went on to trace some of Twiggy's more daring exploits. I scarcely read them. I knew the article was true. She had fallen from the top of the coaster. But it wasn't an accident. She had been pushed.

Vasily Brunov had pushed her.

I growled at myself for not making this connection I was looking for before now—too late to do anyone any good. Early on I had asked Twiggy about the last voyage of the *Stressless I*. The "friend" who drove surfaced. I remember also asking her if she had seen anyone fooling with Ruthie's car on the night of the bombing. She was a poor liar. She hesitated. She had seen Brunov doing just that, guessed he was the friend, and decided to keep that ace up her sleeve. And sure enough, the time came in her life to play the card. It didn't take a lot of imagination to see who "the nasty man" was whom she went to for money. Even though she had killed Selina, it was hard to imagine a more honest and innocent blackmailer. All she wanted, I was sure, was a small stake to get her out of the state, maybe to the Coast. Probably not even four figures. And if she said she'd never come back, she meant it. Pittsburgh held nothing but the rubble of her employment and the ruins of her love. Plus a possible murder rap.

Attorney Vasily Brunov had seen too much of the world. From the attorney's sad vantage point he had peered into the reeking armpit of the worst we had to offer—greed, lechery, lies, felonies. Beyond that there was his own gaudy catalog of crimes. No way could he trust to soiled innocence; his own was too long gone.

I wasted no time calling Charity at 138. No answer. Maybe she'd be home by the time I got there. I packed up my toilet articles and closed the cottage. Inside of forty-five minutes I was home. Charity's car wasn't in the garage. That was annoying because I wanted to share the bad news, see if she had any ideas of where we went from there.

I called out toward her side of the house. As I imagined, she wasn't home. I wandered into the kitchen. It was clean, except for a coffee cup and an open newspaper on the table. I picked up the paper. It was the *Press*, the early city edition. The one I had read.

The article about Twiggy's death was circled in yellow highlighter. So she had read it. The question was, why hadn't she called me? And where was she now? I looked around the kitchen for a note. I found none.

About a half an hour passed before the phone rang. My instincts surprised me. I didn't snatch it up at the first ring. Instead I stared at it as though it were a snake coiled in a narrow forest path. It had to be handled, but one was never in a hurry to deal with trouble. Finally I lifted the receiver.

"Nevsky, you know my voice?"

No mistaking Vasily Brunov's soft tones. "You're—"

"Don't use my name. Or any other names," he said. "That's an order."

"I don't take orders well. Never have."

"You're going to take them tonight, Nevsky."

"Why should I?"

"A friend of yours paid me a surprise visit," he said. "I'm sure by now she wishes she hadn't."

"Ch—"

"We had a discussion."

"Where is she?" I said. "What did you do?—"

"During our discussion, Nevsky—and it was rather a long discussion—I persuaded her to turn over the nasty little trinket from her purse. She gave me rather a scare with it..."

He meant the derringer she carried—and knew how to use. So she was unarmed and in trouble. That too-familiar lead balloon inflated in my stomach. How much trouble was she in?

"...but after that we settled down to questions and answers, Nevsky. At first the answers came very slowly. Your colleague is an unreasonably stubborn woman. She required...persuasion."

Then I saw! He had beaten her. He had beaten what information he wanted out of Charity! My jaw creaked

264

as I bit back my rising rage. The ice was thin. Very thin. I had to be careful.

"Listen up, Nevsky. I want from you. I want you to do some things to get me free of this bronze tar baby I'm touching and can't seem to shake free of."

"I'm not in the mood to help you, friend," I said. "I want to know how my 'colleague' is."

"I'm looking at her. She's looking at me."

"I want to talk to her."

"Look, Nevsky—"

"I want to hear her voice!"

Something in my tone for a moment sent him off his selfish path. There was a long pause. I heard Charity's voice. It was weak. "Yuri, I—I'm sorry. I got ideas. I wanted...personal revenge. You warned me, too, days ago. 'Taking justice into my own hands.'" She had trouble forming her words. I knew he had been beating her face. My anger flared like gasoline on a bonfire. I was totally impotent. Only the thin thread of phone line connected me with the most important person in my life.

Brunov got back on the line. "OK, Nevsky. Now to business. I want the bronze and I want the Twill woman's letter to your colleague."

"I see. What letter?"

"Maybe you didn't know about the letter. Your colleague just got it in this morning's mail. It moved her to pay me a visit. It seems to talk about the Twill woman's suspicions about a car bomb and a visit she planned to make to yours truly. I hadn't counted on that. Your colleague was so impressed with it she came to me personally to persuade me to turn myself over to the police. Not a wise decision for an otherwise intelligent woman. She should have given the letter to the police and let it go at that."

"So you want the letter. Where is it?"

"In your secret room in the basement. With the bronze. I want both."

I hesitated. I wanted to say I didn't have the bronze. I knew that wouldn't work. Brunov had beaten the secret of the White Chamber out of Charity. She had resisted telling him long enough to convince him that, when she gave in, she had told the truth. He wasn't the only one for whom the Sarmatian Demon was a lethal tar baby. "Tell me what you want."

"Put the bronze in your car. Arrange it so I can see it through the windshield. Bring the letter with you. Tape it onto the bronze where I can see it. Got that?"

"Go ahead."

"Drive to the amusement park. It's closed today because of the 'accident.' The west service gate will be open. You'll be able to drive right up to the Hurricane. I'll be on the coaster platform waiting for you."

"What about my colleague?"

"She'll be with me. She'll be where you can see she's all right."

"What's the deal?" I said. "What do I get out of it?"

"You get your lady friend back alive. I get the bronze and the letter. I've got a plane ticket to a faraway land. I need a long vacation. But I need the bronze before I can go. That's the deal."

He was lying, of course. It was a trap. Charity was the bait and I was the hapless two-footed pest. I had to be got rid of, too. So obvious! But what choice did I have?

"I want you here just after dark. And listen, Nevsky—listen close." Brunov's soft voice took on a new, harsh edge—the tones of a desperate man. "No tricks from you. And no men in blue. I've sent four people down the tube. You get cute or call the law and the first thing I do is make your colleague number five. You understand?"

"Sure."

"We'll be waiting." He hung up.

My heart thudded and my hands were slick with sweat. There was some chance I'd freeze right by the phone, so I got moving right away. On the way down to the basement a wash of vexation swirled around me. The point of irritation was...Charity. Why in Heaven's name hadn't she gone to Captain Schlomo Stein with Twiggy's letter? It wasn't like her to try to play heroine. She was too cool for that.

I glanced around the White Chamber, looking for the letter. I couldn't find it. Then I caught on. There was no letter. Charity had seen the article and drawn the same conclusions I had. She had called on Brunov and tried to run a bluff. Sounded like it had been a good one. It would have worked if things hadn't boiled down to physical strength. Now she was badly beaten and in danger.

Yuri Nevsky, the original square peg of caution, was again being forced into the round hole of hero. As my gallant steed was out to pasture and my suit of armor at the body shop, I'd have to do with less glamorous aids. I dug the old Smith and Wesson .38 out of its shoe-box nest of drying packets. I put on my jeans and dark turtleneck. Then I went up to the attic to drag a faithful friend out of his dusty, long drawer-coffin. The body of the dummy I called Charlie McNevsky had been sewn together by Charity. The head was a papier-mâché masterpiece of Ugo DeBrontaigne, a sculptor friend whose work hung in the Carnegie Institute. He had glazed just the right gleam of bald into the lifelike dome. The beard was quality horsehair with just the right Nevsky wiriness to its curl.

Jeans and black turtleneck made me less conspicuous. A dark blue knitted skullcap kept light from reflecting from my balding head. After dark I would be hard to see and unlikely to snag on nails or nasty corners. I wore dark gloves to hide the white of my hands.

I waltzed the Sarmatian Demon out to the car and laid it across the back seat. It was very visible. So was the empty envelope taped to its hammer. I carried Charlie McNevsky out to the garage and smeared Tanglefoot stickum on his palms. I sat him on the front passenger's seat, head down between his knees like an airline passenger in the crash position. I loaded the .38, spun the cylinder. *Clickety-clickety-clickety,* it said. I made sure the safety was on and stuck it behind my belt. That about did it.

I went back into 138 and made two short phone calls. Then I got into the Datsun and drove to Willow Grove. From the road I saw the place was dark. Here and there safety spotlights silhouetted rides rearing up like nightmare beasts from the dimness. I saw the distant white shadow of the Hurricane off in its corner of the park. Darkness hadn't completely fallen. I used what few minutes remained to scout the service entrance. The service road narrowed within the gate. A second pass down the main road at moderate speed showed me the narrowed service road nosed between two shadowy rows of low concession buildings and led to a small plaza. At the plaza's far end stood the Hurricane. I glimpsed the faint glow of safety spotlights somewhere near the roller coaster's rider loading platform.

By the time darkness fell I had decided what I was going to do. I drove very slowly off the main road, lights on, so I'd be seen if Brunov was watching. I stopped right in front of the gate and got out of the car. The hairs on my neck stirred with the dread of a slug ripping into me from the darkness. I was gambling that the attorney wouldn't take the chance of a shot at a distance. He was too desperate for that. He had to make sure.

As he had promised, the gate was unlocked. I shoved it open and got back in the car. I left the driver's-side door slightly ajar. I guided the Datsun toward the narrow way between the rows of shadowy concessions and games. I found the hand throttle mounted on the steering column and turned it just so, till the car crept along at dead low.

When the car rolled into the heaviest shadows I moved fast. I slid out of the car and dragged Charlie McNevsky up and into the driver's seat. Two walking strides beside the moving car were all I needed to wrap his sticky hands over the wheel. His weight would keep the wheel steady enough. I clicked the door shut and did a diving roll into the deepest shadows by the edge of the buildings.

I found a space between two of them and slipped in. Then I sprinted with all the strength in my aging legs through to the next row of concessions. While my car crept toward the Hurricane and held Brunov's attention, wherever he was, I was going to circle around to the side of the coaster. Once past the passenger platform I was going to try to spot him from behind. And perhaps get a look at Charity, too.

My sneakered feet moved quickly and quietly over the asphalt. I had maybe a minute and a half before the Datsun got across the plaza. I made good use of the time and darkness.

In seconds the towering white coaster structure

loomed up just across a narrow walkway. The Hurricane was surrounded by a seven-foot Cyclone fence. The wire across the top hadn't been crimped over. Short, bare lengths jutted up. A good short run, a leap and careful scramble, and I'd be over. I tensed to make that dash. I burst out of my crouch as the night air was hammered by the staccato bursts of an automatic weapon.

The firing was coming from near the platform, aimed elsewhere. I clawed my way up and over the fence. I could have been the Tin Woodman and nobody would have heard me over the gunfire.

By the time the firing stopped I was scuttling on hands and knees through the darkness between heavy steel supports and white wooden beams toward the illuminated platform. I heard a woman groaning. Charity! From a safe spot by a thick steel pier I stopped and peeked. She was in the last seat of one of the Hurricane cars. It sat in the ready-to-roll position by the long wooden starter lever. But the heavy electrical machinery was still. The only sound was her sobbing and saying "Yuri... Yuri... dear *dead* Yuri..." over and over again. The stink of spent cartridges polluted the June night.

I kept low and moved closer to the platform, then under it. Its façade was made of white wooden slats. From all my long days waiting in line to ride the coaster, I remembered there was a small wooden door. I groped swiftly and found it. It was held closed with a thick piece of wire—stuck tight. I wiggled it, cursing under my breath. Finally I worked it loose.

I peered through the slats. There was Brunov! He was in a crouch, moving forward toward my riddled car and realistically slumped Charlie McNevsky. He held a nasty-looking machine pistol at the ready. I opened the door, praying for oiled hinges, and slipped out.

I got to him about ten feet from the car. I jabbed my .38 into his kidney and stepped back. "Don't turn around, Brunov! Drop the ratty-tat-tat or you're dead."

"What the hell...?"

"Drop it."

The machine pistol clattered down. I moved him a half dozen steps back. I jerked the back of his jacket

269

collar down so the sleeves interfered with his arms' movement. He winced and drew breath in through his teeth. "My right arm is messed up," he growled. "The Twill bitch was an Amazon."

"My heart goes out to you, Brunov."

"My right knee, too. I can hardly walk. I nearly went off the coaster instead of her."

"So you have a few booboos, she bought the ranch. And by the way, she didn't send Charity any letter."

He cursed. I frisked him. As my hands moved over his body, I was reminded that he was a powerfully built man. He was carrying only a wallet and a small transister radio. I let him keep both.

He inclined his head toward my car. It leaked fluids like an incontinent old man. "You have really loyal friends, Nevsky. Who was he?"

"Friend named Charlie. I keep him in a drawer. He's my Picture of Dorian Gray. He gets the ugly instead of me. He's a dummy."

Brunov scowled and mumbled.

"Here's what I haven't been able to figure out," I said. "Why were you and Felicia so excited about an ugly statue that was just a copy? Why did you still want it?"

Brunov turned and growled at me. "So you're smart, but not as smart as your whore in the car up there. She figured it out while we had our chat." I glanced toward the roller coaster starting area. Charity's head was lolling. She was hurt. "So fill me in *fast*," I said. "Why did you and Felicia want the statue?"

"It's filled with pure cocaine, Nevsky. Maybe seventy or eighty pounds of it. More than a million bucks worth cut and on the street. The statue's hollow."

I groaned inwardly. Of course! Felicia had dragged the Sarmatian Demon up the walk and into 138 by herself. Trishie had told us it had taken both Count Dromsky-Michaux and Sergei Yelanov, *plus* a dolly, to move her father's version. I should have seen it right away. "You killed Felicia so you could have it all."

"Wrong, Nevsky. What I told you about laying low till the narcs went back in their holes was true. Only Selina, Felicia and I were left. My share of more than a million was plenty. I was happy. Felicia agreed to hide the coke for us. She didn't say where it was. But I trusted her. I knew she was five times more honest than I was. Then she had that accident you said was murder, and all of a sudden I was in big financial trouble. I searched—and trashed—her apartment looking for something that might tell me where she stashed me the dope. I had the key because I was paying for the place."

It didn't take Brunov long to fill in the rest. My pistol jabbed against the back of his neck kept his pauses very short. All the bronzes brought in from Russia were fake. Felicia's husband, Alexey, cast them in a clandestine Georgian foundry. They were modeled after actual art treasures. The hollow demon had been made to order to hide the cocaine. Its age was faked like all the others—every stone and gem were cheap gewgaws. Brunov had found out from Winston where the statue was. But the fat man's blabbing at the funeral fouled everything up. The need for money and fear that Charity and I would soon catch on cost the attorney his cool. He started a chain of rash acts. He called Boothie O'Shea and told him the dope would soon be there, hold on. Earlier he had tried to make Winston part of his scheme. The fat man had been too much of a drunken coward. He had phoned me in panic and said he didn't want anything to do with the bronze. When he told Brunov what he had done, he sealed his doom. He knew too much and was expendable. Brunov shot him after using him to try to scare the bronze out of us. When that didn't work, he put on a fake beard and tried to kill us with the silenced rifle. Judy's shouts had ruined his aim. Once we were dead he planned to search the house and find the bronze. He never dreamed how well it was hidden.

My call telling him Charity and I knew about the cocaine smuggling and the *Stressless I* panicked him further. Even if it meant he'd never find the bronze, we had to be got out of the way. He decided to bomb my car at the party and derotored Charity's distributor. The chance to kill Ruthie, who knew about the coke smuggling, was an unexpected bonus.

"The way things were, my uncle owned me," Brunov said. "I was ready to live with that if I couldn't get back the coke."

"So the mob would have had you where it wanted," I said.

"I was born for a political life. I had no choice. Getting the coke back was supposed to buy back my freedom."

"You were born to go to jail," I said. I had been worried about Charity for hours. During my short chat with Brunov I kept looking toward her. It was past time to have a close look at her. I made the attorney lead the way to the platform. I saw he limped badly. He wasn't lying about Twiggy's desperate handiwork. I wondered how he had overpowered the big woman and tossed her out of a moving coaster car.

Charity was tied. Her face was a horror. I grimaced. Both eyes were black. Blood was caked into scablike crusts under a nose swollen into a bulb. Her left cheek had ballooned to three or four times its normal size. Between lips swollen like sausages I saw gaps where teeth had been. I whirled on Brunov. The pistol came up on its own and centered on his stomach. "In the gut!" I said. "How long would you lie here before anyone found you?"

"I—I gave security the night off." Even in the uncertain light I saw his ruddy face pale. "Nevsky, *don't*."

All my instincts screamed to kill him. He was a murderer and beater of women. He had harmed *my* woman. Pale and pleading now, he would kill me quickly enough if our positions were switched. Long moments passed. I couldn't do it. I suppose it was the conditioning of civilization. With some of us it took and ran deep. I lowered my pistol, understanding why, when each civilization met its Huns, the Huns were six-to-four favorites and a good bet for the smart money.

"Walk down the platform about ten yards," I growled. "Keep your back to me. Don't turn this way or I'll shoot you."

"All right."

"I hope you run for it," I said. "I want to kill you."

"No way."

I turned to Charity, with an eye still on Brunov. She looked up at me out of the pounded tissue of her face. "I'm...OK," she said in a small voice.

"Hell you are. You're hospital bound, lady."

"I thought you were...in the car."

"Charlie McNevsky again."

She tried to smile, I thought. But it hurt too much.

She was well tied in. I glanced at Brunov. He stood still, behaving. I laid the pistol on the seat, where I could reach it in an instant. I went to work on the knots in the stout twine that held her feet. Every five seconds or so I glanced back at Brunov. "Keep your eyes on him," I said to her. "If he moves, scream."

"Um-huh."

I got her feet loose. Her hands were tied to the chrome bar of the seat in front. I had to get into the front seat and stand awkwardly to get at the knots and still keep an eye on Brunov. I took the pistol with me and put it right beside me on the seat.

When the machinery clattered into life, my eyes jerked toward it. Through the heavy wire mesh I saw moving gears and whirling wheels. The car jerked forward. I lost my balance. The pistol slid off the seat and fell by Charity's feet—where I couldn't reach it.

I twisted back toward Brunov. He was coming at me, his big thighs working. He had snatched up a length of pipe in his left hand. I just got my left arm up. I saved my noggin from a fatal lead massage. But it cost me. The wash of sickening pain told me he had broken or cracked one of the forearm bones. I whipped my right arm around his body and pinned his pipe arm. We staggered together into the moving roller coaster car.

I expected him to pummel me with his weak right hand. He didn't. I caught a glimpse of the reason. He was clutching the radiolike object. Too late I understood it was a remote control unit for operating the Hurricane.

A good tug ought to free him from my awkward embrace. He did try to pull his pipe arm loose. But he couldn't get any leverage from his damaged right arm and knee. Somehow I held on. I was surviving on Twiggy's legacy of physical damage.

The car cleared the platform and started the *clickata-clackata* on-chain ride up to the first, tallest height. We swayed in the narrow space in front of the seat like exhausted marathon dancers. Brunov grunted into my ear. "I get rid of you and Day, I'm out of the woods. I buy my soul back. I start *clean* again. I go to Harrisburg!" He shoved me, driving me half out of the car. I held on like a leech. For a moment we both teetered over the edge of battered stainless steel car, our inner ears screaming balance warnings.

Twitching his thick wrist, Brunov slapped at my face with the pipe. I saw stars and turned away. My grip almost slipped as I fell back into the seat. The car had nearly reached the top of the peak. Another few seconds and we would plummet down the dip. However many dozens of rides had made me feel the falling terror, none raised in me the panic I felt now.

The car stopped.

Brunov had touched a stud on the radio control unit. He smiled at me. Then he smiled at Charity behind me. Her hands were still tied to the chrome bar. "The Twill woman took the same ride," he said.

I heaved myself to my feet. Breeze stirred around my sweaty face. Below, the foot of the coaster seemed farther down than any yards could measure. Beyond the coaster and amusement park lay the lights along the Monongahela—traffic moving, mercury vapors, neons peddling gas and beer. Vertigo touched my knees with teasing fingers.

My arm was ballooning up. Too clearly I saw what was going to happen. Brunov was going to work his pipe hand free and beat me silly enough to push me over. Charity would follow. He wanted to finish us high up on the heights—with the car still and steady. I knew why.

He didn't know the coaster.

He had grown up with it, but hadn't ridden it—until last night when he had murdered Twiggy. The roller coaster experience, then, must have been confusing and unpleasant. It wasn't likely he could remember the direction of the deceptive twists and turns of this, one of the world's most famous coasters.

So there was my straw. Either I grabbed it now or he finished Charity and me. I'd have to use my broken left arm. I bit my teeth against the coming wash of agony. Though I could scarcely make a fist, I swung a well-telegraphed roundhouse left. That brought up Brunov's weak right arm in a reflex defense. He held the radio control in that hand. While he blocked my punch-less blow, I probed the exposed right elbow with the quick, strong fingers of my good hand. The sickening pain from the shock to my left arm twisted my stomach in a spasm of nausea. I found the nest of nerves and dug in savagely. I numbed his forearm and hand. An awkward swat of my right hand knocked the radio unit lose. It bounced once on the side of the car.

With a sweep of his arm, Brunov tried to catch it. He had to use his bad arm, the one Twiggy had damaged and I had numbed. For an instant the shiny case slid across the ends of his fingers. He couldn't close his hand fast enough. The unit spun and glinted down into the darkness.

Brunov hissed a curse. When the gadget hit the asphalt the car started down. Soon a speedy descent turned into that steep, terrifying roller coaster plummet. Brunov and I swayed beside each other, trying for balance in the rush of air.

In panic he grabbed at me, probably hoping to wrestle us both down into the safety of the seat or the floor. With my good arm I kept him from closing completely. The wind of descent nibbled at my clothes and hair. The car rocketed toward curve bottom. I remembered the descent was followed by a short jog right, a momentary swing left, then another deeper, sharper dip close to the ground. The surprise was that second right, when the body was braced for a longer left.

I set my feet for the curves I knew. I felt panicky Brunov trying for a better grip. I couldn't allow it, no matter what agonies burned in my broken arm. He stayed upright through the first nasty dip right. Then his weight shifted a little late and too much for the left turn—as I'd hoped. The sudden switch right made him stagger. I coiled my legs and shoved him with all the strength in my right arm. He toppled over the side with a shriek of surprise and fear.

At that point the tracks ran only eight or nine feet above the landscaped bushes. The fall was sure to stun him. Not more. I hadn't had time to think of what could happen when he got back on his feet again. As the coaster car clattered up and down the rest of the run, I imagined his riddling us with his recovered machine pistol as we sailed by like ducks in the closed shooting gallery fifty yards away.

My hope of the coaster car gliding to a halt at the platform was fast dashed. We sailed through the ride line area like the Osaka Express and started the slow climb up again. I started to work one-handed on Charity's knotted hands. She was conscious but shaky. "I hope he landed head first," she murmured.

"Let's try to get a look at him as we go by where he fell out."

We did. It wasn't at all hard. He hadn't hit the bushes or the ground. His momentum had carried him just beyond the bushes to the Cyclone fence. The front of his neck had hit the naked wire ends. They had pierced skin and flesh. He was squirming, caught like a fish on half a dozen hooks. With two good arms and legs he could have lifted himself off. But he had only one of each. He was heaving and kicking, trying to get the round toes of his shoes into the squarish holes in the wire pattern.

We rattled past into the gloom on the way to the rest of the circuit. I untied Charity's hands. She gently touched the swollen meat of her face. She whimpered. "It *hurts*. It hurts *every*where...."

Good thing her handbag was gone. She had no mirror.

I sank back dizzily onto the seat in front of her. My arm was an agony. The jolts of the car shot serious messages of damage into my brain.

On our next pass by Brunov, his struggles to escape had weakened. I thought I glimpsed a dark puddle in the shadows under his suspended feet. Next pass he wasn't moving at all.

Charity looked away. "I want to get away from him. I want this car to stop. I want to get away from him...." Her little litany fit right in with the *clickata-clackata* of the climbing car. The rattling roar of descent silenced her.

I was getting ready to make a daring leap—bad arm and all—out of the speeding car onto the platform. Then

I saw the lights of an approaching car. The bubble gum machine was turned on, but no siren and no speed. Captain Schlomo Stein did all right at following directions.

Chapter Twenty

"Adding a half an hour so I'd show up late!" Captain Stein growled. "So you'd get to play crazy-schmuck-hero-idiot in a moving roller coaster. Look what you got yourself. A busted arm and a dead felon."

"I owed him," I said.

"I owed him, too," Charity said through puffy lips.

"Lady, you should be in the hospital instead of standing nattering around this cruiser."

"We had to tell you what happened," Charity said.

"Well, you told me. Now you need a ride to the hospital. And he needs one to the morgue." He nodded his straw-hatted head toward the body of Vasily Brunov. He hung from his neck on the wire like a fresh beef. And had bled to death like one. The blood lay at his feet in an eight-pint puddle.

A car turned in the service road and nosed through the narrow channel between the concessions.

I answered Stein's questioning stare. "I made two calls," I said.

"Oh, yeah?"

I glimpsed Duke Widemann's white suit at about thirty yards. There was a figure in the other bucket seat. That was a surprise. The small Mercedes convertible pulled up.

Widemann swung his door open and scrambled out.

"What the hell is this, Nevsky? What the hell's the law doing here?"

The spotlights high on the coaster had mercury filaments. They cast a yellowish glow on all our faces. With the pain in my arm and a wave of dizziness breaking over my bomb-bonked brain, the whole scene had the unreality of a grade school play tableau.

The frozen moment was shattered by Trishie Widemann's scream. She threw open the passenger door. "Vasya, *Vasya!*" She ran to the corpse draped down the wire.

Duke looked at us with a tight smile. "I wanted her home. When I told her Nevsky called about Vasily, she had to come." His face hardened in the yellow light. *"Now what the hell have you done to my damn-near-son-in-law?"*

Trishie wailed as she reached the fence. Her sensible shoes splashed in the crimson puddle. She wrapped her arms around his bloody slacks. "Help me get him off!" she screamed.

"I've already checked him, Miz Widemann," Stein said. "He's dead. He bled to death."

Her wail echoed down the long dark midway. My eyes turned to my riddled car where the Sarmatian Demon leered from the back seat.

Trishie's awkward heave at the corpse's legs pressed her face against the soaked trouser cloth.

Duke Widemann called to her. "Don't be foolish, Patricia. The man's already dead. And I think he was up to no good. Come back over here—"

Trishie whirled from the body of her dead lover. Blood smeared her cheek and the front of her matron's dress. "I have a right to my grief! Hear me, you nasty man? *I have a right to my grief!*"

"A little flash of fire left in her yet," Charity mumbled.

Duke looked at Charity for the first time. "My God, woman, your *face*. Somebody better tell me what the hell's been happening here."

So we told him. Agony-armed me, battered Charity and impeccably clad Captain Schlomo Stein sketched in times, motives and victims. We painted Brunov in real, ugly oils. Duke Widemann wasn't an easy man to stun. He had had plenty of shocks and had dished out plenty more. Yet his color, even in the odd light, *did* turn toward his suit's as we cataloged Vasily's murders. *Very* pale.

Still, he held back accepting totally what we said. The last crumb of resistance still lay on the plate. He turned a strained face toward the corpse of his hopes of strong political representation for western Pennsylvania in the embrace of his failure of a daughter. "Proof," he said weakly. "We've got to have *some* proof."

"Follow me," I said. I took steady steps toward my car. My arm dangled down to throb at every footfall. With my good arm I pointed to the Sarmatian Demon. Stein had a light. He shined it into the back seat. One of Brunov's high-velocity slugs had nosed through metal and upholstery to strike the bronze figure on the left side of the chest. More white powder dribbled out of the hole at the vibration of our approach to add to the pile already on the seat.

Duke turned away with a groan. "All right. All right, Nevsky. A wiser man than I'll ever be said dreams die hard. That boy was my dream. We needed the old steel town's voice to be heard. We needed him in Washington."

"We needed somebody *else* in Washington," Charity said. "Not him."

Duke looked at the dangling corpse and at his daughter. Her arms were still wrapped around the bloody slacks. "He could've done so much..."

We followed Captain Stein back to the cruiser. He opened the door and slid in. His arm was halfway to the police radio when Duke grabbed his wrist. The industrialist was a big man. When he tugged the cop's hand gently, it came away from the mike. "What're you thinking about doing there, Captain Stein?" he said.

"Call an ambulance for these two, the meat wagon for your dead Great Legislative Hope."

"I think we should talk that over." I saw Duke shake off the horror and disappointment like so much straw stuck to his back. I understood Important Other Issues had been raised. I caught a glimpse of how rawhide tough was this man in the white suit.

He stroked his chin, tilted his big head up, and looked

at the rising moon. "What we have here, Captain Stein, is some kind of...sad accident."

The captain's snort of astonishment nearly knocked off his straw hat. "Accident? What kind of accident leaves one man hung up bleeding to death like a butchered cow, a woman with her face beat in and another man with a broken arm?"

"Captain Stein, you're well known in the city," Duke said. "Your career in law enforcement's been a long one. It's been a credit to the City of Pittsburgh."

"Th-Thank you." Schlomo had an idea which way Duke's wind was blowing.

"It came to my attention—I have friends everywhere these days, it seems—that you, Mr. Nevsky and Mrs. Day have met on several occasions. I couldn't help but think you might be talking about a subject until recently very close to the center of my interests. Vasily Brunov, that is. So I took the trouble to have some people look you up. That's when I found out about your admirable record and your coming retirement. A well-deserved retirement, from all evidence." Duke led Stein like a child up out of the cruiser seat and back onto the asphalt. His grip on the old cop's wrist was now feather light. "Your plans are...?"

"I'm retiring to Florida. West coast. I have an option on a condo—" Stein's voice was suddenly hoarse.

"I have extensive properties on the *east* coast," Duke said. "Among them some very fine Palm Beach Condominiums—"

"I couldn't afford—"

"One unit in particular I'm thinking of. A small one, set off by itself, landscaped, palms, shrubbery...Ideal for one man. My research told me you're alone."

"Yes, my Sarah—"

"It's possible. *Quite* possible that that particular unit—with a water view and private beach, I might add—could be made available to you for, say, the service fees alone."

"The *service* fees. That's only a few hundred a month."

"Exactly!" Duke waved Charity and me closer. "I know you two should be getting medical attention. But I want to stress the importance of there being absolutely *no* publicity about this evening's circus of violence. Let me explain what I mean and what I could do for you both...."

This visit to the hospital, while not pleasant, had the first one all beat. No pain in my head or loss of memory. Just one bone had been broken in my arm. The cast was lightweight and easy to maneuver. I also had two cracked ribs. A doctor had checked me all over and found me "debilitated." That meant I had to spend some time eating and sleeping and getting my pillow fluffed by cutey pie nurses who seemed to be fond of graying beards and balding heads.

This particular afternoon, the soft sun and blue skies out my balcony doors were even more pleasant than those of the previous two days. Reason: I had a guest. Charity, wearing her familiar light-blue robe, sat across the table from me. She had a mirror in one hand, but it wouldn't yet tell her how good her facial surgeon had been. He was supposed to have been good. He was supposed to have been the best man available in the whole U.S. of A. When her bandages came off she'd be able to decide just how good he was. Right now her eyes peeked like a harem girl's between veils of gauze. Duke Widemann had seen to the surgeon. He had also seen to it we were mended and tended in this place called Pine Mountain Medical Center, a posh clinic well up into the Allegheny Mountains some distance from Pittsburgh.

Charity tried a tentative smile—and quickly closed her mouth. Her missing two teeth would be tended to by a Hollywood-type dentist—also at Duke's expense. But bridgework would have to wait till the bandages came off. She traced the gauze around her mouth with an index finger. "What a con man that Dr. Greenlaw was, Yuri. Bubbling over with confidence. Smooth and convincing and good-looking. A real Don Juan."

"Don Juan was pretty good with a blade, too."

"I hope Greenlaw had a more *refined* touch." She giggled. "Know what he said he'd thrown in at no extra cost?"

"What?"

"A face lift. A little sandpapering here, a little tightening up there."

"What'd you say?"

"Right on!"

"I thought the lines added character," I said.

"Character-shmaracter. Who needs it? Anyhow, they'll be back. I'm thinking of it as a reprieve from the years, not a pardon."

"How you feeling now?"

"About my face? Worried."

We had a visitor. Schlomo Stein. He wore his straw hat and his usual three-piece suit. Summer-weight was his only concession to the heat. He also had his violin case. "A goodwill visit," he said. "To visit the sick earns a man points in Heaven." He asked us how we were doing. We said very nicely, thank you. We'd really know when Charity was unveiled.

"My blessing and mazel tov, gracious lady," Stein said.

We went out on the small balcony. A beach umbrella was set in the middle of a wrought iron table. Its chairs had cushions thick enough to satisfy a princess. Stein tuned his violin and softly played waltzes by Strauss and Lanner. Gay music made for a summer late morning drifted down over the lawns and shrubbery.

Between waltzes Stein chatted about the gullibility of media people and the public at large. Benign misdirection and a few small fibs were all it took to send the bird of truth flying off to permanent freedom. Day security found Vasily on the wire where we had left him. That was all they had found, of course. My wall-eyed pal from Smitty's Auto Parts had got a call from me and hurried out with the wrecker. Before he came we threw a tarp over Vasily. Charity took Trishie on a long walk down the darkened midway. The Sarmatian Demon went into the trunk of the cruiser along with the machine pistol. The cruiser and Schlomo's badge convinced H.J. that the odd-hour tow job was inside the law. Duke's 200-dollar fee spurred his well-developed poor memory. Nor did we use any real names. When the Datsun was gone, despite Charity's pain and mine, we swept up the glass and sanded down the oozes.

Coincidence had it that Vasily had, as he said, sent the regular security men away for the evening. It turned out he had told them he would make their usual rounds for them. He would be there most of the night testing a new radio control unit for the Hurricane. So when he was found dead, it was assumed he had had an accident. It wasn't hard for Captain Schlomo Stein to get himself assigned to investigating any possible relationship between Twiggy's and Brunov's 'accidents' on successive evenings. Nothing turned up. An odd coincidence, nothing more, said his report. Pressure from above, applied by Duke Widemann, took care of the report's being accepted and filed for oblivion.

The obituaries, Stein said, were kind to Brunov. Much was made of his gentleness and betrothal. A first-rate soldier had fallen from the political ranks of Allegheny County....

"Trishie didn't blow it all?" Charity said.

"Trishie left town as soon as the news broke."

"For where?"

"The world. An eighteen-month travel orgy," Stein said. "I got a call from Duke. He said he found two tough, classy broads who had just left their husbands for greener pastures. He made them a little win-win deal just like the ones he had made us."

"He *does* know how to make a deal," Charity said. "I never thought I'd need a *really* good surgeon and dentist...."

"The deal with the classy ladies was they had to stick with Miz Widemann for the duration. If they did, it was carte blanche around the world." Schlomo tapped his violin absently. "I met one of them. *Quite* a hot ticket. Our Trishie isn't going to come back the same naive soul we knew. She has a good chance of coming back with some street savvy—and some spine." He sighed. "The papers and TV said she was 'fleeing her grief.'"

"Doesn't it bother you to...smother the truth, Captain Stein?" Charity sat with swathed face like an oracle at judgment. The aging cop studied his violin's scroll. "Mrs. Day, I'm an old man, an old Jewish man. We're great ones for thinking, we are. I've thought a lot during my forty years in law enforcement. First thing I figured out is gray is everywhere. Ax murderers give kids M & M's and love their mothers. Next thing I figured out was there really isn't any sense to any of it. We're not—none of us—headed anywhere in the big picture of things. We set up *so* many systems. But underneath them all is Jello, Ping-Pong balls in the blower of the Bingo Game of the Cosmos. It's a wonder society works as well as it does. People who try to live by absolute rules are mad—cops especially. How can I take a condominium for keeping my mouth shut? By weighing that against all the times over the last forty years I *didn't* keep my mouth shut. My turn came around. I took it. In the overall scheme of my life, it fits in. Any more questions, Mrs. Day?"

"I have a question—but it's nonethical," Charity said.

"Oh?" Schlomo, who was about to put the violin under his chin, paused with face uplifted.

"You both forgotten? We're not *done* with the mess yet. We haven't found out what started it all—who killed my friend Felicia Semanova?"

"And come to think of it, who was the guy in the JFK mask who Maced me?" I said.

"Let's...think about it," Stein said. He slid the violin under his chin. His bow dug out a largo of one of thousands of Italian baroque sonatas. Leisurely trills and quiet embellishments wound like a web around the sunny summer day. He had been right: it *was* music to think by. When the last note died away amid the distant heat waves, Charity said, "Let's do some fancy supposing. Let's start with one far-out suppose."

"Which is?" I said.

"Let's suppose Count Dromsky-Michaux had just begun to find out his partner, Sergei Yelanov, was cleaning out the business. Maybe he found the first of the emptied accounts, say, and guessed at least part of the situation."

"That's a rather grand suppose, Mrs. Day," Stein said.

"But he *was* awake and at Hermitage late at night when the bronze arrived. The sort of behavior a worried man might show—particularly one who was looking for more evidence to back up a dark, growing suspicion. They say he wasn't all that bright. Just the same, he could probably smell the emotions running when Felicia and Selina dragged in the crate. Remember, they were damp and smelled like gasoline. They had just stood by while Sergei got deep-sixed. And they tore into uncrating the bronze. Maybe he kind of laid low, maybe faked sleep, and saw the Sarmatian Demon go into his employee's car."

I was getting the idea. And the pieces, like those in a run-backward movie of a breaking vase, flew into a whole in an instant. Completely without evidence, of course. "Try this out!" I bubbled. "Count D-M wanted to think Sergei had used the store's money to buy a valuable piece of art. But when he saw the Sarmatian Demon, he knew it was a copy. And, because he had heaved hard on the one for Duke Widemann, he knew the two women couldn't have handled it so easily—"

"He knew it was hollow!" Schlomo Stein brought the bow down in a *sforzato* attack for emphasis.

"By then he probably jumped to the right conclusion—that whatever was inside the statue had been paid for with *his* money." I waved my broken arm. Its strong lightweight cast gave support without bulk. "All of a sudden he was *very* interested in the bronze."

"So he followed Felicia to 138," Charity said. "And she *didn't* lose him. He tracked her right to our door."

"Out of control," Stein said. "You're both out of control." I noticed he was still listening.

"Over the next week or so, the count found out for super-sure that Sergei had liquidated the business under his nose—with Felicia's help," Charity went on. "Much as he could, he probably kept an eye on her and on 138, to see if she hauled out the statue. By then he had a good head of craziness built up. His business was finished. His partner and bookkeeper had done a job on him. So he sawed her steering column—"

My memory sent up a flare from the past. "He told me he was a card-carrying mechanic!" I blurted. "He wanted her dead because only she linked the bronze with Sergei. He thought Sergei had run off and was waiting somewhere for her to sell what was in the bronze. By killing her and then right away grabbing the statue, he thought he could even the score. He figured he could sell what was in it and get his store back. He took the easy way, first, punching holes in walls at 138, trying to find it. Then he took me on with mask and Mace."

Schlomo shook his head and opened his violin case. "So then what happened? Did he all of a sudden lose interest? Why isn't he still trying to get hold of the bronze?"

"What he lost was his nerve, captain." I wandered to the balcony railing and stared down at the near grounds. Two self-propelled wheelchairs with rigged beach umbrellas navigated the smooth asphalt walks. "When Winston mumbled at his sister's wake that we had the Sarmatian Demon, the count guessed other people were involved. Everybody said he wasn't a brave man. He had used a coward's way of killing Felicia. Any ideas he still had died when the bomb went off. He had gone out as far as he could on his own personal limb. So he's reverted to form—lying low and safe. Giving up the store. Taking his losses."

Schlomo clicked home case clasps. "Biggest lot of *un*founded, *un*documented and *un*believable nonsense I ever heard..."

A week later I found out Captain Schlomo Stein had his more-or-less personal cruiser. Beside the expected police radio a Blaupunkt Berlin 8000 AM/FM casette combo brought concert hall realism to law enforcement. Schubert's *Quintet in C* put plucked cellos behind the midway metal mesh with any police guests. I sat with eyes closed and my arms on my lap. I mellowed out.

Moving through traffic we had a chat about music. Schlomo had gone to a conservatory in Austria and had thought about the concert stage. "Didn't have the personality for it," he said. "Wasn't compulsive enough. Too well rounded. Too interested in the world too young."

"Miss it? The crowds? The rep?"

"It's a path I didn't take, Nevsky. One of, say, ten thousand. Look back too much in life and you don't go anywhere."

"The past is over. Tomorrow never comes."

"Street philosophy, Nevsky. Street philosophy."

"Sure, but it keeps the focus where it belongs. Taking charge of now."

Schlomo swung the car into Walnut Street. "Scratch a Russian, find a philosopher," he said. "A bad one."

He pulled into the narrow driveway between shuttered 'sPots and bankrupt Hermitage. It hadn't been a good month for small businesses in Shadyside. There was a van pulled up to the yawning doors of the garage warehouse. He stopped the cruiser short of the parking area. We left it blocking the driveway.

Through the open doors I saw cardboard boxes loaded with odds and ends, the dregs of Hermitage, beneath the contempt of dealers, auctioneers and scavengers. I glimpsed ugly little statues, chipped vases, extension cords with fray around the plugs.

Stein hallooed the little warehouse.

"See my attorney," came a voice from the shadows. "My attorney's handling everything."

"Your attorney's dead. I'd like to talk to you," Stein shouted. "Not about the business."

Count Dromsky-Michaux wandered out carrying a box. Despite the late June heat and the exertion of scraping the last meager tidbits out of Hermitage, he still wore riding boots, knickers, and peasant blouse. The sun accented his Slavic cheekbones. A dribble of sweat curved across the lens of his monocle. "Nevsky, good morning," he said in Russian. "How've you been?"

"Count, this is Captain Schlomo Stein, county police." I used English.

Dromsky-Michaux nodded a greeting. Schlomo dug out his wallet and flipped it open to show his badge. The count waved it back to the inside coat pocket of the captain's three-piece seersucker suit. "I'll take your word for it. What can I do for you, Captain Stein? Whatever it is, I hope it won't take long. I'm about one box and a door slam from the road to Lexington, Kentucky. A friend has a factory filled with heavy machinery. He needs a good mechanic. I'm the man he needs. It's going to be a new life in a new part of the country. It's time for *bon voyage, mes amis.*"

The captain adjusted his straw hat, the gesture somewhere between grooming and apology. "One line you didn't know about has to be cast off before you sail."

"What're you talking about?"

"A little bit of police routine's come up. Nothing much to worry about. Fact is we've known for some time a lady you knew pretty well—Mrs. Semanova—was helped along toward the accident that killed her."

"What?" The count's monocle fell out. It hit the garage's cement floor and shattered. "Felicia *murdered?"*

Schlomo nodded. He hunched his back a bit and cast his lumpy features toward the apologetic. "Lab people been working on the car. Persons unknown sawed her steering column nearly through. They found a fingerprint in the grease of the steering box. I'm making routine rounds of all her acquaintances, work and play. Strictly routine, I want you to understand. Strictly by the book. So I hope you won't get uptight now that's it come 'round to your turn to go downtown for prints."

The count shrugged at Stein's lies. *"Certainement."* His slight bow was sharp and precise. "You'd like to go now?"

Stein nodded.

"No problem. Come up to the office with me. I want to pick up my hat and walking stick and lock up."

Stein and I ambled after the dapper count. The captain unbuttoned his suit coat. I realized he probably was wearing a shoulder holster. We followed the count up the stairs into the stripped office. All the furniture was gone. Two saggy cardboard packing cases were serving as final desk and file. The mustiness peculiar to closed-up places of business already hung in the air. On a wall, near where Ruthie Spires's chair had been, hung a small wooden plaque. What was printed on it sounded like the zany redhead. It read: SOMEBODY SAID CHEER UP, THINGS COULD BE WORSE. I CHEERED UP AND SURE ENOUGH, THINGS GOT WORSE. I missed her. And I missed Judy Larkin. The death that leaked from the Sarmatian Demon still seemed to twine about my days.

The count slid on his gray beret, adjusted it to the proper angle, and picked up his walking stick. It was a long, slender Malacca cane. The head was a handworked boar's head of brass. He touched the tip to the floor, posed jauntily for a moment. "Ready, gentlemen," he said.

He walked by Stein as though headed for the door. The cane was in his right hand. He swung the slender stick in a wide arc parallel to the floor. Midway around the arc, the wooden casing flew free and sailed away to rattle against the far wall. The thin rapier was bare and ready to use.

I saw Stein go for his holster. He was too old and too slow. It had probably been years since he had made a forcible arrest.

Count Dromsky-Michaux skewered him somewhere in the lower bowels. The old cop's knees were buckling before the count pulled out the thin, whippy blade. He cocked his arm to deliver the coup in the heart or stomach.

I lunged toward him. I didn't have a plan and was being dumb. Just the same the count had to deal with me. And he did. He came right at me with a practiced fencing-school lunge. Instinctively I threw up my left arm. The same trick that had cost me a broken bone in it a couple of weeks ago.

The cast was made of reinforced fibery plastic lined with foam. The plastic was like a stiff shell around my arm. The tip of the rapier pierced the plastic, gouged my arm, and exited. For a moment the blade was seized in the plastic. I grabbed my left wrist with my right hand and heaved sharply down.

The blade snapped off. The count's face went slack with dismay. He cursed the stub of blade in his hand in fluent Russian. He broke for the door. I stuck out a quick leg and he tumbled over and down on the bare floor.

He rolled away, scrambling to his feet. I drove the hard tip of my right shoe into the center of his left knee. I felt something give. He howled and froze. I broke his nose with the heel of my hand. Blood gushed from his nostrils. He went down whining and miserable. Inside his knickers his knee was already starting to swell. I knew he wasn't going anywhere.

With a rising sense of gloom I turned back to where Stein lay bleeding on the floor.

Chapter Twenty-One

An iron foundry wasn't a place most people enjoyed visiting in July. Particularly on a Pittsburgh July day when the temperature was around ninety-five and the humidity lay in the river valleys like an Amazon jungle import. Added to that, Charity and I, along with Schlomo Stein, were on a catwalk with a good view of the melting furnace of the Smithson Iron Works. We were roasting half to death.

Charity and I had left 138 an hour ago. We planned to be away for two weeks. She was going to a legal convention, then on to an Arizona spa for "self-study" as she called it. I knew that mostly meant trying to get over Tod Buckcry. She had a physical recovery to make, too, from his abuse and from the damage of Brunov's heavy fists lying deep beneath her repaired face. And repaired it had been. Surgeon Greenlaw had been a wizard. She looked the same—only younger. Only at a certain light angle did I, who had lived many months with her, see shadows of the damage.

As for my holiday, I wasn't sure. The important thing was to be away from 138 to allow the energy engineers and small army of carpenters, technicians and plumbers to install the total climate control system. The deal Duke Widemann had found to make with me would cost him a bundle. The insulation, the solar panels, the micro-computer-controlled heat pumps, the sensors, their circuitry and mechanisms were to be installed with minimum changes in the appearance of the grand old ark of 138. When the preliminary estimates came in, I was willing to let the industrialist back out part or all the way. I didn't know what it meant to be truly wealthy. Duke waved away my mild protests. I had saved him from making a fool of himself too many ways in too many directions for him not to express his gratitude. My remaining weak resistance was swept away when his chief energy engineer promised me a small, tasteful master console for my bedroom. No. 138's year-round environment at my fingertips! Who could resist? Farewell old Gas King Supreme! Hello LED's, microchips, solar cells and computer monitoring!

Schlomo Stein was leaving town today, too—for his Palm Beach condo. I studied his sweaty face, saw new lines and sags in the tissue. The department was right to give him a full retirement a couple of years early. Disability. They had sewed up his gut, but he wasn't at an age to come bouncing right back to a hundred percent. Just the same, he was well enough to have on his usual three-piece suit and straw hat. He was kind to even be here under the searing corrugated tin roof.

The waves of heat from the melting furnace assaulted us like blows. Stein turned his streaming face to mine. "How long do we preview Hell here before the devils appear?"

"Don't know. Eddie's taking care of it."

Eddie DeMarco, owner and manager of Smithson Iron Works, was an expert at taking care of things. His specialty was making things disappear with no trace. It wasn't that Eddie was a magician, or that he was outside the law, or needed money. Making things disappear was a hobby. He liked the mystery and motive behind why people thought things should disappear. He liked to decide whether or not to make something disappear. If he said no, that was it. Once he had said no and some very rough people tried to get him to change his mind. It got ugly. He called me for help. I gave it. So he owed me one.

Today I was to collect.

"You told him not to touch them?" Charity said.

I nodded.

"Did he think you were crazy?" Stein said. "He ought to have. *I* think you're both crazy." He fanned himself with his straw.

"Oh, we're the first to say there's nothing to it. Nothing to copies of an old Russian bronze being cursed or haunted or oozing evil or any of that crap. Right, Yuri?"

"Right." It was good to hear her speaking normally. Her bridgework was a perfect match for her real teeth.

The P.A. system barked to life. All personnel on the shift were to assemble in the manager's office for review of work assignments. When the half dozen men had left the furnace area, a metallic conveyor belt chattered into action.

"Showtime," Charity said.

Schlomo had removed the cocaine bag from the bronze and stored it in the police warehouse. Late yesterday he had filed a requisition to remove it. The cop in charge didn't know he was retired. Duke Widemann gave up his bronze easily. Once he heard it was a copy, he wanted no part of it. Telling him it was also the worst kind of evil-bringer made him laugh. "I don't believe in bad luck," he said. "Just bad planning."

Both Sarmatian Demons made their entrance on the conveyor belt that ran in from the yard. They moved in a stately glide toward the furnace. Their raised hammers and shrieking faces seemed to look for one last human soul to torture. At the bidding of Eddie in the control booth the upper doors of the furnace swung wide. The white heat within drove us back cringing.

There are many ways to destroy things living and dead. Most of them contain the chance of leaving a trace, a clue. The scrap of paper ash finds its way to the police lab. The water-bloated limb floats to the river's surface. But molten metal leaves meager traces indeed. Unlucky steel workers who somehow blunder into hot metal are *gone*. Legend had it that the "remains" are a small ingot poured by a ladle operator with a sense of tradition and buried by a family with a sense of ritual.

The Sarmatian Demons moved toward the searing white heat. Between sweat-slicked fingers pressed to my face I saw the two bronzes glide, glide, glide. Slowly they tipped, one after the other, into a suitable molten hell. Somewhere on earth stood the original. In what surroundings I could not guess. Nor did I want to speculate on what human beings suffered under that parent evil. Or did our dread come from no more than our overactive imaginations and some particularly trying weeks?

"I'm glad they're gone," Charity said cheerily. "Of course I never for a moment thought there was anything to—"

"Me neither."

"Let's get out of here," Stein growled. "I don't know which is worse—the heat or your lies."

We got into our three separate cars. Under the blue July sky the summer seemed to stretch ahead like the tranquil roll of a safe sea. How would I spend it? I thought I knew all along—out at the Murrysville cottage. I would wallow in deep summer. My arm would mend. Memories of death would dim. There were tomatoes to weed, rye to drink and handfuls of starry nights shining their profound messages of proportion down on the sleeping western Pennsylvania hills.

MYSTERIES BY
DIMITRI GAT

NEVSKY'S RETURN   79863-8/$2.50

NEVSKY'S RETURN is the first in a series featuring Yuri Nevsky, a Russian American and top-notch private eye, and his charming, beautiful partner Charity Day. Together they enter the heart of an old Russian neighborhood to search for a missing youth – and find a strange religious sect and murder.

NEVSKY'S DEMON   82248-2/$2.95

When a mysterious bundle is left on his doorstep, detective Yuri Nevsky is thrust into the dangerous world of stolen art and international smuggling. Yuri and Charity Day have become the guardians of a cursed statue that is at the heart of a deadly plot – and they soon discover that there are those who will murder to possess it.

"Mr. Gat is a real writer, and one eagerly awaits the further adventures of Yuri Nevsky."

The New York Times Book Review

AVON Paperbacks

Available wherever paperbacks are sold or directly from the publisher. Include 50¢ per copy for postage and handling. allow 6-8 weeks for delivery. Avon Books, Mail Order Dept., 224 W 57th St., N.Y., N Y 10019

Nevsky 4-83